NO
ALIBI

NO
ALIBI
THE BEST NEW CRIME FICTION

Edited by
MAXIM JAKUBOWSKI

RINGPULL • *Manchester*

First published in Great Britain in 1995 by Ringpull

An imprint of Fourth Estate Limited
6 Salem Road
London
W2 4BU

ISBN 1-89805-151-8

Typeset by Rowland Phototypesetting Limited,
Bury St Edmunds, Suffolk
Printed in Great Britain by Clays Ltd, St Ives, plc

This one's for Robin and Robyn

CONTENTS

INTRODUCTION

Crime and mystery fiction is truly in the midst of a new golden age as the millennium looms on the horizon. Glancing through the bestseller lists, we note the regular presence of many genre practitioners, and an overwhelming percentage of novels belonging to our category occupying in some weeks up to half the charts. These titles range from legal thrillers to psychochillers, police procedurals to female private investigator adventures, forensic detectives to nail-biting suspense, and many mysterious stations in between.

Every succeeding year sees major new talents breaking into print in most countries, a further indication, if any were needed, of the genre's robust health and unflagging energy. Despite a veritable plethora of new titles, the general standards of quality always appear to be on the increase, providing ever fiercer competition for the major awards: the Gold and Silver Daggers presented by the British Crime Writers' Association, the Edgars awarded by the Mystery Writers of America and the Anthonys given out by attendees of the annual Bouchercon, the World Mystery Convention.

In 1995, Bouchercon left American shores for only the third time in its twenty-six years of existence, to deposit its contingent of writers, readers, fans and enthusiasts in Nottingham, England, home of course of that classic rogue, Robin Hood. This anthology which celebrates the art of mystery writing in 1995 takes its inspiration from the event, which will make a small British city the world capital of crime for a long weekend.

Thirty or so leading British and American mystery writers

intending to attend the Nottingham Bouchercon were asked for brand-new stories for this major anthology. They obliged in particularly ingenious ways. Some have dreamed up sinister scenarios, disturbing, even sexy, yarns; others have remained in the traditional realm of the cosy detective story. There are thrills, dastardly puzzles, whodunits and whydunits; dreadful deaths and glimpses of evil; some light humour; policemen and amateur sleuths; victims and perpetrators: in short, there is the whole gamut of human life (and death) that so wonderfully characterizes crime and mystery fiction. None of our sons and daughters of Edgar Allan Poe, Conan Doyle, Agatha Christie, Margery Allingham, Raymond Chandler and Dorothy L. Sayers (add your own favourites to what could be an unending list) disappoint as they demonstrate with bravura how crime and mystery writing satisfies the mind and the soul, combining as it does the art of storytelling with fascinating insights into the shadowy depths of man's fallibilities and errors of judgement.

Our stories criss-cross time and place, with Lindsey Davis penning her first ever story of ancient Rome, H. R. F. Keating allowing us to sit in on an interview in Bombay Police Headquarters and Larry Beinhart taking us back to the burglarious world of Munich in the 1930s, while many of the writers – embracing the Bouchercon inspiration – have chosen Nottingham as the setting for their story.

It is also worth noting that many of our contributors have featured their favourite series character in a new case – another reason why this collection is essential for the crime devotee!

So whether you're newly intrigued by crime writing, or experienced in the language of sleuthing, dip your toes in these murky waters and enjoy the experience. It's a criminal world out there, and none of us have alibis!

Maxim Jakubowski

NOTE ON THE AUTHORS

ROBERT BARNARD, who lives in Leeds, is one of Britain's most accomplished crime writers, with an assortment of awards for novels and short stories on his shelf. The author of almost thirty novels, his latest is *Dead, Mr Mozart*, a historical divertissement written as Bernard Bastable. An accomplished entertainer and previously an academic, with occasional forays into humour, he has also written a definitive study of the works of Agatha Christie, *A Talent to Deceive*.

LARRY BEINHART won the Edgar for his first novel *No One Rides for Free*. Normally a resident of Woodstock, New York where he lives with his wife, crime writer Gillian Farrell, and children, he is currently based in Oxford as the recipient of the Raymond Chandler Fulbright Fellowship. His last novel was *American Hero*, a satirical mystery some critics have likened to *Catch 22*.

LAWRENCE BLOCK was made a Grandmaster by the Mystery Writers of America in 1994. A prolific crime writer who has won most of the awards in the field, he is best known for two series: the bleak, hard-boiled saga of recovering alcoholic sleuth Matt Scudder, last seen in A *Long Line of Dead Men*, and, in a lighter vein, the capers of burglar Bernie Rhodenbarr, a white, Jewish male once transformed by the magic of Hollywood into the black and female persona of Whoopi Goldberg!

LIZA CODY is Britain's most eminent female private-eye exponent and the creator of two unforgettable characters, Anna Lee, a veteran of six fast-moving novels and recently seen (and somewhat betrayed, as is the custom) on television screens as Imogen Stubbs, and, more recently, feisty lady wrestler and amateur sleuth Eva Wylie, who first emerged in *Bucket Nut*. When not putting in strong debating or performing appearances at conventions and mystery events, Liza lives in Somerset.

MAT COWARD is a young British journalist who made his first mystery breakthrough in the *New Crimes* anthology series (also edited by Maxim Jakubowski), which helped him reach the Gold Dagger short-story shortlist on his first appearance. He has since sold stories to many publications. He is a regular contributor to *Mystery Scene, A Shot in the Dark* and is also a columnist for the *New Statesman*.

DENISE DANKS is the first woman to have won the prestigious Raymond Chandler Fulbright Fellowship, which enabled her to spend most of 1994 travelling in the United States. The O. J. Simpson case makes an appearance in her story here, her first directly inspired by the journey. Denise is the creator of Georgina Powers, the most politically incorrect female sleuth in the business, and also, like Denise herself, a computer journalist.

LINDSEY DAVIS is an ex-British civil servant who wrote a romantic tale of ancient Rome, and saw herself adopted by the mystery field as the incomparable Falco began his detecting down those mean Roman streets. He has now featured in six novels, the latest of which is *Time to Depart*, and his love life is still in poor shape. Falco does not appear in this, Lindsey's first ever short story, but Rome does.

MARTIN EDWARDS is a Liverpool solicitor, as is his fictional creation, Harry Devlin. The resemblance ends there – or does it? Devlin has now appeared in four novels, the latest being *Yesterday's Papers*, as well as a handful of short stories which have appeared in British anthologies and *Ellery Queen's Mystery Magazine*. A connoisseur of traditional British mystery writing, Martin won the Crime Mastermind competition at a previous Bouchercon.

CHARLOTTE and AARON ELKINS have collaborated on the novel *A Wicked Slice* (1989), a golfing mystery. They live on an island off Seattle. Aaron won the Edgar in 1988 for *Old Bones*, featuring his series character, anthropologist Gideon Oliver, who has so far appeared in over ten novels, some of which have been adapted for television. His latest novel is *Dead Men's Hearts*.

JOHN HARVEY's short story is only the second to feature Charlie Resnick, his jazz-loving and sandwich-munching Nottingham detective, although the moody cop has already appeared in seven much acclaimed novels and two television adaptations (by John himself, a deft hand at scripting). John is an ex-teacher and prolific writer of Westerns, who often reads his poetry with the jazz band Second Nature, and has recently moved down from Nottingham to London.

REGINALD HILL was awarded the CWA Diamond Dagger in 1995, the highest life achievement recognition in the field. He is the creator of policemen Dalziel and Pascoe, a doughty pair of investigators, soon to have a second chance on television following an abortive first attempt. More recently he also created ex-lathe operator, black Luton investigator Joe Sixsmith, who appears in his story here. Previously a teacher, Reginald lives in Cumbria and is the toastmaster at the 1995 Bouchercon banquet.

EDWARD D. HOCH hasn't written a novel since 1975. He has however written over 750 short stories, one of which has been featured in every single issue of *Ellery Queen's Mystery Magazine* since the mid-1970s, as well as in countless other anthologies. He also edits the respected annual *Year's Best Mystery and Suspense Stories* collection, which has now been appearing for fifteen years. His story collected here brings back one of his all-time favourite sleuths from retirement.

MAXIM JAKUBOWSKI is the owner of London's crime and mystery bookshop Murder One, and a well-known crime editor, critic and writer. Previously a publisher, he won the Anthony award for his *100 Great Detectives*. Stories from his anthologies have won the CWA short story Gold Dagger every year since it was instituted. He writes a mystery column for London magazine *Time Out*, is a contributing editor to *Mystery Scene* and a regular broadcaster.

J. A. JANCE divides her time between Seattle and Arizona, where her two current series are set. Her sleuths are, respectively, Seattle cop J. P. Beaumont and Arizona-based Joanna Brady, whose latest adventure was *Tombstone Courage*. Judy, who sports the distinction of being one the tallest women in the crime field, is also one of its most underrated practitioners. Readers, please take note.

H. R. F. KEATING, currently President of the venerable Detection

Club, is one of the doyens of the British crime scene. The author of over thirty novels in the grand tradition of classic detecting, he is also best known for his creation of the seemingly bumbling but highly efficacious Inspector Ghote of the Bombay police force, who makes another welcome appearance here.

ALEX KEEGAN is a new addition to the ranks of British crime writers. His first two novels, *Cuckoo* and *Vulture*, introduce Caz Flood, a new woman detective in the Brighton police force. Alex is a survivor of the Clapham rail disaster, a veteran top-thirty sprinter and lives in Southampton.

MICHAEL Z. LEWIN is an American writer long since established in Somerset, where he coaches when not penning his soft-boiled Indianapolis thrillers involving Albert Samson, his series character who makes a new appearance here after a detecting sabbatical during which Mike has published two non-series novels, the gritty *Underdog* and the more humorous *Family Business*, which introduces an Italian family of private detectives in Bath of all places.

PETER LOVESEY resides with ease in the top half of the British league of crime and mystery writers. A past winner of Gold Dagger, Silver Dagger and Anthony awards, he has created three successful series featuring respectively Sergeant Cribb; Bertie, Prince of Wales; and, more recently, his contemporary Peter Diamond, who appears in his last novel *The Summons*. An ex-chairman of the Crime Writers' Association, Peter lives in Stratford-upon-Avon.

BARBARA TAYLOR McCAFFERTY and BEVERLY TAYLOR HERALD are both writers and twin sisters, a fact to be borne in mind when reading their story here. As Taylor McCafferty, Barbara has a popular cat mystery series going, which began with *Pet Peeves*, while as Tierney McClellan she mines a traditional whodunit seam in a new series. Beverly writes for the young adult field, and the two writers are collaborating on a novel.

VAL McDERMID is one of the new voices in the feminist sleuthing field. A Manchester journalist born in Scotland, she has created two powerful characters: journalist sleuth Lindsay Gordon who has appeared in four novels, and rowdy but fearless Mancunian private eye Kate Brannigan, who has also reached her fourth caper. Val has recently completed a non-fiction book on American true-life female private investigators.

SUSAN MOODY created Penny Wanawake, a six-foot-tall black sleuth, who was ahead of her time and lost out in the female PI stakes, despite six vigorous novels published between 1984 and 1989. Her new heroine is Cassie Swann, a bridge professional whose card outings inevitably implicate her in crime; Cassie's third appearance was in *King of Hearts*. Susan is also a deft hand at romantic suspense, and was the author of the notorious novel inspired by the Nescafé Gold Blend series of TV adverts.

SARA PARETSKY is the creator of the eponymous V. I. Warshawski, female private eye *par excellence*. Both heroine and creator are based in Chicago where a love of baseball seems obligatory, as her story here attests. The latest novel in the bestselling series is *Tunnel Vision*, and a collection of Warshawski short stories, *V. I. For Short*, is due soon.

IAN RANKIN is Scottish, an ex-journalist and the creator of doughty Edinburgh cop Inspector Rebus. Now living in France, Ian won the 1994 Gold Dagger short-story award for *A Deep Hole*. He also writes fast-paced thrillers as Jack Harvey, which happens to be his son's name! A regular at previous Nottingham events, and an ardent film fan, he did not have to look far for his inspiration when it came to penning his story for this anthology.

CANDACE ROBB, with only three novels to her credit, is effortlessly becoming a leader in the crowded stakes of heirs apparent to the crown of queen of the historical detective novel, currently held by the much loved Ellis Peters. Her gentle medieval sleuth Owen Archer first appeared in *The Apothecary Rose* and is already proving highly popular with readers. Candace lives in Seattle, but often visits England for her research.

PETER ROBINSON was born and bred in Yorkshire, but now makes his home in Toronto, Canada. He does miss the beer, though. His series character, the bluff Yorkshire policeman Inspector Alan Banks, first appeared in *Gallows View* (1987) and has now featured in seven gripping novels, many of which have been shortlisted for the major awards in the mystery field.

Note on the Authors

MARK TIMLIN's south London sleuth Nick Sharman has burst on to TV screens played by rough 'n' smooth Clive Owen in *The Turnaround*, soon to be followed by a further four feature-length episodes adapted from Mark's novels. A latecomer to writing, ex-rock roadie Timlin has quickly established his mark with his fast-paced, brutal, hard-boiled prose which owes somewhat more to Chandler and Hammett than Christie and other attendant British venerables. His latest Sharman charmer is *Paint It Black*.

MARGARET YORKE's subtle novels of psychological suspense have established her as the leading lady in a crowded field. Her impressive career spans a quarter of a century already, and she shows no sign of flagging in her insightful studies of domesticity, common evil and twisted relationships. Her short stories are few and far between, and I am proud that she has joined this collection with another small gem.

FUNNY STORY (for Jurgen Burger)

LARRY BEINHART

My father is visiting for the holidays. He's an old man now. I'm not exactly young either. At least not the way they used to measure men. Pushing fifty. Pushing it quite hard, actually.

My son is six, pushing seven. At that age you can't push hard enough. Time flows like treacle, black, sweet, slow, thick and sticky. You can't move it fast enough. If you charge into it you just get tangled up and slowed down, then you end up having to take a bath.

At my age, when you would give whatever there is to give to slow the metronome down, it seems an enviable state. But try telling that to a kid racing to be a race driver, fireman, policeman, wrestler, Power Ranger, space scientist, karate fighter. Generation upon generation tries to tell their kids that, and each ageing parent sounds like a jerk when he does. Even my father did. I don't mention that, however.

David, my son, spills his juice on the rug. His mother, my wife, starts scolding, and I go to get paper towels to sop it up. 'I told you to be careful of the rug,' she says. 'It's a valuable, very valuable piece. How many times have I told you never to bring drinks on that rug?'

'It's an old rug,' David says. Which is true.

My father looks at me with something less than a wink. Possibly

17

a twinkle. As if to say listen to this, this is how mothers and sons talk, for all time; what a pleasure to hear this.

'The rug was a gift from your grandfather. It's from the old country, and it's a very valuable piece.' What a curious expression, the old country. It makes it sound as if we came from one of those rustic peasanty nations that mercantilism and the Industrial Revolution had more or less bypassed, someplace like Romania, Albania, Ireland or the Ukraine.

'Is it as old as Grandpop?' David says, awe in his voice, that lets us know Grandpop is about as old a thing, let alone as old a person, as he can imagine. Grandpop is pretty old, and he looks old, with wrinkles and liver spots and wisps of hair to highlight the baldness of his liver-spotted, wrinkly dome. Big veins stand out on his hands and his fingers move stiffly and painfully, arthritic, as well as just old.

'Older,' Grandpop says.

'Did you get it new?' David asks.

It's a big old rug, twelve feet by eighteen, a Persian. Handmade, hand-knotted, with an intricate pattern. I've been told how many knots per square inch, but I've forgotten and experts, when they look at it, instantly exclaim things about the pattern and the clan and, most of all, about its probable price. I can't. I just know it's the second most valuable thing we own. It's worth less than the house, but more than the car, a five-year-old Lexus. But, like the good old Persian it is, in a house with a son and a daughter and a dog and a cat and, from time to time, rabbits, gerbils and wounded birds, it looks old and faded and worn and as comfortable as a home.

'No, not really,' Grandpop says.

'Did you get it at, like, a garage sale, or an auction?' David asks. He's been to lots and lots of both. We've furnished the house, except for the rug and one or two other bits, from garage sales and auctions. This is not to say that it looks like Levittown leftovers. My wife is a woman of terrific taste which she combines with immense ferocity in her search for true value. For her, anything short of getting a 1400-dollar chair for 225 dollars is a furnishing defeat.

'Would you like me to tell you a story about that rug?' Grandpop says.

David looks doubtful. Furniture acquisition stories don't thrill him. He's really had his fill of them. When my wife does make a furnishing score she not only brings the item home, she brings the tale of its purchase with it: the days, weeks, months of searching; the revelatory moment of finding; the strategy and tactics of the negotiation and a blow-by-blow of the bargaining.

'You'll like it, it's a funny story,' his grandfather says.

David is not convinced. Then I, like a schmuck, which means jewel in German but schmuck in English, say 'That's not a good story for him.'

'Tell me, Grandpop,' David says.

'Pop,' I say. Why I imagine I can still head this off, I don't know. Maybe I don't. Maybe I just think it is the responsible, parental thing to try.

'What? The boy shouldn't know?'

Maybe he shouldn't. 'He's a little young.'

'Maybe I won't be here next year to tell him.'

Try to argue with that. But, none the less, I did. 'You will. I say he's not ready. If, God forbid, you're not here, I'll tell him. When the time comes.'

'Tell me,' David says. Of course. 'I want to know.'

'What's this "God forbid" stuff?' my father asks me.

'It's a turn of phrase.'

'It's superstition,' he says, more fiercely than seems called for.

'OK, it's superstition. I'm superstitious, I would like you to come back next year and for many years to come.'

'How did you get the rug, Grandpop?'

His grandfather gets out of his chair with creaks and groans and sighs. Not the furniture, the man. And gets down on his knees on the floor. He rolls back a corner of the rug. 'Look at this,' he says. 'This is fine, fine wool. Strong wool. It wears like iron. Woven by hand, the threads are tied by hand. The dyes they use in this, they'll last hundreds of years. Today they make millions of everything, carpets, cars, toys, pens, books, chairs, glasses, silverware, they make it fast, they make it cheap. I'm not saying that's bad, or that the stuff they make is bad. I'm not an old curmudgeon, can't move with the times, stuck in the past, can't appreciate progress. I like progress, I like to see everybody, every working man and woman, with washers and dryers and summer clothes and sports clothes and ski clothes and running shoes, walking shoes, aerobic shoes, tennis

19

shoes, dress shoes, shoes with winking red lights in the heel. Them I like especially.

'But you should understand, boy, that once upon a time, not everything came out of a plastic extruder by the twenty millions. Once things were made by hand. One at a time. And there weren't so many, many, many things. There were just a few things. Even for rich people there weren't so very many things. So each thing became more important. Can you imagine going to the pawn shop . . . does he know what a pawn shop is?'

'Ask him, not me,' I say.

'What's a pawn shop, David?'

'I don't know.'

'It's a place where you leave something valuable and they loan you money.'

'Dad just uses his card at the bank.'

'Right,' Grandpop says, 'I understand. Me too. But once, they didn't do that. When you borrowed money you had to leave something tangible behind. Something that the person who loaned you the money could hold on to, even sell if you didn't pay it back. In the old days, you could leave a coat and borrow money.'

'A coat?' David says, incredulous. As well he might in these days of cheap, and truth to be told, disposable clothing.

'Right, exactly. Material things, they had value. Not just big things like cars, but watches and jackets, even hats. And rugs.'

'How did you get the rug, Grandpop?'

I just sighed and shook my head.

'I stole it,' he says.

I throw up my hands, make a sound of exasperation, drop my hands and shake my head.

'You stole it?'

'Pop, do you have to do this?'

'Yes, I stole it,' David's grandfather says without a trace of shame. Or even embarrassment. Without a thought of discretion.

'What kind of role model, what kind of ideas are you putting in my son's head?'

'Just truth,' he says.

'It's not funny,' I say.

'There's funny and there's funny,' he says.

'My dad says not to steal things. He makes me give things back when I steal them,' my wonderful son says.

'Your father is absolutely right,' the subversive old man says without a hint of sincerity.

'Did you steal a lot of things?' my son asks.

'You bet,' his grandfather says.

'Great, just great,' I say.

'Really, Grandpop?' David says, as wide-eyed and fascinated as you would expect.

'Really, David,' Grandpop says. 'I was a thief.'

I suspect that damage is being done here that will take me years to undo. A rogue, an absolute rogue.

'I was more than a thief. I was about the best thief in Munich. Which was a very great place to be a thief because it was then, as it is now, a very rich city. With many rich people who loved expensive things. As they do now. Even though then there was a depression and what is called hyperinflation. Do you know what hyperinflation is?'

'He's six, for God's sake,' I point out.

'Like in Brazil,' my son says. What does he know about Brazil? The kid hardly knows how to buy a candy bar and get the correct change.

'It means that every day the money is worth less. Yesterday a candy bar is fifty cents, tomorrow it costs a dollar. A week later, you need two dollars. Then five dollars. In two, three weeks, a candy bar costs ten dollars. Then twenty. That's hyperinflation. So it was better to have things than to have money. I never stole money. You understand why?'

'Stealing money is bad?' my son offers as a reason not to steal money. That's the reason he learned at home.

'Because when you have hyperinflation money is worthless. It's junk. It's garbage.'

My wife, listening to this, begins to gesture at me frantically. This is a conversation I'm not looking forward to. I'm a fairly weak-willed fellow, or, if you wish to be polite, easygoing, and I tend to go whichever way the wind blows. What it is, I'm actually pretty resilient and self-satisfied, so a lot of things just don't matter to me because there is something at the center that stays fairly pleased with itself even when the weather changes. And they are both, my father

21

and my wife, very strong-willed people. I have never been able to silence either one of them or stop either one of them from saying what they thought needed saying, however little it actually needed saying.

'I'll make some tea,' I said. Why? Why not say, Pop, I'm going into the kitchen so my wife can tell me to tell you to shut up because this is most emphatically not a story for a six-year-old boy. Theft is just the beginning. There's violence and despair and murder.

'He's six years old, for God's sake,' my wife says. Severely.

'No shit,' I say.

'Well, aren't you going to stop him?'

'Why don't you stop him?' I say.

'He's your father,' she says. This is marital tennis. Not a match game by any means, really just a warm-up, stroking matters back and forth.

'He knows David is six. So maybe he has some reason for telling it now.'

'Don't be ridiculous, what reason could there be for telling a six-year-old his grandfather was a thief, a professional thief.'

'He was, to hear him tell it, the prince of thieves. He was a cat burglar. Actually he rather relishes himself as Cary Grant in *To Catch A Thief*.'

'That doesn't make it better,' my wife says.

I say 'Achievement is always to be admired.'

She is not amused. She says so. She is frequently not amused. I frequently dream about being away from news of her non-amusement.

'Maybe he wants to tell David to always be the best you can be, no, the best there is, no matter what your field of endeavour. And do it with style and panache. I mean, my father was no worse, or not much worse, than D'Artagnan.' David and I are reading *The Three Musketeers* together. What a revelation to rediscover them. Athos, Porthos, Aramis and D'Artagnan were appalling by contemporary standards. They're all common brawlers who go around drinking in bars then refusing to pay, and then getting into knife fights and stabbing people, sometimes to death. All right, the knives are really big and they call them swords, but I can't see the difference. On the moral plane at any rate. Porthos and Aramis both live off women. D'Artagnan claims to be in love with one woman, makes

love to another without a moment's hesitation, then jumps all over
the second woman's maid, not even out of lust, but so he can use
her. I am more than faintly envious. Athos, the most noble and
sensitive and aristocratic of the bunch, murders his wife. Twice.
Why? Because he discovered that she had once been convicted of a
crime and had been branded, as in having a brand burnt into her
flesh with a hot iron just like they do to cows in cowboy movies.
The only remotely moral message implicit in these events seems to
be to get it right the first time.

'Tell him to stop,' she says.

'No.'

'Tell him,' she commands. Demands. Requires.

'Why don't you tell him?' I suggest, sensibly, thoughtfully, fairly.

'He's your father,' she says.

I resist the temptation to say, I knew that. I say, 'Exactly.'

'So? You have to stand up for your family, and this is your family,
your wife and your child . . .' This is just the wind-up, a prep-
ositional phrase, as it were, for a lengthy and major statement which
will be delivered with such fervor and eloquence that, right or wrong,
I will certainly feel that her position is unassailable and not to be
denied.

There is only one chance, and that is to head her off at the pass,
fire off a few shots, spook the lead animal and turn the stampede in
a different direction.

'It's because he's my father that you should tell him,' I say. 'My
emotional involvement and his, the roles, father and son, parent and
child, are permanent, you know. They never go away. You can't
unravel them with your parents, in spite of four years of therapy.
I'm not criticizing you,' I hasten to add. Though I probably am.
Though I couldn't say what I need to say without saying it. So what
do you do with that? It is a huge amount of work to have a conversation with my wife. I'm tired of it. 'I'm just saying that if I say it,
we get involved in a whole to-do about the parent–child relationship
and lots of emotional shit. If you tell him, you can tell him adult to
adult, in fact you will probably assume the dominant role as parent,
which you are to David, and since my father's really playing a boy-to-
boy thing with David, that puts you in a superior position.'

'It's your responsibility,' she says.

'Morally, that's true. I agree with you a hundred percent.' That's one of my best tactics with her. It's very important to her to be right and morally correct. 'However, pragmatically, if we want him to stop, he's more likely to listen to you.'

Her mouth opens. She wants more to come out.

'You're absolutely correct,' I tell her, before more comes out. 'It is my responsibility. But if I do it, it won't work. If you do it, it will.'

'All right,' she says. Disdainful of my ineffectuality – but not unbearably so, this time – she goes back into the living room.

As we go back in we hear David ask, 'Why did you steal? Was it because you were hungry and your children were starving?' He has heard that some people steal because they must. This is the legacy of liberalism in our immediate culture and in our house: criminality comes from deprivation. When, and if, it is ever true, I suppose it imparts more than an excuse, it imparts a certain legitimacy, even nobility, to theft. *I would steal before I would let my family starve.* Don Corleone morality. However it is rarely true. The starving tend to just go on and starve and to the degree they steal, it is to snatch the bread off the plates of those starving beside them, not to launch daring raids on the manor house on the hill.

'I stole because I wanted to,' my grandfather tells my son.

'Isidore,' my wife says commandingly.

'One minute,' Izzy says. 'You see, I came from a fine family. My grandfather – you see, I had a father and he had a father, I know that you know that but to think about it and see it in your mind, that's something else – my grandfather was a rabbi. And he had three sons and one daughter.

'His youngest son was a doctor . . .'

My wife doesn't interrupt, even though her command has gone unheeded. Perhaps because this part is all right, this is a sort of noble family history, roots, capable of generating lots of sentiment, and she likes that sort of thing.

'That doctor was my father. He was very scientific, very secular and very assimilated. Do you know what assimilated means?'

'Or secular, for that matter,' I put in.

'No,' my son says.

'Do you know what a rabbi is?' my grandfather asks.

'Yes,' my son says. 'He's like a priest. For Jewish people. And I'm part Jewish.'

'Right,' my wife says. She's the one who's brought him to temple, though she's not Jewish at all. I'm totally secular. As was my father. Totally. Even adamantly.

'And assimilated, it means that we became, as much as we could, just like the other people around us. You are completely American. We were as German as Germans could be. We loved Bach and Wagner and read Goethe and respected learning and orderliness. Except . . .'

'Except what?'

'Except for me,' Grandpop says. 'My father had three sons. One became a medical doctor, as he was. One became a professor of chemistry, and the third became the black sheep of the family.'

'And that was you!' David cries with delight.

'Isidore, would you come into the kitchen? Now,' my wife says.

'What for?'

'I don't know how you like your tea.'

'A little bit of cream, two sugars,' he says. 'Cubes, if you have them. I like sugar cubes.'

'Because I want to talk to you,' she says.

'All right,' he says, getting up off the floor with even more creaks and sighs than he required to get down there. 'There was so much goodness and orderliness around,' he says. 'And I had so much sap in me, I just couldn't stand it.'

'Now. Please,' my wife says.

'Is Mom going to let Grandpop finish his story?' David asks me as they disappear into the kitchen–conference room.

'I wouldn't like to bet on it either way,' I say. I'm curious myself, who's going to win this little to-do.

'Dad, can we go to the video store?' he says.

'Sure.'

'I want to get a movie called *To Catch A Thief*,' he says. 'Have you ever seen it?'

'Yes.'

'Will I like it?'

'Well, if I remember, it's got a lot of love-stuff in it . . .'

'Yucky.'

'. . . but aside from that, you should like it.'

They return from the kitchen. My son and I look toward them, searching their faces for clues as to what will ensue. It's real clear.

My father has a slight smile on his face. If you're in a bad mood it
can look like a sneer. I remember it well from growing up. And how
it used to infuriate me. My wife, on the other hand, looks pale and
chastened. I wonder what he could possibly have said to her. I've
never achieved that effect. I guess I still have something to learn
from the old man.

Isidore lowers himself slowly down to the floor. More creaks,
groans, sighs. My wife goes back into the kitchen, hastening, it turns
out, to bring him his tea, as he likes it, though not with sugar
cubes. We've never had them around. I suspect we are about to start
stocking them. She also brings a plate of some not very sweet, adult
sort of cookies for Grandpop to share with David.

From where I sit the Christmas tree more or less frames the two
of them. Strings of light, little wooden sleds and santas and elves all
made cheaply in China hang from the branches, along with glass balls
and an eclectic assortment of thisment and thatment of ornaments
assembled over the years. Presents in patterned paper and glittery
ribbons are spread out on the floor behind them.

'Christmas was our best season,' Grandpop says. 'I had a partner.
A young man named Jurgen. This was a very strange time. Germany
had its Jew laws – these were laws that were separating out the Jews
from the German people. For us this was very confusing, because
we saw ourselves as Germans, and as Jews hardly at all. But Jurgen
and I had become friends before all that and we stayed friends,
chasing girls together – you're too young for that, yes?'

'I like girls,' David says.

'But not like that,' I explain. Though it should not need explanation. 'He means he hasn't reached the age where he won't play
with girls, not that he's reached the age, which comes after that,
where all he wants to do is play with girls.'

'Of course,' Grandpop says. 'We liked what kids nowadays call
life in the fast lane. Cash, clothes, cars.' As if suddenly remembering
who is in his audience, he adds, with an admonishing finger, a gesture
he has surely copied from somewhere because I know it is not innate
to him (when he wanted to make a point, a hit, though open-handed
and mild, was more his style). 'Of course, I would be very unhappy
if you were to be that way. You should be more like my brothers.
Students. Men of learning. Respected. You understand?'

'Sure,' David says, tuning right in to his grandfather's conspiracy to commit hypocrisy. In his short life the only things he has ever expressed a desire to be when he grows up are things that are defined as testosterone-driven activities, things with fighting, fires, vehicles, guns. From today we can add stealing.

'Jurgen was the outside man. I was the inside man. He had a way with serving-girls that you would not believe. They loved him. They had but to meet him and their eyes would get big and round like cows' eyes and they would look up at him like this.' He rolls his head around with a motion that quite definitely evokes mooing and cud-chewing. 'And they would tell him everything. What the family they worked for was buying as presents, when they were going visiting, when the houses would be empty. I was helping Jewish families sell their jewelry, so I knew a lot of the jewelers. I would get information from them about people buying expensive jewelry. Also there were several that were not so honest who would buy from us the jewelry we stole.

'Finally there were a few who worked with us. When they sold expensive pieces they would tell us. Then we would steal it and we would sell it back to them.'

'Cool,' David said.

'Isidore,' my wife said, very sternly. It is a tone of voice I have come to loathe.

'Sorry,' Grandpop said, sounding just like I do when I'm making a meaningless pro forma acknowledgement. My wife glared at me. Of course.

'Anyway, Christmas would come, and we would have our houses picked out. We would know what was inside, or enough to know it was worthwhile taking the risk. And how to get in and when the house would be empty. The maids' rooms in big houses were usually way up on top, and sometimes a window would be left open for us.

'I was the cat,' he says, leaning forward, smiling and immensely pleased with himself. 'I could climb, I could get my fingertips into the smallest crack, I could stand on the narrowest ledge. And I could jump from one hold to the next. To do this you have to be two things: fearless and skinny. I was both.

'Other times I would pick the lock . . .' He looks down at his cramped old hands and sighs for the dexterity that they once had, and the youth that it represented and all that went with that youth. 'Or cut the glass. There were many ways. None of which a

27

well-brought-up young man like yourself should know,' he adds. No need to mention that he had been as well brought up as David. Better in fact. Isidore was the son of a doctor, grandson of a rabbi. David was the son of a composer of advertising jingles, grandson of a thief.

'Anyway, we had costumes. Jurgen would dress as Father Christmas, Santa Claus. I would dress in very dark, dark green. Almost black, so that I would be invisible in the dark; and smear dark green make-up on my face so even the white of my face would not catch the light; but, but, if a policeman were to stop us, I would say that I was one of the elves from the Black Forest, one of Father Christmas's helpers. Most of the things we stole would still be wrapped, you see, so we would say we were going to a party and bringing the gifts.'

'Did that actually work?' I blurt out, incredulous.

'Only once was it put to the test,' he says.

'Why are you filling our son's head with this, this terrible nonsense,' my wife says.

'It's the story of the rug,' he says. Innocently. 'It's a funny story.'

'Is this true?' she asks.

'As God is my witness,' my father says. And who knows what that means. To whatever degree he believes in God, he is very, very angry with Him. And finds His deeds unforgivable. At least that's what he's told me.

'Can we at least not wallow in the details,' my wife says.

'Of course, Moira,' he says. 'Not an unnecessary word. I will cut to the chase.'

'Thank you,' she says.

'So, on this particular Christmas, we are doing pretty well. We get into this big mansion that is close to the Englischer Gardens, which is a big park in Munich, like Central Park in New York or Golden Gate Park in San Francisco. What I'm there for is a diamond bracelet, I forget now the details of carats and number of diamonds, but this was worth, today, fifty, sixty thousand dollars. Lots of diamonds, lots of glitter, a real show-piece. Also there was, hidden away, a lesser piece, worth maybe fifteen, twenty thousand. One was for the wife, one was for the mistress. Plus there were many other things, the silver, small art pieces, whatever was small and valuable. Plus they had children. Close to the ages of my children then who were – one was younger than you and one, the girl, was exactly your age. Very pretty she was, and like you she had blond hair. So did I, when I was young and I had hair. Not these white wisps . . .'

The phone rang. I went to answer it. I knew the next bit. My father saw the rug there. He recognized it. It had belonged to a very rich Jewish banker in Munich, someone very well known at the time but whose name meant nothing to me and would mean nothing to David. My father recognized it because he had robbed the previous owner some years earlier. He had admired it then. It was, he said, the best Persian he had ever seen. Now he could not resist it.

The phone call was from one of our neighbors, a sweet young woman named Elaine. She's a widow, but reasonably well off, very attractive, with dark eyes, black hair and a full figure. Our daughter is visiting her daughter and Elaine is calling to find out if I will be coming over to pick Susan up or if she should deliver her. I say I'll come over, which I know is what she wants to hear. It's easier for her, and means that we might be able to spend a few adult minutes together. I tell her it will be an hour or so. Elaine says to come whenever I can, when I can will be all right.

When I hang up the phone Moira is standing there. She has that I-have-things-to-say look in her eye. Actually it is a look that is rarely absent, even when she is saying the things.

'What,' I ask her, pre-emptively, 'did my father say to you? To blackmail you into letting him finish telling this tale of the Yiddisher–Deutscher Robin Hood?'

'He said that he had been to the doctor and that he doubted he would be here another year and that he wanted David to know his story, from his lips.'

'Can't argue with that,' I say, somewhat surprised. He hasn't said anything to me about exceptionally imminent death. He looks pretty damn good. For his age. And, of course, he is prone to dramatization and exaggeration. Especially when he wants to get his way.

'No,' she says.

'I have to confess,' my father says as we walk back into the room, 'that although I had a very lovely wife, who was incidently a perfect mother to my two children . . .'

'Is that my grandmother?' David asks.

'No. That was my first wife,' my father says. 'The banker, who originally owned the rug, had a very beautiful daughter. Like a princess in a fairy tale. She had spurned me, and I thought it would impress her for me to have the rug.'

'Do we have to go into that?' my wife asks.

'It's the story of the rug,' my father says as if the rug has its own life, its own fervent history crying out to be told, a tale that it needs to pass on to posterity. 'I'm just trying to be fully honest here.'

'Don't,' I say. 'Don't overdo it.'

'OK,' he says. 'I can see that it is time to make a long story short. I will not thrill you, little David, with how I slipped out the back door, crept through the bushes and trees on the ground carrying not just my usual swag, but this huge rug on my back. And how Jurgen, my partner, swore at me as a madman when I brought it to the car. How I was adamant that we take it. Why? I don't know why. We all need a little mystery in what we do. Isn't that correct?

'This was Christmas Eve. Jurgen and I, we split up our take, which was considerable. Very considerable. It was late and he took me home. I had the rug of course.

'I went upstairs with all my things. My wife, Sarah, was waiting. My children, David and Judith, were sleeping. I kissed my wife and then went, right away, just as your father does with you, to see my sleeping children. There is something about coming home and finding your children safe and sound, healthy, asleep in their beds, blankets tucked around them, that is better, I think, than almost anything else in the world. Ask your father if this is not true.'

David looks at me. Moira likes this part. She beams. 'Yes,' I say, 'it's true.' It's true, and yet there are fathers, and mothers, who give it up. Or who give up a lot of it – except for alternate weekends, a week in the summer, and practically never on Christmas – because baser emotions like lust and anger are stronger than the sentimentalities of our higher feelings.

'I kissed them on their foreheads,' my father says. 'Then I added their extra gifts, those I had picked up from rich people's homes in the course of the night, to the ones we already had. I put them under the tree, just like you have here. Then I sat with my wife and we counted our blessings. Our children being the chief ones.

'Not long after we went to bed there was a commotion in the street. Noise downstairs. Then at the door. It sounded like someone was kicking the door down.'

'Was it the cops?' David asks.

'I thought so. But I was ready for that. I was prepared, I had a plan, I had an escape route.

'We lived on the top floor. I always kept the stolen stuff, the valuable stolen stuff, if it was in the house at all, in one bag. I could get out to the roof from the window. Once I was on the roof, I was free and clear. Remember, I was the cat. I could jump from our roof to the next building, then the next, and down the drain-pipes into the alley. From the alley I could get into the basement of the apartment building across the way. And soon I would disappear.

'So I turned to Sarah and I said, "Don't worry, it's me they want. You just tell them I'm not home. You haven't seen me." I looked at the rug. I wondered if it would give me away. The thing about Persian rugs is that, for the most part, you have to know something about them to be able to tell if it's a good one or a bad one or a real one or a fake one. So, quickly, even as we heard the footsteps on the stairs, we spread it across the floor. It was a little bit too big, so we just folded the end under. I was certain that no one would recognize its value or think it was stolen.

'Then, just as the knock on the door came, I went out the window with my bag of swag, and took off across the rooftops.'

'Did you get away?' David asks.

'Yes,' my father says. 'I got away.'

'Is that the end of the story?' my wife asks.

'It can't be,' David says. 'What about the rug?'

My father smiles. Or rather his mouth twitches toward a smile and the smile, that smirk that used to infuriate me so, dies, stillborn. As well it should.

'I went back in the morning.'

'Christmas,' my wife says.

'Yes. Christmas. Sarah, and David and Judith, were gone.'

'Where? Where did they go?' my son asks.

'The knock on the door. That wasn't the police looking for a thief. It was the Brownshirts, the Nazis, looking for Jews. And they found some. Two of them sleeping, waiting to wake in the morning to see what gifts Father Christmas had brought them in the night. Two of them and their mother. They took them away.'

'What happened to them?' David asks.

'Immediately? I don't know,' my father says. 'In the end, the camps. The ovens. I don't know. Disappeared. Never to be seen again.'

My son looks at me. He's not following this. He doesn't have enough information to know what the camps and the ovens mean. To him, camp is a place to go and play. Summer camp, arts and crafts, learning to swim, dodge-ball. Ovens are where cakes are made and bread is baked. So now I have to tell him.

Which I try to do as simply as possible. 'Not very long ago,' I say, 'when your grandfather was a young man, the people of Germany decided they wanted to get rid of all the Jews. To kill all the Jews. They did this very methodically. As if they were building cars. It was a very terrible thing.'

'Why?' my son asks.

'People do terrible things,' I say. 'Very terrible things. This was one of the worst. But there are others.' It is one of those things, of course, for which my father will never forgive God. I tend to agree with him.

'Was that your mommy?' David asks.

'No,' I say. 'Grandpa married another woman later.'

'They took the children's toys, all the Christmas gifts. They left our little tree. And the rug.'

Now what's odd is that my father finishes the story there. He hasn't really told the story of the rug. And there is a story of the rug and it's quite a tale. Like many other Jews, especially assimilated Jews who thought of themselves as more German than most of the Germans they knew, he thought that this anti-Semitism was just a bulge in the political hieroglyphics of history and that, like many other excesses, it would reach a high tide and recede. At that point he suddenly understood that things were much, much worse and much more permanent than that.

He and his friend Jurgen, who adamantly did not want to be drafted, decided to escape Germany for Switzerland. It was not so easy then as it is now to cross a border. Also, neither of them wanted to arrive in a new country totally broke. They wanted to get away with their loot. Jurgen had at one point worked for an industrialist who had a vacation château on Lake Lucerne. Then they thought of the rug. They could put their loot – and Isidore – in the rug, the rug in a truck and claim they were delivering it to the château.

This they proceeded to do.

I've heard my father tell this tale more than once. Sometimes there is a policeman in it. A German cop who catches them at a roadside inn just at the moment when Jurgen is bringing food out to the truck and Isidore is crawling out of the rug.

They kill the cop.

They are afraid that the corpse will be found and that they will be caught in the ensuing hue and cry. So they drive off with the corpse, looking for a place to dispose of it.

Somehow, when you're looking to do something like that, there never seems to be a right moment at the right place. At every right place there are people present. Whenever you're alone there's no place. The nightmare continued, hour after hour, as they approached the Swiss border. Finally they were out of time and out of possible places to dump the dead. They wrapped the cop in the rug – along with Izzy – and crossed into Switzerland, the dead German lying snug beside the running Jew.

That is the story of the rug. Usually.

But my father doesn't say any of that. He ends it there and says, 'A funny story, no?'

'No,' Moira says. 'I don't see anything funny about it at all.'

'Well, it's a Jewish story,' Grandpop says. He shrugs. 'Some people don't get them.' But that's because he has not laid the punch-line on us yet.

He gets up from his sitting position, to his knees, on the rug, and puts his big, old, veined and spotted hands on my son, touching his shoulders and the fine, soft hairs on his head, which still, sometimes, even now, on the odd and special day, have the sweet smell of puppy fur. 'I was a very wild young man,' he says. 'I did many, many things that were bad. Things that you should never do. If only because I don't think . . . I don't think the rewards are worth the risk.

'Still, I don't regret them.

'I regret only one thing. That I abandoned my wife and my children. I pretend to excuse it in that I couldn't know what would happen. But really, you see, the statement should go the other way. If you are a man. A real man. You should never leave your wife and children alone, exactly because you do not know what will happen.

'In this,' he tells David, 'you are very lucky. Because your father is a better man than I am. He will never abandon you. He will never leave you alone. This I know.'

My father is a wily old man. As well as having been a wicked one. But how has he divined that that is exactly what I want most to do in the world? Is his telling the tale this way, with this moral, some random event that I am, in my guilt, very attuned to? Is he a messenger sent by fate, not knowing what he is really saying, sent to warn me of the consequences of my action? Or is this David's grandfather, quite conscious of what he is doing, wily and manipulative, cleverly herding David's father back into line?

I had gathered my strength, my strength for coping, once again, just to make it through the holidays, planning my escape for the cold clarity that I anticipate for January. There's a sweeter woman who flushes with warmth when she sees me and welcomes me in, into her arms, into her heart, into her body. Dark eyes that seem to swallow me whole and flood me with endorphins or whatever chemicals the chemistry of love consists of, so that I feel free of pain and fear. Away from the spats and the sniping and the sword that lies down the middle of the bed where my heart and Moira's used to lie entwined.

My father, who brought this rug to America – where he gave up his thieving ways, he says, and opened a jewelry store – and gave it to me as a wedding gift, has come about the other gifts he has given me.

Among those other gifts he has given me are loyalty, love of family, and the cherishing of children. I didn't know that those gifts came with an enforcer who would show up at the crucial moment with a warning parable. He has put a kinehara on me. I suddenly feel that if I leave them, the evil that men do will come and steal them away and kill them, leaving the weight of their fate on my soul, a curse for which I can never forgive God.

I look at Moira and wonder if there is any way, any way whatsoever back to the garden?

I look at my father, expecting that infuriating smile to be on his lips and see, instead, only pleading eyes, and I know that I will stay at home. With my family and the goddamn rug.

DEXTERITY A Resnick Story
JOHN HARVEY

If Resnick had bumped into Nicky Snape early that Saturday morning, he could have become the proud owner of a bargain-price, next-to-new CD-player, fully programmable, random play facility, digital filter, the whole 16-bit. And all for thirty quid. Twenty-five, should that have been all the cash Resnick could lay his hands on at the time.

True, there were one or two things missing, bits and pieces really, incidentals. No manual, but then anyone with a bit of intelligence could work out which switch did what for himself. And the box: no, there was no box. Who needs a box, when the whole unit tucked so neatly under the front of a loose-fitting leather jacket, or, for ease of carrying, under one arm? The remote-control transmitter, though, Nicky had to admit that was more of a problem; nobody wanted to be jumping up out of the armchair every few seconds to fiddle through the tracks by hand. But he'd dropped it, hadn't he? Sliding his skinny arse back out through the bathroom window, the remote had squeezed out of his hand like a bar of soap and landed in the open toilet bowl with a splash.

Shit!

Legs waving in the wind, CD clutched to his chest, Nicky had not reckoned the risk of going back for it. Especially considering where it had fallen. Given on a quiet night he could hear the Turveys farting from four doors away, Nicky didn't fancy diving his hands into their khazi without a pair of rubber gloves.

No matter, he'd boost one from the electrical shop on the corner, one of those universal jobs that lets you programme everything from the telly to the microwave. Legs up on the settee with a can of Tennents, few flicks of that and you could tape *EastEnders*, listen to a tasty bit of Jungle, and make yourself a toasted ham sandwich all at the same time. Meet us here tomorrow and it's yours for a tenner, right? Five, then. Five, OK? Five. Do without, you tight cunt!

But Resnick had neglected to make his way into the city via Radford Road and so missed sampling the sales patter and burgeoning entrepreneurial skills of the fourteen-year-old Nicky Snape. What Resnick did was leave his car in the Central Police Station car park, nip into the market for an espresso, then wander down Market Street to SuperFi and purchase a brand-new Rotel RCD965BX at fifteen per cent off, last year's model. Box, manual and remote control included.

Now at last he had something on which to play the Billie Holiday boxed set he had bought himself the Christmas before last.

One thing Nicky was good with, his hands. Arms, too. Slide them down inside the smallest window crack, delve into the deepest letterbox, ease back the tightest bolt, slip the toughest lock. Like most things, it came with practice.

When Nicky got back home that Saturday afternoon he was feeling cool. Black denim shirt loose over baggy black jeans. Reversed on his head, the Chicago Bulls baseball cap he'd swapped with some kid from school. Music zapping through his Walkman at nearly 200 beats per minute and bright new Reeboks on his feet. Nicky felt like . . . Nicky felt like a fucking star!

Then smack! Three paces into the room and his mother caught him such a round-arm slap that he went stumbling sideways, legs jellying under him, cap flying and one earpiece of his headphones all but piercing his inner ear.

'What? What the fuck was that for? What?'

Norma hit him again: once for asking stupid questions and once for using language like that inside her house. 'Don't you come in here swearing at me, you loundering trail-tripes, don't you bloody dare! This is your mother you're talking to and don't you bloody forget it!'

Nicky pulled off his headphones and, scooping up his cap from the floor, jammed it back on his head. 'What?' he shouted in his mother's face. 'What?'

At five-foot-eight, Norma Snape was a couple of inches taller than her youngest son and outweighed him by some forty pounds. It should have slowed her down more than it did. The next blow Nicky ducked, but not the one after. Norma's open hand struck him on the same side of the face, right around the ear, and Nicky's skin burned red.

'What the fuck've I done now?'

'Didn't I just tell you . . . ?'

'Don't!' When Nicky scrambled back around the settee, he was close to tears.

'For fuck's sake!' shouted Nicky's seventeen-year-old half-brother, Shane. 'Why don't the pair of you cut it out and let me watch this in peace?'

Neither paid him the slightest heed. The four o'clock at Kempton was under starter's orders and Shane had a twenty each way riding on the second favourite.

'Look,' Norma said, pointing at her youngest son's feet. 'You think I'm blind or stupid or what?'

'What?'

'Jesus and Mary, can't you ever say anything but that?'

'If I knew what you were talking about,' Nicky said, 'I might.'

Norma narrowed her eyes as if she were in pain; someone knocked at the front door and she yelled at them to go away. 'Those shoes,' she said. 'Those trainers you've got on your feet. They're new, aren't they? Brand sodding new.'

'So?'

'So you picked 'em off the trees alongside the Park and Ride, did you? You thieving little bowdykite, you've been up the Viccy Centre, thieving again, that's what.'

Nicky's face contorted into a smirk. 'Yeah, well, that's just where you're wrong, 'cause I never nicked them at all.'

'And I've told you before, I'll not have you lying to me.'

Nicky tried vaulting his brother's legs in a dash for the kitchen door, but Shane's kick caught him high on the back of the thigh and brought him low. 'Get out the bloody way!' The leaders were only at the second furlong mark and Shane's horse was back amongst the stragglers already.

'Right. Now, you listen.' Norma had Nicky jammed up against the open door, holding him by his hair. 'You're going to get those off your feet and take them back right now.'

'No way.'

She pulled his head back before slamming it against the door. 'You'll do what you're sodding told.'

Nicky wriggled the fingers of his right hand down into the back pocket of his jeans and came up with a crumpled receipt. 'Don't believe me, look at that.' There were tears in his eyes now and no mistake.

'What?'

'Now who can't say nothin' else?'

Norma slapped him for being smart and took the receipt. 'One pair Reebok training shoes, forty-nine pound, ninety-five.'

'Yeah, and today's date, see there, today's date, date and time, where and when I bought 'em, today.'

'Forty-nine, ninety-five.'

'Yes.'

'Almost fifty quid.'

'Yes.'

'For those?'

'Yes.'

Norma punched him so hard in the chest that Nicky nearly stopped breathing. 'Where in the name of buggery did you get fifty pound to spend on your scuttering feet?'

It had been snowing when Resnick arrived back at his car; just lightly, a thin skein of flakes filtering down from an almost blue sky. Careful, he had locked the CD-player inside the boot, knowing better than to tempt providence, even in the police car park.

Phoning through to his own CID room at the Canning Circus sub-station, he half smiled at Kevin Naylor's diffident voice, asking him to please hold. Blurred down the line, he heard the fall and rise of voices, the scrape of chairs, the computer printer's broken rhythm, the sound of whistling that could only come from Graham Millington, a shrilly confident version of 'The Way We Were'.

When Naylor returned to the phone it was to report the normal mix of break-ins and minor assaults, drunk and disorderlies, and vehicles taken without consent. Like CID teams up and down the country, those of Resnick's officers who were not hard-pressed by long-term investigations were busy sweeping up the leftovers of another urban Friday night. And there was still Saturday to come: the traditional weekend of two halves.

'Not at the match, sir?' Naylor asked.

Resnick hung up. These past weeks of the season, frustrated by a series of games in which, if their visitors could not find a way of doing it for themselves, his team's defence had all but kicked the ball into their own net – and sometimes done exactly that – Resnick had voted with his feet and stopped attending. Since when, predictably, although County were still in prime relegation position, they had achieved some memorable results. Had actually won matches.

With a small degree of guilt, Resnick thought that, had he stopped going sooner, the team might have had a chance of staying put.

To cheer himself up he set out for the old market square, spurred on to brave the youth of the city, clustered with numbed insouciance around the listening posts in the Virgin Megastore, and brush his way into the jazz section at the rear in order to supplement his meagre collection of CDs.

There were times when Norma Snape thought that if she'd not come south from Huddersfield, things would have been all right. No one had told her that, aside from being the self-confessed 'poetry capital of the country', Huddersfield had recently been voted the town in which folk were most likely to be burgled. West Yorkshire police statistics, official. Put her Nicky in with a chance of knocking off another sonnet or knocking over the corner shop, it didn't take fourteen lines of iambic pentameter to tell which was the most likely.

At least tonight she knew where he was, playing pool with his Uncle Vic and under pain of death to be back in the house before eleven. Shane was . . . well, the Good Lord alone knew where Shane was . . . and Sheena – Sheena was sitting here alongside Norma, sipping a rum and Coke to make it last, knowing after that she'd be on halves of lager like everyone else.

'Where you off to now?' Norma asked, as Sheena shuffled from her seat, smoothing her skirt down in the far direction of her knees.

'Loo.'

'Be sharp, then. Karaoke's set to start any minute.'

Sheena made a face and wiggled away, more than half the eyes in the pub turning to watch her go. Norma had put her on the pill to celebrate her fifteenth birthday, but knew that was never enough. Times had changed since she was a lass herself, and there were things far worse you could catch now than a baby.

'Been gone long enough to piss for me too,' Norma said, as Sheena finally returned. Up at the mike a Barton bus driver, still wearing his uniform trousers, was making a passable meal of 'The Green, Green Grass of Home'.

'Party upstairs,' Sheena said, sitting down. 'Cheryl Rogers's eighteenth.'

'Not a mate of yours, is she?'

'Can't stand her, stuck-up cow. And her vol-au-vents taste like cardboard stuck round sick.' Sheena leaned back and used a chipped fingernail to pick some shredded chicken from between her teeth.

For Resnick, it was a pretty basic sandwich. Ham, a few slices of strong Lancashire, some shallots, what remained of a green pepper and a smear of mustard pickle. The bread – his favourite caraway and rye – he had toasted on one side. Lately, he had been drinking Worthington White Shield.

The Billie Holiday tracks with Ben Webster and Barney Kessell were coming to an end, and he was looking at his purchases from Virgin, wondering how on earth you were supposed to read the notes on CDs without a magnifying glass. He turned the cases over in his hand. Spike Robinson: *The Gershwin Collection*. Spike, who had dedicated a number to Resnick's late friend Ed Silver from the stage at Ronnie Scott's. Monk, of course. The set of piano solos which included 'Memories of You'. Duke Ellington's *New Orleans Suite*, with Johnny Hodges playing one of his last solos on 'Blues for New Orleans'. And Charlie Parker – Bird – the *Dial Masters*. Resnick set the disc to play.

Broadway at 38th Street in New York, 28th of October, forty-seven. A Tuesday. Duke Jordan at the piano, Max Roach on drums. Miles Davis was just twenty-one. The rolling, rubato opening to 'Dexterity', before muted trumpet and alto play the theme, a little riff repeated clean and simple before the band drops out and leaves

Parker wheeling through space alone, fingers, breath and soul manoeuvring together with agile blue grace.

Smiling, Resnick touches the remote and plays the track again.

Norma and Sheena had arrived home a shade after ten-thirty to find that Nicky was already there, head bent over some new computer game or other, can of Coke close to hand. He barely shrugged when his mother and sister came in.

'Where's our Shane?' Norma asked.

'In his room.'

'What doing?'

'Sara Johnson.'

Norma's coat dropped to the floor. 'He better not gecking be! He . . .'

She was at the foot of the stairs before Nicky's laughter stopped her in her tracks, Nicky all but doubled over, Sheena joining in with it, pleased to see their mum caught out.

'You little bugger!' But Norma was laughing too, pleased she could still see the funny side.

'What's all the racket?' Shane asked, appearing in the doorway, magazine at his side.

'Never mind,' Norma said happily, picking up her coat. 'Sheena, just set kettle on, there's a love.'

'God,' said Sheena, 'why's it always me?' But it wasn't a real protest, only routine. 'Maybe we could all watch a video?' she called from the sink.

'What? Like together?' Shane laughed. 'What d'you think this is all of a sudden, happy families?'

'Why not?' Norma said.

The tea hadn't had time to mash before Pete Turvey and his cousins were hammering at the front door.

The Turveys, all three of them, along with their respective wives, had spent the early part of the evening in their local before moving on to Radford Boulevard and Cheryl Rogers's birthday party. Cheryl's mum and Pete Turvey's wife worked the early shift at Player's, grateful to be hanging on to their jobs longer than most.

'Come back the house after,' Bev Rogers had said. 'Trevor's got some drink in, haven't you, Trev?'

Cheryl's dad had nodded with less than enthusiasm. What the chuffin' hell did she want to be asking that pack back for? Piss up your leg as soon as look at you, most of the time. But all Pete Turvey had done was drop a shoulder in Trevor's direction and nod his head. 'Nice one, Trev. We'll be there, no problem at all.'

'Look here,' Bev said, once they had all arrived and were standing, the three Turvey men close to six foot apiece, planted in the centre of the Rogers's living room with glasses in their hands. 'This lot of presents our Cheryl got. Too much really. Way over't top. But then, like I was saying, you're only eighteen once.'

'Aye,' Pete Turvey had said, lifting his glass and winking in the girl's direction. 'Sweet eighteen and scarce been kissed.'

Cheryl's face and neck showed several shades of red and Turvey, who knew a few things about her that her mum did not, grinned and winked again.

'See what her dad give her, here, look,' Bev said from across the room. 'Stereo, all of her own.'

Turvey could see it right enough, units stacked on one another, not quite matching: twin-deck Technics cassette-player, JVC amp, Kenwood tuner and, perched on top of them all, a Panasonic CD-player, almost new.

'Nice,' said Turvey, moving in for a closer look.

''Course,' Bev said, 'Trevor had to match them up himself, piece by piece, didn't you, Trev?'

'Very nice,' Turvey said over Trevor's grunt. 'CD, specially.'

'That was what I really wanted most of all, wasn't it, Dad?' Cheryl said, colour almost back to normal.

'Shame,' Pete Turvey had said, turning back into the room, 'the one he got you had to be fucking mine!'

'Let me get my hands on the bastard!' Pete Turvey said now, pushing his way across the Snape's front room; but he had Norma to get by first and then there was Shane. 'Thievin' shitarse!'

'Let him be.'

Eyes wide, Nicky was crouching down beside the TV.

'Sort him out of there,' Turvey said to his cousins, pointing, but when one of them moved there was Shane to block him and the other one stood his ground. 'Go on!'

But nobody did.

'Happen,' Norma said, 'you should tell us what this is all about.'
'I'll tell you what it's all about,' Turvey shouted.
'Right. Then why don't we all sit down first?'
'I don't want to fucking sit down!'
'Suit yourself.'

From the kitchen doorway, Sheena glanced over at Nicky and saw that Nicky was fit to piss himself with laughter. 'I don't suppose anyone'd like a cup of tea?' she asked.

Nicky clapped a hand across his mouth and headed for the door.
'You stay bloody there!' Pete Turvey called.
'Nicky, stay there,' Norma said.

Still fighting the urge to laugh, Nicky leaned against the wall.
'Tell 'em what happened,' one of Turvey's cousins said.
'What happened,' said Pete Turvey, 'is that sniggering little toerag over there broke into my place Friday, stole the CD and sold it to Trevor Rogers for thirty quid so's Rogers could give it to his kid for her soddin' birthday.'

Now it was Shane's turn to laugh.
'Shut it!' Norma said. And then, 'Nicky, is that true?'
''Course it isn't.'
'Don't you lie to me now.'
'I'm not.'
'He fucking is!' Turvey made to get at him, but this time the settee was in the way. The settee and Shane.
'You bring him round here, this bloke then,' Shane said. 'Rogers, that his name? Get him round here tomorrow, first thing. Say it all to Nicky's face. And mine. If he does and Nicky's lying, we'll sort it out.'
'How?'
'We'll sort it out.'

Turvey stared hard into Shane's face, but Shane didn't waver. Turvey knew he was heavier, older, taller; he had to ask himself if he fancied it, and the truth was he did not. Not there and then.

'Right,' Turvey said, backing off. 'Tomorrow, right?' He nodded at his cousins and with a hunch of their shoulders they turned and went, slamming the door at their backs.

Norma moved fast and she had hold of Nicky before he could dodge from the room.

'Mum!'

43

She slapped him both ways with her open hand, both cheeks, forward and back. Then slapped him again, tears hot against the laughter that still clung to the corners of his eyes.

'Tea's cold,' called Sheena from the kitchen.

'Then mash some more.'

Shane Snape was known. One conviction for aggravated burglary and with the next one he would do time. Serious though, Shane, about some things – money in his pockets, Special Brew, screwing Sara Johnson, supporting Mansfield Town, politics of a sort. Responsibilities, he was serious about those too. Norma didn't ask him where he was going, didn't want to know, although, of course, she knew.

Shane hammered on the Rogers's front door until Bev came down.

'Trevor, I want to see him.'

'It's past one in the morning.'

'I don't care if it's past Monday. Get him down here now.'

The two men stood, uneasy, in the cold back room; Bev, too nervous to go back to bed, sat on the stairs behind the closed door. Trevor old enough to be the other's dad.

'Pete Turvey,' Shane said, 'he was round ours earlier tonight.'

'Yes.'

''Bout something you said.'

'Yes.'

'Me, I think he must've heard you wrong.'

Trevor Rogers looked into Shane's eyes and remembered what he'd been told. How Shane had put this bloke in hospital for letting his dog piss on Shane's foot while he was waiting in the betting shop. Two weeks in intensive care. Definitely touch and go. It didn't matter that it wasn't true. What mattered, he believed it, Trevor, staring into Shane's unsmiling face, his unfaltering grey eyes.

'Yes,' Trevor said, 'he must've got, you know, wrong end of the stick.'

At the door, Shane turned: 'I was you, Trevor, I'd see Turvey got his CD-player back.'

So Cheryl said goodbye to the most prized part of her stereo without ever having heard it; Trevor bunged Pete Turvey an extra twenty and mumbled something about one bloody kid looking much like another, must've made a mistake. 'Right,' said Turvey, copping the player and the twenty and gobbing full in Trevor's face, 'that's what you did all right.'

'You,' Shane said, wrenching Nicky's arm up high behind his back. 'Next time you shit on your own shoes, you can wipe it off yourself.'

'I hope you realize,' his mum said, 'just how lucky you are.'

Nicky did: and he thought it was never going to change. He lay low for a couple of weeks, swapping comics, playing the same old computer games, bunking off school and nicking stuff from shops, nothing out of the way. Then he broke into the Turvey house again and stole their CD-player for the second time.

Pete Turvey did something he thought he'd never see himself do – he went to the police.

'What you goin' to do about it, that's what I want to know. What you goin' to fuckin' do?'

From the door to his office, Resnick looked across the CID room to where Kevin Naylor, seated at his desk, was trying to calm an irate Pete Turvey into being rational. About thirty years, thought Resnick, and three bites at the education system too late.

'Kevin,' Resnick said from near Turvey's shoulder, 'anything I can do?'

'This gentleman . . .' Naylor began.

'What you can do,' Turvey said, 'is get that little arsehole Snape up in court and this time, instead of feedin' him with lollipops and promises and pats on the head, stick him inside so the rest of us can step out the house without comin' back and findin' anything not bolted down's been nicked.'

'This isn't Shane?' Resnick said. 'This is Nicky?'

'Christ!' exclaimed Turvey. 'I must've come to the wrong place. Someone who knows what he's on about.'

'Why don't you,' Resnick said, 'let DC Naylor have an accurate list of dates, what's been taken, anything else that's useful? I'll go along and have a word with the Snapes myself. OK?'

'Yeh,' said Turvey. 'Right. Yeh, right.' And, wind from his sails, he took a seat at Naylor's desk.

*   *   *

Resnick had known the family for a long time, through a whole catalogue of case conferences and supervision orders, periods for all three of the kids in local authority care. He knew Norma and liked her well enough, though he would never have been as foolish to think that she liked him. Why would she? From where Norma was standing, trouble came in shiny suits and waving warrant cards.

Like him or not, she made him a cup of tea. Pointed at the best chair for him to sit down in.

'How's Sheena?' Resnick asked, balancing the cup on one raised knee. At one side of the room, the television was switched on, an Open University broadcast on engineering Resnick doubted anyone was following.

'Is it her you've come about, then?' Norma asked.

Resnick shook his head.

'It's those Turveys, isn't it?'

'Is it?'

'Putting in their spoke where it's not wanted. Stirring trouble.'

'They're making it up, then? About Nicky?'

Norma's expression changed, sour, as if she had found something floating on the surface of her tea. She sighed. 'What's the caufhead done now?'

Resnick voiced the complaint: the constant break-ins, the CD-player stolen twice.

Norma shook her head. 'Even our Nicky wouldn't be that daft.'

Resnick let it ride. He knew there was no evidence, only Turvey's suspicions, though for himself, he thought they were probably correct. But if the machine had been taken it would have been offloaded within hours; the one risk Nicky would have kept to a minimum was being caught with it on his person.

As Resnick sipped the strong tea, he could feel it forming a lining inside his stomach. Silent, Norma lit one cigarette from the butt of another.

'You can see where it's heading, Norma. Clear as I can myself.'

She shook her head and tilted it back, eyes closed. 'You think I haven't told him till I'm blue in the face? Eh? Pleaded with him, belted him, tried shutting him in his room? Doesn't do a ha'p'orth of good.'

Resnick doubted Norma was old enough ever to have seen a halfpenny. 'Do you want me to talk to him? D'you think that might help?'

Norma let herself slump forward. 'If you can find him, why not? One thing sure, it can't make nothing worse.'

Nicky was in town, standing with a crowd of youths in the amusement arcade on the north side of the square.

'Let's go outside, Nicky,' Resnick said. 'Sit in the car.'

'Fancy me, then, do you?' Nicky grinned, adding a slight lisp to his voice. 'How much is it worth?'

Ignoring the laughter, Resnick took hold of his arm. 'I'll not ask twice.'

Leaving the arcade, the boy turned back to his friends and laughed, miming masturbation with his hand.

He listened to Resnick for ten minutes, biting his already too-short nails and fidgeting with the ring in his left ear. All of the time his attention seemed to be outside the car, watching whoever was passing by; Resnick doubted if he'd heard one word in ten and was certain he didn't care.

'Nicky, have you heard what I've been saying?'

''Course,' Nicky smiled. 'Not stupid, you know. I can listen.'

Yes, Resnick thought, but not to me. 'OK,' he said, 'you can go.'

Through the mirror, Resnick saw the boy stick two fingers high in the air before going back into the arcade.

'You've talked to him?' Turvey said, incredulously. 'What sort of soddin' good's that supposed to do?'

His complaint would still be looked into, Resnick explained, the details of the missing property would be logged and if it turned up, of course, Turvey would be informed.

'And Snape?'

'We'll keep an eye on him.'

'What you mean,' Turvey said, 'you're not goin' to do a bare-arsed thing.'

Resnick shook his head. 'We'll do what we can.'

'Well, then,' said Turvey, puffing out his chest. 'I know someone who'll do a whole lot more.'

'I have to warn you,' Resnick said, 'about taking the law into your own hands.'

'Yeh?' Turvey said. 'Yeh? The law? What's that then, round here? The law? What's that? You, that what it is?' He laughed. 'Look around you. What d'you think?'

Resnick couldn't remember who it was had told him the best place to keep vodka was in the freezer, Russian vodka, at least. Whoever it had been, he was grateful. It was close to midnight, but somehow he didn't want to go to bed. In the living room, he turned off the central light and sat with one of the cats curled in his lap, another stretched out, long and slim, along one of the arms. The vodka glass was cold against his hand. He thought about Norma Snape, struggling to bring up three kids against all the odds. Then he tried not to think about it. There was a ballad track on the *Dial* set and he played it now, only the occasional flutter of notes embellishing the melody, the sharp edge of Parker's tone cutting all but the smallest residue of sentimentality away. When it came to an end, Resnick cued it again. 'Don't Blame Me'.

Nicky knew he was late and his mum would give him a thorough bollocking and he didn't care. The rhythm that tore through his headphones was fast and ragged and it seared his mind clear of everything else but the warmth of the cigarette he lifted to his mouth as he walked towards his home. He didn't hear the car approaching, didn't hear Pete Turvey's angry shout, the whoosh of the bottle as it sped, flaming, through the air, nor the crash of glass as it shattered at his feet.

What Nicky saw was the burst of flame as the petrol bomb exploded, and all he knew beneath his screams was the pain which claimed his hands and face and which clung to his legs like blistering skin.

MY SHIP IS COMING IN

MARTIN EDWARDS

The Tall Ships had returned to Liverpool and for days the city had been buzzing with excitement. Smart young men in naval uniform strutted along the streets near the river, talking in strange accents and flirting in sexy broken English with the local girls. Crowds flocked to the waterfront to see the proud square riggers which had crossed the Atlantic before mooring in the docks on the banks of the Mersey. The ships had retraced their route of olden days, when Liverpool had been the second city of the British Empire and its exports had found a ready market in the Americas. So much had changed since then, but everyone seemed to be relishing a brief glimpse into a glorious past and even that old skinflint, the sun, had shone down all week on the celebrations.

Harry Devlin's morning in court had ended earlier than expected, and so he found himself wandering over to the Pierhead to look at the ships. Tomorrow would see the final sail-past and he and his partner Jim Crusoe had been invited to join a party of lawyers and businessmen, accepting the hospitality of a financial services outfit newly arrived in the city. He loathed the superficial small talk that characterized such events, and had intended to discover an alternative engagement and watch the ships instead from the vantage point of his flat in the Empire Dock development, with only a six-pack of bitter for company. But taking in the scene and the sunshine, he changed his mind. The weather was too good for delight in it not to be shared.

When he arrived back at his office at Fenwick Court, the face of Suzanne, Crusoe and Devlin's receptionist, was aglow.

'I'm afraid I've got some bad news for you,' she said.

Suzanne specialized in *schadenfreude*. Her cheekiness was exceeded only by her indolence, and if he and his partner had been less soft-hearted, they would have sacked her after a month's employment. But Harry was well aware of the length of the city's dole queue, and against his better judgement he had more than once persuaded Jim Crusoe not to add Suzanne to it. Anyone who lost a job in Liverpool these days did not easily find another.

'What's the problem?'

'Well,' she said, a smile creeping across her face. 'It's about me.'

Bad news about Suzanne? His mind boggled: was she proposing to work longer hours? He returned her smile noncommittally and waited.

She took a deep breath. 'I've decided to leave you.'

The words had the same effect upon him as might the announcement that his 100–1 flutter in the Grand National had romped home five lengths ahead of the favourite. She sensed at once that he was struggling to contain his emotions, but misinterpreted their nature.

'I'm sorry, Mr Devlin, it's no good pleading with me to stay. My mind's made up.'

He racked his brains for a suitable response, reluctantly ruling out a yell of jubilation. 'Well, Suzanne . . . this does come as a surprise.'

She nodded. 'I've kept it to myself, but I have been thinking about it for some time. No disrespect, Mr Devlin, but the wages here are pretty lousy and let's face it, the working conditions are hardly plush.' She waved a hand towards the out-of-date magazines cluttering up the battered occasional table and the dusty yucca in the corner of the reception area. 'Besides, I want to get on. I'm ambitious, I want to make something of myself.'

A couple of practical suggestions sprang to Harry's mind, but he kept them to himself. 'So where are you moving to? Windaybanks? Maher and Malcolm?'

'God, I wouldn't dream of going there. It would be a case of out of the frying-pan and into the fire. At least you and Mr Crusoe aren't stuck-up. No, I've had enough of the legal profession. It's not exactly glamorous, is it? So I've decided to make a career in corporate hospitality.'

Harry gaped at her. Daphne du Maurier's Mrs Danvers would, he thought, have made a more congenial hostess.

Again she misread his expression. 'Yes, it's true: even in this city there are one or two wonderful opportunities. For the right person, that is.'

She smiled for a moment and Harry suddenly realized that, in the right mood – which seldom seemed to have struck her during their years together – she could be likeable enough. When her features were not screwed up in a spoiled-brat frown, when the near-constant note of complaint left her voice, she was simply another Scouse girl who kept dreaming of a better life. A little plump, perhaps – too many chocolate bars munched while the phone kept ringing – but attractive for all that. How typical that it was not until now that it had occurred to him. All the same, he had no intention of trying to talk her out of her decision to quit. Besides, the change of job might indeed be the making of her.

'A company has made me an offer I can't refuse,' she confided. 'There is a catch, though.'

Harry had *known* it was too good to be true. 'What is it?'

'They are organizing a marquee for people coming to see the Tall Ships tomorrow. Everyone who is anyone will be there. So they really would like me to start straight away.'

'I don't think that will be a problem,' Harry said.

'But what about my month's notice?'

'Jim and I wouldn't wish to stand in your way when you have such a marvellous chance.'

'Fantastic! I knew you would understand! I've always said, Mr Devlin may seem to stagger from one crisis to another, but beneath it all he has a heart of gold!'

Harry didn't know what to say to that, but Suzanne saved him the trouble by rushing on. 'There is just one more thing. If you don't mind me mentioning it.'

'Go on.'

'I'm supposed to be meeting my new boss at twelve so that I can give him my answer. Would it be all right if I took an early lunch?'

'Take as long as you like,' said Harry, with all the magnanimity at his command.

He felt the first faint twitches of regret at his generosity when, at half past two, his secretary complained that Suzanne had still not come back and that, in deputizing on the switchboard, she was getting behind with his typing.

'It's the not knowing I don't like,' said Lucy. 'You'd think she would at least have had the decency to call.'

'She's excited,' said Harry. 'I expect she's lost all track of time as her new employers wine and dine her.'

Lucy grunted. She was no admirer of Suzanne. 'That girl has never had the slightest consideration—'

'Look,' he said gently, 'a few hours' inconvenience isn't too high a price for us to pay, is it?'

She gave him a slow smile. Although they had worked closely together for years, he had made it a rule not to express even a hint of the depth of his dissatisfaction with Suzanne. But perhaps no one would have needed a degree in psychology to guess it.

'I suppose you're right,' she said, and he went back to his work.

Half an hour later she buzzed him again. 'Harry, I'm getting worried about Suzanne.'

You think she may have turned the job down? he was tempted to ask. But all he said was: 'Don't be. It's beginning to look as though she's decided to take the rest of the day off.'

'I can't believe even she would do that. Anyway, the drawers of her desk are cluttered with her rubbish. There's no way she'd leave without stuffing it all into half a dozen carrier bags.'

'So perhaps she'll turn up for it on Monday.'

'I don't know. Keith, her boyfriend – you know, the hefty lad with the motor bike – has rung in. She promised to call him at two o'clock on the dot to let him know how her meeting with her new lord and master had gone. But he's heard nothing at all.'

'Perhaps she forgot.'

'He reckons she would never let him down.'

Harry shrugged. In both his personal and professional experience, most people deluded themselves about the constancy of their loved ones. 'I didn't press her to come back promptly, you know. Quite the opposite. She was obviously thrilled with this new job. After all, I've never offered her a single lavish lunch outside of Christmas. You can understand her making the most of this one.'

'Keith is bothered. He says she's never broken a promise to ring him before. And she does it all the time, I can tell you. God knows what the firm's phone bill looks like. Besides, she also promised to call her mum. According to Keith, she hasn't done that either. He's so het up he's even going to ring round the local hospitals.'

'Suzanne's a big girl, Lucy. She can look after herself.'

'You really think so? She's only twenty-two. And there are some funny people out there.'

I know, thought Harry, *most of them are our clients*. 'Come on,' he said calmly, 'what do you think has happened to her?'

'I've no idea, but I'm sure we ought to try and find out.'

He groaned. 'OK, but I'm telling you, it's a complete waste of time.'

Elaine, his partner's secretary, had taken over on the switchboard. He was startled to see her dabbing a tear from her eye.

'For heaven's sake, Elaine. Let's get all this in proportion. Suzanne is probably still charming the pants off the feller who has offered her this new job. Hasn't anyone thought about ringing his company?'

'That's just the problem,' said Elaine. 'We can't trace them. If you ask me, they don't exist.'

Suzanne had been talking for some time, he soon learned, about making a break with legal work. The boss, he reflected, is always the last to know about these things: much the same as a cuckolded spouse. The publicity surrounding the return of the Tall Ships and all the entertainments associated with it had persuaded her that corporate hospitality offered career prospects as exciting as they were remunerative. She had prepared a c.v. – an exercise in creative writing, Harry suspected – and sent it out to the specialist firms listed in the Yellow Pages. The previous afternoon, a call had come through for her at a time when Elaine was in the reception area making a vain attempt to water some life into the yucca. Suzanne had not disguised her glee at the phone message, and whilst she held the receiver in one hand, she used the other to beckon her colleague over to share the good news.

'They've picked me from over fifty applicants!' she had whispered, covering the mouthpiece. 'And the pay is twice the measly sum I get here! Listen, I'll put him on the speaker.'

Elaine had heard the managing director's voice loud and clear. His tone was self-confident, bordering on the brash.

'You sound like our sort of executive, Suzanne my dear. Attractive and outgoing. Interpersonal skills are so important, of course, in our line of business. We deal with leading decision-makers, you know, so we have to maintain high standards. Think you can cope?'

'Oh yes, Mr Sachs. I'm sure of it.'

Her simple assurance had seemed to be all he needed to hear. 'Call me Charles, please. Very well, Suzanne, I think I can say even at this stage that the job is yours if you want it. And so the only question is, when can you start?'

'Well, when do you want me?'

A chuckle from Charles Sachs. 'As soon as ever possible, Suzanne. As I mentioned, this Saturday will be a very busy day for us. If you could join us in our marquee, I would be most grateful. After that, there will be a string of other events for you to organize. As you know, the Old Trafford test match is not too far away.'

'Oh yes,' agreed Suzanne, who barely knew what a test match was, let alone where she might find the ground at Old Trafford.

'Would you be able to start with us at once, then?'

'Oh . . . well, yes, yes, I'm sure I can.'

'Splendid! So there is no difficulty with your present employer?'

'None at all,' Suzanne assured him. 'After all, I've worked my fingers to the bone for them these last few years. They owe it to me not to stand in my way.'

'Excellent. In that case, the sooner we can get together the better. Naturally I'm looking forward very much to our first meeting. Perhaps you would like to join me for lunch, say? How does tomorrow sound?'

'That would be lovely.'

'Then it's a date. I'll pick you up outside the Liver Building on the stroke of twelve.'

'And how will I recognize you . . . er . . . Charles?'

An easy laugh. 'Quite simple. I shall be driving a red Jaguar.'

As she put the phone down, Suzanne shot Elaine a glance of triumph.

'You've certainly landed on your feet,' the older woman said.

'Doesn't he sound dreamy?'

'Don't let Keith hear you say that.'

'Oh, don't be a spoilsport. What the eye doesn't see . . .'

And Suzanne had giggled with pure delight.

'What makes you think the company was phoney?' demanded Harry.

'I've spoken to all but one of the corporate hospitality places in the book,' said Elaine. 'None of them has heard of Suzanne. Nor of a Mr Charles Sachs – with or without a red Jaguar.'

'You don't know the name of Sachs's business?'

'No, but Keith is certain that Suzanne only sent out half a dozen job applications. There aren't too many Liverpool firms who specialize in corporate hospitality.'

'And the company you haven't called?'

'The number was unobtainable.'

'That must be the one. Try again.'

Elaine did so and Harry listened in. It sounded as if the line had been disconnected.

Harry checked the Yellow Pages. 'The Glad Hand Partnership. If Charles Sachs is connected with them, they can scarcely have disappeared in the space of twenty-four hours.'

'What do you think we should do?'

'First things first. We don't even know if she actually met Sachs. I'll nip over the road to see if Bill Dawkes can tell me anything.' He grimaced and added reluctantly. 'In the meantime, check the hospitals again.'

Bill Dawkes sold fresh fruit from a barrow which he stationed each day outside the Liver Building. But even on good days – and there had been a few of them lately, thanks to the crowds swarming to see the Tall Ships – when he managed to get rid of his stock by mid-afternoon, he would always hang around until the rush hour had passed. He was a widower who had been working in the city centre for close on forty years, and Harry guessed that even if he never flogged another banana, it would take an earthquake to prevent him from turning up and chatting to all and sundry between nine and half five. If anyone was likely to have seen Suzanne at the time of her intended meeting with Charles Sachs, it was Bill.

And the old man did not disappoint. "Course I saw her,' he confirmed. 'Not that she had time to say hello. Soon as I spotted her, I reckoned she was meeting a feller.'

'How on earth did you make that out, Bill?' asked Harry, in his best Dr Watson voice.

'Never seen her hair done so nice in all the years I've known her,' said the old man simply. 'And was I right? 'Course I was. She looked up and down the Strand for a couple of minutes, and then blow me down if a Jag doesn't pull up right next to her.'

'A Jaguar?' So she had met Sachs after all.

'Red 'un. The window wound down and she said something to the feller inside, then opened the door and hopped in. They headed off towards the docks.'

'You didn't by any chance catch sight of the car driver?'

Bill didn't let him down. 'No more than a glimpse when he leaned across to speak to her. Youngish feller by my reckoning. Fair hair, salesman's smile.'

'You're very observant.'

The old man shrugged. 'Got nothing better to do all day, have I, but keep my eyes open.' He paused. 'What's the problem?'

'She's leaving us. The man you saw was her new boss. He was supposed to be giving her lunch, but she's not come back or let anyone know where she is.'

'Think she's got herself in a spot of bother?'

'I wish I knew,' said Harry, although in his heart of hearts he thought he did.

His next stop was the address for Glad Hand, which he had memorized from the Yellow Pages. It was close to the Dock Road, a small business park with one-storey units and a forest of To Let signs. Leaving his car in one of the empty marked spaces at the entrance to the park, he walked along the pavement, checking off the names over the doors. The fifth bore a signboard which proclaimed The Glad Hand Partnership – Specialists in Corporate Entertainment. Harry tried the handle. It was locked.

A tubby middle-aged woman poked her head round the door of

the adjoining unit, a place rejoicing in the name of Anguish Alarms. 'Looking for someone, love?'

'Glad Hand?'

'Thumbs Down, more like. Sorry to disappoint you, love, but they've gone bust. Owe you money, do they?'

'No, but I'm surprised by what you say. They offered a friend of mine a job only yesterday.'

The woman shook her head. 'Must be some mistake. The Azha brothers – the people who ran Glad Hand – did a flit weeks ago. They'll be back in Bangladesh by now if I know anything.' A dreamy look came into her eyes. 'Rascals, of course, but gorgeous blokes, all the same. They told me they were princes in their home country. But if they're royalty, I'm the Queen Mother.'

'And Charles Sachs? Did he work for them?'

She gave him a baffled stare. 'Never heard of him. No, the brothers had a couple of young girls working for them, but no one else that I ever knew.'

So: a dead end. Harry groaned as he racked his brain, trying to salvage something from his visit. 'Could it be that someone has been using the premises since the Azhas fled?'

'No chance,' she said with unmistakable pride. 'They invested in one of our latest alarms. State-of-the-art technology, I can assure you. No one could get in next door without half the neighbourhood hearing of it. My husband hasn't disconnected the system yet, even though they never paid us everything they owed, I might add. He's soft-hearted is my—'

'So there's no way anyone could be operating the Glad Hand business, or any other, from these offices?' Harry interrupted.

'No way in the world,' she assured him.

'Oh well. Thanks anyway. I must be going . . . wait a minute!'

In turning to leave, he had glanced over to the opposite side of the road. A lorry was parked in front of a couple of the units, obscuring parts of the signboards. The first said Charles and the second Sacks. As Harry's mind whirled, a man in overalls jumped into the cab and the lorry moved off, revealing the full signboards. Charles Kahn – Brushmaker and Kirkdale Sacks respectively.

'Are you all right, love?'

'I'm fine,' he said slowly. 'Listen, I'm sure the chap I'm looking for – he did call himself Charles Sachs, but that's not his real name – is familiar with this place. He may even be based here. Tell me, do you know anyone who drives a red Jaguar?'

The woman frowned. 'There's Mr Lovell, of course.'

'And who is he?'

She gestured to a separate block further down the road. 'He's one of the directors of Beagries, the developers who own this whole park. Those are their offices.'

'So I can find him over there?'

'Not today you can't. He and his wife have been invited to one of these Tall Ships jamborees by the Lord Mayor.'

As one door opened, another shut. 'And his Jaguar? Any idea where that may be?'

'You'd have to ask Carl. That's Mr Lovell's chauffeur. He was banned from driving, you know, Mr Lovell. They caught him in the Mersey Tunnel one night after he'd been at some posh dinner. So he had to hire Carl Shadford.'

Harry scratched his head. 'This may seem a strange question, but is it possible that Carl Shadford might have had access to mail sent to the Azha brothers?'

'Since you mention it,' said the woman, amiably blunt, 'it seems more than strange, and it makes no sense to me whatsoever . . . But you're not the first person to come here who's been ripped off by the Azhas. I know how you feel, believe me. You can't imagine how much one of our latest alarms . . .'

'I'm sorry to press you,' said Harry, 'but this is rather urgent. About the mail . . .'

'Oh yes, I'm a great one for sidetracking, my husband's always telling me so. Well, their mail is being held by Beagries. The letter-box is sealed up, as you can see, and the postman delivers it to the admin block. So I suppose it's possible Carl could have—'

'What can you tell me about Carl?'

The woman's face darkened. 'I'll be straight with you. I don't care for the man. Thinks a lot of himself, if you ask me. Talks posh, but Thelma, the girl I know at Beagries, was telling me she's heard rumours that he's been inside. Don't ask me what for.'

'Can you describe him? Believe me, it is important.'

Her powers of observation might not have been quite in Bill

Dawkes's class, but they were good enough. Shadford was in his early thirties, fair-haired, tall and broad-shouldered. He was a natty dresser and she reckoned he had ideas above his station. She'd once seen him carrying a slim attaché case bearing his own initials in gold lettering.

'C. S.,' said Harry to himself. 'Carl Shadford – or Charles Sachs. A very convenient alias.'

'Pardon?'

'Nothing. I wonder, have you seen him this morning?'

'I think he said hello just before nine. When Mr Lovell's away, he has a few odd jobs to do around the offices, but I don't think they stretch him. He seems to loaf around a lot, killing time.'

Killing time. For once the commonplace phrase made Harry shiver. Where had Carl Shadford taken Suzanne?

'Does he live locally?'

'I've no idea,' said the woman. 'You'd have to ask Thelma.'

'I'd like to do that. Can you introduce me?'

She folded her arms. 'Don't you think you ought to tell me what this is all about, Mr . . . ?'

'Devlin. Fair enough. But can we walk as we talk? Somehow I feel I haven't much time to lose.'

In half a dozen sentences he explained how Suzanne's disappearance had brought him here. The woman – she told him her name was Margaret – paled as she absorbed the implications of his story. But Harry sensed she was one of those people who was good in a crisis. Her mouth compressed into a thin line and she wasted no more words as she led him to Reception in the business park admin block.

'Thelma, this is Mr Devlin. He needs to find Carl Shadford.'

'He's welcome to him.' The girl's grimace robbed the Welcome sign on her desk of its sincerity. Harry was for a moment reminded of Suzanne, but he banished the thought at once. For the first time in his life, he wanted nothing more than to see his sulky receptionist again.

'Any idea where he might be?'

Thelma spread long bare arms. 'Search me. He lives in a bedsit just off Smithdown Road. I heard him say something about having to take the car back to the Palace, but that was hours ago. If you ask me, he's probably driving up and down ogling at girls in short skirts as per bloody usual.'

'The Palace?'

'Mr Lovell's house. He lives out near Halsall. It's a real mansion, by all accounts. Nine bedrooms, swimming pool, tennis court, you name it. Though who needs nine bedrooms in this day and age, I've never managed to work out.'

A place that size might come in very handy, thought Harry, for someone impersonating a company boss and wanting to impress a gullible girl. Especially on a day when the owners of the house were out.

'Would you mind if I called my office?'

'What's this all about?' Thelma asked. But he left it to Margaret to explain while he rang to update Lucy.

'Can you tell the police and let them know what's happened, please?'

'Keith's already done that,' his secretary said. 'He turned up here five minutes ago in a right state. What are you planning to do now?'

'I think I may take a look at Lovell's house. On the off chance.'

'Oh God, Harry, I hope she's all right.'

'I'm sure she is.'

'Liar,' Lucy said bluntly. 'You sound worried sick.'

A couple of minutes away from the address Thelma had given him, Harry caught sight of something that almost made him swerve into a ditch. As he rounded a bend on the country lane that led to Lovell's house, he saw sunlight glinting on the bonnet of a red Jaguar. The car was parked on a grassy verge at a point where the road skirted a spinney. He pulled in behind it and sprinted round to the driver's door. The car was empty, but on the back seat he could see the attaché case Margaret had mentioned. A useful prop, of course, for a man playing the part of a company boss.

A footpath signpost pointed the way to Button Spinney. He clambered over a stile and followed a dirt track curving between the trees. The low branches scraped his scalp, forcing him to duck and slow his pace. Because it had not rained since the last test match (all five days washed out without a ball being bowled) the dried mud of the track was unmarked by footprints. Yet where else could Shadford have taken Suzanne?

Harry strained his ears in a vain attempt to hear something other than the whistling of unseen birds. His palms were as damp as his lips were dry. He could only hope that he was not too late.

Suddenly he heard a woman cry out. Suzanne, it had to be Suzanne.

He hurried forward, oblivious of the leaves brushing into his eyes, the wood scraping the skin of his cheeks. He was almost bent double, crouching like an animal about to pounce – but on what?

The path twisted again and at once he was in a clearing. Carl Shadford was on the ground with Suzanne. But the only act of violence to which Harry had become witness was the raking of her long red fingernails down the bare back of her lover as he reached a shuddering climax.

'You should have made your excuses and left,' said Jim Crusoe the following afternoon. They were standing outside their hosts' marquee, watching the Grand Parade of Sail. Unable to contain his delight, Jim had put his glass of Pimm's down on the floor while he listened to Harry's account of the unfolding drama at Button Spinney.

'I've never known a confrontation like it. Albert Campion never had this trouble. It's difficult to take a culprit seriously when his trousers are down around his ankles. It was almost a relief when Keith arrived.'

'All hell broke loose, I gather.'

'And Shadford's jaw was broken, more to the point. I'll never forget the scene, with that big lad in leathers wrestling a half-naked Lothario and Suzanne screaming blue murder while she struggled to get her knickers back on. I don't think I've ever been so glad to see the police turn up in my life.'

'How did they get there?'

'Lucy had persuaded them to take Suzanne's disappearance seriously, but by then Keith had already decided to follow me up to Lovell's place on his motor bike. The police car passed the same way and even they couldn't miss my car, a red Jag and a Harley Davidson crammed together by the side of the road. So they decided to investigate.'

'And what have they done with Shadford?'

'Once his jaw had been wired up at Sefton General, they invited him to assist with one or two inquiries.'

'Is it true he has a record?'

'Fraud and theft and even a driving-while-disqualified. Oddly enough, he was no more entitled to drive the Jag than the man from Beagries. They didn't check up on him properly when he applied for the job. Apparently, he even managed to gull a hardbitten businessman like Lovell by touching his forelock and flashing a couple of forged references. Charming the pants off Suzanne was plain sailing by comparison.'

'So no history of violence or offences against women, after all?'

'None known. Keith's the one who faces a wounding charge, although my guess is that the Crown Prosecution Service will want to soft-pedal on that one. And yet . . .'

'Yes?'

'Ah, forget it.'

He sipped at his drink and looked out towards the river. Thousands of people were packed on each bank and their excited chatter almost drowned out the crackle of the commentary on the parade. He could see a cutter, a sloop, a three-masted schooner and a barquentine, elegant vessels that had crossed half the world to be here today. And yet his mind was elsewhere as he wondered what might have happened once Suzanne had learned the truth about Carl Shadford's deception of her. He imagined her fury provoking the chauffeur and . . . well, for all the farce of the showdown at Button Spinney, Harry would never regret what he had done.

He arrived early at work on Monday morning, anxious to catch up on work ignored during Friday's drama. Suzanne was standing next to the desk in Reception and she greeted him with a smile that surprised him with its warmth.

'I wasn't expecting to see you here this morning,' he said.

'I do want to thank you for – for everything. Keith and I – we're very grateful.'

'You've kissed and made up? That's good news.'

'And I've got some more good news for you,' she said, beaming. 'I've decided to withdraw my resignation. It's the least I could do after you helped to save me from that – that bastard. I've realized the grass isn't always greener on the other side. Never mind what I said about the wages here. Money isn't everything. I can promise you, Mr Devlin, this time I'm here to stay.'

Harry slowly took in her unshakeably magnanimous expression and, despite himself, began to laugh.

ONE THOUSAND DOLLARS A WORD

LAWRENCE BLOCK

The editor's name was Warren Jukes. He was a lean, sharp-featured man with slender, long-fingered hands and a narrow line for a mouth. His black hair was going attractively gray on top and at the temples. As usual, he wore a stylish three-piece suit. As usual, Trevathan felt logy and unkempt in comparison, like a bear having trouble shaking off the torpor of hibernation.

'Sit down, Jim,' Jukes said. 'Always a pleasure. Don't tell me you're bringing in another manuscript already? It never ceases to amaze me the way you keep grinding them out. Where do you get your ideas, anyway? But I guess you're tired of that question after all these years.'

He was indeed, and that was not the only thing of which James Trevathan was heartily tired. But all he said was, 'No, Warren. I haven't written another story.'

'Oh?'

'I wanted to talk with you about the last one.'

'But we talked about it yesterday,' Jukes said, puzzled. 'Over the telephone. I said it was fine and I was happy to have it for the magazine. What's the title, anyway? It was a play on words, but I can't remember it offhand.'

'"A Stitch in Crime,"' Trevathan said.

'Right, that's it. Good title, good story and all of it wrapped up in your solid professional prose. What's the problem?'

'Money,' Trevathan said.

'A severe case of the shorts, huh?' The editor smiled. 'Well, I'll be putting a voucher through this afternoon. You'll have the check early next week. I'm afraid that's the best I can do, Jimbo. The corporate machinery can only go so fast.'

'It's not the time,' Trevathan said. 'It's the amount. What are you paying for the story, Warren?'

'Why, the usual. How long was it? Three thousand words, wasn't it?'

'Thirty-five hundred.'

'So what does that come to? Thirty-five hundred at a nickel a word is what? One seventy-five, right?'

'That's right, yes.'

'So you'll have a check in that amount early next week, as soon as possible, and if you want I'll ring you when I have it in hand and you can come over and pick it up. Save waiting a couple of days for the neither-rain-nor-snow people to get it from my desk to yours.'

'It's not enough.'

'Beg your pardon?'

'The price,' Trevathan said. He was having trouble with this conversation. He'd written a script for it in his mind on the way to Jukes's office, and he'd been infinitely more articulate then than now. 'I should get more money,' he managed. 'A nickel a word is . . . Warren, that's no money at all.'

'It's what we pay, Jim. It's what we've always paid.'

'Exactly.'

'So?'

'Do you know how long I've been writing for you people, Warren?'

'Quite a few years.'

'Twenty years, Warren.'

'Really?'

'I sold a story called "Hanging by a Thread" to you twenty years ago last month. It ran twenty-two hundred words and you paid me a hundred and ten bucks for it.'

'Well, there you go,' Jukes said.

'I've been working twenty years, Warren, and I'm getting the same money now that I got then. Everything's gone up except my income. When I wrote my first story for you I could take one of those nickels that a word of mine brought and buy a candy bar with it. Have you bought a candy bar recently, Warren?'

Jukes touched his belt buckle. 'If I went and bought candy bars,' he said, 'my clothes wouldn't fit me.'

'Candy bars are forty cents. Some of them cost thirty-five. And I still get a nickel a word. But let's forget candy bars.'

'Fine with me, Jim.'

'Let's talk about the magazine. When you bought "Hanging by a Thread", what did the magazine sell for on the stands?'

'Thirty-five cents, I guess.'

'Wrong. Twenty-five. About six months later you went to thirty-five. Then you went to fifty, and after that sixty and then seventy-five. And what does the magazine sell for now?'

'A dollar a copy.'

'And you still pay your authors a nickel a word. That's really wealth beyond the dreams of avarice, isn't it, Warren?'

Jukes sighed heavily, propped his elbows on his desktop, tented his fingertips. 'Jim,' he said, dropping his voice in pitch, 'there are things you're forgetting. The magazine's no more profitable than it was twenty years ago. In fact we're working closer now than we did then. Do you know anything about the price of paper? It makes candy look pretty stable by comparison. I could talk for hours on the subject of the price of paper. Not to mention all the other printing costs, and shipping costs and more other costs than I want to mention or you want to hear about. You look at that buck-a-copy price and you think we're flying high, but it's not like that at all. We were doing better way back then. Every single cost of ours has gone through the roof.'

'Except the basic one.'

'How's that?'

'The price you pay for material. That's what your readers are buying from you, you know. Stories. Plots and characters. Prose and dialogue. Words. And you pay the same for them as you did twenty years ago. It's the only cost that's stayed the same.'

Jukes took a pipe apart and began running a pipe-cleaner through the stem. Trevathan started talking about his own costs – his rent, the price of food. When he paused for breath Warren Jukes said 'Supply and demand, Jim.'

'What's that?'

'Supply and demand. Do you think it's hard for me to fill the magazine at a nickel a word? See that pile of scripts over there? That's what this morning's mail brought. Nine out of ten of those stories are from new writers who'd write for nothing if it got them into print. The other ten percent is from pros who are damned glad when they see that nickel-a-word check instead of getting their stories mailed back to them. You know, I buy just about everything you write for us, Jim. One reason is I like your work, but that's not the only reason. You've been with us for twenty years and we like to do business with our old friends. But you evidently want me to raise your word rate, and we don't pay more than five cents a word to anybody, because in the first place we haven't got any surplus in the budget and in the second place we damn well don't *have* to pay more than that. So before I raise your rate, old friend, I'll give your stories back to you. Because I don't have any choice.'

Trevathan sat and digested this for a few moments. He thought of some things to say but left them unsaid. He might have asked Jukes how the editor's own salary had fluctuated over the years, but what was the point of that? He could write for a nickel a word or he could not write for them at all. That was the final word on the subject.

'Jim? Shall I put through a voucher or do you want "A Stitch in Crime" back?'

'What would I do with it? No, I'll take the nickel a word, Warren.'

'If there was a way I could make it more—'

'I understand.'

'You guys should have got yourselves a union years ago. Give you a little collective muscle. Or you could try writing something else. We're in a squeeze, you know, and if we were forced to pay more for material we'd probably have to fold the magazine altogether. But there are other fields where the pay is better.'

'I've been doing this for twenty years, Warren. It's all I know. My God, I've got a reputation in the field, I've got an established name—'

'Sure. That's why I'm always happy to have you in the magazine.

As long as I do the editing, Jimbo, and as long as you grind out the copy, I'll be glad to buy your yarns.'

'At a nickel a word.'

'Well—'

'Nothing personal, Warren. I'm just a little bitter. That's all.'

'Hey, think nothing of it.' Jukes got to his feet, came around from behind his desk. 'So you got something off your chest, and we cleared the air a little. Now you know where you stand. Now you can go on home and knock off something sensational and get it to me, and if it's up to your usual professional standard you'll have another check coming your way. That's the way to double the old income, you know. Just double the old production.'

'Good idea,' Trevathan said.

'Of course it is. And maybe you can try something for another market while you're at it. It's not too late to branch out, Jim. God knows I don't want to lose you, but if you're having trouble getting by on what we can pay you, well—'

'It's a thought,' Trevathan said.

Five cents a word.

Trevathan sat at his battered Underwood and stared at a blank sheet of paper. The paper had gone up a dollar a ream in the past year, and he could swear they'd cheapened the quality in the process. Everything cost more, he thought, except his own well-chosen words. They were still trading steadily at a nickel apiece.

Not too late to branch out, Jukes had told him. But that was a sight easier to say than to do. He'd tried writing for other kinds of markets, but detective stories were the only kind he'd ever had any luck with. His mind didn't seem to produce viable fictional ideas in other areas. When he'd tried writing longer works, novels, he'd always gotten hopelessly bogged down. He was a short-story writer, recognized and frequently anthologized, and he was prolific enough to keep himself alive that way, but—

But he was sick of living marginally, sick of grinding out story after story. And heartily sick of going through life on a nickel a word.

What would a decent word rate be?

Well, if they paid him twenty-five cents a word, then he'd at least be keeping pace with the price of a candy bar. Of course after twenty years you wanted to do a little better than stay even. Say they paid him a dollar a word. There were writers who earned that much. Hell, there were writers who earned a good deal more than that, writers whose books wound up on best-seller lists, writers who got six-figure prices for screenplays, writers who wrote themselves rich.

One thousand dollars a word.

The phrase popped into his mind, stunning in its simplicity, and before he was aware of it his fingers had typed the words on the page before him. He sat and looked at it, then worked the carriage return lever and typed the phrase again.

One thousand dollars a word.

He studied what he had typed, his mind racing on ahead, playing with ideas, shaking itself loose from its usual stereotyped thought patterns. Well, why not? Why shouldn't he earn a thousand dollars a word? Why not branch out into a new field?

Why not?

He took the sheet from the typewriter, crumpled it into a ball, pegged it in the general direction of the wastebasket. He rolled a new sheet in its place and sat looking at its blankness, waiting, thinking. Finally, word by halting word, he began to type.

Trevathan rarely rewrote his short stories. At a nickel a word he could not afford to. Furthermore, he had acquired a facility over the years which enabled him to turn out acceptable copy in first draft. Now, however, he was trying something altogether new and different, and so he felt the need to take his time getting it precisely right. Time and again he yanked false starts from the typewriter, crumpled them, hurled them at the wastebasket.

Until finally he had something he liked.

He read it through for the fourth or fifth time, then took it from the typewriter and read it again. It did the job, he decided. It was concise and clear and very much to the point.

He reached for the phone. When he'd gotten through to Jukes he said, 'Warren? I've decided to take your advice.'

'Wrote another story for us? Glad to hear it.'

'No,' he said, 'another piece of advice you gave me. I'm branching out in a new direction.'

'Well, I think that's terrific,' Jukes said. 'I really mean it. Getting to work on something big? A novel?'

'No, a short piece.'

'But in a more remunerative area?'

'Definitely. I'm expecting to net a thousand dollars a word for what I'm doing this afternoon.'

'A thousand—' Warren Jukes let out a laugh, making a sound similar to the yelp of a startled terrier. 'Well, I don't know what you're up to, Jim, but let me wish you the best of luck with it. I'll tell you one thing. I'm damned glad you haven't lost your sense of humor.'

Trevathan looked again at what he'd written. *I've got a gun. Please fill this paper sack with thirty thousand dollars in used tens and twenties and fifties or I'll be forced to blow your stupid head off.*

'Oh, I've still got my sense of humor,' he said. 'Know what I'm going to do, Warren? I'm going to laugh all the way to the bank.'

THE MAN WHO SPOKE

H. R. F. KEATING

'I can tell you exactly when it all began,' the man said. 'It was just three days ago. In Madras. I had arrived from London late that evening. I work for Indihols, the UK travel firm in Nottingham, you know. We're preparing a new itinerary starting from Madras, The Glory of India South. I've come to India to – did I say it's my first time here, my first ever? Did I?'

'Yes, yes. You were stating such, just only as you came inside.'

'Yes. Of course. But, as I was telling you, when I arrived in Madras – it was late in the evening, just three days ago, three days ago only – I was met at the airport by a car arranged by our Delhi office. It was to take me to my hotel. I was sitting in the back as we drove in, and after I had exchanged a few words with the driver – his English was first class – I just sat there in silence. I was very tired. From the flight, you know. And then—'

He came to an abrupt halt.

'Yes? And then?'

'Then suddenly I leaned forward and spoke. I spoke.'

'You spoke, yes? But what it was you were saying?'

'I – I don't know. Or at the time I didn't know. Not at all. Words came out of my mouth, but I didn't know what they were. But then

– then my driver turned back to me and answered, in the same rather rapid sort of speech. Tamil, as I learnt later. But – but, you see, I don't speak so much as a word of Tamil. I don't understand it. I told you: I've never even been to India. None of my family – my father, my mother, uncles, anybody – has ever been here. I don't – I didn't even know, as far as I can remember, that Tamil was the language they spoke in Madras. They told me back in Nottingham everybody I would have any dealings with in South India would speak good English. But – but there I was, sitting there, in that car, in the dark, speaking in Tamil and – and understanding it.'

Inspector Ghote, regarding his visitor from behind his desk in Bombay Police Headquarters, saw a westerner who looked, for once, truly white. White as if some violent vacuuming force had sucked the very blood out of him.

'But sir,' he said, somewhat puzzled at distress so altogether excessive, 'you must . . . sir, you may please not be so much upset. There would be some simple explanation.'

'Oh, yes, Inspector. There's an explanation all right. But it's hardly one that's simple. Or reassuring, I promise you. But let me go on. It's probably best if you hear everything just as it happened. Before you make up your mind about me. Yes.'

He gathered himself together.

'So, as I said, Inspector, I spoke. I uttered those words, those sounds. I had asked a question. In Tamil. I had asked, just making casual conversation, if the monsoon rains had come to an end, and the chap had replied that there hadn't been any rain for three days. And I had understood. Totally extraordinary. But believe me, Inspector, it happened.'

He shook his head in recollected bewilderment. And then went on.

'That was all that happened. Then. Just that single exchange of casual remarks. I was, frankly, too stunned even to open my mouth again, and before I knew it we were at the hotel, the Connemara, and I was, still in a sort of daze, being given my key at Reception. It was just like an ordinary door key; I recall being slightly surprised and kind of intrigued by that; and after trailing along a maze of corridors behind a porter and going up and down various flights of stairs, we reached my room and I just collapsed on to the bed and at once fell into a deep sleep.'

'You were not at all having some dreams?'

'No, no. Or, if I did, I don't remember. And, in fact, when I woke up next morning I came to the conclusion that all that business – speaking Tamil – must have been something I actually had dreamt. In the car. Because I was certainly very tired then and could have dropped off.'

'Yes, yes. That is the simple explanation only, yes?'

Ghote had been on the point of ringing for his peon to fetch this foreigner a soothing cup of tea. But what the man said next made him swiftly change his mind.

'No, Inspector, that was only the beginning of it all. I want to – I think I want to – Inspector, I have come here because I want to confess to murder.'

'Murder? You are saying and stating you have now committed some murder?'

'Yes. No. No, it wasn't me. Not . . .'

'Not you? But you are confessing only? I am not at all understanding.'

'God, Inspector, I wish I understood. I wish I had some idea whether it all was even possible. I wish – I wish I had never set foot in India at all.'

Abruptly he plunged his head between his hands and sat huddled in silent misery.

Ghote considered him for a while. Then he pulled a pad towards himself, took up a ball-point and, with a little bark of a cough, reclaimed his visitor's attention.

'Sir,' he said, 'I think it may be better if we would begin at whatsoever beginning there may be. What, sir, is your good name?'

The man in the chair opposite slowly raised his head and gave himself a little shake.

'Yes,' he said. 'Right. Yes, my name's Williamson. It's Tom Williamson. I am Tom Williamson. I must be. I must be.'

'Yes, yes. If you are saying it. Now, kindly state your present address here in Bombay.'

'It's – yes, there's that. I'm staying at the President Hotel. Yes.'

Tom Williamson seemed to gain some reassurance from having produced an incontrovertible fact.

'Yes, the President,' he went on. 'I arrived in Bombay early today and booked in there. Yes. Look, I think I'd better tell you, in the right order, everything that happened to me after – after that odd event in the car in Madras on my way to the Connemara. You see, something else happened later that first morning. It was like this. No appointments had been arranged for me that day, so I set off to have a look round the city for myself. See what sort of impact it might have on one of our customers coming to Madras for the first time. Just like me.'

Calmer now, he went on with increasing coherence.

'I had really succeeded by that time in putting that whole Tamil-speaking business out of my mind. So I took one of those what-d'you-call-'ems, autorickshaws, and asked the driver to take me to Fort St George. I'd gathered from a brochure in my room, you see, that the Fort was one of the main sights of Madras. Off we went, and I was perfectly happy sitting there in that little sort of carriage behind that rather noisy motor cycle, taking in the passing scene. You know, the old buildings half hidden in that terrible way by those enormous crude film hoardings. Or – or, one I remember in particular, not for a film but saying in huge letters, in English, Bath Tubs for the Genteel. It's things like that, I thought then, that give a place that touch of the different, the exotic, the odd, that our clients like.'

For an instant he seemed to become aware that Bombay was also a city equally lavish in huge crude film hoardings. He made a slight gesture of apology.

'But there I was,' he went on quickly, 'bowling along perfectly happily and certainly not understanding one word of all the Tamil I heard from bystanders whenever the traffic brought my auto-rickshaw to a halt. And then – then another extraordinary thing happened. Inspector, I suddenly knew what it was that we would be coming to in just a minute or two. There, in Madras. A place I had never been to in all my life. I knew I would see the statue of a man on a horse. And, more, I knew the man would be a certain Governor Sir Thomas Munro and – odder even than that – I knew he would be perched on his horse with no saddle and no stirrups. And, yes, almost at once we went over a bridge across a river, and there was that statue. Exactly as I had known it would be. A man in a long cloak on a horse without a saddle or stirrups.'

He leaned forward over the desk, his face dazed with bewilderment.

'Inspector,' he said – shouted almost – 'don't you see? That made it totally certain. What I had refused even to let myself believe before. Inspector, in another life, in the past, I must have been an Indian, a Madrasi, a Tamil-speaker.'

'Well, yes,' Ghote agreed with caution. 'Such things have been known to happen. There are many evidences. But, my dear sir, kindly do not take it so much to heart. If you were some Tamil gentleman in a former life, it is no more than a matter of some interest. There is no need for so much of shock.'

'But Inspector, there is. There is. You see, the very next day I found out just who it was that I – that I had been. Just what it was I had done. And that was when I felt I had to come here, to Bombay, to – to make absolutely certain. That was when—'

But now, once more, the young Englishman seemed unable to continue.

'That was when . . . please?' Ghote prompted at last.

'When? Oh, yes, when I set out to go to the hospital here in Bombay, where I used – that is, I went this morning and made some inquiries at the – let me get the name right – at the Gokaldas Tejpal Hospital.'

'The G. T. Hospital, yes. Just only round the corner from here itself. In Lokmanya Tilak Road.'

'Yes. Yes, but, you see, it was then that I began to think it really might be true. When someone told me Lokman-whatever Road was once called Carnac Road. You see, it was Carnac Road I had been trying to find.'

'Sir, still I am not at all seeing. Yes, it is true, Lokmanya Tilak Road was formerly known, from British days itself, by the name of Carnac Road. But I am not at all understanding why it was that this was so much of shocking for you. Sir, kindly begin once more.'

'Yes. Yes, I must. I must. How else are you going to believe me?'

'Very well then, sir. Please tell.'

Tom Williamson sat up a little straighter in his chair and took a deep inward breath. Ghote settled himself, ball-point poised, to listen.

'It was like this, Inspector,' his visitor said at last, 'during the rest of that day, my first day in Madras, after I had seen the Munro statue, I felt much as you did just now. That it was an extraordinary experience, but one that I could eventually come to terms with. Even make a good story out of, when I got back home to Nottingham. So, though I was a bit disturbed, I just went on looking round Madras. I went all along that huge beach there and visited the Theosophical Society's gardens and looked at a temple with some unpronounceable name. And, as I didn't have any other – what shall I call them? – bursts of recall, I almost forgot about the experience with the statue. But next day, the day before yesterday in fact, I had a 10 a.m. appointment at the Tourism Development Corporation. Do you know Madras, Inspector?'

'No, no. Not at all.'

'Well, the tourism offices are in something called C-in-C Road. I'd gathered that stood for Commander-in-Chief Road. And, as I saw from the map in the brochure in my room that it wasn't far, only just on the other side of the river there, the Cooum, I decided I'd walk. While it was still comparatively cool. And—'

Tom Williamson came to a full halt. His face, which had slowly begun to regain a healthy pinkness, abruptly lost its colour once more. A sheen of sweat appeared on his forehead.

'Inspector,' he croaked out eventually, 'I had just got across the bridge and turned in the direction I wanted to go, and I was looking vaguely down at the river and the rough ground sloping towards it, when – when I knew that it was there where we had put the body.'

'The body? What body it is?'

'The body of the man I killed, Inspector.'

'But when? When were you killing this individual? You were not saying you had done this while you were just only looking round Madras itself.'

'No, no. It wasn't me who – that is, I didn't kill the fellow when I was me. I mean – oh, let me explain.'

'Kindly do.'

'Yes. Yes, well, you see, it was when I saw that sloping ground going down to the Cooum that I suddenly knew who I had been. When I could speak Tamil. Then. All those years ago. Some time in the 1930s. I was then, if you can believe it, a certain Dr Ammayappa Pillai. It's a name I've never even remotely heard of. Why should I have done? But I knew I was – that I had been – a doctor, a surgeon. And I've never had the least interest in surgery, or medicine, or anything of that sort. I know nothing about it. But at that moment I knew I was a surgeon, so skilful in fact that I had found

a senior post in Bombay. At the Gokaldas Tejpal Hospital. But –
but, back in my native Madras, I had been – Inspector, back in
Madras I was obsessed with love for a very much respected dancing-
girl, one Komalam by name.'

Ghote realized now that this Englishman's voice had imperceptibly
taken on an Indian lilt. Yes, he registered, I am being spoken to
now by Dr Ammayappa Pillai from Madras.

He sat perfectly still, half wishing that the modern ball-point he
still held poised over the name and address, which was all he had
managed to write on his pad, could somehow be transformed into a
thick 1930s-style fountain pen. Something that would not jerk his
visitor back to the present time.

But, once embarked on his story, it seemed nothing was going to
halt Dr Pillai. If Dr Pillai he was.

'And, because of my love, my passion, for Komalam, one day
about midday when I had left the Tejpal at the start of a short period
of leave and was walking along Queen's Road to my lodgings, at a
moment's notice I hailed a passing victoria and told the fellow to go
fast as his horse would take us to the Victoria Terminus station.
There I was just in time to catch the Madras mail. And, a little less
than thirty-six hours later, I had arrived at Egmore station – I had
changed on to that line – and was making my way on foot along
the deserted night-time streets of Madras to Komalam's house, just
behind C-in-C Road. I had expected her to be alone. I had arrived
on her fast day when she never entertained and, though I knew she
would admit me as a friend, I knew too I would have to wait an
hour or so, till past midnight, before she would let me make love to
her.'

Dr Pillai – Ghote thought of the man opposite now as the Madrasi
doctor of the 1930s and no one else – paused for just a moment and
then, eyes blazing, resumed his story.

'But when I reached the house I found the watchman, whom I
had often treated very generously, strangely reluctant to let me in.
But I insisted, brushed past him and ran quickly up the stairs to
Komalam's room. There was no one there. But from the bedroom
just beyond I heard sounds. I thought it was Komalam protesting
at something, perhaps to her old maidservant. Without thinking, I
swept aside the door-curtain. Komalam was there on the bed with,
above her, an almost naked Englishman. And on the floor beside

the bed were his clothes, the dress uniform – I recognized it – of an officer of the Dorset Regiment, stationed at the Fort. And beside that heap of scarlet cloth was his dress sword, in its scabbard.'

He came to a full stop then.

Ghote heard himself asking, in a voice he scarcely recognized, what had happened next, though he already had more than a notion of what he would be told.

'The man,' Dr Pillai, or perhaps Tom Williamson, went on, 'jumped from the bed when he heard me. *Get out of here, you filthy black swine,* he yelled. He dived then for his sword, naked as he was. But I – I was quicker. I snatched it by the hilt. It came free of the scabbard. The English officer – it was only afterwards that I learnt he was one Captain Maurice Fanshawe – was at least a brave man. He squared up to me. I could see he intended to wrench the sword from my grasp. And so – so I thrust it at him. His own sword. And it pierced his throat. His blood gushed out. There was no question then but that he was dead. That I had killed him.'

And somehow, at that moment, Ghote knew Dr Pillai had become once again the young man from the English travel company who had come to India for the first time just three days earlier.

'Sir,' he said, 'what was happening after that? Are you knowing itself? Or is that the end only of what you have recalled of that former life?'

Tom Williamson gave a prolonged sigh.

'I don't know, Inspector,' he answered. 'I discovered later from the files of *The Hindu*, the English-language paper there in Madras, that Captain Fanshawe's body was found the next day. On the bank of the Cooum at, so far as I was able to tell, the exact place my eye had fallen on as I had walked towards the Tourism Development Corporation. But what I don't really remember is helping Komalam's watchman carry it there, as I suppose I must have done. It could be that at *The Hindu* – I had not been able to keep my 10 a.m. appointment, as you may well understand – I read so much about the affair, every word I could lay my hands on, that I came to believe I had actually participated in all of it, that the scene in Komalam's bedroom was more than just an extraordinary flash of – of transferred memory or something.'

'Yes, yes. Finding out that such a murder case had occurred,'

Ghote reasoned, 'does not at all mean you yourself were that murderer.'

'No, Inspector, that is what I came to think in the end. What I came to convince myself of. To convince myself. I told myself that there was not necessarily any such person as Dr Ammayappa Pillai. Because, you see, no murderer was ever apprehended. No one, except Komalam and her servants, had, I imagine, seen me – had seen Dr Pillai in Madras that night. So even though I had discovered that, back in the 1930s, there had been the body of a stabbed man found beside the Cooum where I had had that flash of recall and had remembered seeing it, that did not necessarily mean I was the man who had stabbed that fellow. Or, in fact, that there had even ever existed a Dr Ammayappa Pillai. I could, through some extra-ordinary trick of the mind, have imagined or invented the whole thing.'

But now Ghote recalled the chalk-white face of his visitor as he had come stumbling into his office not half an hour before.

'However, you were finding out something more,' he said. 'You were coming here to Bombay and going to the G. T. Hospital.'

'Exactly, Inspector. As you seem to have guessed, I felt I must find, if I could, some solid evidence to say whether Dr Ammayappa Pillai had or had not existed. Whether there was really a surgeon of that name at a Bombay hospital in the mid-1930s. So I abandoned everything in Madras and flew here. And – and at the G. T. Hospital, just a quarter of an hour ago, I discovered that, yes, at that time there had been a surgeon there whose name was precisely Ammay-appa Pillai.'

A twisted grin showed itself on the paper-pale face on the other side of the desk.

'So that is why I am confessing to murder. Because I did kill that man, didn't I? In a previous life, if you like. But it was me that did it. Dr Pillai is me. He must be. For me to have known what I found I knew.'

In the face of this, Ghote sat silent, deep in thought. Minutes passed. One. Two. At last he looked across at Tom Williamson, his mind made up.

At the corners of his eyes, if nowhere else, there was the merest hint of a smile.

'Mr Williamson,' he said, 'when I was just only a boy I was most fond of stories concerning one Mr Bulldog Drummond. In one of such there was a saying I have never forgotten. A very, very English saying, I am thinking. Mr Williamson, it is this: *Your secret is safe with me.*'

SECOND FIDDLE

J. A. JANCE

As a homicide detective, I've always viewed myself as something of a white knight riding off to defend truth, justice and the American way, although sometimes the results on that score are less than satisfactory. And though I've been called to hundreds of crime scenes over the years, it isn't often the murder victim turns out to be someone I know.

Both those circumstances came together in one case when I was called to a late-January homicide along with my partner, Sue Danielson. The victim had been found in a vacant lot next to the railroad tracks in a neighborhood called Georgetown – a mostly industrial area directly south of downtown Seattle.

The victim lay on her back, pale blue eyes reflecting back the cold winter sky. I recognized her the moment I saw her slack, upturned face. 'Erica,' I said.

'Erica?' Sue echoed. 'You know her?'

I nodded. 'She goes to one of my AA meetings.'

Sue looked down again at the corpse – a white, middle-aged female, with an ugly bloodstain in the middle of her left breast. Despite the cold, she was dressed only in a long-sleeved flannel shirt and worn jeans – not the fashionably-worn kind people buy from speciality boutiques. This woman's jeans had become frayed the old-fashioned way – by long wear. The same held true for her shoes – shabby Nikes with most of the tread rubbed off the soles.

A small-calibre handgun lay just beyond the fingertips of her outstretched right hand. The mangled palm of the left one struck me as a classic defensive wound. When faced with a pointed gun, victims instinctively hold up a hand in hopes of deflecting the bullet. It hadn't worked, of course. The amount of blood that had flowed from both wounds told us the woman hadn't died right away. My guess was that she had bled to death.

'Erica what?' Sue asked.

Outsiders must think the words 'Alcoholics Anonymous' constitute some kind of gimmick. But use of the word anonymous is not an empty figure of speech. What makes it possible for an ex-boozer like me to spill my guts in front of roomfuls of strangers week after week is the fact that none of those people know my name, and I don't know theirs. Don't ask me why it helps, but it does.

'Just Erica,' I said. 'She claimed she'd been sober for two years.'

'And dead four days minimum, Detective Beaumont,' Doc Baker added, walking up behind us. Startled, I turned toward the King County Medical Examiner. Baker seldom shows up at ordinary crime scenes these days.

Noting my surprise, he brushed it off. 'It's always a good idea for the head honcho to keep his hand in. Better for morale. I was just leaving at a meeting down at Boeing Field when the call came in. I've already taken a look. Bet you lunch at Vito's that my time-of-death estimate isn't off by twelve hours in either direction.'

Doc Baker always tries to sucker the newer guys. 'Don't bet him,' I advised Sue. You'll lose.'

The ME gave Sue Danielson an appraising once-over. 'Maybe not,' he said. 'Not with new guys who look as good as she does.'

At sixty-two and nearing retirement, King County's medical examiner is an unreconstructed male chauvinist pig. He still thinks Bobby Riggs should have, to quote him, 'whupped Billie Jean King's ass'. Vaccinated against the rising epidemic of political correctness, Baker displays an engraved brass plaque on his desk, *You Can't Teach an Old Doc New Tricks*. As far as the ME is concerned, that says it all.

A less self-possessed woman might have taken offence. Sue handled Baker's leer by ignoring it. 'What do you think we've got?' she asked.

He shrugged. 'Looks self-inflicted to me. No sign of struggle. Lots of blood, so it took a while for her to die.'

I looked down at the immediate area surrounding the corpse. Seattle was having one of those rare patches of cold, late-winter sun with no rain for over a week. Without cloud cover, night-time temperatures had plummeted into the upper teens. The frozen earth around the body was littered with trash and punctuated by patches of winter-dry weeds, but no nearby plant stalks showed evidence of having been recently broken, nor could I see any lingering signs of footprints.

'Her name's Erica, by the way,' I told Doc Baker. 'An acquaintance of mine.'

'Last name?' he asked.

'Sorry,' I said. 'No idea.'

'Typical,' Doc Baker groused.

The crime-scene investigation team showed up then, along with the police photographer. We spent the next bone-chilling hour scouring the area, looking for evidence. When attendants from the ME's office came to retrieve the body, Sue and I retreated to our car to thaw out our hands. The attendants were loading the corpse on to a gurney when Baker came rumbling across the lot, marching toward us like a fast-moving thundercloud. His shock of white hair stood on end. His face was red; his forehead creased by a dangerous frown.

'Oops,' I said to Sue. 'This looks like trouble.' And it was.

'I thought you said her name was Erica,' he growled accusingly when Sue and I stepped out to meet him.

'That's the name I know her by,' I countered.

'Well, we found this in her hip pocket.' He held up something that looked like a credit card. 'Says here her name's Georgina Elisa Carver.'

The rectangular piece of plastic he handed me was an official, state-issued photo identification card – the kind non-drivers can obtain from the department of motor vehicles in lieu of a driver's licence. It offers the cachet of an official ID for people who, for one reason or another, don't drive. Looking down I saw a photo of the woman I had known as Erica smiling back at me over the name Georgina Elisa Carver. The card listed a Bellevue address.

After examining the card, I passed it along to Sue. 'Wait a minute,' she said. 'I remember this name from yesterday's briefing. It was unusual enough that it stuck in my head. Wasn't she listed as a missing person?'

As soon as Sue jogged my memory, I knew she was right. It took only a matter of moments for Sue to keyboard the victim's name into our new, in-vehicle laptop. Seconds later we had our answer. Georgina Carver had, indeed, been reported missing Sunday evening by her sister, Gail Mathers. When Georgina had left home on Saturday and didn't return that night, Gail had worried. Georgina still wasn't home by Sunday evening. That's when Gail had called the police. The MP report listed both a work and a home number. The address listed matched the one on Georgina Carver's ID.

'Off to Bellevue, then?' Sue asked me.

'Sounds like,' I told her.

Bellevue, a suburb Seattleites used to denigrate as nothing but a 'well-to-do bedroom community', is now a major city in its own right, complete with a fairly respectable skyline of high-rises. It's touted as being a relatively crime-free haven of rich Republicans, but in recent years Seattle street gangs have joined more traditional commuters in going back and forth across Lake Washington on the I-90 bridge. Which means that Bellevue isn't nearly as crime- and drug-free as it used to be.

'Let's go,' I said. 'You drive. I'll navigate.'

Because it was a weekday morning, we decided to track down the work number first. That led us to a place called Tyee Middle School. Sue's inquiry about Gail Mathers provoked both a broad smile and a shake of the head from the school secretary.

'I'm afraid Ms Mathers doesn't work here any more.'

'But she did as late as last week,' Sue objected.

'That's right,' the secretary answered. 'But she called in on Monday morning and said she wouldn't be in for the rest of her life. She won the Lotto jackpot Saturday night. Seven million dollars' worth. With that much money, why would anyone want to keep teaching seventh-grade math?'

Sue, who has her own junior-high-school-aged son named Jared to contend with, glanced at me. 'Why indeed?' she said.

We headed off to track down Gail Mathers's home address.

'You hear a lot of stories in AA meetings,' I told Sue as we climbed back into the car. 'After a while they all start to blend together, so

I may have my wires crossed. But I seem to remember Erica saying that she had been in prison at some point and that she was writing a book about the experience.'

Sue frowned thoughtfully. 'If Georgina went to prison for an alcohol-related offence, that might explain why she had an ID card in place of a driver's licence.'

While Sue drove, I checked with Records. Georgina Elisa Carver had done fifteen months at Purdy for vehicular homicide and driving under the influence.

'That was a pretty good guess,' I told Sue with a grin. 'Ever think of trying your hand at being a detective?'

'I'll take it under consideration,' she returned.

Gail Mathers's house was a modest one on a wooded hillside east of Bellevue Way. The woman who answered the door looked enough like Erica that they might have been twins. She peered out at us anxiously from behind a partially opened door.

'Gail Mathers?' I asked, showing her my ID and badge.

'Yes.'

'I'm Detective J. P. Beaumont. This is my partner, Detective Sue Danielson.'

'Is this about Georgina? Did you find her?'

'I'm afraid so,' I answered. 'Although we don't yet have a positive identification.'

Gail Mathers blanched, clutching at the doorknob for support. 'Is she dead?'

'Please, Ms Mathers. It would be better if we didn't discuss this here on the porch. Do you mind if we come in?'

Gail turned and fled sobbing across the room, leaving us to find our own way. The living room was clean but cluttered, filled with more than enough yellow and orange plaid, colonial-style furniture to fill two large living rooms rather than a single small one. Gail threw herself down on a couch and huddled there weeping. Taking turns, Sue and I briefed her on the situation.

'How can this be?' Gail Mathers wailed as we finished. 'Just when things were starting to get better – for her; for both of us. How can Georgie be dead now? When did this happen? Where?'

'In a vacant lot south of downtown Seattle,' I explained. 'We won't know when until after the autopsy. We'll need you to come downtown as soon as possible to give us a positive ID.'

'What do you mean about things getting better?' Sue asked. 'The jackpot?'

Gail nodded. 'Things have been awful for Georgie for years now, ever since the accident. First Hal died – Hal was Georgie's husband, you see. He was thrown from the car when it slammed into a tree. She was driving. Hal lingered in intensive care for weeks before he died. Then there was the trial. When that was over, they shipped Georgie off to prison, even though she'd paid a fortune for that quack of an attorney. She spent every last dime she had, but she went to prison anyway. Then, while she was locked up, our mother died of Alzheimer's.

'I think Mother's death was the last straw. When Georgie came home from prison, she was different somehow – all closed up. There were times she told me she couldn't see any reason to go on living. That's understandable. She had lost her life's work. She couldn't go back to being a psychologist. No one would have her. People told me that sometimes they'd see her in downtown Seattle, holding one of those "Will Work For Food" signs. That was a scam, of course. She always had food to eat and a roof over her head here with me.

'I kept hoping that if I was patient, eventually she'd pull out of it. My birthday was last Thursday. It broke my heart when the day came and went with no acknowledgement whatsoever. I thought she had forgotten it completely. Not that I wanted much. Money's tight for her. A card would have been plenty. Then, Sunday morning, I found this out in the kitchen inside the coffee canister.'

Gail took a basket off the coffee table and thumbed through a number of cards before retrieving one and handing it over to me. The card a small but flowery one; the verse on the outside simple. 'In an uncertain world, sisters are forever.' Inside it said, 'Thanks for being mine.' It was signed, 'Love, Georgie.'

'There was a Lotto ticket for that week's game tucked inside the card,' Gail continued. I went right to the Sunday paper and checked the numbers. When I realized we'd won, I couldn't believe it. I went racing down the hall screaming like a banshee. "We won! We won!" And I did mean we, because I would have shared the jackpot with Georgie. But she wasn't there. Her bed hadn't been slept in. I waited all day Sunday on needles and pins. I could hardly stand not being able to tell her right away.

'It meant we'd both finally be able to do the things we'd dreamed of doing – like buying nice clothes and traveling. I've always wanted to go to New York and to see something live on Broadway. And Georgie always dreamed of visiting the British Museum. When she still wasn't home Sunday night, I called 911 to report her missing.

'The officer was very nice, but he said the police would have to wait a full twenty-four hours before they could do anything. He asked me if Georgie had a problem with drugs or alcohol. When I told him she used to drink, he said maybe she'd fallen off the wagon and gone on a bender. After thinking about it a while, I decided maybe he was right. So Monday I took the day off and went down to Olympia to pick up our first check. Since Georgie wasn't there, I had them make the whole thing out to me.

'I spent all day yesterday resigning from the school district and making arrangements to put the money in the bank. Handling that much money is really complicated, you know. I wanted Georgie with me when I made all those decisions and transactions. She's always been smart about things like that, even when she was drinking.'

'I met your sister a time or two,' I said. 'She called herself Erica instead of Georgie. Do you have any idea why she might have done that?'

A frown flitted across Gail's somber face. 'When we were little we used to pretend we were someone else. I was always Suzanne – I liked that name better than plain old Gail. And Georgie always picked Erica. It drove our mother crazy. We'd go for days at a time without breaking character. It was like a contest to see which of us could outlast the other.'

'And she claimed to be working on a book,' I added. 'Do you know about that?'

'Georgie, writing a book?' Gail asked. 'You must be mistaken. If she had been, I certainly would have known about it.'

'And you didn't?'

'No. Where would she have done it? When?'

'Maybe in her room,' Sue suggested quietly. 'Is it possible for us to see it?'

Gail rose to her feet. 'Of course,' she said. 'This way.'

We made our way through the cluttered house. It wasn't messy so much as overstuffed. The dining room held two full-size dining-tables and a jumbled collection of stacked chairs. The family room held two television sets and two pianos – an enormous old upright and a smaller, more modern spinet.

'Half of these are Mother's things,' Gail explained as we threaded our way down the hall. 'I didn't want to get rid of anything without Georgie's approval. While she was in prison I couldn't consult her. And now that she's out, she's . . .' Gail lapsed into silence, finally adding lamely, '. . . she hasn't shown any interest.'

Compared to the rest of the house, Georgina Carver's bedroom was monk-like in its spare simplicity. There was a single, well-made bed under the window, a chest of drawers and a small desk with a straight-backed chair pushed under it. Nothing was out of place except for a single piece of paper lying on the desk.

Meandering over to the desk, I glanced down. One of the few benefits of encroaching middle age is an increasing ability to read things at a distance. That may be bad for reading newspapers and books, but it's good for reading papers off tables without having to pick them up.

In this case, I was looking at the monthly newsletter from something called the Washington Center for the Book, at the Seattle public library.

'What's this?' I asked.

Gail shrugged. 'Georgie's mail. It came this morning. She went downtown on the bus almost every day. I always wondered where she went and what she did down there. Maybe she spent her time at the library.'

And at AA meetings, I thought.

'What about your sister's friends?' I asked. 'Did you know any of them?'

Gail shook her head. 'Georgie and I were worlds apart when it came to that. I didn't approve of hers, and she certainly didn't like mine.'

'So you didn't necessarily chum around much,' Sue offered. Gail nodded. 'But were you and your sister friends?' Sue pressed.

A anguished look flashed across Gail Mathers's face. 'Not really. You know how it is.'

'How what is?'

'Georgie always thought Mother liked me best; that she always played second fiddle to me. She shouldn't have been jealous. Georgie was always smarter than I was. And prettier.'

And deader, I thought, edging around the worrisome hunch that was beginning to grow in my gut. 'Do you happen to keep any weapons here in the house?' I asked.

'Only a .22. For protection,' Gail Mathers added. 'I bought it last year. Georgie thought that two women living alone ought to have some kind of weapon, but she couldn't buy it in her own name. Not with her record.'

'Could we see it, please?' Sue asked.

'Sure,' Gail said easily. 'It's in the nightstand in my bedroom.'

But, of course, it wasn't there. Gail made a show of searching for it but finally gave up. 'Maybe we ought to go down to the medical examiner's office now,' I suggested.

'I'll get my car keys,' Gail said.

'Don't bother. We'll drive you downtown and bring you home afterwards,' I said.

Sue and I waited outside by our car while Gail closed up the house and switched on the alarm. 'Seven million dollars,' Sue mused thoughtfully. 'What if that Lotto ticket never turned up in a birthday card? What if it really belonged to Georgina and Gail stole it? You combine that much money with a years-old sibling squabble, and what do you have?'

'A female Cain and Abel?' I offered.

Sue nodded. 'The thought had crossed my mind,' she said.

'So far, that's strictly speculation.'

Sue Danielson's face was grim. 'My guess is it won't stay that way long.'

The trip to the morgue was like countless other awful victim-identification trips. The moment the lab tech whipped the sheet off Georgina Carver's pallid face, Gail Mathers fainted dead away. She was still quivering and semi-hysterical when we dropped her back to the house in Bellevue. Sue and I offered to stay until a friend or family member could arrive, but she wouldn't hear of it.

That was just as well. I was anxious for us to head back downtown. 'What's the hurry?' Sue asked.

'Let's hit the Seattle public library,' I told her. 'We'll check out the Washington Center for the Book.'

'What does that have to do with the price of peanuts?'

'If Georgina Carver went downtown every day, if she hung out down there without any kind of job, she must have been doing something. The library seems like as good a place to start as any. If nothing else, we know she's on their mailing list – under her real name.'

'Oh,' Sue said.

At the library it was only a matter of minutes before we were directed into the office of Nancy Pearl, the executive director for the Washington Center for the Book. I gave the preliminaries short shrift before plunging into the pertinent questions.

'Do you know someone named Georgina Carver?' I asked.

'Of course,' Nancy answered directly. 'She doesn't go by that name here. We've all been asked to call her Erica. She's using one of our carrels this time around.'

'Carrels?'

'Desks,' Nancy Pearl explained. 'So many would-be writers are stymied by the lack of a decent place to work. They can apply to use one of our work spaces in the C. K. Poefratt Writers' Room for up to as long as a year at a time. We provide a warm, well-lighted quiet place in which to work, along with a locker for storage so they don't have to carry things back and forth. For the time period of their grant, our mostly not-yet-published writers can work here as much or as little as they like.'

Nancy Pearl paused for a moment and studied me with a puzzled frown. 'But why are you asking me about Georgina . . . about Erica, I mean?'

'She's dead,' I said. 'We found her body this morning.'

Nancy didn't seem surprised. She leaned back in her chair, closed her eyes, and shook her head. 'Erica was so frightened that would happen. And it did, no matter how hard she tried to prevent it.'

'What are you talking about?' I asked.

'It's the sister, of course,' Nancy answered briskly. 'Erica showed me some of the passages from her diary. She was culling entries and editing them into a book. She told me on more than one occasion how afraid she was of her sister, the teacher. What's her name?'

'Mathers. Gail Mathers.'

'Right. That's the one. Erica told me that if anything ever happened to her, I should tell the detectives to check on Gail, that she wasn't to be trusted.'

'Did Georgina say why?'

'She said her sister always hated her, something about their mother. Georgina and I had lunch together several times, the last time just days ago. She seemed desperately frightened – literally afraid for her life. She told me that shortly before Christmas Gail bought herself a gun.'

Sue Danielson and I exchanged glances. 'Do you have any idea what kind?'

'She didn't say, and it wouldn't have made any difference if she had. I don't know anything at all about guns.'

'Going back to the project she was working on. You say she kept a diary?'

Gail nodded. 'I'd call it more of a journal. I believe she started it while she was incarcerated. It must have been very painful. There was an accident, you see, several years ago on New Year's Eve. Georgina was driving when her husband was killed. She served time in prison, lost her job, everything. I think writing the book was her way of driving out the demons, of trying to make sense of it all.'

'Is there any way for you to open her locker?' Sue asked.

'Not without a court order,' Nancy responded. 'Confidentiality, you know.'

She said it so firmly that we didn't even bother trying to change her mind. Getting a court order took several hours. When we finally had one, Nancy led us into the wood-paneled, carpeted room. Several of the desks were occupied by people who looked up at us, frowning at the interruption.

The locker, when Nancy opened it, was as spare and uncluttered as Georgina Carver's bedroom. There were four spiral notebooks and a ziplock bag full of lottery receipts, twenty-six separate tickets in all. At two games per week, that meant thirteen weeks of Lotto games in which Georgina had played the same two sets of identical numbers over and over. Only the receipt for that last Saturday's game – the winning ticket – was missing.

Exchanging the contents of the locker for a receipt, Sue and I headed out the door. The library is only a few blocks from the department, but I didn't want to go there. Not right away.

'Aren't you hungry?' I asked Sue. 'Shouldn't we stop off for a bite to eat before we head back?'

'I'm starved,' she agreed with a knowing smile.

Over a meal that was too late for lunch and too early for dinner, we skimmed through the first few notebooks and devoured the last one. The story was there in painstakingly unflinching detail – from the grim entries relating Hal Carver's appalling injuries to Georgina's terror at the idea of Gail being armed with a gun.

One passage, written in early January, hit me especially hard. 'I've talked to N. P.,' Georgina wrote, referring presumably to Nancy Pearl. 'She says just because Gail and I are sisters doesn't mean it isn't domestic violence. N. P. thinks I should move out or go to the police. If I left, where would I go? And if I went to the cops, who would they believe? The nice lady schoolteacher, or the ex-con straight out of the slammer?'

I passed the notebook across to Sue and waited while she read it. 'What do you think?' I asked.

'I think it's time to talk to Captain Powell.'

It was several days before we had the autopsy results back and enough probable cause to return to Bellevue. The next time Sue and I showed up on Gail Mathers's doorstep, we came armed with a search warrant and accompanied by officers from the Bellevue Police Department. At first, while we conducted the search, Gail sat quietly watching the process and acting as though she had no idea why we were there. Sue was the one who found the jacket in the front hall closet – a leather jacket with what looked like powder burns on the front and sleeves.

When we started reading Gail her rights and placing her under arrest, she went ballistic. It took all four of us – Sue and me and the two Bellevue cops as well – to restrain her.

The case came together quickly after that. Gail Mathers's arrest was followed in short order by a grand jury indictment, a preliminary hearing and eventually a trial. All the while Gail loudly proclaimed her innocence. The prosecutors didn't believe her. The jury didn't, either.

Admittedly, most of the evidence was circumstantial. There was no eyewitness who saw the murder go down, but the powder burns on the jacket found in the closet did connect Gail Mathers with firing the fatal weapon. Entries from Georgina's diary were allowed into evidence. As the prosecutor read the agonizing passages that spelled out the victim's fear of death at her sister's hands, the words fell upon a hushed courtroom with the undeniable weight of fulfilled prophecy.

Gail Mathers was convicted and sentenced to twenty years to life for first-degree murder. Before corrections officers moved her out of the King County Jail, she asked to see me.

'You know Georgie staged her own suicide as murder just to set me up, don't you?' she asked. 'The Lotto jackpot made it that much easier for her to win.'

'Win!' I objected. 'What do you mean, win? The woman is dead.'

'My sister was a pathological liar,' Gail replied calmly. 'She must have worked on this scheme for months, maybe even years. She'd go to any lengths to get even, and look what's happened. My teaching career is over. The jackpot money's gone as far as I'm concerned. The IRS claims I lied about Georgie giving me the ticket. That will make the entire jackpot flow through Georgina's estate. The feds want the estate taxes, and they want them now. Georgina's will named me as primary heir and the Seattle public library as contingent beneficiary. Since I've been convicted of her death, everything that doesn't go for taxes will go to the library. Instead of being a millionaire, I'm a pauper. It'll take everything I own to pay my lawyer.'

'Would Georgina be that diabolical?' I asked. 'Why would she go to that much trouble?'

'Because she hated me,' Gail answered simply.

'Oh, please. Don't give me that old line about your mother liking you best.'

'No, because Georgina held me responsible for Hal's death.'

That one stunned me. 'How could that be? She was the one driving the car.'

'Did you read the notebooks?' Gail asked. 'Her diaries?'

'Sure, but . . .'

'Did she ever say where the party was held that New Year's Eve?'

'No.'

'I'll tell you where it was, Detective Beaumont. At *my* house. Georgina and Hal both got drunk drinking *my* booze at *my* party. It's taken this long for her to get back at me, but that's all right. I can be a graceful loser.'

'What do you mean by that?'

'I'm not going to appeal my conviction. Why bother? I don't have any money left or a job or even a house to live in. This way I may not get to travel, but I'll have food to eat and a roof over my head. I'm looking forward to twenty years of reading books without having to put up with other people's rotten kids. But you're wrong about one thing.'

'What's that?'

'Mother always did like me best.'

I left the jail feeling odd, as though I had been sucked into a war between two crazed women, and I couldn't tell who had won or lost. Heading back home, I remembered a verse my mother told me once, although I can't remember exactly where it's from:

> It needs more skill than I can tell
> To play the second fiddle well.

I have a terrible feeling Georgina Carver played one hell of a second fiddle.

INVESTIGATING THE SILVIUS BOYS

LINDSEY DAVIS

The location of the crime was critical. The scene was a marshy river valley, between low but significant hills. Alongside the river ran an ancient salt road. It came up from the coast, about twenty miles away, then continued into the interior towards a city which at that time ruled the neighbourhood. In a wide curve of the river lay an island which offered the first crossing point inland. This bridgehead made a natural halt, for it was about one day's journey for the beasts bringing salt from the sea. These factors had encouraged settlement. The hills were crying out to be defended – and someone had just begun surrounding them with a rampart wall. In the footings of the new wall the investigator had seen a recent corpse.

There had been no attempt to hide the body. As soon as he asked, bystanders told him freely that the victim was one of the two Silvius boys. They also admitted quite openly who had battered him to death. One of the oldest crimes in the world: a young man had quarrelled bitterly with his brother and killed him with a building tool.

That was when the investigator should have gone home. He was a visitor who had come merely to sightsee. But he knew something of the family involved and so he found himself intrigued. Being drawn in despite himself was a hazard of his profession. Once his interest had been caught there was no escape.

The purist inquirer likes a date for a murder. That posed a problem. Time had no set limits. The tribes north of the river maintained a rough calendar by banging a nail into a temple door every year. It worked well, unless the temple burned down, as happened fairly frequently. Here the people were more primitive. Even so they were practical, and quite capable of devising their own methods of reckoning. Very soon they would calculate everything from the most important date they had. So if you wanted to be pedantic, you could say that the man who was killed by his brother had died in the year time began.

Well, that was the kind of easy-to-remember fact which helps keep casework archives neat. This was, without any question, Case Number One.

Number One – with no arrest foreseeable. It did not bode well for the future of the profession.

On the driest and highest of the hills above the river's marshy floodplain stood a group of shepherds' huts. They had a venerable, weathered air – and the shepherds who lived in them had a reputation for beating up strangers. As he climbed the hill, which was harder going than it looked, the investigator sighed. He hated shepherds. This collection were known to be formidable. They did not wait to be raided by bandits, like most countrymen who knew their lot was to lead a hard life and suffer. These themselves rode out in armed groups, attacked the bandits vigorously, and shared out their spoils. They were famous for flouting authority. They had found themselves young leaders who encouraged them to plunder the herds of neighbouring landowners, even including the royal estates. The investigator knew this because he worked for the king.

As he climbed towards the hilltop he noticed a flurry of movement. They had seen him coming. They knew exactly who he was. They also knew he was at a disadvantage. As he came up, gasping, he saw only a huddle of hostile people in rough sheepskin dress, who all looked surly and all looked the same. To a city man they had an obtrusive smell of woodsmoke and lanolin. It made him feel his own habits were over-fastidious.

'I need to speak to Faustulus.' He felt a taut knot in his belly. It was always the same at the start of something: dread of the unknown.

'What do you want?'

'Someone is dead.'

'What's it to you?' The man who spoke was being no more obstructive than usual. He just belonged to a group who took pride in being blunt. Like all such groups, outsiders judged them plain rude.

Faustulus himself had come out of a hut. The investigator knew him already because Faustulus was the previous king's herdsman. This had made for complications during the raids on the royal estates – for Faustulus was also foster-father to the ringleaders who organized the raids. Now nearing the end of his working life, he was hardy, skilled and too intelligent for his own good. The stubborn, confident type, the type who breaks the rules. Twenty or thirty years ago he took home two abandoned infants when any sensible man would have left them to die. They grew up to be the Silvius twins.

It was clear from his eyes that Faustulus already knew that one of his rowdy foster sons was now lying alongside the new rampart with his head cracked open, and that the other was responsible. Those eyes said that, like any man who brought up children who came to grief, he was now wondering why he had bothered. But there was a hard defiance in their gaze as well. He would stand by the survivor.

The investigator gave him a courteous nod, then braced himself. 'Where's Romulus?'

A murmur ran through the crowd. 'Go back to your work,' ordered the investigator. 'Disperse. There's nothing to see.'

A woman rushed to the front, tear-stained and shrieking abuse. He ought to have known Larentia would not be far away. 'Get out of here! You're not wanted. Get back to Alba.'

She was younger than Faustulus, but well matched in spirit. She had a reputation for putting herself about too much. Maybe she did, though in a small, and small-minded, community any woman with character risks jealous talk. This one had never cared what others thought.

'Larentia, I'm sorry to find you in this trouble.' She checked herself, seeing that the investigator was a quiet and steady man who would not be swayed from his purpose. 'I have to see Romulus before I leave,' he told her levelly. He could take his time. Romulus belonged right here. He would not flee.

Larentia still looked ready to fly at him. If she appealed to the others the investigator would be lost. He knew this was the most dangerous moment. Walking up the hill alone had been stupid. His mouth dried, as if he had been chewing grapeskins to nothing. If these people decided to tear him apart he had no means of defending himself.

'Let Romulus be. He's grieving for his brother,' Larentia cried.

'I can understand that,' the investigator said.

'You don't understand anything!' Behind the spitting rage of a creature defending her young lay darker feelings. She was standing apart from Faustulus as if pain had erected a barrier between her husband and herself. She also knew that whatever happened she had lost not one, but both her boys.

'I'm trying to understand,' said the man from Alba Longa. 'Maybe the best thing is if Romulus himself stops hiding in the hut behind you and comes out to explain.'

Romulus emerged of his own volition. If he wanted to remain a power in the community there was no alternative. Once he looked like a fugitive he would lose all powers of leadership.

Pushing past his knee as he ducked out of the hut came a large dog, growling fiercely at the stranger. The investigator stood his ground. Presumably a man who had been suckled by a she-wolf was good with animals.

The watchdog sat on its tail and and fell silent. Romulus came further forward. He was strong and fit, past boyhood but still young. His expression was dark, but otherwise unfathomable. People said he made a happy companion exchanging stories around a campfire, but if you met him at market you would not attempt conversation. He was rural and close. That was how he set out to be, even normally, let alone on the day he had killed his twin brother.

Seeing him, the crowd relaxed. No one, including the foster parents, made any move to intervene when suspect and investigator walked to another part of the hilltop where they could talk in privacy. The two men were now looking south, across a deep cleft which divided the hill that would be known as the Palatine, the hill where the twins had been brought up, from the crag called the Aventine.

'I don't have to say anything to you!' declared Romulus. He sounded like anyone caught poaching on the royal estates.

'That's right.'

'You're wasting your time.'

'It goes with the job.'

The investigator surveyed him thoughtfully. Hardened and self-opinionated. A fighter, who could devise a plan and then organize the muscle to carry it out. A young thug. But then what else could he be, with that background?

The Silvius family, now the hereditary kings of Alba, claimed descent from Aeneas, that pragmatic old hero who escaped from Troy then pushed his way to power in Italy without a by-your-leave. His descendants were never renowned for peaceful living. The twins' grandfather had been shoved off the throne by his brother, who methodically killed all his nephews, then ordered his niece to become a vestal virgin. Instead of sticking to her intended life of chastity she let herself be raped – or, according to her, she was deflowered by Mars, the god of war (good story: a quick-thinking girl). The resultant sons had been ordered to be drowned in the Tiber, but the job had been bungled and Faustulus had found them in the flooded fields, being suckled by a she-wolf.

Well, the she-wolf tale was a ludicrous rumour. Romulus and Remus were just one more set of tearaways: a violent background, mother no better than she should be, unknown or absentee father, children pushed around between foster parents, unusual relations with animals. They had been brought up in dirt and poverty, always dreaming of the better life and striving to grab it the fastest way. Now one had come to a sticky end. The other was implicated. How long before he too met some sordid fate?

'What are you thinking about?' asked Romulus.

'I saw you, that night in Alba,' the investigator told him. 'The night the old king was killed.'

'Oh, that night!' exclaimed the old king's nephew in a soft, bitter voice. He seemed much older than he should.

'It looked like a happy ending for you and your brother.'

'Do you believe in happy endings?' Today, with Remus dead, Romulus clearly did not.

'I believe in order,' the investigator said. 'So when people get killed, I believe in calling the perpetrator to account.'

'You'll wear yourself out!' jeered the tearaway prince. 'I'll stick with believing in fate.'

Fate had certainly seemed to be on their side when he and his brother had come to Alba. At that time the twins had been at the height of their success as community heroes attacking bandits. One group, however, had set a trap for them. Remus had been captured by these robbers and handed over, first to the king of Alba, then to his deposed brother whose estates had been raided by the twins. So Remus had come face to face with his grandfather for the first time. The grandfather started to think.

Faustulus, who had long ago worked out the twins' royal origin, realized the truth was bound to come out. Back in the shepherd's hut there was urgent discussion. Romulus knew he had to act. With typical flair he infiltrated the city, rescued his brother, killed the usurping king, and saw their grandfather finally reinstated as monarch.

'So what went wrong?' mused the man from Alba. 'You had been greeted in triumph. You were princes restored to your heritage.'

'You can never go back,' said Romulus darkly. His expression cleared a little: 'We wanted space. We were uncomfortable in the old city that had once rejected us. We wanted our own territory.' He spoke as if fleeing the nest were some new idea. The investigator smiled. Alba was sorely overpopulated, all agreed. And the Silvius boys had always looked as if they were driven by unusual strength of will.

'So here you are. Back where you were found in the floods and brought up. About to found a new city that could rival all others – but now Remus is dead. Do you want to tell me about it?'

'No.'

The eyes of Romulus seemed to glitter as he stared out across the river. Was this simply the madness of a born killer? Or was it the set face of a man who had committed a horrific act by accident against the person he had always been closest to, a man who knew he now had to live with that for the rest of his life?

'It would be better if you told me,' repeated the investigator quietly. The forces of right and wrong fought their old battle in silence.

Despite his previous refusal, the surviving twin began speaking. His voice was controlled but tense. 'The situation was impossible. No city can have two founders.' Why not? Well, any idea of partnership had always been lost on the Silvius family. Suggesting notions of brotherhood was just asking for a black eye. 'Because my brother and I were twins there was no seniority. We decided to ask the gods of the countryside to say which of us should govern the new city, and give his name to it.'

'So you chose to use augury?'

'One has to be civilized.'

'Of course.'

Augury was a rural art. In theory it was scrupulously impartial. To the sceptic from Alba it was open to misinterpretation, otherwise called fraud. The diviner foretold the future by looking at flight patterns of birds. That was random enough. The trickery entered when the diviner gave his opinion of what the patterns meant. At this point human error was inclined to creep in.

'I stood upon this hill here; Remus was on that one.' Romulus gestured to the Aventine. 'My brother spoke first. He had seen six vultures.'

He fell silent. The investigator had already heard what happened next. Immediately after Remus had made his pronouncement, Romulus doubled the tally and saw twelve birds. Well, that was what he said. Presumably Remus soon realized he had walked right into that one.

'Your brother's followers claimed priority for him, on the grounds that he had seen his sign first?'

'Yes. While mine did the same on grounds of number.'

'So nothing was solved!'

'Fighting broke out,' Romulus confirmed wryly.

'And is that when you killed him?'

'No.' Had the rediscovered prince not been so heavily sunburnt after his life as a shepherd, he might have looked as if he were blushing. An admission of the stupidity of it found its way into his voice: 'The majority seemed to agree that I should be the city's founder. I harnessed an ox and ploughed a furrow to set out a boundary. Then I set to, building a rampart. That was when Remus came over and jeered at my work. He jumped over the half-built wall, scoffing. I lost my temper and went for him.' Dangerous places, building sites. Not a sensible playground for such a pair of squabbling brothers.

To his credit, Romulus was not the type to inaugurate his city by sitting on a stool in a clean tunic giving orders from a chart. He would have been right in there with a hod or a mattock, stretching his muscles and getting his knuckles grazed. When his brother came and kicked at the newly mortared stonework with a maddening laugh, Romulus would have been hot, sweat-stained and covered with dust. After their tussle over the augury, his temper must have been stretched to breaking point. Remus never stood a chance. Still, he should have known that.

'So Remus is dead. What's your plan now?' asked the investigator cautiously. He thought he knew the plan. It could be unwise annoying a man who had just put a shovel through his own twin brother's skull for interfering.

'The plan,' stated Romulus, who also realized the fine points of the situation, 'is the same as before: I am founding a city. I mean it to rival all other cities. I shall fortify the hill on which we are standing, enclose ground, and attract manpower.'

'Mould the rabble into a body politic?' suggested the man from Alba.

'Your terms are a bit Etruscan,' said Romulus drily. He was referring to the tribesmen from north of the river, who traded with Greeks and had absorbed some exotic practices.

'Founding a city's more complex than herding sheep.'

'I realize that.' The prince was grim.

'For instance,' said his companion, 'you will have to address the issue of social order. Cities need rules. One rule which you may want to suggest to the community is "Don't murder each other."'

'I shall insist on it,' said Romulus calmly.

'Oh I see: "Don't do what I do, do what I say"?'

'That seems a nice definition of civic authority.'

'Now we're getting somewhere!' scoffed the investigator, who was after all a city man. He had a highly developed sense of irony, and was wary of people in charge.

Romulus had caught him gazing across the unwelcoming landscape. 'I'm going to make something of this place,' he declared. His tone was that of a visionary, as if he dreamed of ineffable empire. But since he came from rural stock, out loud he made only cautious claims: 'All you see now is wild country peopled by lawless tribes, but it will become far greater.'

'I wish you every success.'

'Why have you come to challenge me, then?'

'If whatever you're planning is meant to improve standards, maybe a murder is a bad way to start!'

'Prevent me founding my city, and there never will be anything here but the wilderness,' warned Romulus. 'You'll be interfering with history.'

'As special pleading, that's certainly different!' The investigator smiled. 'Normally when I tackle a suspect he says, "Put me away, and one dark night my pals will get you!" I have to admit, I wasn't expecting anything subtle from one of the Silvius boys . . . but it still leaves me as the high-minded idiot who has to allow you your second chance.'

There was a theory that if you gave hoodlums from a deprived background something to care about, they would come good. The man from Alba doubted it. On the other hand, not many roughnecks from difficult families were offered the chance to establish an empire as their sweetener to reform themselves.

'Think of it as an investment in the future,' said Romulus. Adding, 'As for me, I shall atone for Remus by devoting my life to the new city.'

'Ah – community service!' replied the investigator, inventing a dubious concept without intending to.

There was a short silence, which was not unfriendly.

Romulus stirred. As a man with a nation to found, he rarely stayed still for long. 'So is that all you wanted to ask me?'

'Yes.' The investigator's tone had a decisive note. 'Well, there's just one more thing—'

Romulus stared at him, unfamiliar with the concept of an investigator suddenly turning back with the unexpected question that overturns the alibi. Even so, he had a feeling he was about to be tricked. 'What's that?'

'Only—' For the first time a slight note of bashfulness entered the investigator's voice. 'If you're founding a city, you're going to need law enforcement—'

'So?'

'So I wondered if there might be a job for me.'

*   *   *

105

Decades later two grizzled investigators were comparing notes. The elder, retired now but still an expert in his own eyes, tried to cheer up his colleague by relating his own worst experience.

'Believe me, I know the nightmare: the witnesses clam up and the prime suspect is boasting that you can't touch him. There's unavoidable publicity; the whole population is watching and waiting for your big mistake. Mine had a royal connection – in fact, even the gods were taking an interest, according to some.'

'So what was this – a family case? Gang warfare? Or a business partnership that went wrong?'

'Oh, all those! I'm talking about the Silvius brothers.' The name meant nothing. Time had moved on. There were new villains now. 'I knew who did the killing. There had been plenty of onlookers. He admitted the crime. The problem was, I couldn't touch him.'

'They all say that,' the young man disagreed. 'It's standard: "You've nothing on me! You'll never make it stick!" Normally once you've got as far as accusing them, you know you'll take them all the way to court.'

'Mine,' smiled the old expert, 'was never a normal case.'

'No case is normal,' snapped the rookie impatiently, as they turned down an alley (looking twice in case of muggers) then peeled off into a favourite bar. Immediately they both wondered why it had become such a favourite. The frosty girl who took their order growled with irritation at their greeting. She hated men in their line of business; well, she hated men in any line. She was suffering from an appalling cold. Her bar-room etiquette was to cough all over any drinks she was serving, then she coughed all over the customers. When they paid up, she fiddled the money.

Some things never change.

'No case is normal,' agreed the retired agent with a smile. 'Especially if you try and arrest Romulus!'

His young companion was choking on his drink. 'Romulus!' Now, sitting in Rome, which was already a leading city amongst its neighbours, with Romulus the great leader after a lifetime of wise public service, the idea of anyone taking him to task seemed unbelievable.

'He killed his brother. I thought he should account for it.'

'You set about him like a suspect – and then he gave you a job?'

The old expert looked diffident. When he had risked the question, Romulus had suddenly smiled – the calm, confident smile of a man who knows he will fulfil his destiny. 'He said I had the right attitude.'

The young one spluttered again, but subsided in awe. 'Well, it all worked out.'

'Letting him off? Well, he wasn't going to offend again. We agreed what happened to Remus was all in the family – the fighting Silvius brothers doing what their ancestors did best. Unless their mother, the vestal virgin, had secretly borne triplets to the so-called god of war, Romulus had run out of brothers. I had two options: I could arrest him – if I wanted to be thrown off a crag by the mob. Or I could give him his chance.'

'So why do you call the case a problem?'

'I hate loose ends. Even when Romulus gave the city laws and made the populace respect them, when his own reputation had become impeccable, I could never forget that Remus was dead and nobody had answered for it.'

The younger man laughed. 'You're obsessed!'

'That's why it's a problem,' agreed the other quietly.

'Madness! He's built the greatest city in Italy. You're vindicated.'

The rookie's friend felt obliged to be fair: 'There was the business of the gang rape. I was never happy with our result on that.'

'The Sabine girls?' Surprised at first, the younger colleague forced himself to take the professional view. 'Well, yes; I can see there was a case – against Romulus as the ringleader, and every male in the city.'

'There had been a prior conspiracy; and the women were abducted and held against their will.'

'But when their fathers made a complaint, surely the victims all refused to testify?'

The retired officer shrugged. 'Marital rape is always tricky to prove in court.'

'They knew when they were well off,' said the young man, taking the robust Roman view. 'Husbands who were not bad, and life in a bright modern city.'

'Oh I'm sure that's how they saw it,' agreed the old expert gravely. For a moment his young friend felt disconcerted. He sympathized with Romulus all those years before, standing on the edge of the Palatine and hearing this stubborn maverick suggest that the dead Remus should perhaps not be lightly passed off as a mere hitch on the road to destiny.

'Don't tell me you're still hoping to get him one day?'

Without comment, the retired investigator smiled and made ready to leave. In the doorway he paused for a moment. An old habit. Rome was

107

a city, so it was full of thieves and fraudsters and people knocking each other on the head; sometimes there was a reason, but sometimes they did it just because they felt like it. Anyone who knew what he was doing stopped to sniff the air and look down the street before he stepped outside. That's what cities are like.

After he had gone, the younger man sat on, finishing the wine. When he rose, fumbling reluctantly for money, the miserable barmaid spoke: 'Your friend left a tip. He's not in the same line as you, is he?'

'He was once.' The rookie chortled, still amused by the story. 'That's the investigator who once tried to arrest Romulus!' The girl appeared impressed for a moment so the man added, 'Just think; if Romulus hadn't bashed his twin brother, we could be living in a city called Reme.'

'Get away!' said the girl.

'My pal would still arrest him, if he had a chance.'

'Too late.'

The rookie paid the waitress more attention. Rome's law-enforcement men had already learned the fine principle of picking up information from bored girls in tawdry bars. 'Why's that?'

'Romulus has gone.'

'What do you mean?'

'He vanished. Did you notice that nasty storm this morning? Romulus was out reviewing some troops on the Plain of Mars. A thick cloud of mist enveloped him, so nobody else could see him. When it cleared, he had disappeared. They reckon he was taken up to heaven in the whirlwind, and that that's the last we shall ever see of him.'

'Carried off by a whirlwind, eh?' The rookie sighed. 'You're right, it's too bad.'

He stood at the counter, staring into his own thoughts. The barmaid pretended to wipe down a table.

People don't just disappear. Being carried off by a whirlwind was about as likely as being suckled by a she-wolf.

Romulus had been a popular ruler, but only among the common people to whom he gave his own loyalty. The young man knew that Romulus had attracted jealousy from some of the city senators. Could it be that the senators had set upon Romulus and despatched him secretly? There would be a body somewhere; someone just had to hunt for it . . . The insistent voice of his profession suggested that the Plain of Mars incident should be looked into.

Another voice told him not to be a fool. Law and order men are not required to involve themselves in politics. This was one case for which he would never get civic funding. And if he was right, even if he discovered the truth, he would never be allowed to make it public or take any credit.

He knew what a sensible man ought to do. But when he walked from the bar, his feet were taking him towards the low plain alongside the river where Romulus was supposed to have vanished. His head was full of unanswered questions, and in his eyes was the haunted expression of a man obsessed.

CARRION
PETER ROBINSON

Isn't it strange the way two people might strike up a casual acquaint-ance due simply to a quirk of fate? And isn't it even stranger how that innocent meeting might so completely alter the life of one of them? That was exactly what happened when Edward Grainger and I met in a pub one wet September lunch-time, only weeks before his tragic loss.

I work in a bank in the City. It's a dull job, livened up only by the occasional surge of adrenalin when the pound takes yet another plunge on the foreign exchange markets, and most lunch-times I like to get out of the office and take refuge in the Mason's Arms.

As a rule, I will drink half a pint of Guinness with a slice of quiche or a cheese roll, say, and perhaps, once in a while, treat myself to a steak and kidney pie. As I eat, I work at the *Times* crossword, which I never seem able to finish before my glass is empty, and after my meal I enjoy a cigarette. I know the vile things are bad for me, but I can't quite seem to give them up. Besides, how bad can one cigarette a day be? And only five days a week, at that.

Given its location in the City, the Mason's Arms is generally busy, noisy and smoky by half past twelve on a weekday, and that suits me just fine. Lost in the crowd, buffeted by conversation and laugh-ter that requires no response on my part, I can concentrate on my crossword or allow my mind to drift in directions that the constant application of the little grey cells to columns of figures precludes.

That particular lunch-time, I found myself leaving the office a few minutes later than usual due to an important telephone conversation with an overseas client. The short walk also took longer because I had to struggle against the wind and rain with a rather flimsy umbrella. When I got to the Arms, as I had taken to calling it, I found my usual little corner table already taken by a stranger in a pinstripe suit. I could hardly tell him to sod off, so I carried my drink over and sat opposite him.

As he read his *Times*, I studied his features closely. I would guess his age at about forty-five – mostly because of the wrinkles around his eyes and the grey hair around his temples and ears – but having said that, I would have to admit that the overall effect of his face was one of youthfulness. He had bright blue eyes and a healthy, ruddy complexion, and he showed no sign of that dark, shadowy stubble that makes some men look rather sinister.

After I had finished my ham roll, I lit my cigarette and wrestled with eight down, letting the ebb and flow of conversation drift over me, until a voice seemed to single itself out from the crowd and speak directly to me.

Startled, I noticed the man opposite looking at me in a way that suggested he had just spoken.

'Pardon?' I said. 'I was miles away.'

'Crippen,' he said. 'Eight down. "Quiet prince upset for this murderer." It's an anagram of "prince" and "p" for silent.'

'Yes, I do see that, thank you very much.' If my tone was a little frosty, it served the bugger right. I hate it when people solve my crossword clues for me, the same way I hate anyone reading over my shoulder. Takes all the fun out of it.

His face dropped when he saw the look I gave him.

'I'm sorry,' he said. 'Very rude of me. Didn't think.'

'It's all right.' I put the crossword aside and flicked a column of ash at the floor.

'Look, you wouldn't happen to know anything about septic tanks, would you?' he asked.

'I'm afraid not.' As far as conversational gambits went, this fellow wasn't exactly heading for the top of the class in my book.

'Oh. Pity. You see, we're having one installed in a couple of weeks, my wife Harriet and I. I'm just not sure what kind of mess to expect.'

'Well, I suppose they'll have to dig the garden up,' I told him. 'But I can't honestly say I've ever seen one, so I don't know how big they are.'

He smiled. 'Well, that's the point, isn't it? You're not supposed to *see* them. We're moving to the country, you know, to Hampshire.'

'Why are you moving?' I asked. And though I surprised myself by asking such a personal question of a complete stranger, it felt natural enough.

He sipped his gin and tonic before replying. 'It's for Harriet, mostly,' he said. 'Wants the country air. Not that I'd knock it, mind you. And it's a beautiful cottage, or will be after the renovations. Seventeenth century. I'll keep the flat in town, of course, go down to the country at weekends. Yes, I'm sure it'll work out.'

'I hope so,' I told him. Then I excused myself and headed back to the bank, it being almost one-thirty and Mr Beamish, the branch manager, being a real stickler for punctuality.

As time went on, our conversations became a regular feature of my lunch-time visits to the Arms, though I would be hard pushed now to think of everything we discussed: politics, of course, on which we disagreed; books, on which we agreed far more than we would have imagined; and marriage, about which we couldn't quite make up our minds. Sometimes we would just work on the crossword together in silence.

He also talked about weekends at the country house, of autumn walks in the woods, the occasional hovercraft trip to the Isle of Wight, quiet nights with a good bottle of claret, a hefty volume of Trollope and log fire crackling in the hearth.

Though I had never fancied country living myself, I must admit that Edward's accounts made me quite envious. So much so that when Evelyn brought up the subject at home after watching a documentary on the Cotswolds, I thought it might become a real possibility for us too, in a year or two's time.

Edward and I never arranged to meet at any other times or places – ours was a purely casual acquaintance – but I like to think that a sort of friendship developed. Sometimes he didn't turn up at all. He worked in international finance, he told me, and now and then he had to sacrifice his lunch-hour for emergency meetings or telephone calls from strange time zones. Occasionally he had to go abroad for a few days. But when he did come, we usually contrived to sit together and chat over our drinks and rolls for half an hour or so.

During that time I didn't find out very much more about his private life, and if I were to come to any conclusions, they would be owing entirely to my reading between the lines.

I didn't ask Edward about his wife's occupation, for example, but somehow I got the impression that she spent most of her time at home, cooking, cake-decorating, cleaning, sewing, knitting and such. What people used to call a housewife in the old days. I suppose now she could call herself an estate manager, down in Hampshire. As far as their relationship went, it sounded perfectly normal to me.

Though I had never met Harriet, I'm sure you can imagine how shocked I was on that bright, windy Thursday in early October when Edward came in a quarter of an hour later than usual, looking drawn and haggard, and told me that his wife had disappeared.

Naturally, I tried to comfort him as best I could over the following weeks, at least as far as our brief and irregular meetings allowed. But there was little I could do. For the most part, I could only look on sadly as Edward lost weight and his former ruddy complexion turned wan. Soon he came to remind of the wretched youth in Keats's poem, 'Alone and palely loitering'.

Weeks passed, and still there was no sign of Harriet. Theories as to her disappearance varied, as they do in cases like this. One tabloid speculated that she had been abducted by a serial killer, then chopped up and buried somewhere. A local doctor suggested that she could have suffered some form of amnesia. If so, he went on, she might easily have wandered off and ended up living on the streets of London with the thousands of other lost and lonely souls. One neighbour, Edward told me, speculated that Harriet could have been actually *planning* her escape for some time and had simply taken off to America, Ireland or France to start a new life under a new name. With a new man, of course. Astonishingly, Edward also told me that even *he* had come under police suspicion at one time, albeit not for long.

Christmas came and went. It was about as cheerful as a wet weekend in July, the way it usually is for families whose children have all grown up and left home. Edward seemed to have gained a little colour when I saw him after the holidays. Or perhaps the Arctic winds we had that January had rubbed his skin raw. Anyway, it was around then that he started dropping in at the Arms for lunch less and less frequently.

By the beginning of February I hadn't seen him for three weeks, and I was slipping easily back into my old routine of doing the crossword over lunch. I missed his company, of course, and I was certainly curious about Harriet, but we are creatures of habit, are we not? And old habits are deeply ingrained.

It was near the end of March when I saw him next, but it wasn't in the Arms. No, I had come into the West End shopping one Saturday afternoon, mostly to get out of the way while Evelyn was busy planting the herbaceous borders. I hate gardening, and if I'm around I usually get roped in.

Anyway, I was browsing in the fiction section of Waterstone's on Charing Cross Road, when I saw Edward across the table of new releases. It took me a moment to recognize him because he was wearing casual clothes and seemed to have done something to remove the grey from his hair. He was also fingering the new Will Self paperback, which one would hardly expect of a Trollope man.

On second glance, though, I realized it was definitely Edward, and that the pretty young blonde with the prominent breasts didn't just happen to be standing beside him; she was *with* him. Surely this couldn't be the elusive Harriet?

Then a strange thing happened. Edward caught my eye as I walked over, and I saw a very odd look pass over his features. For a moment, I could have sworn, he wanted to turn tail and avoid me. But I got to him before he could retreat.

'Edward,' I said, 'it's good to see you.' Then I looked at the blonde. I could see her roots. 'I see Harriet has turned up, then,' I said with a smile.

Edward cleared his throat and the blonde merely frowned. 'Well . . . er . . .' he said. 'Not exactly. I mean, no, she hasn't. This is Joyce.' He put his arm around the blonde's shoulders and looked down at her with obvious pride and passion.

I said hello to Joyce as Edward haltingly explained our relationship, such as it was; then he made excuses and they hurried up the stairs as if the place were on fire. That was the last time I ever clapped eyes on Edward Grainger.

*   *   *

About a year after the incident in Waterstone's, something so profound, so shocking and so unexpected happened to me that my life was never to be the same again. I fell in love.

Like most people my age, I had long thought myself immune to powerful passions, long settled into a sedate and comfortable existence with little in the way of strong emotion to upset its even keel. If I have unsatisfied or unrequited hopes and wishes, then I am in good company, for who hasn't? If I regret some of the sacrifices I have made for the comforts I have gained, who doesn't? And if I sometimes feel that my life lacks adventure, lacks spice, then again, whose doesn't? In all that, I felt, I was perfectly normal.

Life, it had come to seem to me, was a slow betrayal of the dreams of one's youth and a gradual decline from the desires of one's adolescence. Little did I know what a fragile illusion all that was until I met Katrina.

Imagine, if you can, my utter amazement when the bells started to ring, the earth moved and a sudden spring came into my step every time I saw her. Absurd, I told myself, she'll never pay the least attention to an old fuddy-duddy like you. But she did. Oh, indeed she did. Love truly must be blind if such a gorgeous creature as Katrina could give herself to me.

Katrina came to work for the branch in the summer, and by autumn we were meeting clandestinely whenever we could. She lived alone in a tiny bedsit in Kennington, which was convenient if a bit cramped. But what is a little discomfort to a pair of lovers? We were consumed with a passion that could no more be stopped than an avalanche or a tidal wave. It picked us up, tossed us about like rag dolls and threw us back on the ground dazed, dazzled and breathless. I couldn't get enough of her sad eyes, her soft red lips, her small breasts with the nipples hard as acorns when we made love, her skin like warm brown silk.

Needless to say, this affair made life very difficult both at work and at home, but I think I managed to cope well enough under the circumstances. I know I succeeded in hiding it from Evelyn, for I surely would have felt the repercussions had I not.

We went on meeting furtively for almost a year, during which time our passion did not abate in the least. Katrina never once asked me to abandon my marriage and live with her, but I wanted to. Oh God, how I wanted to. Only the thought of all the trouble, all the upheaval that such a move would cause prevented me. For Evelyn wouldn't take it lying down. So, like many others embroiled in affairs, I simply let it run on, perhaps hoping vaguely that some *deus ex machina* would come along and solve my problems for me.

Then, one day, after an excruciatingly painful Christmas spent away from Katrina, Evelyn reminded me of a conversation we had had some time ago about getting a country cottage, and pointed out the ideal place in an estate agent's brochure: a run-down, isolated cottage in Oxfordshire, going for a song.

Furiously I began to think of how such a move might prevent me from seeing Katrina as often as I needed to. We would have to sell the Dulwich house, of course, but the Oxfordshire cottage was indeed going for such an unbelievably low price that I might be able to afford a small flat in town.

At a pinch, however, Evelyn might suggest I commute. The thought of that was unbearable. Though Katrina and I wouldn't be separated totally, anything other than a quick session after work before the train home would be impossible. And neither of us wanted to live like that. A quickie in the back of a car is so sordid, and we were passionately, romantically in love.

On the other hand, I could hardly crush Evelyn's dreams of a place in the country without thinking up a damn good explanation as to why we should simply stay put. And I couldn't. The price was right, and we might not have another chance for years. Even with the renovations that would need to be done, we worked out that we could still easily afford it.

And so we took the plunge and bought the cottage. To say I was a soul in torment might sound like an exaggeration, but believe me, it doesn't even come close to describing how wretched I really felt as I signed on the dotted line.

We had sent Sam Halsey, a jack of all trades in the renovation business, over to Oxfordshire on a number of occasions to assess what needed doing and how it could be done to our liking *and* to our budget. One of his complaints was that, due to its isolation and to the odd whims of its previous owners, the toilet arrangements were far from adequate.

After much deliberation, one afternoon at the house in Dulwich, Sam said, 'Of course, you could have a septic tank put in.'

'A what?' I said.

'A septic tank. Perfectly respectable. Lots of country folk have them. Of course, you'll need some carrion.'

'I'm sorry, Sam, I don't follow you.'

'Carrion. To get the whole process going. Some of the younger chaps in the business will tell you a bit of compost will do the job just fine, but don't believe them. Don't you believe them. My old boss told me—'

Sam's voice faded into the background as, suddenly, it hit me. I thought of my old lunch-time companion, Edward Grainger, and that guilty look that flitted across his features the time I saw him in Waterstone's with Joyce, the blonde.

I remembered the tragedy of his wife's disappearance, and how, after that, I saw less and less of him.

And I remembered how the disappearance occurred around the time they were having a septic tank installed at their cottage in Hampshire. Carrion indeed.

And then I thought of my Katrina, my beautiful, beautiful Katrina, who took my breath away with her sad eyes and her skin like warm brown silk.

And lastly, I thought of Evelyn. Life just isn't fair, is it? Some people don't simply fade away quietly into the obscurity from whence they came when you want rid of them, do they? No, they have to cause trouble, create scenes, make unreasonable demands and generally do their damnedest to ruin your hopes of a decent and happy future without them. They just *won't go away*. Well, as I have already explained, Evelyn is one of those people. I'm certain of it.

On the other hand, people disappear all the time, don't they? And people change. Harriet changed into Joyce, didn't she? Sometimes you just have to give a little kick-start to get the process going, like the carrion in the septic tank, and then nature takes care of the rest.

'Penny for them?'

'What? Oh, I'm sorry, Sam. Miles away.'

'That's all right. I was just saying as how you'll need some carrion for the septic tank. My old boss swore by it, he did.'

At that moment, Evelyn passed by the open french windows in his shabby beige cardigan, secateurs in hand. Wisps of grey hair blew in the March wind like spiders' webs, and his glasses had slipped down his nose. Yes, people disappear all the time, don't they? And if it can happen to wives, I thought, then it can bloody well happen to husbands too.

'Yes, Sam,' I said slowly. 'Yes, I suppose we will. Don't worry. I'll take care of it.'

THE GUILTY PARTY

SUSAN MOODY

MAN FOUND HANGED, I read. *Refugee Takes Own Life.*

At first I wondered why my mother should have kept this cutting when, as her death approached, she had thrown so much else away. I thought she had long ago forgotten the events of that distant summer, though I had never done so; now it seemed she had not. Afterwards she had never explained, and I had never asked. In those days, children did not question. We did as we were told, we accepted.

But now, reading the piece of worn newsprint, the questions rose in me again like bile.

I was eleven, that July. It was one of those long hot summers soon after the war, the sort which linger on in the memory and stand as the paradigm of all the summers of our youth. Day after day the sun blazed from an empty sky, turning our grey Kentish sea to an almost Mediterranean turquoise. We spent every day on the beach, swimming or endlessly competing against each other to see who could throw a stone the furthest, who could hit a floating piece of driftwood first, who could chuck a pebble into the air and hit it with another.

Although I was a girl and the rest were boys, we competed on equal terms; sex had not yet sneaked into our consciousness. There was no television to make us precocious before our time, and although we were permitted to go to the cinema once a week, we groaned when the hero kissed the heroine, or looked away, embarrassed. We were not allowed to read Enid Blyton; sweets were still rationed; strawberries were only available in season; appearances mattered.

We wore shorts and Aertex shirts. On our feet were Clark's sandals or white tennis shoes which we Blanco'ed vigorously when they grew grubby, setting them out on a window-sill overnight to dry a stiff chalky white. We never wore black plimsolls: black ones were common. Fish and chips was also common, and so was eating in the street. So the pleasure and delight of buying three pennorth of chips and devouring them, hot and vinegary, straight from the newspaper wrapping, was made all the more delicious by the guilty fear that our mothers might see us.

It was always our mothers we worried about. Fathers were non-existent or rare. We never asked about them, partly because, in those years following the war, they were not a species to which we were used, and partly because the answer might be too painful to give or to receive. My brother and I had a father, though we scarcely knew him; David and Nicholas and the brothers, Charles and Julian, did not. Ours was still in Germany, helping, so my mother said, to rebuild it: whenever I thought of him, which was seldom, I envisaged my scholarly father in his shirtsleeves, setting bricks into mortar.

This was a naval town and there had been many local casualties. Looking back, I imagine the mothers had nowhere else to go and so they stayed on, tucked inside their private griefs, bringing up their orphaned children, contriving to send them away to the kind of schools their officer husbands would have wanted, making do, drawing only a modicum of comfort from each other. Our accents were middle-class, our poverty genteel.

Why my mother had chosen to come here while she waited for my father to return from rebuilding Germany I am not sure. We had no local connections and she hated the sea, the corrosive salt air, the lumps of tar we tracked in from the beach to ruin her worn carpets, the gales which prowled beneath the roof tiles and brought the prospect of unpayable bills.

We, on the other hand, loved it. It was an extravagant town to

122

spend our holidays in. From the windows of our vast houses, which were separated from the beach only by a quiet road and a stretch of green, we had an extensive view, bounded at one side by a chalky headland covered in a cap of bright grass, on the other by a pier broken in two halves. As summer lengthened, the vista simplified itself into parallels of colour: blue sky, turquoise sea, butterscotch shingle, the parrot-green grass, silver railings. Beyond the pier wallowed a rusting hulk, the victim of enemy action. On the horizon, the spars of wrecked ships stuck up like the arms of drowning men, and when the light was right, you could see across the Channel to France, maybe even Dunkirk. On the esplanade, a red-painted land-mine solicited alms for shipwrecked sailors. Although it was never spoken of, the war was part of our lives.

In winter, the wind was so strong you could spread your arms and lean back on it. There was a lifeboat, too, and sometimes we would be wakened by the sound of the maroon going off to call in the lifeboatmen. At night, bugles from the barracks played the last post: every morning, we were woken by reveille.

But that summer, as we waited for adolescence, we were bored. There were still weeks to go before we returned to the routines of boarding school. Apart from the weekly visit to the cinema, nobody offered us entertainment; we made our own from such pinchbeck as was available. Our perpetually anxious mothers were not involved with us; although they fed us, saw that we washed our hair regularly, got us up in the morning, they did not talk to us. In those days, the adults in our lives ended at our eye level: I cannot remember ever seeing my parents' faces, only their clothes. My rarely glimpsed father, I remembered, had a penchant for Leander-pink ties; my mother wore crossover flowered dresses, but what their faces were like I can only reconstruct from looking at photographs.

My brother and I had a wind-up gramophone, and half a dozen records which we played endlessly that summer: the 'Teddy Bears' Picnic', 'In The Mood' and 'Jealousy' and the drinking song from *The Student Prince*, over and over again until one dramatic afternoon my mother rushed in like a whirlwind and hurled whatever was on the turntable to the ground, where it smashed into several shiny black pieces. To our surprise, we saw she was crying. 'For God's *sake*!' she shouted. Our homes were full of hidden tension.

*   *   *

Quite why my mother had decided I was to take piano lessons with Mr Hartman, I don't know. Perhaps she had decided I was becoming too much of a tomboy. Perhaps she was worried that when I went away to my new school in the autumn, I would be found wanting. Perhaps it was because Mrs Summerfield was sending her daughter Rosie to him.

Whatever the reason, I found myself one hot afternoon standing in the fusty front room of Mr Hartman's flat, in the house four down from ours. A grand piano dominated most of the bay window. Through it, I could see the heads of the boys down on the beach, aimlessly chucking stones into the sea. Vaguely I understood that Mr Hartman had come from Germany before the war. He had a foreign accent and wore a Fair Isle pullover with holes in the elbows. His teeth were the colour of honey.

How old was he? Now, I can see that he was probably in his late thirties, but at the time he seemed immeasurably aged in his grubby uncollared shirt and round tortoiseshell spectacles. My brother had a similar pair: I knew that you could prise the tortoise-shell off, like a scab. I wondered if Mr Hartman had discovered this.

That first afternoon he sat down at the piano stool and placed me between his knees. 'We shall start with the scale of C,' he announced, and proceeded to play it. He put a warm hand over mine and bent my fingers one after another up the keyboard and down again. 'Up,' he said. 'And down again. Up – and down.'

His cluttered room smelled of coffee and tobacco and aniseed. It was an alien smell, and curiously exciting, quite different from other houses I had visited. Bookcases overflowed with volumes in German; a sabre hung from the wall with a little blue velvet gold-tasselled cap tied to it. There were faded sepia pictures on the walls of naked girls gazing into streams or leaning pensively back against pillows. Records in tattered brown slip-covers lay piled on the floor; a rack of china-bowled pipes stood on the mantelpiece and beside it, a tin where Mr Hartman kept tobacco, with a girl painted on it, her long hair rippling over but not hiding her unformed body. A red glass decanter stood on the window-sill and, instead of lying on the floor, an oriental carpet was fixed to the wall.

A record-player in a shiny wooden cabinet stood beside the fire-place: whenever I climbed the stairs to his flat, I would hear him playing Schubert's *Trout Quintet* and for me, now, that music is inextricably associated with guilt and Mr Hartman. On top of the record-player stood a primitive radio, with antennae protruding from the top, and beside it lay a pair of headphones.

Twice a week that summer I walked out of our gate and down to Mr Hartman's flat. I progressed from scales with one hand to scales with both, and then on to arpeggios and the ripple of chromatics. I could pick out 'Twinkle-Twinkle Little Star' on the piano in my own house, and 'Three Blind Mice'. One afternoon, Mr Hartman declared that I should learn a simple tune, which I would play first with one hand and then, when I had mastered it, with both. '*Müss i' den, müss i' den, zum stätle hinaus,*' he crooned into my ear. He gripped me between his knees as he put his hands inside my shirt and squeezed my waist. 'You will like this, I think.' His hands were warm and slightly rough; a finger moved slowly over my bare skin. '*Und du, mein schatz, bleibst hier.*'

The boys were waiting for me when my hour with Mr Hartman was up. Why did they choose that afternoon to scoff at me and at him? They had never done so before. Jealousy, perhaps, or a recognition of the fact that I was changing?

'Silly old Hartman,' jeered my brother, as loudly as he dared, glancing up at Hartman's window.

'Hartman, fartman,' said Julian, older than the rest of us, and more knowing.

The boys found this deliciously comic. 'Hartman, fartman,' they said. 'How can you *bear* it, stuck up in some stuffy old flat all afternoon with a horrible *German*?'

'A beastly Hun.'

'A bloody,' Julian said daringly, 'Kraut.'

And why did I choose that afternoon to say: 'I think he's a spy'? Was it from boredom? Or a desire to establish that I was still one of them? Or was it from some deeper alarm? As soon as I had uttered the words, I wanted them unsaid, but it was too late.

The boys pounced. 'A spy? What do you mean? How can he be? How do you know?'

My credibility was at stake. 'He's got a radio,' I said, 'one of those ones that spies use, with bits sticking out of the top. And headphones.'

'Headphones?' The boys stared at each other.

'There's still lots of spies about,' Charles announced. 'I heard about it at school. It's to do with the Cold War.'

We could see that he did not know what the Cold War was, and politely refrained from asking him.

'Do you think national security could be at stake?' asked Nicholas, made knowledgeable by the *Rover* which he borrowed surreptitiously from a friend.

'I think we ought to investigate old Fartman,' said my brother. 'I mean, if he's a spy, and everything.'

'How're you going to do that?' I asked scornfully. I wished I had never spoken. All I'd seen was the radio and some German books; all I had was a sense of something about Mr Hartman which might be dangerous.

'We could keep a watch on him,' said Julian, importantly.

And that's what we did. We hung about on the green, swinging on the silver railings, staring up at his window. We followed him when he walked past the lifeboat into town; we followed him home again. Julian produced a notebook and a pencil and we kept a record of his comings and goings. We noted the arrival of Rosie Summerfield, and her departures. Darkness fell late, and our mothers, preoccupied, knowing we would not, in any case, sleep, did not insist on early bedtimes. We were out there every evening, watching him.

Because his flat was on the first floor, we could not see into his room but occasionally he came to the window and stared down at us. And once, Julian, balancing on the railings, claimed he could see him, with his headphones on, tapping away at something.

Once, Mr Hartman asked me what we were doing. 'Come here,' he said. He sat down in the armchair beside the cold fireplace and I sat on his lap. His warm rough hands held my thighs. I liked him; I wondered if my father would have this same male smell when he came home. 'What are you children doing, playing outside my window all the time?'

'Nothing,' I muttered. If I told him we believed he was a spy, he might stop my piano lessons, or move away. I would miss him. I realized then that I missed my father.

He seemed sadder than usual. 'I don't like being watched,' he said. 'I have been watched too much.'

Was this a threat? When I reported back to the boys, they grew excited. 'He's obviously been under observation before,' Julian, our ringleader declared. 'We'll keep a watch at the back of the house as well as the front. We'd better be a bit more careful.'

We skulked behind lampposts and gates; we stared up at Mr Hartman's windows from behind hedges and garden walls. When he walked, we darted from doorway to doorway behind him, our breath coming faster when he paused or looked behind him.

He never challenged us. When I went for my lesson, he stood behind me at the piano, his hands on my shoulders or slowly stroking my bare arms. Sometimes his hands moved to cover my Aertex-shirted chest. He kept me longer, afterwards, leaning back in his armchair with me astride his thighs, his hands clasping my legs, a finger slowly climbing higher and then returning. Sometimes he bounced me up and down, and sighed.

'It's only a game,' he said to me one afternoon. Outside, the sun whitened the yellow shingle; between the red velvet curtains a shaft of light was solid with dust.

'What is?'

His hands cradled my buttocks. 'Life,' he said. 'You, my dear, and me. It's only a game. And sometimes I am tired of playing it, of moving on, of keeping to the rules.'

I had no idea what he meant.

One day, Julian announced that he had sent Mr Hartman an anonymous letter, had pushed it through the front door of the house the evening before, then ran like the wind before anyone saw him. He had cut the words out of a newspaper, just like they did in books.

'What did you say?' We gasped at the daring.

'I told him we were on to him,' said Julian. 'Told him we knew exactly what he was up to.'

'He'll probably make a bolt for it now,' said Charles.

'Where would he bolt to?' I said. I could hear in my head his sad voice, singing. *Und du, mein schatz, bleibst hier.*

'Back to his paymasters,' said Nicholas.

'Who're they?' I demanded. I was frightened; Julian had gone too far. It was supposed to be a game, wasn't it? And now it had become serious.

'The Russkies, I should think.'

'We ought to send a letter to the police,' Julian said.

'Anonymous, do you mean?' asked my brother.

'Yes. That'd scare him, if the police came round, asking questions.'

'We'd probably get a medal or something,' Nicholas said.

'How can we, if the letter's anonymous?'

'Fingerprints,' Nicholas said.

When I came home from my next lesson, my mother was waiting. 'How're you getting on?' she said.

'All right.'

'Why don't you play me something,' she said.

I was embarrassed, unused to so much attention. I launched into 'Three Blind Mice'. If she was impressed, she didn't say so.

'How do you get on with Mr Hartman?' she asked. There was something about her demeanour which made me uneasy.

'Very well,' I muttered. 'He's nice.'

'Does he ever . . .'

'What?'

'Touch you?'

'Of *course* not.' And, to put her off, I added: 'The boys think he's a spy.'

'Silly things. He's a refugee. Poor Mr Hartman. Do you want to go on with the lessons?'

'Yes please,' I said.

But I never went back to Mr Hartman's flat.

He hanged himself that night, using a tie, in the big old wardrobe of his bedroom.

I cried. The boys were subdued. All of us blamed Julian for precipitating the suicide, but we knew ourselves to be equally guilty. We had driven him to it, watching him, dogging his footsteps, never leaving him alone. It was only a game; we knew perfectly well that he was not a spy, poor Mr Hartman who had been forced to flee his country by the Nazi threat and find refuge and safety in England.

MAN FOUND HANGED.

I read the cutting again. Why had I never asked? And why had my mother never explained, never reassured? Was she afraid of what I would tell her? She knew I blamed myself for the suicide. She knew that. Now, for the first time, I read the evidence given at the inquest by Mrs Mary Summerfield, the last person known to have seen Mr Hartman alive. She stated that she had gone round to discuss a certain matter concerning her daughter, Rosemary Summerfield, aged ten; that the discussion had grown heated, that she had threatened to inform the police if he did not in future keep his hands to himself.

My mother had known all this, so why did she not speak of it to me? And if she had, what difference would it have made? I thought I had killed him by accusing him of being a spy. I believed that between us, the boys and I had driven him to his death. And now, after all, I had discovered that if there was a guilty party in all this, it was not I.

If my mother had explained to me then, had put aside her own worries and looked at mine, would I have married, had children, lived the kind of life which might have been anticipated for me that summer when I was eleven?

Or would I always have feared that if I ever again let a man put his hand on my thigh, or touch my breasts, he would kill himself?

ROBIN HOOD'S RACE

EDWARD D. HOCH

It was Simon Ark's long time interest in mazes and labyrinths that brought us to the Nottingham area in the first place. I'd been attending a small Eastern European book fair in my position as senior editor of Neptune Books, and I'd stopped in London on my way home. Nothing could have surprised me more than to have Simon seek me out at my hotel.

When I heard his voice on the telephone my first reaction was 'Simon! What are you doing in London?'

'I'm on my way to Nottingham. They're rebuilding Robin Hood's Race. Come with me and we'll have a fine old time.'

Until then my British travels had been confined to the London area. I knew about Robin Hood, the Sheriff of Nottingham and Sherwood Forest, but I was only vaguely aware that the place was actually a good-sized city. 'I can't, Simon,' I insisted. 'I'm only here briefly. I'll be flying back to New York tomorrow.'

'Phone the office and tell them you'll be back Monday instead. You are a senior editor, aren't you?'

I was, and before the day had ended I was on the phone telling them just that. I'd known Simon Ark for nearly forty years, since I was a cub reporter just out of school, and he was always able to lure me off on new adventures. My wife Shelly often despaired when I chased off after this mystic wanderer who sometimes, in all seriousness, hinted at being two thousand years old, but I would go anyhow. This time was no different.

The trains for Nottingham left from St Pancras station every hour. On the way up there was mention again of Robin Hood's Race. Simon Ark had settled back in his seat in the first-class carriage and was commenting on the passing countryside. Suddenly he changed the subject and came to the reason for our journey. 'Outside Nottingham they're rebuilding Robin Hood's Race.'

'A race track?' I suggested in my innocence.

'A labyrinth! A maze! It is sometimes called Shepherd's Race, but the Robin Hood name has obvious local connections.'

I nodded. 'You mean one of those winding paths through tall hedges where people are forever getting lost.'

He smiled. 'There are many of those in England, my friend, but Robin Hood's Race was a different sort. It was a curious maze, cut into the ground, with intricate winding pathways totaling some 535 yards in length. This is no garden of forking paths, however. There is only one winding route through the labyrinth. Its purpose was to serve as a complex running course for young men and boys, to develop agile bodies.'

'Was it something from Roman days?' I asked.

'Probably only from the early fifteenth century, judging by its location and the crosses carved in the turf at each corner. Certainly it predates the Reformation, and was probably the work of some priests living nearby. It was on common ground. The alternate names suggest it may have been used for grazing sheep in Robin Hood's time.'

'And when would that be?' I asked with a smile. 'Before or after King Arthur and the Round Table?'

'Quite a bit after,' Simon answered seriously. 'Surely you know that Arthur was first mentioned in a Welsh poem dating from around the year six hundred. The Robin Hood legend dates only from the fourteenth century. Long before that mazes and labyrinths had acquired a mythic reputation – a dwelling place for minotaurs and virgins. Perhaps devils too, if one remembers Dante's nine circles of Hell.'

The city of Nottingham was larger than I'd expected. We took a cab from the station near the canal, driving past an impressive old castle which apparently housed an art gallery and museum. Our hotel was near the Royal Centre, but Simon planned to spend little time there. As soon as we were unpacked, I made arrangements to rent a small car to take us out to our real destination. It occurred to me that Simon Ark might have wanted more than companionship out of me. He never drove a car in America, so I was certain he wouldn't be trying out the right-hand drive on British roads. I was a bit uncertain myself, but I'd done it before and I was at ease after the first ten minutes.

Simon had explained that the new maze was not to be in the original location but further out in the countryside. He seemed to know the directions, but as we turned off the main road on to a country lane we found the way blocked by two police cars. 'What's this?' I asked, pulling to a halt just in time to avoid a collision.

A young uniformed officer came up to the car. 'Sir, you'll have to take another road. This one's closed off.'

'We're seeking the site of the new Robin Hood's Race,' Simon told him.

'Well, that's right here, but the entire area is cordoned off. We're investigating a death.'

'I see.' Simon was peering out at the field even as he spoke. A small circle of men, uniformed and in plain-clothes, were standing around something not quite hidden from view. A photographer was busily recording the discovery from every angle.

The officer turned away as I manoeuvered the car off the road and headed back the way we had come. 'Did you see it, my friend?' Simon asked before we'd gone twenty feet.

'I don't know what I saw.'

'Pull off here,' he said sharply. 'We'll walk back.'

'They'll arrest us, Simon.'

'We will take that chance.'

'Nice of you to include me in your plans.'

We left the car near the intersection and headed back across the field toward the group of men. Almost at once the young officer spotted us and called out.

'Take me to your superior,' Simon instructed him.

The officer shifted uncertainly.

'It is important I see your superior at once.' Simon stared at him unblinkingly.

'Wait right here! Don't move!'

He consulted with the others and presently an older man in plain-clothes came over to speak with us. 'My officer tried to make it clear that we're investigating a suspicious death. Unless you have information that would assist in the investigation I must ask you to leave.'

'We may have information,' Simon told him. 'Who is the dead man?'

I could almost imagine the thoughts running through the detective's mind, confronted as he was by this tall old man in a black coat, asking for a look at the body. He showed great restraint when he only asked, 'What is your name, sir?'

'Simon Ark. This is my friend, a senior editor at Neptune Books back in New York.'

Perhaps that impressed him somehow. I'll never know. 'I'm Detective Inspector Staples. Do you have information which could assist us?'

'I am here to study Robin Hood's Race, both in legend and reality. I understand the original maze is being recut at this new location.'

Before Detective Inspector Staples could reply, the uniformed officer came running up. 'We have an identification, sir.'

'Very good.' He turned away, then back to study Simon's craggy face. 'Do you know anything about Robin Hood's Race?' he asked.

'Quite a bit. I've made a study of mazes and labyrinths.'

'Come along then, but keep back and don't touch anything.'

A young woman had appeared from somewhere, and as we approached the circle of men her agitation seemed to increase. 'Catch her!' one of the officers shouted.

They lowered her gently to the grass. With the circle broken we now had a better look at the thing we'd only glimpsed before. It was the body of a man in work clothes, sprawled across the freshly cut sod of the maze. The body lay like a limp pincushion, pierced on all sides by a score of arrows. It was as if he'd been executed by a firing squad of bowmen, or caught by a bandit gang which had despatched him with ease before vanishing back into the woods.

'Robin Hood!' DI Staples spluttered a short while later. It was the first time anyone had given voice to the thought. The body had been removed and the young woman who'd identified it had recovered her composure enough to speak with the detective. Simon and I were making a pretence of examining the newly-cut portions of the maze, but both of us were listening to the nearby conversation.

'Well, you think of such things in Nottingham, don't you?' the young woman said. 'It's all around us here.' Her name was Marcia O'Banyon and the murdered man had been living with her for the past year. He was Jeffrey Barlow, and he'd been hired by the local tourist office to cut the turf for the maze, following a pattern spray-painted on the grass.

'But the *ghost* of Robin Hood?' Staples asked. 'Such things don't happen these days, if they ever did.' Still, there was an uncertainty about his voice, a protest that seemed more like an effort to convince himself.

'Jeff told me he was worried about it. He wished he wasn't out here alone all the time. It is sort of remote, you know.'

'The lane is just over there and the road is not a hundred feet away,' Staples pointed out.

'But these trees hide it, don't they? And after the other killing—'

Simon Ark perked up at those words. He gave up the pretence of examining the maze and walked over to the detective and Marcia O'Banyon. 'There was a previous killing?' he asked.

The young woman nodded. She was still in her twenties, and I suspected this was the first close loss she had ever experienced. Her red-rimmed eyes reflected a grief that seemed very real. 'David Mills, the farmer who owned this property. He and a neighbor were attacked near here last month and the neighbor was killed.'

'With arrows?' Simon asked.

'Mr Krupper was shot in the back with an arrow. Mr Mills broke his arm fleeing from the scene,' Staples told us, taking over the narration.

'Then this is the second attack. Was the other also in daylight?'

'At dusk,' Staples replied. 'David Mills had brought Krupper out to show him the markings for the maze.'

'Mills once owned this property?'

The detective inspector was reluctant to talk further. 'Are you a newspaper publisher?' he asked me.

'Books,' I assured him. 'We're not reporters.'

He nodded. 'Thought you were a bit old for that game. What are you – professors?'

'I have done some teaching,' Simon told him. 'But I believe we might help with your crime wave.'

'How's that? You had any experience with Robin Hood?' There was a shadow of sarcasm in the question.

'Not exactly. Tell me about the crime scene in the city.'

'We have it, like everyone else. Not with bows and arrows, though, and not usually out here in the country.'

Simon Ark nodded. 'This man Mills seems to have witnessed the earlier attack and lived to tell the tale. I think I should speak with him.'

'His house is about a half-mile down the lane, on this side. Talk to him all you want, Mr Ark, but I warn you this is police business. I want no meddling.'

We returned to the car just as the body was being removed. I wondered what they would do with all those arrows.

The home of David Mills was an eighteenth-century stone farmhouse that had been restored and added to over the decades. Mills himself was walking in his garden, easily recognized by the plaster cast on his left arm, extending from elbow to fingers. He walked with a cane in his right hand, but despite his infirmity I guessed him to be around fifty at most. The dark hair on his head had thinned, though the face below it still held the memory of youth.

'Visitors, so late on a sunny afternoon! This is a treat, gentlemen.' He walked over to greet us.

Simon introduced us and he invited us in, making a half-hearted offer of tea. 'What's happening down the lane?' he wanted to know, seating himself before a great stone fireplace that had seen frequent use. 'I heard sirens earlier.'

'There's been a killing,' Simon told him, lowering his bulk into a chair our host had indicated. 'A man cutting turf for the maze was shot with several arrows.'

'Another one,' Mills said softly. 'Are you police? Reporters?'

'Neither,' Simon assured him. 'We came here to study the maze, but a supposed sighting of the ghost of Robin Hood is certainly of interest.'

'Who said anything about a ghost?' the man countered. 'If people start talking about ghosts, it'll drive down the property values here.'

'Surely you don't believe—' I began.

He seemed startled that I had spoken. 'Folks in these parts believe lots of things, especially out in the countryside.'

'We would like to hear about the attack on you and Mr Krupper,' Simon interrupted. 'I understand he was killed.'

David Mills stared at the floor, remembering. 'Poor old Krupper. He was my neighbor across the lane. The two of us had gone down to look at the maze.'

'This was on your property?'

'It was a separate field I hadn't farmed in years. When the council decided they wanted to buy that property for a restoration of Robin Hood's Race, I was against it at first. Finally I agreed, and that evening when Krupper told me they'd been marking off the plan of the maze with spray paint, I wanted to see it.'

'This was at twilight?' Simon asked.

The farmer nodded. 'It was just getting dark. I had my cane along because my bum leg bothers me sometimes. It's not far, of course, but Krupper drove us there in his car. We'd got out and were looking around when suddenly I heard a noise and a grunt from Krupper. I looked up from the digging to see him pitch forward, an arrow in his back. I must have panicked then. I turned to run and my bum leg just gave out on me. I tried to break my fall and broke my wrist instead.'

'Did someone find you there?'

David Mills shook his head. 'I knew I had to get out of there or I'd be a dead man too. I managed to reach Krupper's car and drove it down the lane. When I got here I phoned the police.'

'And you saw no one?'

'No one. Certainly not the ghost of Robin Hood.'

'Do any of your neighbors hunt with a bow and arrow?' Simon asked.

'The Randolph boy used to. I haven't seen him with it lately. He's pretty far away up the hill, though.'

'Boy?'

'I shouldn't call him that. He's eighteen now, going to start at Cambridge in the autumn.'

'Where does he live?'

David Mills gestured with his good arm. 'Keep going on this lane. You'll come to a left turn going up a slight rise. Follow that to the top and you'll be at the Randolph place. The boy's name is Rob.'

'Thank you sir,' Simon Ark told him, and we returned to the car.

As we drove along the lane, following directions, I asked, 'Simon, what business is this of ours? I've stuck with you on wild goose chases before, but we don't belong in this one.'

'The scent of evil is strong in these parts, my friend. Perhaps the devil wears the guise of an archer.'

'More likely this boy, Rob Randolph, let loose an arrow by accident.'

'One arrow is accident, twenty arrows are demonic.'

As I parked the car in front of the old farmhouse, we saw a slender youth in the yard, stretching a longbow and letting fly an arrow at a circular straw target. 'That was a good shot,' Simon Ark said, walking toward him.

He put down the bow. 'Are you police?'

'Only two strangers travelling through your country. You would be Rob Randolph.'

'That's right. A friend called to tell me there'd been another killing.'

'At Robin Hood's Race. Do you know the place?'

'I know it.' His eyes were sharp and very blue. I imagined he could pick off a grouse in flight with one of his arrows. 'It is a mistake to cut a new maze at that place.'

'Why? Do you believe the area is bewitched?'

'I believe that arrows fly without archers,' he replied, 'and that legends sometimes come to life.'

A middle-aged woman came to the back door of the house. 'What do you want here?' she yelled at them. 'Leave us alone!'

The young man picked up his bow and notched another arrow into the string. Simon walked toward the woman in the doorway. 'Are you his mother?'

'Yes. I'm Selma Randolph. Who are you?'

'We are examining the recutting of Robin Hood's Race, the maze down on David Mills's property.'

'That does not concern us,' the woman said. She had large eyes and she might have been pretty once. Now she had grown puffy-faced and overweight.

'Do two murders concern you? They should.'

'I know nothing about that,' she replied.

Rob Randolph let loose another arrow, sending it thudding into the very center of the straw target. With the woman waiting for us to leave, there was no chance to question him further. Simon and I returned to our car.

As we drove down the hill Simon asked, 'Do you think Rob is short for Robert?'

'I'd say so, yes,' I replied.

Simon stared out the window at the passing trees. 'In this region, perhaps it's more likely short for Robin.'

Mrs Randolph had phoned Detective Inspector Staples about our questioning her son, and he was not pleased when we returned to the site of the maze. 'You'd both better come with me,' he told us. 'I'm going back to the office. You follow along and we'll have a talk.'

Twenty minutes later we were seated in his cramped and uncomfortable interrogation room. He came right to the point. 'We don't like people snooping around in the middle of murder investigations. You do more harm than good. Why did you go up to the Randolph place?'

Simon Ark answered before I could speak. 'You have two men killed with arrows. It seemed reasonable to question any bow hunters in the area. Mr Mills mentioned young Randolph's name.'

'The boy is not a suspect,' Staples answered firmly. 'I talked to him after the first killing and he was at home with his mother.'

'You may have a so-called serial killer on the loose here. It wouldn't be wise to wait for a third killing.'

Staples was not convinced. 'We're interested in finding a killer, not in sensationalism. Talk like that comes and goes. The press has a field day for a week or so and then it fades away. A few years back some teenage girls disappeared and the press got worked up. Nothing came of it.'

'Were they ever found?'

He sighed, perhaps reminiscing on the folly of wayward youth. 'One turned up in London, the other three never came back but they probably headed that way too. It's the siren song of the big city.'

'Spoken like a philosopher,' Simon Ark told him.

'Or like a father and a police officer who's seen it all.'

'Tell us some more about the first killing.'

'Here, now! I'm supposed to be questioning you!'

'We're questioning each other. Isn't that the way to true knowledge?'

'I already told you about it. And what I didn't tell you Mills probably did. Krupper was killed and he broke his arm.'

'You questioned young Rob Randolph. Forget about what his mother said. Couldn't he have been bow hunting in that area?'

'We checked all that.' He walked to the wall and indicated a large map of Nottingham and its environs. 'This area is the land owned by David Mills. Robin Hood's Race is being rebuilt in this portion here. Mills still farms the area to the north of the house. Mainly he hires local people to do most of the actual work. He's what some would call a gentleman farmer. But you'll notice that the fields are between Robin Hood's Race and the Randolph place further up the hill. On the evening of the first murder, if Rob had been out hunting he almost certainly would have crossed the freshly plowed fields of Mills's farm at some point. My men surveyed the fields carefully. The only footprints were those of Mills and Krupper on their way down to the site of the maze. Rob Randolph never crossed that field. If he was hunting on the night in question it was in a different area.'

Somehow Simon had turned the tables on him. The detective was discussing the case as he would with an equal or a superior. But the moment soon passed and he recovered himself. 'Stay out of my hair,' Staples told us. Since he was nearly bald, it seemed like an easy request to honor. 'I don't want any more of these Robin Hood killings. People are already talking about abandoning the maze, or finding another location for it.'

'Never fear,' Simon stated flatly. 'No more arrows will fly. By morning I will deliver the killer to you.'

Detective Inspector Staples all at once looked tired. He dismissed us with a wave of his hand. 'Close the door on your way out. If you have information you can phone it in.'

Outside, as we walked toward the car, I said, 'That's one promise I don't think you'll be keeping.'

'On the contrary. I know the identity of our deadly archer, and I have only to confirm the motive for the crimes. We must hurry to a hardware store, my friend, before they close.'

We purchased a pick and shovel, and a bright battery-powered lantern that could be seen from some distance away. These were stored in the trunk of our car. 'They call it the boot over here,' Simon corrected me. 'The tools will be safe there until we finish dinner.'

'Then where are we going?' I asked, but of course I knew.

'To Robin Hood's Race. There is much work to be done if the maze is ever to be completed.'

'You're going to dig sod in the middle of the night?'

'Well, I was hoping you would do the actual digging.'

'While you do what?'

'Protect you from the ghost of Robin Hood.'

It was already dark, and after a bite of food we drove back out to the site of the maze. Police markers were still up, warning us off the crime scene, but we ignored them. Using the lantern, Simon led us to the very center of the maze, still marked out on the grass with spray paint. 'Here is where we will dig,' he told me.

'For what? A pot of gold?'

'For a murderer. Don't worry. You will not have to dig long.'

He moved the light several times as I ripped the turf with pick and shovel. Often it was not even angled toward me, and I had the impression it was not shining for my benefit at all. A couple of times Simon held up his hand and I stopped digging while he listened, but then he gave the signal to resume. The night had turned cool and I felt a chill down my spine. Overhead there were no stars.

After a half-hour of digging I could see that even Simon was beginning to question his theory. There was no sign of Robin Hood's ghost or young Rob Randolph or any other sort of archer. When another light finally appeared from across the field, and then grew closer, it proved to be David Mills, leaning heavily on his cane and cradling a flashlight with the cast on his left arm.

'What are you two up to, anyway?' he asked. 'I saw the light from my house.'

'Only digging,' Simon told him.

'It's dangerous to dig here after what's happened.'

'Dangerous for you perhaps, Mr Mills. We are seeking evidence of murder.'

'The police found nothing.'

'They did not look deep enough. I am concerned with past murders, not the present ones.'

'Past—'

Simon Ark faced him and said, in a voice of judgement, 'You

killed at least three young women and buried them here. That was why Krupper and Barlow had to die, before the truth was dug up.'

'You're mad!' David Mills growled. 'Mad! Do you think I could even hold a bow and arrow with my arm in a cast?'

'They weren't killed with a bow and arrow. I believe they were killed with a sword cane.'

As Mills cursed and pulled the blade free, it glistened as it caught the light of our lantern. Perhaps he'd forgotten my presence, as people often do. He lunged at Simon with his weapon, and I hit him with my shovel.

Simon was not even surprised when Detective Inspector Staples and two of his men appeared out of the night to take charge. They'd followed us, of course, as Simon had guessed they would. 'You owe me an explanation,' the detective told him as his man hurried David Mills off for medical attention.

'It was not difficult to settle on Mills as the killer,' Simon Ark explained. 'But the motive was something else again. It seemed the killings were aimed mainly at frightening people away from this particular field, and you confirmed today that some thought the maze should be moved to another location. I remembered Mills telling us that he was against selling the property at first, and that added to the possibility that he had something to hide. It was something dangerous to him, possibly buried but not too deep, if he feared the removal of turf for the maze might reveal it. You mentioned the missing girls and that seemed a likely possibility.'

'If he killed Krupper, how did he get the broken wrist?' Staples asked.

'Somehow Krupper was suspicious of him and they struggled. Mills fell and broke his wrist but still managed to kill the man. It was something else that turned my suspicions toward Mills, though. When we spoke to him he told us he and Krupper drove down the lane to the maze because his leg was bothering him. But you told me this afternoon your men found their footprints in the plowed field, walking from the house to the maze. Why would Mills lie about such a small point? I could think of only one reason. He wanted to emphasize his bad leg, to explain why he had the cane along. I started thinking about that cane. Even if a bow and arrow had been used for the first murder, Mills couldn't have used it a second time to kill Jeffrey Barlow as he dug the maze. With his arm in a cast, firing even one arrow would have been next to impossible, to say nothing of twenty. But suppose the cane hid a slender sword, used by Mills to stab his victims at close range. He could then plunge arrows into the wounds to hide the original sword thrusts. The use of twenty such arrows in the case of Barlow was an act of sheer terrorism, to frighten people into abandoning the maze.'

'After the first killing he said he drove the car back to his house.'

'He had to explain why it wasn't at the scene, didn't he? He might have saved himself these lies by simply not admitting he had the cane with him, but he feared you'd see its imprints in the soil and wonder about it.'

'And the arrows without their bow?' Staples asked.

'Hidden beneath his jacket, or more likely hidden in advance behind bushes near the maze. Perhaps he was trying to cast suspicion on the Randolph youth while at the same time creating a ghostly figure of Robin Hood. The broken wrist didn't hinder him with the sword. As we saw tonight, he could draw it with one hand.'

Staples nodded. 'My men will be digging up this area in the morning. I hope you're wrong about those girls' bodies. Though my guess is you're not. I doubt if they'll want to put the new Robin Hood's Race here after all.'

'That's a shame,' Simon remarked. 'I came to Nottingham to see it.'

'You're not far from Lincoln here,' Staples pointed out. 'There's a nice turf puzzle maze at Doddington Hall.'

Simon Ark looked at me and smiled. 'We still have a day, my friend. Perhaps we could drive up to Lincoln in the morning.'

THE CANCELLATION

REGINALD HILL

'Hello.'

'Who's that?'

'It's Joe, Aunt Mirabelle.'

'You sure? Why didn't you say so before?'

'Because it's my phone in my office, Aunt Mirabelle. I always answer it.'

'Not when you know it's me ringing, you don't, boy.'

Joe Sixsmith sighed. As a leading light among the black PIs of Luton who'd served their time as lathe operators, he felt entitled to a little respect.

'What do you want, Auntie?'

'You know Mr Tooley's funeral?'

'We talked about it last night. You said it couldn't be till next Thursday 'cos they'd had a rush on at the crem. and I made a note and said I'd definitely be there. Remember?'

'Of course I remember. Well, it's this afternoon. Half past three.'

'Today? But you said—'

'I know what I said. And I told that funeral director friend of yours it was a crying shame that folk had to be kept lying around so long, especially when they'd only got one frail old sister who'd travelled all the way from Belfast to sort out the effects and had neither the money nor the strength to be travelling back home and back here again in the space of a week . . .'

'Yes, Auntie,' said Joe, risking an interruption. 'You said all this. So what's changed?'

'Mr Webster from the parlour rang this morning to say there's been a cancellation and did we want it?'

'Lou said a cancellation? Of a funeral? You sure?'

'Don't you start again, Joseph. Just be here three o'clock sharp. Don't want that old lady going home saying they don't know the meaning of good neighbourliness here in Luton.'

Joe grinned broadly as he replaced the receiver. It was true that for many years Mirabelle had undoubtedly been a good neighbour to old Mr Tooley, making sure he continued to be well fed even when, as often happened, he contrived to lose most of his pension at his much loved dog track by the middle of the week. But this argosy of Christian charity to a miserable sinner was at risk of foundering on the rock of old Miss Tooley, the grieving sister, who, so far as Joe could judge, had no intention whatsoever of travelling home to Belfast and back in a week. On the contrary, she seemed more than content to fill her brother's place, resting in his flat with Good Neighbour Mirabelle coming round with three hot meals a day, in between which she spent most of her time on the good neighbour's line, pouring out her woes to her numerous acquaintances back in Belfast.

So news of the cancellation must have come like a gift from God to Mirabelle.

Possibly as compensation for these uncharitable thoughts, and in spite of the shortness of notice and the fact that, at ninety-three, old Mr Tooley had outlived most of his two-legged friends, Mirabelle had managed to drum up a fair turnout, enough to fill both funeral cars with Joe having to squeeze in the front seat of the hearse next to Lou Webster whom he'd known since schooldays.

'OK Lou?' he asked.

'Fine. Yourself, Joe?'

'Fine. Get a lot of cancellations in your line of business, do you?'

'Not a lot. In fact it takes something unusual.'

Joe contemplated eternity for another dignified furlong. But his mind kept drifting back to the cancellation.

'So what was unusual about this one?' he asked.

'Mr Tallas? For a start, he died abroad.'

'You say he was called Dallas?'

'Tallas. It's Greek. That's where he was, in Greece, visiting his family. But seems he'd been born here, had British nationality, and wanted to be buried here. So the insurance company rang to say it had to be postponed. Family complications. I wasn't best pleased, I tell you. One thing you can't afford in our game is smell.'

Joe tried eternity again but it was no good.

'Smell?' he said.

'You know. Bad meat smell. Mr Tallas died in a car accident, probably all cut up and left out in the sun till they got round to shovelling him into a coffin – you know what these wops are like, all *mañana* out there.'

'Think that's Spain, Lou,' Joe pointed out gently.

'Is it? Won't fall out about a couple of miles. Anyway, first thing I noticed when I picked him up at the airport was the pong. You had to get up close but I've got a nose for it. I thought, hello. Don't want you lying around in my parlour too long.'

Joe shuddered and looked behind him.

'No need to worry about Mr Tooley. Time I'm finished with a client, you could sit him in your living room and keep him there for a month without anyone noticing except he didn't move much.'

'Got a girl on the cheese counter at the hyper like that,' said Joe. 'So what did you tell this insurance guy, Smith?'

'Said nothing till he rang to cancel this morning. I mean, he's paying. Has paid. Top dollar. But soon as he said there was a family travel problem and the funeral would have to be cancelled, I said that'll be extra for the inconvenience, and I'm not keeping him any longer than tomorrow else I'll have the Health round. I didn't tell him I'd already moved the coffin out of the chapel of rest and into my workshop.'

Joe said, 'How're you going to manage tomorrow? Not another cancellation?'

'No. We're doing first of the day, parish job, some poor derelict. Push him through in five minutes flat, slip the cream soup a bung, and we can easily fit in another long as they don't want no Friends, Romans and half the Messiah. Smith said fine, and if the family didn't make it, go ahead anyway.'

Joe thought about this, slowly as was his wont. It took him half a mile to work out that the cream soup was the crem. sup., i. e. the crematorium superintendent. But there were other puzzles.

He said, 'So if Smith's not that worried about the family making it, why not go ahead today anyway?'

'Don't ask me. All I know is he's paying. Also it gave me a chance to do your auntie a favour. Wise man doesn't miss a chance like that.'

Joe took his point. Mirabelle blacking an undertaker in Luton was like the bailiffs moving in.

He sat back and looked forward to the service.

It was more entertaining than he anticipated.

First off the chaplain, due doubtless to a late rebriefing, seemed unsure as to whether he was bidding farewell to Daniel Tooley, retired car mechanic and greyhound enthusiast, who'd died in the fullness of years, or David Tallas, company director, who'd been cut off in his prime. In the end he settled for David Tooley a.k.a Daniel Tallas who'd been good to his family, generous to his employees, loyal to his friends and kind to dumb animals, by all of whom he would be deeply missed.

If employees covered bookies, it would do for old Mr Tooley, thought Joe.

Old Miss Tooley certainly showed no unease until the moment approached for the final curtain. But now she prodded Mirabelle in the ribs and hissed, 'When will we be having 'Danny Boy', Bella?'

Mirabelle, who hated being called Bella, asked what she thought she was talking about. Old Miss Tooley said it was universally known that Daniel wanted 'Danny Boy' sung at his funeral. Mirabelle said it was the first she'd heard. Old Miss Tooley said Daniel wouldn't rest in his grave and *she'd* be laid low for weeks if the song wasn't sung. And Mirabelle, feeling the implied threat and nobly resisting the temptation to point out that, as old Mr Tooley had expressed a wish for his ashes to be scattered over trap 3 at the Luton dog track, resting in his grave hardly applied, looked at Joe.

'No,' said Joe.

'You got no problem singing it down that hell-hole drinking den you frequent, I see no reason for you to be shy in the house of the Lord,' said Mirabelle.

And two minutes later Joe found himself standing alongside Mr

Tooley's basic-package coffin, assuring its inmate that the pipes, the pipes were ca-alling.

In fact it was no problem. As a long-time baritone in the famous Boyling Corner Chapel Choir and a popular contributor to karaoke night at The Glit, Joe could hold a tune and had performed before audiences more interactive than this. And size-wise it wasn't bad either. In fact there seemed to be quite a lot more people in the congregation than the nine or ten Mirabelle had crowded into the funeral cars. Perhaps she'd sent out a three-line whip throughout her wider sphere of influence beyond the Rasselas Estate. But Joe doubted it. There were folk here who didn't look like they belonged to Mirabelle's flock. Men in sharp suits with fifty-quid haircuts. Women to match.

As the final words of the song faded away, one of the mystery mourners, a handsome redheaded woman of about forty whose elegant silk suit showed she'd kept her figure in a way which Mirabelle probably considered an affront to both Nature and God, began to applaud.

Mirabelle turned and glowered, but nothing abashed, she got in three or four more hearty claps and gave Joe a smile whose warmth he felt like a turned-up fan heater.

Beside him, the coffin was on the move. He returned to his seat leaving the bemused chaplain to resume centre stage. A blessing, a few moments of silent prayer, then they were filing out to the piped strains of some mournful muzak.

'Was I all right, Auntie?'

'All right for your drunken friends, maybe. No place in church for them vibratos. If you can't hit the note you shouldn't be singing,' she said sharply. Then, relenting, she said 'No, you were fine, Joe. I'm just mad at that *person* putting her hands together like she was at some pop concert.'

A hand tugged at Joe's sleeve, a waft of powerfully musky perfume tugged at his nostrils and he turned to find himself looking at that *person*. Behind her at the crem. door he could see her male companion talking agitatedly to Lou.

'Looks like there's been a real cock-up,' said the woman in a smoke-roughened voice which rubbed you up the right way. 'Seems we've come to the wrong funeral, but it was worth it to hear you sing. Don't do gigs, do you?'

'No,' said Joe flattered by her implication and fluttered by her scented proximity. 'Karaoke night down The Glit, and I'm in the Boyling Corner Choir.'

'Never heard of them,' she said. 'I'm Mandy Levine, I run a little club out Barnet way. Thursday night's old-time night, always get a good crowd in, you'd go down well there. Here's my card if you think you might fancy it.'

She laid her hand on his arm, gave him the warm smile plus a promising squeeze and a saucy wink, then turned to join her friend, who seemed to be bringing the rest of the mystery mourners up to date. After a while they moved off *en masse* to the car park and dispersed in a snarl of Jags and BMWs.

On the way back Joe said to Lou, 'What was all that about then?'

The funeral director said, 'Don't know and I don't want to know, and unless someone's paying you a lot of money to find out, I reckon you don't want to know either.'

One of Joe's great strengths as a PI was that he never let bafflement bother him in the line of business. If, as often, he couldn't see the wood for the trees, he was usually quite content to rest peaceful in a clearing, confident that luck or instinct or a passing lumberjack would show him the way out.

But puzzles that were none of his concern either personally or professionally fascinated him.

He took out the card the woman had given him and studied it. It read *Mandy Levine, The Green Hat* plus a telephone number.

'That woman offered me a spot at her club,' he said.

'Mandy Levine? I'd steer clear there.'

'Why's that, Lou?' said Joe, getting a bit pissed off with all this gratuitous advice.

'Because if it's your deep brown voice she's after, she'll rip you off. And if it's your deep brown dick she's after, Arnie, her husband, will do the ripping off.'

'Arnie Levine? Sounds familiar. Tell me about him.'

Lou laughed shortly. Perhaps it was OK once you'd got rid of the coffin.

'Nothing to tell,' he said. 'Except that colleagues of mine in north London reckon him and his mates are good for business.'

Joe digested this. It was like ripe Camembert – nasty smell but compulsive.

'And that was Arnie giving you a row at the crem.?'

'That's right. He and his friends were pissed off at not being told Mr Tallas had been postponed.'

'So why'd you not tell them?'

'Didn't know they were coming, did I? Mr Smith from the Insurance said quiet do, family only.'

And his family lived in Greece. Where he'd died. Funny.

The funeral tea was a great success, mainly because old Miss Tooley had insisted on laying in a supply of bottled Guinness and Irish whiskey. When Mirabelle, who was as near teetotal as wouldn't have stirred the needle on a Breathalyser, looked disapproving, Miss Tooley said, 'Two things Daniel asked for in his will: one being the scattering of his ashes at the dog track – the other being that his friends should drink him *slainte*, and you can't do that in tay!'

Mirabelle took her revenge when the old lady, in response to a question about her travelling plans, announced that to be sure, she ought to be getting back, but the planes to Belfast were so packed now the peace was here, she doubted if she could get a seat for several days more.

'I've some good news for you there, Miss Tooley,' said Mirabelle, who'd just returned from her flat next door looking triumphant. 'I've just been phoning my old friend Mrs Marley's daughter who works on the booking desk at the airport, and when I told her how desperate you were to get back home, she played with that machine of hers and came up with a ticket for you on the eight-thirty flight tomorrow morning.'

'Eight-thirty?' said Miss Tooley in dismay. 'Now how am I going to get up and find my way to the airport at such an ungodly hour?'

'Don't you fret, my dear,' said Mirabelle. 'I'll see you don't over-sleep. And Joe here will drive you to the airport, won't you Joe?'

Joe, having once again been given the proof that no one messed with Mirabelle, eschewed even token resistance and said 'My pleasure, Miss Tooley.'

It looked like game, set and match to the home team till at the height of the what was now undeniably a party, Miss Tooley screamed, 'The ashes! I can't go without scattering dear dead Daniel's ashes!' and collapsed in a fit of what Mirabelle termed the vaporizers.

Joe knew what was going to happen before it happened, and

was already heading out of the Tooley apartment when his aunt announced: 'Don't you give that no nevermind, Miss Tooley. Joe will fetch them. And if you set out half an hour earlier, you'll have plenty of time for the scattering.'

Joe looked at his watch. Quarter to seven. Would the ashes still be at the crem. or would Lou have had them collected? Either way, would there be anybody in either spot to hand them over? For once in his life he acted sensibly and dived into Mirabelle's flat and picked up the phone.

It rang ten times before it was picked up and Lou's professionally sepulchral tones announced, 'Webster Funerals. How may I help you?'

'Lou, it's Joe. Listen, you got Mr Tooley's ashes yet?'

'Yes. Made sure of it. Mirabelle said the old lady would be flying home very soon.'

'Sooner than she thinks,' said Joe. 'Listen, we need 'em now. Any chance you could bring them round?'

'No way. It's the annual LAUFS dinner and I'm giving the address.'

'Laughs?' said Joe. 'Didn't know you did comedy, Lou.'

'Luton Association of Undertaking and Funeral Services,' said Lou. 'And I'm late.'

'Sorry,' said Joe. 'Anyway, can I collect them myself? It's a matter of death and death.'

He'd hit the right note.

'What I'll do is leave the key to the workshop entrance, that's round the back by the garages, on the ledge above the door. The urn will be just inside. Lock up behind you and push the key through the front door. And don't hang about getting here. I get burgled, it's down to you.'

'Thanks, Lou. I'll be there five minutes tops.'

It was a lie. He knew it was a lie as soon as he got out into the cold night air and realized just how much he'd enjoyed of old Miss Tooley's Irish hospitality. The car was out, and the Rasselas Estate was not the kind of place that taxis cruised.

He set off walking, wasted time waiting for a bus, saw three sweep by in convoy when he was between stops, took a short cut, got lost and was resigning himself to the last indignity for a PI of having to ask the way when he saw the sign, Webster's Funerals.

He made his way round the back. There was a car parked in the shadow of the garages, a BMW. Lou must be doing well, thought Joe, glad it wasn't a hearse. He took out the pencil torch he carried and ran its finger of light over the door ledge till he found the key.

As he took it down and poked the finger of light into the keyhole, a distant clock struck eight.

Superstitiously, he felt mightily relieved it wasn't midnight.

The relief was short-lived.

Midnight was nothing, a time to frighten kids with, telling ghost stories round the fire.

When you were standing outside a darkened funeral parlour and the door swung open at the mere touch of the key, didn't matter what time of day it was, that was really scary.

He stepped inside, telling himself Lou had been careless and forgotten to lock the door. He didn't believe himself but that didn't always mean he was wrong, any more than believing himself had ever meant he was right. He was in a long stone-flagged corridor. His torchlight dribbled on to an urn standing against the wall. He picked it up and gave it a little shake. It was full, presumably of Mr Tooley.

Now was the time to withdraw, lock the door, and if in the morning it turned out someone had stolen all Lou's gilt-edged coffin handles, say, 'Hey man, I'm sorry, but I didn't notice a thing.'

He took a step backward. And heard a noise.

It was not the kind of noise you wanted to hear in the kind of place he was hearing it in. It was sort of frictional, like wood being dragged across wood as in, say, a coffin lid being dragged off a coffin. Also it was so loud you couldn't pretend you hadn't heard it, though he was doing his best.

Then came a second sound, this one human, like a gasp or a groan, perhaps even a *yuck!*

Joe went cataleptic for thirty seconds – or it might have been thirty minutes. When the power of thought returned he wished it hadn't, for it was a funny thing, but, now he was *really* scared, there was no choice but to go forward and take a look. Something wrong there, surely?

A lesser man might have used this interesting psychological

contradiction as an excuse to stand still and ponder, but Joe's anti-intellectual feet were already carrying him steadily down the dark corridor. As he moved he felt his senses sharpened by fear. He could feel the sensuous curve of the urn he was still carrying like a cupped breast; he could hear smaller sounds, rustling, heavy breathing sounds; he could see the outline of the door behind which they were being made, and he could smell a whole complex of smells. In it were woodshavings and embalming fluid, the things you'd expect in such a place, plus a heavier, muskier and somehow familiar perfume. And finally, as he gently pushed on the unresisting door, blotting all these out completely, he was hit by the foul and foetid stench of rotting flesh!

On the last turn of the hinge the door squeaked, and so did the redheaded woman standing by an open coffin with a funerary urn in her hands and, on her handsome face, lurid in the light of a fluorescent lantern perched on a workbench, an expression of mixed shock and guilt.

'Hello Mrs Levine,' said Joe. 'Still looking for talent?'

She recovered quickly, you had to give her that.

'Jesus Christ, it's you, the baritone blackbird! What the hell are you doing here? Not where you work, is it?'

As she spoke she put the urn on the workbench and from a large canvas toolbag removed a long slender screwdriver which glinted like a stiletto in the light. Joe eyed it uneasily.

'No,' he said. 'Actually I'm a PI, a private investigator.'

And not someone you should mess with, was his intended implication, but instead it sent her into peals of laughter.

'Hey, that makes you the Singing Detective,' she gasped. 'Even better billing than the Baritone Blackbird. Why don't we clear up here and go somewhere to talk about your career?'

'First you tell me what makes you so keen to take a last look at your friend Mr Tallas,' he said.

She smiled and glanced fondly into the coffin.

'David and I were once very close. Arnie never knew – he'd have killed me if he'd found out. So you see why I wanted to pay my last respects alone.'

It was clearly crap, but spoken with such sincerity that Joe wasted a second working out the odds it was the truth. His abacus mind had difficulty computing the figures, and the effort of concentration must have switched off his fear-heightened senses for a second, because it was the change in Mandy's expression rather than what must have been the not inconsiderable noise made by a man walking on crutches that alerted him to the danger behind.

He twisted round, fast enough to see but not to avoid the blow from the crutch handle. But at least the movement diverted it from the back of his head where it might have produced unconsciousness, to the side of his face where it just felt like he'd been kicked by a misanthropic mule. As he fell back the man swung a plaster-encased leg at him. Joe scrabbled backward across the tiled floor and more by chance than judgement his left foot hooked around the man's other crutch, now bearing all his weight, and pulled it from under him. The man teetered for a moment and Joe, supine, hurled Mr Tooley's urn at his chest.

There wasn't enough force in the projectile to do any damage but the impact was enough to tip the balance, and with a shrieked word which Joe didn't recognize but which sounded like an oath, his attacker fell backward like a felled pine.

Joe closed his eyes in relief and opened them again to find the gleaming tip of Mandy Levine's screwdriver poised three inches above his left eye, of which, it being the stronger, he was particularly fond.

She was holding the implement in both hands, and he did not doubt that the full weight of her generously structured upper deck could drive it via his eyeball into his almost paralysed brain.

But she wasn't looking down at him, she was looking towards the fallen figure of the intruder. Joe did not dare raise his head to follow her gaze, but his straining ears could hear no sound to indicate the man was preparing to return to the attack.

Then the bright blade wavered and the woman rose. Joe sat up quickly too, and winced as he found that Mr Tooley's urn, as though in revenge for being so impiously misused, had rolled back between his legs. Holding it, Joe got groggily to his feet.

Mandy Levine was kneeling by the fallen man.

'Bring the light,' she commanded.

She was, Joe guessed, a woman accustomed to being obeyed. He, being from long practice a man accustomed to obeying women accustomed to being obeyed, swapped the urn for the lantern and carried it over to her.

Expertly she raised the man's eyelids, examined his eyes, felt for a pulse in the neck and said flatly, 'Dead. You've killed him. Cracked his skull.'

'Hang about,' protested Joe. 'It was an accident. He's dead, I'm sorry, but it wasn't my fault. Who the shoot is he, anyway?'

He knew the answer before she said it. Sometimes the impossible is also the inevitable.

'Tallas,' she said. 'David Tallas.'

Joe went to the coffin and shone the lantern into it.

'Shoot,' said Joe. Mirabelle's soapy mouthwash aversion therapy had made this his strongest oath, but under provocation he could utter it with an intensity that would have won him style points at Billingsgate.

The coffin was a showy mahogany affair, with ornate gilt handles and the kind of brocaded silk upholstery which, even though ripped so that the stuffing trickled through, must have cost an arm and a leg. Of arms there was no trace, but there were legs a plenty, four to be precise, all belonging to a deceased and decomposing goat.

It wasn't very big, barely more than a kid, but its bouquet was enormous.

'Mrs Levine,' said Joe, gagging. 'Maybe you ought to tell me what's going on.'

The woman slowly rose. Her foot kicked against one of the crutches. She picked it up and held it two-handed as she eyed Joe calculatingly.

Joe would have liked to be sure she was merely working out what to say to him, but the memory of the screwdriver poised over his left eye was still strong, and he had an uneasy feeling that she was still weighing war against jaw.

Words won, temporarily at least.

'I'll give it you straight, Joe,' she said in that husky caressing voice. 'The reason David here went to Greece was as agent for a little syndicate put together by my Arnie and his friends. He was good at that sort of thing, David. Could sell false teeth to tigers and buy their stripes at the same time. There was a fair amount of money involved, hard cash money which he took with him, so imagine how Arnie and the others felt when they heard the news. David driving from the airport in a hire car had swerved on a mountain road to avoid a goat, bounced down the hillside, got thrown out, hit a rock and broke his neck, while the car had gone up in flames. Nothing left but unidentifiable ashes.'

'To avoid a goat?' said Joe glancing at the coffin.

'Yeah, that's what I thought. More chance of David avoiding a dirty weekend at the Ritz than swerving to avoid a goat. Came in useful though.'

'So he faked his death to pocket the syndicate money?'

'You got it, Joe,' she said admiringly.

'Must've taken some doing,' said Joe dubiously. 'I mean, even in Greece there must be regulations . . .'

'Sure there are. But the cousin who's his closest relative over there happens to be a police chief out in the sticks. Just the guy to know all the forms and formalities as well as all the fiddles. Wait till the goat's beginning to pong a bit so no one wants to get too close to the coffin, screw it down and send it home. Easy.'

Joe pondered this, conscious of the woman's eyes upon him. He didn't have the kind of detective mind which made connections like a digital exchange, but put a goat in his path and he'd fall over it.

He said, 'Easy, yeah. But not so easy as fixing a fake funeral in Greece. Lot less risky too. And why'd he come back himself? And how come if he faked the accident he's up to his hams in plaster? And why did he cancel the funeral today? And why's he hobbling round here trying to kill people? And just what the shoot are *you* doing here, Mrs Levine?'

'Mandy,' she said. 'Call me Mandy. I like to be on first-name terms with people I do business with.'

'We're doing business?' said Joe. 'Have I missed something?'

She smiled and said, 'Come on, Joe. No need to play quite so dumb, even when you've got the face for it.'

She really did believe he knew what was going on. It was quite flattering. He turned away from her so that the bewilderment on his face didn't show quite so bright. And he found himself looking into the coffin again . . . the torn silk lining . . . the stuffing oozing out . . . powdery, white . . . what kind of stuffing did these Greek undertakers use anyway?

He licked his finger, touched it to the powder, tasted the grains on his tongue. They said it helped you see things clearly. It certainly worked for Joe Sixsmith.

'Smack,' he said. 'That's what he went to buy.'

'That's right. Greece has got borders like a lace curtain. Most of the stuff pouring in from Pakistan and the East hits Europe there. But moving it on to where the big markets are is a lot harder, especially for the small-time operators. So David set up a deal to pay his cousin what was a small fortune in his terms, and buy enough shit to make Arnie and his chums a large fortune in their terms. It looked an all-round winner. Only David fancied a bit more than his commission. In fact the lot, not just the money but the sell-on profit. And he could only get that by selling the stuff here.'

'So he had to come back. And he used his own coffin to carry the heroin. Smart,' said Joe, with genuine admiration. 'But what went wrong?'

Mandy laughed.

'Apart from you cancelling his ticket, you mean?' she said. 'Silly bugger got himself involved in a real accident here before he could arrange for a bit of quiet meditation by the dear deceased's coffin and remove the shit. He realized last night he was in no state to come and collect for himself, so he rang me at the club. I nearly had an accident too when I heard his voice, I tell you.'

'Why'd he ring *you*?' asked Joe.

She smiled and gave him her saucy wink.

'Like I said, we were quite close once,' she said.

'You didn't think of telling Arnie he was alive?'

'Why would I think of that? He'd just want to sort Dave out, and Dave's not such a gent he wouldn't let Arnie know what we'd been up to before he went under. No, keep stumm seemed best. I went to see him. Couldn't do anything last night, I was meeting Arnie later. So we fixed for him to cancel this morning, then he discharged himself from hospital this evening and I brought him along here. Don't think he trusted me by myself. He was sitting in my car; must have seen you coming in after me and thought he'd better hobble to the rescue, poor bastard.'

'Doesn't sound like you're going to miss him.'

'A bit. But I've mourned for him once, haven't I? And that's enough for any man. Question now is, what are we going to do, Joe?'

'No question,' said Joe. 'I'm going to go out of here and ring the police.'

'No,' she said, hefting the crutch. 'Don't think so. Anyone rings the police, it's me.'

'Sorry?'

'Mobile in the car. I go out there, say I think something terrible's happening. Got this call from David asking me to pick him up at the hospital. Didn't know what to make of it. He asked me to drive him round here, saying he'd explain everything. And we arrived to find the door already open. He went in. I heard a scuffle and rushed in to find you here, the coffin open, and David dead upon the floor. Think about it, Joe. Man just out of hospital against advice, in plaster and on crutches, gets cancelled by fully fit, highly qualified PI. What kind of questions would that make the police ask, eh?'

Joe guessed that the main kind of question it would make the local force ask was, what the shoot did she mean by 'highly qualified'?

But qualified or not, he knew a deal when he was being offered one.

'What's the alternative?' he asked.

'Well the way I see it, Joe, is we've got a coffin with contents all legally certified as the body of David Tallas, deceased. And we've got the body of David Tallas deceased.'

It took his breath away, which he didn't mind as it gave a respite from dead goat.

'And the stuff in the coffin?'

'Plenty of room for both of them,' said Mandy.

'I didn't mean the goat.'

'Oh, the shit. Straight split? Or I'll take the lot, sell it and then split the divvy with you?'

Joe considered for a moment.

There was a lot to be said for not getting mixed up with the police, some of whom would be glad of a chance to think the worst of him. Also once it got public, however it panned out, he was going to end up as the man who'd made Arnie Levine unhappy, which he didn't mind doing so long as Arnie took his unhappiness to jail. But there was no offence he'd committed here.

He said, 'You may be on to something, Mandy. Hang about.'

He turned to the canvas toolbag on the workbench. She'd come well equipped. He took out an old-fashioned auger, drew a deep breath and, leaning over the coffin, began punching holes in the lining.

She watched approvingly for a while, then approval turned to puzzlement as he ran his tiny torch beam along the shelves which lined the wall till he saw what he wanted.

And puzzlement turned to horror as he unscrewed the top off a carboy of formalin and began to pour it into the coffin.

'What the hell . . . !'

'Nice mix,' he said. 'Mainline this and you'll get a high that will last for ever!'

For a second he thought she was going to come at him and possibly hope that the coffin would take two. Then she shook her head and began to laugh.

'OK,' she said. 'Do I take it this means I've got half a deal?'

'Why not?' he said. 'I don't approve of wife-beating.'

'Arnie got wind of any of this, beating would be the easy option,' she said grimly. 'You want to take his feet? OK. Lift!'

Five minutes later they were on their way out. As Joe locked the door he asked, 'How'd you get in anyway?'

She raised the canvas bag in which she was carrying her tools and lantern.

'Skeletons,' she said. 'Fitting, huh?'

'Don't get stopped,' warned Joe. 'Going equipped's a crime.'

'Hope not, Joe,' she laughed. 'I always go equipped. Like a lift?'

'No thanks. I'm parked round the corner,' he lied.

'OK. Take care, Joe. And if you ever did decide you'd like a try-out at my club, you've got my number.'

He watched the car lights vanish out of the yard, then took a deep breath of the lovely cold odourless night air. It felt good to be out here alone, with Mandy Levine moving away from him at a rate of knots and a strong locked door between himself and that coffin with all its grisly freight . . .

And the thought put him in mind of Mr Tooley's ashes, resting quiet in their urn, back inside on the workbench top where he'd left it.

'Oh shoot!' said Joe Sixsmith.

Next morning he stood with old Miss Tooley in front of starting gate 3 at the Luton dog track.

Joe tested the wind with a damp finger and said, 'I think we'd be better the other side.'

'I take your point,' said Miss Tooley. 'Dearly though I loved Daniel, I don't fancy taking him home in my eye. Give us the urn, Joe.'

He handed it over.

She said, 'Thanks, Joe. And thanks for everything. You've all been so kind to me. I'll miss you all like my own legs. But it's no distance at all now I've found you. Tell Mirabelle I'll be back to see her as soon as I can manage.'

'She'll look forward to that,' said Joe.

'I know she will. Soul of hospitality, your aunt. I didn't think I would take to her so much at first, but it shows how wrong you can be about people, doesn't it, Joe?'

'It certainly does,' said Joe. He was thinking of Mandy Levine. OK, he wouldn't have liked to have given her the choice of himself dead and David Tallas alive. But he could admire a realist, someone who could look at how things stood, and accept whatever the fates threw up with a smile. She'd taken his trick with the formalin pretty well considering he'd ruined what must have been close on a million quid's worth of dope, street value. Yes, a feisty lady, as they said. Perhaps he would take up her offer of a spot at her club . . . after all, it had been made before any of that business last night . . .

Miss Tooley had unscrewed the top of the urn and was peering inside.

'Ah, that's good,' she said. 'You hear such tales of people finding eggshells and clinker, but I see that Daniel's burnt down to a fine white ash, just as I'd have expected. You can see the pure living just by looking at what he's become.'

She held out the urn so Joe could share the experience.

He looked at the fine white powder it contained with the rapt expression of a man seeing eternity.

What he was actually seeing was Mandy Levine when he first interrupted her in the funeral workshop. She'd been holding an urn which she had then placed on the workbench. Where he later had placed Mr Tooley's remains.

No wonder Mandy had taken his sabotage of her hopes of great profit so well! Not trusting the slippery Tallas to give her the promised split, she'd already stashed herself a nice little nest egg in the nearest handy receptacle. But she'd picked up the wrong urn.

Reginald Hill

Joe hoped that she'd discover her mistake before she tried to trade old Mr Tooley on to some hard-nosed dealer.

Whatever, he thought it best to postpone his professional singing début just a little while longer.

He settled down to watch that remarkable old lady, Miss Tooley, scatter about a hundred grand's worth of pure smack into trap 3. The wind carried most of it away, but not all.

They stood with their heads bowed for a moment.

Old Miss Tooley said, 'I'd have liked him to have some sort of lasting monument, but this is what he wanted. And I'm sure his friends will not forget him.'

'No indeed,' said Joe. 'In fact I was thinking I might come here tonight and back the three dog through the card, just as a kind of tribute.'

'Now that's a lovely thought,' said old Miss Tooley. 'You're a darling boy, Joseph. Put a fiver on for me, for I'm sure the Lord will be after smiling down on such a kind and loving gesture.'

And Joe, looking down at the scattering of white over the ground inside trap 3 said, 'I think He's smiling already, Miss Tooley.'

GUILT TRIP

VAL McDERMID

As neither of my parents was too bothered about religion, I managed to miss out on Catholic guilt. Then I found myself working with Shelley. A guilt trip on legs, our office manager. If she treats her two teenagers like she treats me, those kids are going to be in therapy for years. 'You play, you pay,' she said sweetly, pushing the new case file towards me for the third time.

'Just because I *play* computer games doesn't mean I'm qualified to deal with the nerds who write them,' I protested. It was only a white lie; although my business partner Bill Mortensen deals with most of the work we do involving computers, I'm not exactly a techno-illiterate. I pushed the file back towards Shelley. 'It's one for Bill.'

'Bill's too busy. You know that,' Shelley said. 'Anyway, it's not software as such. It's either piracy or industrial sabotage and that's your forte.' The file slid back to me.

'Sealsoft are Bill's clients.' Brannigan's last stand.

'All the more reason you should get to know them.'

I gave in and picked up the file. Shelley gave a tight little smile and turned back to her computer screen. One of these days I'm going to get the last word. Just wait till hell freezes over. On my way out of the door and down the stairs, I browsed the file. Sealsoft was a local Manchester games software house. They'd started off back in the dawn of computer gaming in the mid-eighties, writing programs for a whole range of hardware. Some of the machines they produced games for had never been intended as anything other than word processors, but Sealsoft had grabbed the challenge and come up with some fun stuff. The first platform game I'd ever played, on a word processor that now looked as antique as a Model T Ford, had been a Sealsoft game.

They'd never grown to rival any of the big players in the field, but somehow Sealsoft had always hung in there, coming up every now and again with seemingly simple games that became classics. In the last year or two they'd managed to win the odd film tie-in licence, and their latest acquisition was the new Arnold Schwarz-enegger–Bruce Willis boys 'n' toys epic. But now, two weeks before the game was launched, they had a problem. And when people have problems, Mortensen and Brannigan is where they turn if they've got sense and cash enough.

I had a ten o'clock appointment with Sealsoft's boss. Luckily I could get there on foot, since parking round by Sealsoft is a game for the terminally reckless. The company had started off on the top floor of a virtually derelict canalside warehouse that had since been gutted and turned into expansive and expensive studio flats where the marginally criminal rubbed shoulders with the marginally legitimate lads from the financial services industries. Sealsoft had moved into modern premises a couple of streets away from the canal, but the towpath was still the quickest way to get from my office in Oxford Road to their concrete pillbox in Castlefield.

Fintan O'Donohoe had milk-white skin and freckles so pale it looked like he'd last seen daylight somewhere in the nineteenth century. He looked about seventeen, which was slightly worrying since I knew he'd been with the company since it started up in 1983. Add that to the red-rimmed eyes, and I felt like I'd stumbled into *Interview with the Vampire*. 'Call me Fin,' he said, with no trace of any accent other than pure Mancunian as we settled in his chrome and black leather office, each of us clutching our designer combinations of mineral water, herbs and juices.

I resisted the invitation. It wasn't the hardest thing I'd done that day. 'I'm told you have a problem,' I said.

'That's not the word I'd use,' he sighed. 'A major disaster waiting to happen is what we've got. We've got a boss money-earner about to hit the streets and our whole operation's under threat.'

'From what?' I asked.

'It started about six weeks ago. There were just one or two at first, but we've had getting on for sixty in the last two days. It's a nightmare,' O'Donohoe told me earnestly, leaning forward and fiddling anxiously with a pencil.

'What exactly are we talking about here?' He might not have anything better to do than take a long tour round the houses, but I certainly did. Apart from anything else, there was a cappuccino at the Atlas café with my name on it.

'Copies of our games with the right packaging, the right manuals, the guarantee cards, everything, are being returned to us because the people who buy them are shoving the disks into their computers and finding they're completely blank. Nothing on them at all. Just bog-standard, high-density preformatted unbranded three-and-a-half-inch disks.' He threw himself back in his chair, pouting like a five-year-old.

'Sounds like pirates,' I said. 'Bunch of schneid merchants copying your packaging and stuffing any old shit in there.'

He shook his head. 'My first thought. But that's not how the pirates work. They bust your copy protection codes, make hundreds of copies of the program and stuff it inside pretty crudely copied packaging. This is the opposite of that. There's no game, but the packaging is perfect. It's ours.' He opened a drawer in his desk and pulled out a box measuring about eight inches by ten and a couple of inches deep. The cover showed an orc and a human in mortal combat outlined in embossed silver foil. O'Donohoe opened the box and tipped out a game manual, a story-book, four disks with labels reading 1–4 and a guarantee card. 'Right down to the hologram seal on the guarantee, look,' he pointed out.

I leaned forward and picked up the card, turning it to check the hologram. He was right. If this was piracy, I'd never seen quality like it. And if they could produce packaging like this, I was damn sure they could have copied the game too. So why the combination of spot-on packaging and blank disks? 'Weird,' I said.

'You're not kidding.'

'Is this happening to any of your competitors?'

'Not that I've heard. And I would have heard, I think.'

Sounded as if one of Sealsoft's rivals was paying off an insider to screw O'Donohoe's operation into the deck. 'Where are the punters buying them? Market stalls?' I asked.

Head down, O'Donohoe said 'Nope.' For the first time I noted dark shadows under his eyes. 'They're mostly coming back to us via the retailers, though some are coming direct.'

'Which retailers? Independents or chains?' I was sitting forward in my seat now, intrigued. What had sounded like a boring piece of routine was getting more interesting by the minute. Call me shallow and superficial, but I like a bit of excitement in my day.

'Mostly smallish independents, but increasingly we're getting returns from the big chain stores now. We've been in touch with quite a few of the customers as well, and they're all saying that the games were shrink-wrapped when they bought them.'

I sat back, disappointed. The shrink-wrapping was a clincher. 'It's an inside job,' I said flatly. 'Industrial sabotage.'

'No way,' O'Donohoe said, two pale pink spots suddenly burning on his cheekbones.

'I'm sorry. I know it's the message no employer wants to hear. But it's clearly an inside job.'

'It can't be,' he insisted bluntly. 'Look, I'm not a dummy. I've been in this game a while. I know the wrinkles. I know how piracy happens. And I guard against it. Our boxes are printed in one place, our booklets in another, our guarantee cards in a third. The disks get copied in-house on to disks that are overprinted with our logo and the name of the game, so you couldn't just slip in a few blanks like these,' he said contemptuously, throwing the disks across the desk.

'Where does it all come together?' I asked.

'We're a small company,' he answered obliquely. 'But that's not the only reason we pack by hand rather than on a production line. I know where we're vulnerable to sabotage, and I've covered the bases. The boxes are packed and sealed in shrink-wrap in a room behind the despatch room.'

'Then that's where your saboteur is.'

His lip curled. 'I don't think so. I've only got two workers in there. We've always had a policy of employing friends and family at Sealsoft. The packers are my mum and her sister, my auntie Geraldine. They'd kill anybody that was trying to sabotage this business, take my word for it. When they're not working, the door's double-locked. They wouldn't even let the parish priest in there, believe me.'

'So what exactly do you want me to do?' I asked.

'I don't want you questioning my staff,' he said irritably. 'Other than that, it's up to you. You're the detective. Find out who's putting the shaft in, then come back and tell me.'

When I left Sealsoft ten minutes later, all I had to go on was a list of customers and companies involved in returns of Sealsoft's games and details of who'd sent back what. I was still pretty sure the villain was inside the walls rather than outside, but the client wasn't letting me anywhere near his good Catholic mother and auntie Geraldine. Can't say I blamed him.

I figured there wasn't a lot of point in starting with the chain stores. Even if something hooky was going on, they were the last people I could lean on to find out. With dole queues still nudging the three-million mark, the staff there weren't going to tell me anything that might cost them their jobs. I sat in the Atlas over the coffee I'd promised myself and read through the names. At first glance, I didn't recognize any of the names of the computer suppliers. We buy all our equipment and consumables by mail order, and the only shop we've ever used in dire emergencies was the one that used to occupy the ground floor of our building before it became a supermarket.

Time for some expert help. I pulled out my mobile and rang my tame darkside hacker, Gizmo. By day he works for Telecom as a systems manager. By night, he becomes the Scarlet Pimpernel of cyberspace. Or so he tells me. 'Giz? Kate.'

'Not a secure line,' he grumbled. 'You should know better.'

'Not a problem. This isn't confidential. Do you know anybody who works at any of these outlets?' I started to read out the list, with Gizmo grunting negatively after each name. About halfway through the list he stopped me.

'Wait a minute. That last one, Epic PC?'

'You know someone there?'

'I don't but you do. It's wossname, the geezer that used to have that place under your office.'

'Deke? He went bust, didn't he?'

''S right. Bombed. Went into liquidation, opened up a new place in Prestwich a week later, didn't he? That's his shop. Epic PC. I remember because I thought it was such a crap name. That it?'

'That'll do nicely, Giz.' I was speaking to empty air. I like a man who doesn't waste my time. I drained my cup, walked up the steps to Deansgate station and jumped the next tram to Prestwich.

Epic PC was a small shop on the main drag through Prestwich village. I recognized the special-offer stickers. It looked like Deke Harper didn't have the kind of fresh ideas that would save Epic PC from its predecessor's fate. I pushed open the door and an electric buzzer vibrated in the stuffy air. Deke himself was seated behind a PC in the middle of a long room that was stuffed with hardware and software, fingers clattering over the keys. He'd trained himself well in the art of looking busy; he let a whole five seconds pass between the buzzer sounding and his eyes leaving the screen in front of him. When he registered who his customer was, his eyebrows climbed in his narrow face. 'Hello,' he said uncertainly, pushing his chair back and getting to his feet, 'stranger.'

'Believe me, Deke, it gets a lot stranger still,' I said drily.

'You live out this way, then?' he asked nervously, hitting a key to clear his screen as I drew level with him.

'No,' I said. Sometimes it's more fun to let them come to you.

'You were passing?'

'No.' I leaned against his desk. His eyes kept flicking between me and his uninformative screen.

'You needed something for the computer? Some disks?'

'Three in a row, Deke. You lose. My turn now. I'm here about these moody computer games you've been selling. Where are they coming from?'

A thin blue vein in his temple seemed to pop up from nowhere. 'I don't know what you're on about,' he said, too nonchalantly. 'What moody computer games?'

I rattled off half a dozen Sealsoft games. 'I sell them, sure,' he said defensively. 'But they're not hooky. Look, I got invoices for them,' he added, pushing past me and yanking a drawer open. He pulled out a loose-leaf file and flicked through fast enough to rip a couple of pages before he arrived at a clutch of invoices from Sealsoft.

I took the file from him and walked over to the shelves and counted. 'According to this, Deke, you bought six copies of Sheer Fire II when it was released last month.'

'That's right. And there's only five there now, right? I sold one.'

'Wrong. You sold at least three. That's how many of your customers have returned blank copies of Sheer Fire II to Sealsoft. Care to explain the discrepancy? Or do I have to call your local friendly trading standards officer?' I asked sweetly. 'You can go down for this kind of thing these days, can't you?' I added conversationally.

Half an hour later I was sitting outside Epic PC behind the wheel of Deke's six-year-old Mercedes, waiting for a lad he knew only as Jazbo to turn up in response to a call on his mobile. Amazing what people will do with a little incentive. I spotted Jazbo right away from Deke's description. A shade under six feet, jeans, trainers and a Chicago Cubs bomber jacket. And Tony Blair complains about Manchester United's merchandising.

He got out of a battered boy racer's hatchback clutching a carrier bag with clear, box-shaped outlines pressing against it. I banged off a couple of snaps with the camera in my backpack. Jazbo was in and out of Epic PC inside five minutes. We headed back into town down Bury New Road, me sitting snugly on his tail with only one car between us. We skirted the city centre and headed east. Jazbo eventually parked up in one of the few remaining terraced streets in Gorton and let himself into one of the houses there. I took a note of the address and drove Deke's Merc back to Prestwich before he started getting too twitchy about the idea of me with his wheels.

Next morning I was back outside Jazbo's house just before seven. Early risers, villains, in my experience. According to the electoral roll, Gladys and Albert Conway lived there. I suspected the information on the list was well out of date. With names like that they might have been Jazbo's grandparents, but a more likely scenario was that he'd taken over the house after the Conways had died or suffered the fate worse than death of an old people's home. The man himself emerged about five past the hour. There was less traffic around, but I managed to stay in contact with him into the city centre, where he parked in a loading bay behind Deansgate and let himself into the back of a shop.

I took a chance and left my wheels on a single yellow while I walked round the front of the row of shops and counted back to where Jazbo had let himself in. JJ's Butty Bar. Another piece of the jigsaw clicked into place.

Through the window I caught the occasional glimpse of Jazbo, white-coated, moving between tall fridges and worktops. Once or twice he emerged from the rear of the shop with trays of barm cakes neatly wrapped and labelled, and deposited them in the chill cabinets

Val McDermid

round the shop. I figured he was good for a few hours yet and headed back to the office before the traffic wardens came out to play.

I was back just after two. I kept cruising round the block till someone finally left a meter free that gave me a clear view of the exit from the alley behind the sandwich shop. Jazbo emerged in his hot hatch just after three, which was just as well because I was running out of change. I stayed close to him through the city centre, then let a bit of distance grow between us as he headed out past Salford Quays and into the industrial estate round Trafford Park. He pulled up outside a small unit with Gingerbread House painted in a rainbow of colours across the front wall, and disappeared inside.

About fifteen minutes later he emerged with a supermarket trolley filled to the top with computer-game boxes. I was baffled. I'd had my own theory about where the packaging was coming from, and it had just been blown out of the water. I hate being wrong. I'd rather unblock the toilet. I let Jazbo drive off, then I marched into Gingerbread House. Ten minutes later, I had all the answers.

Fintan O'Donohoe looked impressed as I laid out my dossier before him. Jazbo's address, photograph, phone number, car registration number and place of work would be more than enough to hand him over to the police, gift-wrapped. 'So how's this guy getting hold of the gear?' he demanded.

'First thing I wondered about was the shrink-wrapping. That made me think it was someone in your despatch unit. But you were adamant it couldn't be either your mum or your auntie. Then when I found out he worked in a sandwich shop, I realized he must be using their wrap and seal gear to cover his boxes in. Which left the question of where the boxes were coming from. You ruled out an inside job, so I thought he might simply be raiding your dustbins for discarded gear. But I was wrong. You ever heard of a charity called Gingerbread House?'

O'Donohoe frowned. 'No. Should I have?'

'Your mum has,' I told him. 'And so, I suspect, has Jazbo's mum or girlfriend or sister. Probably took him along to help them carry some gear. It's an educational charity run by some nuns. They go round businesses and ask them for any surplus materials, and they sell them off to schools and playgroups for next to nothing. They collect all sorts – material scraps, bits of bungee rope, offcuts of

170

specialist paper, wallpaper catalogues, tinsel, sheets of plastic, scrap paper. Anything that could come in handy for school projects or for costumes for plays, whatever.'

Fintan O'Donohoe groaned and put his hands over his face. 'Don't tell me . . .'

'They came round here a few months ago, and your mum explained that you don't manufacture here, so there's not much in the way of left-over stuff. But what there was were the boxes from games that had been sent back because they were faulty in some way. The disks were scrapped, and so were the boxes and manuals. If the nuns could make any use of the boxes and their contents . . . They've been dropping them off once a fortnight ever since.'

He looked up at me, a ghost of an ironic smile on his lips. 'And I was so sure it couldn't be anything to do with my mum!'

'Don't they say charity begins at home?'

MARBLES
MARGARET YORKE

Why couldn't she just let him go?

There were other prisoners in the room. Two goldfish swam round and round in a glass globe on a shelf at his eye level, mesmerizing him as he watched them circling hypnotically and staring back at him. A few weedy strands of greenery swayed to their movements. She'd put them there, saying they would be company for him.

Now she was moving round the room. He swivelled his gaze to follow her actions. What was she planning? She wouldn't tell him. It would just happen. She'd haul him up, drape his floppy body against her muscular torso and dump him in the wheelchair. Then she'd push him along the passage and out of the bungalow, bump, bump, down the steps to the gravel path and over the lawn, if she thought he could be aired sufficiently there while she worked in the garden, or along the road to the shops, if that was her plan. She never used the planks someone had arranged as a ramp by the steps; she knew he could feel the jarring as she heaved him up or down. She was very strong now; her shoulder and arm muscles had developed since his illness.

He could no longer speak. Grunting sounds were all he could manage, though in his head he could recite large chunks of poetry learned in youth: how Horatius held the bridge, and about the Ancient Mariner. So he hadn't lost his marbles, as she told everyone he had. But she knew he hadn't; that was what made it worse. All

173

this was intentional, and there would be no end to it because, as everyone declared, she was marvellous, and managed him so well.

There had been some damage to his memory; he couldn't recall everything he wanted to remember, nor what had happened just before he had his stroke, but there had been a row. What was it about? A woman: that was it. It was always a woman, even though he was now so old. He couldn't think who this last one was, which was sad: if he were able to picture her it would be comforting. Brenda had said dreadful things about her, and told him that his conduct was disgusting at his age. A man was only as old as he felt, however, and until this had happened, he had felt quite young – well, not young exactly, but in his prime, and virile, certainly.

There'd been so many women in his life. He'd known just how to make them warm to him; the chase was the best part, selecting the quarry, then ensnaring her. He'd usually tire first of the entanglement, finding a new attraction to pursue and making an art of bidding the current one goodbye. Was Muriel the latest? Was she the one he'd taken on the river, down near Marlow? They'd fumbled in a punt beneath a willow. She'd giggled and pretended to be cross, then given in. They all gave in, eventually. Muriel's face swam before his gaze, briefly replacing the goldfish bowl: her eyes shone; she was young and excited. She couldn't be the last one; she was a girl from long ago, and it had been a bit of fun, not serious.

Brenda, though, had always been suspicious whenever he was late home from the office or away on business. She'd seen him as a catch, because by capturing him she'd vanquished the competition, for he'd been quite a fellow in his day and she was determined not to lose him.

He'd felt proud, in those days. She'd been a lovely girl, tall and slim, with long legs and gorgeous golden hair, sleek and shining, softly waved in the fashion of the day. Her hair was golden still, but now it was a bright brassy colour, and tormented into a frizz of corkscrew curls around her head. She'd filled out, too: her legs were sinewy and her body thick.

He had heard the doctors say that he was unlikely to improve much more and could remain in this condition for some years. He did not want to struggle on with such a meaningless existence, attempting to move his wasted limbs in response to the ministrations of a physiotherapist – though she, a pretty woman, came no longer: Brenda instead moved his legs and arms around and massaged him with horny, heavy fingers. He was tired of being spoonfed, like a baby, with a towel, bib-like, round his neck; of being washed by Brenda's hostile hands. Thank goodness shaving him had been abandoned; a neat grey beard now adorned his chin. She trimmed it and his hair at intervals, tweaking both. When the district nurse, on a regular visit, performed any of these services, it was an entirely different experience.

Managing to turn his head away from the bowl of fish, he watched her as she looked through the picture window, studying the garden. She did it all herself; it was something she could manage while she cared for him, she said, when praised by her bridge-playing friends. Ever since his return from hospital he'd spent Thursday afternoons in front of the television, tuned to BBC 2, while Brenda and three other women played bridge for four hours or more in the dining room.

'It's a minder for him, poor darling,' Brenda had said about the television, and she would leave the handset beside him though she said he couldn't use it. 'He doesn't understand a thing we're saying, do you, dear?' she would add, beaming at him, but with steely eyes because she knew he did. The knowledge gave her power; she had complete control.

Now and then she sent him to a nursing home so that she might have a rest. He hated it, because the routine and the faces were unfamiliar, but during these breaks he was spared her rough treatment; the strange nurses were quite kind and gentle, though they were always in a hurry. He never knew where she went or whom she met at these times; perhaps she stayed at home alone. Perhaps she had a lover.

Had she? Surely, if that were so, she'd let him go, cease caring for him quite so conscientiously; perhaps even try to hasten his death by some mild, undetectable form of neglect. It wouldn't be too difficult. He longed for her to do it, to release him from this mortal coil. After all, she'd have everything he left: the bungalow, his savings and a good pension. She could enjoy it with another husband, if she could find one. But perhaps she had a married lover and needed him alive, providing cover for their intrigue. He knew all about that – hadn't he used the same excuse himself, to avoid commitment? He'd declared he couldn't leave poor childless Brenda, who had only him.

How she'd worshipped him, at first! And he had been obsessed with her for months. But when that ended, he could never leave her, however great the temptation, because she blamed him for the baby's death, and perhaps it was his fault. Brenda had gone to visit her mother, who was in hospital, leaving him in charge. Because she couldn't drive she'd gone by bus. He'd popped out in the car to meet his latest lady. He hadn't been gone long – they'd driven up to the common and it had been a hasty coupling in the car, a challenge and an opportunity. When he got home he didn't think about the baby, supposing that she'd cry when she felt hungry. It was Brenda who had found her, after; and by chance she'd touched the bonnet of the car, which was still warm. The silent baby, though, was dead. One little hand, outside the covers, was quite cold.

No official blame was attached to him. Cot-deaths still happened to this day and were inexplicable, but Brenda was wild with rage and grief. She never forgave him, and it was the one misdeed for which he had not forgiven himself, though even if he'd stayed at home it might have made no difference.

It could have done, however. That was the point. And so he had to endure his eternal punishment.

In recent weeks he had regained some extra movement in his arms, but he hadn't let her understand how much. He could rotate his wheelchair now, a fraction. He practised secretly, and clenched his fists, or tried to: a feeble contraction, but improving. While she read to him, he tested out his fingers and his neck, managing to work them just a little. Now he complied with her exercise routine, for though it was a torment to him, it was helping him regain strength, and he would use it when he could. She'd sit there reading sentimental novels to him while he schemed. His chosen literature was the *Financial Times* or political memoirs. He knew she did not like the romantic novels any more than he did: it was a penance she inflicted on him, one she was prepared to endure herself. Sometimes, lulled by her monotonous voice, he slept, and she would rouse him by tapping him quite sharply on the head and becoming more animated in her reading of the tale. When, after tortuous misunderstandings, the lovers were united, she would make waspish comments about how he had never known perfect passion.

He'd tried to give up, allow sleep to swallow him, to let his frailty overcome him, but she would not let him go.

'I won't permit you to die. That's too easy. You will live, serve out your life sentence, and I'll go on receiving praise for how I tend you. I'll make you carry on,' she'd say, knowing he could understand.

At intervals he could not keep track of what was going on around him; his lucidity was variable, and he was fearing that his foggy spells were growing longer, but he knew his body was not failing yet; the doctor was extremely pleased with how his heart and lungs were working.

'You're a credit to your nurse,' he'd say.

Why couldn't she release him? All she had to do was be more casual in her care, let standards slip. He hated her now. He loathed her ugly, brassy hair, her coarse laugh, the crude comments she made about his feeble body and its functions. In a sense, she was as firmly trapped as he, but he was the captive, she the jailer.

Now she'd decided on her programme. It was fine enough to take him for a trundle. She scooped him up and hauled him into his wheelchair, a helpless, septuagenarian infant in its pram, but she never strapped him in, tipping him backwards as they tackled steps and slopes. She tucked a rug around him, then left him on the lawn while she went to fetch the mower.

So spring had come again. Vaguely he noticed the yellow of daf-fodils, the reds of early tulips, in the borders. Every year she did this to him: parked him on the rise above the lawn, moving him when she'd cut a wide swath, keeping him close as she went up and down, the mower's droning sound an angry hornet, a buzzing fortissimo, hurting his ears. Before his illness, when he cut the grass himself, its noise had irritated him and he had planned to get a new machine, one which ran more quietly. Now the sound pierced his skull as she went to and fro, as close to him as possible, moving him nearer after every three or four promenades past him. Once or twice, while she was at the far end of the lawn, he nodded off, only to start awake again as she approached.

How long had this been going on? How long had he been ill? It felt like years and years. When would it end? Only when she no longer had the power to hold him back from the grave, and that time might be far distant. He was condemned for ever to her care, her cutting of his toe- and fingernails, her trimming of his hair and beard, her dealing with his most intimate bodily needs.

177

She stopped below him to empty the grass-box, stooping over the barrow which she had left beside the pond. There were no fish in there; a pity, he had always thought. He'd made it years ago, when they first bought the bungalow for their retirement, and he'd put lilies in, in weighted baskets.

His hand was already on the wheelchair brake. He freed it, not sure if gravity would set him rolling fast enough. He tried to propel the chair into motion as she spread the mowings so that another boxful could be added without it overflowing. As his chair started running towards her he held on grimly, aware that the impact might not be enough to kill her, but if he struck her hard she'd be immobilized, giving him time to drag himself, somehow or other, to the pond.

Above the mower's noise she never heard him.

They found him drowned in two feet of water, his face among the lily leaves, his wheelchair on top of him, pinning him down, his head immersed.

Brenda was barely even bruised, though she had been briefly winded. They wouldn't believe her version of the story, that she must have left off the brake on the chair, and it had run down the slope. She insisted that she'd tried and tried to save him, and indeed, when help arrived, her feet and clothes were soaking. She tried to haul him from among the leaves and lily stems, but, with the chair on top of him, he'd been too heavy and she couldn't move him.

She faced a charge of murder, though some of the papers called it a mercy killing.

SHAFTED
CHARLOTTE AND AARON ELKINS

There aren't that many people around these days who can say 'Pshaw' and get away with it, but take my word for it, Henry Weaver is one of them.

'Pshaw, Ben,' he said, slapping the morning *Herald* on to my desk and scattering the files I'd been working on for two hours. 'Whole thing's all bollixed up. Completely turned around. Absurd.' And again for good measure: 'Pshaw.'

This, you understand, was by way of greeting. Henry has never been famous for his way with words, and age has failed to mellow him. People in Scallop Bay often think of him, with a certain tolerant fondness, as a man with a crusty exterior and a heart of gold. The crusty part I can confirm, but I'm not so sure about the other. Not that I mean to say there's any real meanness in him, but good God, if you want to talk about cranky, know-it-all, interfering old buzzards . . .

'Anything in particular, Henry?' I asked pleasantly – as pleasantly as could be done through clenched teeth – 'or do you just mean generally speaking?'

'Whole damn thing. Read it.' A knobby finger tapped the boxed article on page one.

'I've read it.' Hell, I'd practically written it.

Imperiously the horny fingernail tapped again. 'Read it.'

I read it.

CORONER RULES MURDER-SUICIDE IN SEA EAGLE DEATHS

SCALLOP BAY. The deaths of a prominent Sea Eagle Golf and Country Club couple have been ruled a murder and a suicide.

Dune County Coroner Simon Galumbie this morning said that Adele Haskell, 66, was murdered by her husband Stanley, who then committed suicide. Haskell, 84, who had made his fortune in pharmaceuticals, was well known for his extensive collection of golf memorabilia.

Scallop Bay Police Chief Ben Rinucci said that Mrs Haskell had been killed with a single blow by a club from her husband's collection. The hickory club, an 1854 niblick made by the renowned Scottish clubmaker Hugh Philp, was broken in the attack and lay beside her. Mr Haskell then shot himself in the head with his own Smith and Wesson revolver, which was still in his hand at the time the bodies were discovered in the couple's seaside mansion, according to Rinucci.

Rinucci believes the two deaths were the result of a domestic dispute.

'Well?' Henry said when I looked up.

'Well?' I said.

'Domestic dispute,' he muttered, oozing scorn. 'Preposterous.' (Henry's also pretty good with 'preposterous'.) One tangled white eyebrow shot up and quivered. The red-rimmed, pale-blue eye underneath glared at me. 'Bungled it, Ben. From start to finish.'

'Oh?' I said with what I hoped was a receptive smile. 'Could you be a little more specific?'

No doubt you've been wondering about this stoic reserve that I was so manfully displaying – well, there were reasons for it. First of all, there was Henry himself. The old boy had done more than his share to put Scallop Bay on the map. We all owed him a debt. It was Henry and a small group of cronies who had come together forty-three years earlier to purchase the wild strip of coastal land that they had then developed into the Sea Eagle Golf and Country Club, which in turn had transformed Scallop Bay from a crossroads smattering of fruit and vegetable stands into one of the south coast's premier residential communities, with a tax base to knock your eye out.

But that was a long time ago. A *long* time ago. Then, at an age when he should have been basking in the mellow, reflective sunshine of his golden years and dangling his great-grandkids on his knee and so on, suddenly and cantankerously he decides that the town is in need of his presence again. At eighty-one he runs for the five-member city council against the advice of his family, his friends and his doctors. He runs, and dammit if he doesn't win. That was two years ago, and ever since he's been the terror of the city's departments. Lately, to my unending grief, he's turned his attention from parks and recreation (leaving the director a gibbering wreck) to the police department. Nowadays it's rare that three days go by without his coming in to sputter, not very coherently, about the mishandling of one case or another.

But until this happened, it's never been anything more important than a traffic violation or a domestic dispute (of the non-lethal variety), and it was always possible to mollify or even accommodate the old guy once I could figure out what he was prattling about. But this was the most sensational crime in Scallop Bay's history. Newspapers across the country were covering it. Nothing remotely like it had ever happened here; in my fourteen years on the job it was only my third murder, and the first two had involved transients, so they didn't really count.

'Specific?' Henry said, and issued one of his infrequent complete sentences. 'Stanley never killed her, how's that suit you for specific?' Then, more characteristically: 'Out of the question. Plain as can be. Damn well see it for yourself.'

I took a deep breath. It didn't help, but a moment's reflection did. Of course he was upset. Who wouldn't be? With Stanley's death, all of his contemporaries were gone. And Stanley had been more than a contemporary; he'd been an amicable competitor. Henry was a collector of golf antiques too, if not quite in Stanley's league, and the two of them could be seen on the club terrace on sunny afternoons, drinking their straight-up Martinis, watching the golfers come in and arguing happily or at least spiritedly about the relative values of smooth versus knife-cut gutty balls, or James McEwan versus Robert Forgan long-nose woods. Once upon a time they'd both been avid golfers, but for many years now their collections had been considerably more exciting than their golf games.

'Well, I certainly see your point, Henry,' I said, sacrificing honesty for diplomacy, 'but the thing is, the paper didn't report everything. Let me fill you in on our investigation.'

That was always a good ploy, making the old gaffer feel he was privy to inside information. I explained the facts of the case: there had been no break-in, there were no items missing, no sign at all of burglary. The club had Stanley's fingerprints on it; the bullet wound in his temple had powder burns around it, indicating that the shooting had been at point blank range; the gun was still in his hand—'

'Already read that,' Henry interrupted testily. 'I can read, can't I?'

'The coroner says—'

'Simon Galumbie's a fathead,' opined Henry – the first words with which I was in total agreement. 'Ought to get a second opinion. Somebody higher up.'

'There isn't anybody higher up than the coroner, Henry. He's elected, remember? The only thing I could do would be to call in the state medical examiner's office—'

'Then do it,' Henry snapped. 'I want this looked into.'

This was pushing it. I bristled. 'Well, now, just one—'

Henry bristled right back at me, that scrawny jaw thrust forward, the tendons standing out on his neck like braided strings. 'You have a report ready at the next commission meeting, Ben, or I'll want to know the reason why.'

I could feel my eyes, which tend to be a little protuberant anyway, bulge a little more, but in the end I sank back in my chair, a beaten man.

Ah, the joys of serving at the pleasure of a city council. Where else did you have not one, but five different bosses to keep satisfied, every one of them a raving independent? Of course Henry was only one vote, and an eccentric one at that, practically always at odds with his fellow members, so there was little the old coot could do besides make things unpleasant, which he regularly did anyway.

But there was another reason for my tiptoeing around him. The fact is I'm a pretty avid golfer myself, and I'd been giving a lot of thought to applying for membership at Sea Eagle. Myra was after me all the time about it, and now that she had inherited from her mother, we could actually afford it. And to be honest, it appealed to me too, not that I'd ever admit it to Myra. I grew up in the old Scallop Bay, you know – my father was one of those fruit peddlers – and between you and me, it seemed like it'd be a hell of thing for a ragtag kid christened Beniamino Enzo Guglielmo Rinucci to get into a blue-blood kind of outfit like Sea Eagle. I sort of felt like I owed it to my father, if you know what I mean. But election to the country club needed approval by the directors, any one of whom could blackball me. And Henry, as a club founder, was a lifelong ex-officio member of the board . . .

'Yes, sir,' I mumbled at last. 'I will.'

'Speak up,' he said. 'How do you expect me to hear you?'

I supposed that the gritty sound in my ears was my teeth grinding. 'Yes, sir,' I said more clearly, but then I couldn't stop myself from adding: 'You wouldn't care to tell me who did murder her, would you? If Stanley didn't?'

Henry was all ready with his answer. 'Who inherits?' he said. 'That's where I'd start.'

Ordinarily, I think of myself as a pretty thick-skinned guy, not the type whose ears get singed by anybody very often, but the next afternoon they were burning for the second day in a row. This time the heat came from Davis Kornbloom, newly-appointed Deputy State Medical Examiner, who had taken less than two hours at the morgue to arrive at his preliminary conclusions – the mind-boggling upshot of which was that Henry had hit the nail on the head. Stanley Haskell had been the victim, not the perpetrator, of homicide.

'But . . .' I stammered, '. . . but what about the gun? He still had it in his hand.'

But, Kornbloom had pointed out (pretty smugly, if you ask me), the victim's hand was the last place you would expect to find it. In suicides with handguns, the weapon was generally thrown several feet, or at least dropped, when the shock to the nervous system caused the victim to fling out his arms. If a weapon was found in a suicide victim's hand, it was usually due to the hand's having been fixed or supported in some way. Hadn't the chief known that?

Well, no, I guessed I hadn't.

And as for those powder burns, explained Kornbloom, they

merely indicated that the gun was fired at close range; they didn't indicate who pulled the trigger. True, murderers didn't generally manage to get their guns right up against their victim's temples without a substantial struggle (of which there was no sign at the Haskells'), but a frail, eighty-four-year-old man would hardly have given an able-bodied killer much trouble.

'Sure, OK,' I said, 'but that's not enough to prove murder. You said "usually", didn't you? In other words, "not always", right?'

Kornbloom, not yet thirty despite his balding blond pate, and with the ink barely dry on his Ph.D. in Forensic Pathology and Criminalistics, beamed patronizingly at me.

'No, no, there's more, of course. Let me try to explain,' he said kindly.

That's what started my ears tingling. *Try* to explain?

Possibly, Kornbloom said speaking slowly and clearly, the chief remembered that there was a considerable amount of blood on Haskell's right hand; the hand with the gun?

Yes, I said sharply, I remembered quite well. There was a lot of blood in a lot of places. Bullets had a way of doing that.

Of course they did, said Kornbloom, but while finding blood on the back of a suicide victim's hand was common, finding it on the *palm* was not, inasmuch as the hand would have been wrapped around the weapon's grip at the critical moment. Had the chief not been aware of that?

Well, no, I supposed I hadn't. Scallop Bay is a pretty peaceful place, although it picks up some in the summer, when we have to hire a couple of temporaries. But even then, there isn't too much in the way of either gunshots or suicides, and no one could call me an expert, least of all me. That's why I have to rely on experts. Like Galumbie.

And in those few handgun suicides where the palm *was* blood-spattered, Kornbloom continued, one would expect that the patterns of blood on the hand and the grip would match. If they didn't, surely Chief Rinucci could see that it indicated that the gun was placed in the deceased's hand later, after the blood had begun to dry.

Well, yes, I supposed I could see that. And the patterns didn't match, is that what Kornbloom was getting at?

Indeed, that was what Kornbloom was getting at. They didn't

come close to matching. He would go into it more thoroughly in his written report. But in the meantime the chief would do well to get started looking for his double-murderer. Statistics showed that every day a homicide went unsolved, the probability of eventual resolution dropped by another twenty percent.

Had the chief been aware of that?

No, the chief hadn't been aware of that, and he didn't much give a damn. My problem wasn't statistics, my problem was that I'd screwed up – royally; like a green kid on his first beat. When Galumbie told me it was murder-suicide, 'A no-two-ways-about-it, open-and-shut case', I'd bought it. I'd known the Haskells hadn't been getting along too well, and what with the findings at the scene . . . Lordy, I muttered at myself as Kornbloom left, would there ever come a time when I would learn, really learn, not to jump to easy conclusions?

I creaked back in my swivel chair, lit one of the *Antonio y Cleopatras* that Myra wouldn't let me smoke at home, and gave myself up to thought.

Who inherits? Henry had said.

Well, I already knew who inherited. Not because of any painstaking investigation, I'm sorry to say, but because I'd happened to run into Ed Massie, the Haskells' lawyer, the day before and I had asked, out of nothing more painstaking than curiosity, to whom they'd left their money.

'It's a little complicated,' Ed had said, 'because they had mutual-beneficiary reciprocal wills, y'see, but the upshot is that Adele's money, of which between you and me there isn't all that much – a million would be pushing it – mostly goes to Grinnell, her old college in Iowa. Now, Stanley's – and here we're talking major numbers; probably fifteen million by the time all's said and done – that goes, kit and caboodle, to his nephew in Kensington. Everything but that golf collection, which goes to a museum.'

'His nephew Monte?'

Ed had nodded. 'Only nephew he had. Sole living blood relative.'

So there it was: the sole individual to profit from the Haskells' deaths was Stanley's nephew Monte. But as a suspect Monte was a dead end. For one thing, he was a prominent commodities trader in the City and very probably even richer than his uncle; as a murderer for profit, he was an unlikely candidate. More significantly, Stanley had recently been diagnosed with an inoperable liver tumor and had been told that he wasn't likely to live more than six months at the outside. Monte knew that as well as anybody else – it wasn't any secret. So why would someone who knew that he was in line to inherit a fortune feel impelled to commit murder – double murder – to speed up the process by six months or so?

In my view that let Monte out, or at least moved him a long way down the list of contenders. But there was someone else, someone right up at the top, and let me tell you, my scalp was crawling at the thought that I'd had him right in my hands and sent him merrily on his way.

At eleven o'clock on the morning of the murders – about two hours after the Haskells had died, according to Galumbie – a couple of bicyclists had seen an old blue pickup truck streak out of the Haskell driveway and roar down Fiske Road. I started a search for it, of course, and the driver turned himself in the next day when he heard we were looking for him. He was a spacey, bearded twenty-six-year-old loner named Clete Lane, who had been in small-time trouble with the law since he was thirteen, beginning with joyriding and then moving on to drunk driving, auto theft, and breaking and entering, for which he'd gotten out of county jail only a few months earlier. He'd been working as a gardener and handyman for the Haskells two or three days a week. His story was that he had reported for work, gone to the house and seen Haskell's bloody body through the den window. He had panicked and fled, assuming that the first thing we would have done would have been to arrest him.

Which it damn well would have been.

But everything he said checked out – where he'd stepped, what he'd touched, what he hadn't touched, what he'd seen and not seen – and I told Sergeant Tustin to let him go. By then Galumbie had presented his open-and-shut case, so what was the point of holding him? Besides, my instincts told me Lane was just a strung-out, essentially harmless pothead, not a vicious double-murderer.

Well, I sure had my doubts about my instincts now. I drove out to the beat-up trailer that Lane lived in near Bailey's Pond, but the place was locked up and deserted, the pickup truck nowhere in sight. Terrific.

But I thought I knew where he might be, or at least I hoped I did. If I remembered right, he usually worked at Haskell's nephew's place in Kensington on Thursdays. So I got back in the car and drove down Beach Highway to Kensington, which is even tonier than Scallop Bay, with ten-foot shrubbery walls hiding the mansions from the eyes of the idle curious. They don't even have street addresses there. Monte's place just has this little sign on the gatepost out front that says 'The Cottage' in Olde English letters. Then you drive in and you find out that The Cottage is a two-year-old, two-storey fieldstone house with something like 12,000 square feet and God knows how many bathrooms.

Monte was home, which wasn't all that unusual with his working hours, and the first thing he did was thank me for all my kindnesses to him regarding his aunt's and uncle's death, and especially for bringing the case to such a rapid conclusion, so that everyone could put this terrible tragedy behind them.

You can imagine how good that made me feel. 'Maybe we better sit down,' I said.

In the oak-floored living room with its twenty-foot-tall, green marble fireplace, with cups of coffee brought to us by an actual maid in an honest-to-God uniform and even one of those little caps, I explained as delicately as I could that the case wasn't exactly closed and that things weren't exactly the way we thought.

'Stanley didn't kill Adele?' he murmured when I'd finished, his round, normally ruddy face pale. His cup shook so much on its saucer that he had to put it down. 'Stanley didn't commit suicide? Somebody *murdered* him?' He put his hand over his eyes. 'Thank God!' The color came back to his face with a rush. 'I mean—'

I smiled. 'I know what you mean.'

'Do you know who did it?'

'We're working on it. Look, Mr Haskell, is Clete Lane around somewhere? I'd like to talk to him.'

'No, he usually doesn't show up for another couple of—' He stared at me. 'It was *Clete*?'

'Well, I just want to—'

'I can't believe it!'

'I didn't say—'

'But Clete's so . . . so timid. I mean, I can't imagine him getting up the nerve to walk into my aunt's bedroom, let alone to . . . to do what he did. It just seems . . .' He spread his hands.

I put my cup and saucer down on the glass-topped end table. 'What makes you think it was in the bedroom?'

The room suddenly seemed very quiet. 'What do you mean?' Monte asked. 'I read it somewhere.'

I shook my head. 'No, you didn't read it anywhere.'

'So where was she killed then? What difference does it make? Oh, the library, I suppose – where he keeps the clubs.'

'No,' I said, 'it was the bedroom, all right.' I stood up and gave him my Sergeant Friday look. 'Sir, I think it'd be a good idea to go down to the station and talk about this some more.'

Monte drew himself up in his chair and glowered at me, his face all hard planes now. He started to say something, changed his mind, clamped his mouth shut, took two slow, raspy breaths, and spoke like the Wall Street veteran he is.

'I want my lawyer there, Rinucci.'

Let me make a long story short. This is supposed to be about Henry Weaver, not about me, although I can see why you might not think so by this time.

Anyway, I had my man, but I wasn't all that proud of myself. I'd gone to Kensington to arrest Clete Lane, not Monte, after all, so I could hardly claim superior detective work when he promptly delivered himself into mine hand, as you might say. Also, I didn't have answers to some pretty important questions: if money was the motive, what was Monte's hurry? Why kill two people instead of just sitting tight for six more months until Stanley made a natural exit? And why kill Adele at all, why not just Stanley? And why go through the risky, complicated folderol of concocting that murder-suicide scenario instead of, say, simply making off with some silver, or a valuable golf club or two, so it looked like an interrupted burglary that blew up into a double murder?

I'm embarrassed to admit it, but Ed Massie had already given me the answers. Remember those mutual-beneficiary reciprocal wills that Stanley and Adele had? What that means, I finally learned, is that the Haskells' immediate heirs were each other. Adele's will left everything to Stanley, and Stanley's left everything except his collection to Adele. Only in the event that the other person was no longer alive would the money go to the college in Adele's case and to Monte in Stanley's.

So: the reason that Monte was in such a hurry was that if he waited for Stanley to kick the bucket on his own, then Adele would have inherited, and goodbye fifteen million bucks as far as Monte was concerned. And I think you can see why Aunt Adele had to go too, right along with Uncle Stanley. If Monte had left her alive, Haskell's fortune would have gone straight into her lap.

As for making Haskell out to be a murderer, in a sense, that *cost* Monte money because the law prohibits a murderer from inheriting from his victim and thus Adele's money was barred from coming to Monte via Stanley. But Monte wasn't interested in his aunt's piddling million or so; he was after his uncle's fortune. So what he absolutely had to demonstrate was that Adele 'predeceased' Haskell, as Ed Massie later put it, so the money would go straight to Monte and not into his aunt's estate.

And what was the surest way to establish it? Obviously (he says now), to make it appear that it was Stanley who killed her.

Simple.

Oh, yes, the point of it all? Why would a rich Wall Street trader be in such dire need of money? It didn't take long to find out. Monte, it seems, had personally poured between ten and twenty million dollars of his firm's money down the drain in some spectacularly bad trading decisions on the European futures market and was desperate to cover the losses before anyone found out. My best guess at this point is that he went to see his uncle to ask for an 'advance' on his inheritance, or maybe a loan, and Haskell wouldn't budge. In anger or panic Monte killed him, then did some fast thinking about mutual-beneficiary reciprocal wills and went upstairs to Adele's bedroom to finish the job.

Let's hope we can prove it in a court of law.

That still left me with one burning question. How the hell did Henry Weaver know about it? Or *did* he know about it?

The next afternoon I found him on the sun-soaked flagstone terrace of the club, at the table he'd shared for so long with Stanley, downing a solitary Martini and abstractedly watching the day's incoming golfers meet their final challenge (or final humiliation) on the sweeping eighteenth green below.

I cleared my throat. 'All right if I sit down?' While Henry might see no problem with barging into my office, scattering my paperwork and plopping uninvited into a chair, he could be pretty touchy about 'his' table.

'Um? What? Oh, Ben.' He gestured at a chair and grunted, which I took as an affirmative.

He tutted as a grim, red-faced woman in plaid Bermudas botched a fifteen-inch putt. Without looking at me he said, 'Here to play some golf, are you?'

'Uh, no, I'm not. Not right now.' Not in my uniform and with a .38 on my hip, I wasn't. Not at the Sea Eagle Golf and Country Club.

'Planning to play in the Jubilee Tournament, though, aren't you?'

'I'm not a member here, Henry.'

'Nonsense. 'Course you are.'

'No, honestly—'

'Sh. Now watch this fellow. Seen him before. Ought to chip to the green, right? Won't do it. Use a wedge, try to pitch it up and on, and wind up in the left bunker. Now you just watch.'

Into the left bunker it went.

'Ha,' said Henry with deep satisfaction, and finally turned to me. Clearly he was in one of his mellower moods. Possibly this was his second Martini. 'Well, if you're not a member, you ought to be. Could use some young blood. Be glad to put you up if you like.'

'Thank you, Henry,' I managed to get out. I began to think that the heart-of-gold people might have something after all. 'And there's something else I have to thank you for.'

He sipped his Martini, watched the action on the green, and listened while I told him about Monte.

'Well, fine,' he said. 'More like it.'

'Henry, I have to ask you something. Did you actually *know* it was Monte?'

He seemed genuinely surprised. 'Now how would I know a thing like that?'

'You told me to start with the inheritance.'

'Well of course. Only makes sense.'

'Did you know about the reciprocal wills?'

'The what?' His attention returned to the green.

'Well, did you . . . was it the gun being in his hand?'

'Gun?' he said. 'Hand? Now look at that putt, did you ever see a thing like that? Time for Wally to put up the clubs, I'd say.'

'Henry,' I said, my voice rising in spite of myself, 'how in the hell did you know that Stanley didn't kill her?'

He turned from the green and gave me his full attention at last, with a probing, earnest look that said he was wondering how in the world I'd ever gotten to be a chief of police.

'*Club* his wife to death?' he cried. 'Stanley Haskell? Are you mad?'

'Well, I know you two were friends, but—'

'Good God, man!' He rose trembling from his chair and stared at me, aghast. '*With an 1854 Hugh Philp hickory-shafted niblick?*'

NEWS, AS IT HAPPENS

DENISE DANKS

The one anchor who had arrived early was three storeys up in the scaffolding tower smoothing down her sharp red suit. Tanned legs set firmly apart, she framed herself against the white, honeycombed structure of the criminal courts building in downtown Los Angeles. Below her open-air studio, the technicians sat in the shade of their satellite trucks, eating boxed lunches that had been delivered courtesy of the networks. It had been a quiet morning at Camp OJ, but it was gone midday now. The tarpaulin roofs sucked in and out with the breeze. The dark sun radiated through the haze. Across the street, tension had begun to rise.

'A lawyer or someone, maybe a juror's gonna come out. They gotta eat like the rest of us,' said someone behind me.

'They didn't come out yesterday. They brought it in,' said another.

There was a hopeful murmur as a group of suits came out of the glass doors below. The news photographers shuffled into a line at the top of the stairwell, just in case. The television cameras owned by the channels were already in position. They had been lined up on their tripods on either side of the stone steps since early morning. Their operators were studying the group too, but they were keeping cool in the shade below. Only their fellow freelancers were squeezing in between the snappers on the hot sidewalk, hustling for a clean shot, a face that would make it for them. The group passed by, untroubled. They were lawyers mostly, but not the right ones.

Someone poked my back and I turned around to see a lanky man in a plaid shirt holding a light meter against my T-shirt.

'I want you two guys and the two down there to white down. This is white. What do you think?' he said.

'It was clean on this morning,' I said.

'What do you think?' he said to the men, who held their cameras like flame-throwers and could be trusted to understand his technical request. One of them, the shorter and more muscular of the two, I found very attractive. He wore sunglasses: Oakley E-wires with socket-shaped lenses that hid his eyes and made him look mean. I had no idea what he had asked, but I recognized a confrontation when I saw one. The unsuspecting man in plaid was plainly in the line of fire. He repeated his request but made the radical mistake of using the wrong tone. The taller of the two cameramen then obliged him with a fast, flowing, confident answer that contained far more numbers than words.

'Way over my head, man. What does that mean?' the man replied, sweeping his hand in low flight above his crisp hairline.

'It *means*, the way we're set up, it won't make a bit of difference,' said the shorter cameraman. He made a movement with his mouth that made it seem as if he was chewing gum, but he wasn't. The man in plaid waited and took a deep, calming breath, thrusting his palms before him like a frustrated artist.

'So what am I running around here doing this for?' he said.

There was no reply unless the big smile that the shorter man gave him, and held a fraction longer than geniality called for, counted. I was about to suggest to the man in plaid that he could make them all white down to those grinning, oh so shiny bright teeth, but I lost my opportunity. There was a scuffling of chairs down below and he was gone, swept away by the rush of bodies and bobbing microphones that surged down the stone steps towards a single door that had opened at the far end of the building. I followed and stepped over him on my way down.

As it happens, it was a false alarm, a disappointing non-event. A nobody, a juror rejected from another case, had ambled out into the air, blinking at the sunlight and flashbulbs like a recently awakened marmoset. The cameramen and news teams hustled back to their positions. The man in the plaid shirt hobbled around in a haphazard circle looking down on the ground around him for his light meter, and cursed as passing feet crushed his fingers and toes. The cameraman with the E-wires and the wonderful teeth stood up on the top step looking down at the glass doors. There really was nothing doing.

I'd picked a mediocre day for sightseeing. I'd spent the morning snapping cops and traders and news teams but no real celebrities, no Shapiro, no Cochran, no Clark. I hadn't expected OJ. OJ would go in the back way, if he was there at all. I'd have been satisfied with a juror though, as would everyone else. I did buy an essential commemorative T-shirt from Mr Disaster Wear. He had the appearance of an entrepreneurial beach boy and sold slogans in blood-red and bone-white lettering that cried out: Don't Squeeze the Juice, Dateline OJ Simpson 1994 Trial, OJ Guilty or Not?

'I do quakes, fires, hey, even floods but not admitted killers. The Menendez Brothers? No way. Charles Manson? No way. Forget it,' he told me, emphasizing his business ethics while taking my fifteen dollars. 'I got the Heidi Fleiss case coming up soon, but with OJ on at the same time, I don't know about her, without him on every day, she would have been a big draw.' He shrugged as people in the risk business do.

'Stress biz,' he said.

'For sure,' I replied and walked away. I'd been happy to part with my money. It was a good deal for a high-quality, black all-cotton button-through shirt that depicted the entire story of the alleged murder right through to the trial, and featured all the participants on the back, including beautiful Nicole and the hapless Goldman. The hat man twenty feet away wanted forty dollars for a gaudy sequin-encrusted 'OJ is Innocent' baseball cap. It wasn't good value. He wouldn't even let me photograph his hideous life-size cut-out of OJ wearing it unless I paid him ten dollars. I declined, that and his invitation to a party for the courthouse street traders at the Comedy Store that evening.

As for the 'OJ Juror Reject' button from an old boy on the corner, I didn't fancy that at any price. He told me he was retired and lived between Hope and Sinatra in Palm Springs. He earned 200 dollars a day and saved his CIA pension. As an alternative to the Juror Reject button, he offered me a 'Screw Baseball League 1995 for

What They Did in 1994' button, which he said was the Next Big Thing. I wasn't investing in baseball, I said, and he let me take his photograph without charge.

When the working crowd settled down, it was quiet again but for the faithful shuffle of a frowning Christian who held up a scrapbook depicting Christ's agonizing journey to the Cross. *Cristo El Rey! Viene Ya*, his poster cried out. I took a photograph of him for free too.

'Can I take a picture of you?' I said, turning to the cameraman. He pretended he hadn't heard, so I persisted as politely as I could.

'Excuse me.'

I pointed my autofocusing Olympus at him and took two snaps.

'Why're you taking photographs?' he asked.

'I'm on holiday.'

'You been to Disneyland?'

'Of course.'

'What about Universal Studios?'

'I'm saving that for later.'

'Don't miss it. It's very cool.'

'So, what do you think?'

'About what?'

'Did he do it?'

'OJ? Hey, I don't know, lady. I wasn't there.'

'You must have an opinion.'

'I must?'

'Yes.'

'Well I don't . . . have an opinion.'

'Neither do I. In fact, I don't really know what the fuss is about.'

The cameraman turned his mean sunglasses my way.

'You're English, right?'

'I am.'

'Let me explain,' he said pointing at the courthouse. 'This is a world event. Inside there is possibly the greatest footballer in the world, and he stands accused of murdering his wife. That's big news in any language. Even your English.'

'He's not the greatest footballer in the world.'

'OK, he comes close.'

'He's not even a proper footballer.'

'You don't think OJ Simpson is a proper footballer?'

196

He was being sarcastic.

'Maradona is a proper footballer.'

'The soccer player you're talking about? That loser? We had him here for the World Cup. Guy took drugs.'

'He didn't kill his wife, not even allegedly, and he was one of the greatest players in the world, ever. Everyone but the Americans knows that,' I said. 'Now, if you had, OK, let's say Pele, in there, the whole world would be here. That's if the Brazilians would let you take him, of course. That would be a truly international emotionally charged news event,' I said, waving my arm towards the cameras and the traders, 'not merely a business opportunity in LA.'

We stood in silence for ten minutes. We watched the cafeteria windows for signs. Sometimes the attorneys would eat there, but everyone felt the situation was hopeless. There was going to be no action that day.

'You going to be here a while?' the cameraman said, turning to me.

'I was going to get something to eat now,' I replied.

'I have to go to my truck. Could you watch my camera?'

I thought about it for a moment. I was in no hurry.

'Sure,' I said.

I watched him go. Broad shoulders, nice broad shoulders that I liked, and an easy walk. He would have to be strong to lift the twenty-three-pound Sony Betacam and run with it, up flights of stairs, anywhere. I wasn't strong at all. I tried to lift the thing and couldn't easily, so I leaned against the wall in the shade until the Latino came up beside me and stuck a gun in my ribs.

There was a cop twenty feet away but he didn't notice. He had his hands full controlling the crowd of news professionals and lunch-time rubbernecks on the steps and sidewalks around the courthouse. The Latino was my problem. I couldn't let him just walk with it, without saying anything, without some protest. My hair was on end. I was afraid, but I found the words to point out that the camera did not belong to him and that I was looking after it for the person to whom it did belong.

The Latino was short and chunky, with dark, darting eyes that faced mine once as he said '*No hablo inglés*,' and hoisted up the camera, taking it briskly up the hill, past the cop, the news crews and the souvenir hunters until he turned the corner, out of sight. I looked about, speechless at the simple expediency with which the crime had taken place. Everyone looking for incident had been watching the courthouse. They had all been present at the scene of a crime but not one knew it. Not one had recorded it. No one but me knew what had happened. The Latino had stuck a gun in my ribs and I now stood open-mouthed, looking hither and thither for some reassurance. I thought that perhaps I should leave too, but if I did, I'd be like the man in the white Ford Bronco, a fugitive from justice. The cameraman would give the police my description. I was a tourist so I'd be easy to find. I was perspiring with the heat and aggravation. If I had had a cigarette I would have smoked it. I leaned against the wall and waited, until the cameraman, who no longer had a camera, crossed the street and walked up the slight incline towards me. He was holding a large brown paper bag.

'I got some juice, OJ of course, ha, ha, and a choice, pastrami or cheese and salad. You get first pick.'

I took the pastrami and bit into it. He looked down at my feet.

'Where's my camera?'

I swallowed.

'Some guy came by and picked it up,' I said.

'Some guy came by and picked it up? Are you nuts?'

'A Latino,' I said, taking another bite.

The cameraman had one hand on his hip and the other was pinching the bridge of his nose under the glasses, which bobbled up and down as he massaged the tension that was building in his brow.

'Were you, uh, distracted?' he asked. He didn't raise his voice at all. He was calm and reasonable but the sunglasses that disguised his eyes and made them look mean gave a more accurate impression of his feelings.

'A bit,' I replied.

'What distracted you?'

'The gun he was pointing at me. That distracted me initially, and then when I pointed out that the camera was not his, the fact that he didn't speak English.'

'He didn't speak English.'

'He spoke Spanish. He said *"No hablo inglés."* I understood that.'

I drank some juice and rested the paper cup on the wall while I finished my sandwich. My companion did not appear to be hungry in the least. As I wiped my mouth he looked at the ground and shook his head before dropping the brown paper carton to his foot and drop-kicking it high into the air. The cheese sandwich and the OJ didn't leave the arcing bag until it hit the sidewalk thirty feet away. They have laws for most things in America and at that moment I was sure there was a law against that. A cop started towards us.

'You did nothing?'

'He had a gun.'

'Fifty thousand dollars' worth of equipment and you did nothing?'

'Be reasonable, please, what would you have done?'

The cop was a Latino too, in an impossibly tight uniform festooned with terrifying weaponry and communications technology. He asked the cameraman sans camera what he thought he was doing. He called him sir. The cameraman told him what had happened and pointed out, not unreasonably in my opinion, that the policeman had got over real quick for a suspected case of littering but where the fuck had he been when a 50,000-dollar piece of equipment took a walk. The cop said that, in *his* opinion, the cameraman had a bad attitude problem and that his advice to him *right now* was to chill and watch his mouth. There was a shout before the cameraman could reply. The press corps had begun to move down the steps towards whoever was leaving the building flanked by their attorneys. The cop told us to wait exactly where we were and hurried in the direction of everyone else.

'Shit, shit, shit,' the cameraman said as we watched the action around the first OJ trial juror reject of the day.

'I did do something,' I replied when I'd finished snapping the mêlée around the juror. The cameraman turned to me.

'What? What did you do?'

'I took a photograph,' I said.

The dark lozenges of glass that had reflected my image caught the sunshine and flashed like a bulb. After a few seconds they turned away as he looked up the street.

'Do you know where the camera is right now?' he said drily, still not looking at me. I said I had no idea.

'It's on its way to Mexico. Everything gets down there one way or another. Most of the cars that get stolen in this state end up down there. Sometimes they don't even change the plates because the authorities don't care. Hell, the Mexican *police*'ll buy a stolen four-wheel-drive off-road vehicle and won't bother to change the plates. The police drive around in stolen cars, can you believe it? Cars that belong to American citizens.'

'Unbelievable,' I said.

He looked at me sharply, perhaps hoping to measure the sincerity quotient by the look on my face.

'Maybe we should give the police what we've got,' I suggested. 'The man's mug shot might be in their records.'

Other cameramen were beginning to notice my companion's plight. Some commiserated in the best way they knew how.

'Hey man, guy at KTVK-TV got suspended because his camera got stolen. We're going to have to chain the equipment up,' was one contribution.

'Man, I never leave mine, take it to the can with me. Seen a guy throw dollars on to the floor to distract people so he could take a camera. Never leave it. No way, man,' was another.

My friend gritted his wonderful teeth.

'Will you lose your job?' I whispered.

'Already did. I'm freelance,' he replied, 'I got to get back to the rental company and break the news.'

I did feel sorry for him.

'Are you insured?'

'Sure. Can you give me the film?' he said.

I thought about it.

'All my snaps are on it, and the film isn't finished.'

'My camera cost fifty thousand.'

'I still want my snaps. I want my snap of him especially. I'll give you a duplicate, how about that?'

'OK, come with me, I know a quick turnaround place.'

We walked up the hill away from the courthouse.

I pointed to a tall building like the Empire State with a sunny beach scene four-square under the Doric columns of the upper levels.

'That looks familiar,' I said.

'*LA Law*,' said my companion, who was hurrying me along.

We walked briskly past a parking lot. The metal bonnets reflected

200

the sun and the windscreens the blue sky and its insubstantial clouds.

'Can I come with you to the police?' I asked.

'You'll have to.'

'Good. I was going to go up to the house, but I can do that tomorrow.'

'Whose house?'

'OJ's.'

'My, you're a real tourist, aren't you?'

I had the feeling he didn't approve.

'Where are you parked?' he asked.

I pointed a couple of blocks south. He said it was nearer than his pickup and we should go to my car.

'So, is the rental company insured or are you?'

'I take out insurance when I rent it. I'm OK,' he said, moving quickly again. I found myself sprinting after him, my face red with exertion.

'So who buys them in Mexico?' I said, panting behind him.

'Huh?'

'Who buys the cameras?'

'I don't know. Porno rings buy them here.'

'So it could still be in town.'

'What?'

'Not in Mexico.'

'Right.'

'Do they ever try to sell them back?'

'What?'

'To the rental company. Where do rental companies buy the cameras?'

'The manufacturers. Distributors.'

'Yes, but what if this guy tries to sell it back to a rental company? The rental firms should have copies of his photo too. If he sells it to anyone, how much do you think he'll get?'

He walked on ahead until I asked him to stop for a moment. The sun was burning my back through my T-shirt and I had to look around and get my bearings. I took a few deep breaths to control my shallow breathing. Driving everywhere that's more than ten yards away in an air-conditioned car does not improve a body's stamina. The parking lot was behind the justice department and Camp OJ. I could see then that it would have been easier to go down the hill and cut through under the scaffolding studios and past the satellite trucks. I wondered why he'd taken me this way. I shaded my eyes from the sun to be sure I'd picked the right lot and saw the Latino. He was pulling out from a meter bay in a Ford Blazer four-wheel drive.

'That's him,' I said excitedly, memorizing the number and digging in my bag of souvenirs for a pen and some paper. I found a postcard of Laguna Beach and wrote the number down on the back. The cameraman took the card from me, indifferently. Now he seemed chatty.

'You staying here, in Laguna?'

I replied that I was.

'It's all fagged out down there.'

I didn't understand.

'Gays.'

'There is a lot of beach volleyball,' I said, not knowing quite what I was expected to say. In the distance I could see the Ford Blazer doing a U-turn in the street. The cameraman saw that I had seen it and became as tense as I was.

'What's going on?' I said. 'We've got to get out of the way? What does he want?'

'Give me the camera quickly,' he replied. I handed it over as the Blazer pulled up beside us. The cameraman stepped to one side. The Latino stared at him and then pointed his gun directly and unimpeded at me. He wasn't as close as before but this time he fired. I saw the flash and felt the blow like a tremendous punch to the body. I didn't feel myself fly or fall but I was on the ground looking up at blue sky and the poisonous sun burning through the yellow haze like a small black ball of treacle. The cameraman's head blocked the sunlight and shaded my face. His sunglasses stared down at me, his eyes blanked by the mean lenses of his thin wired Oakleys. I don't think it was pain I was feeling more than an overwhelming lack of trust. He had insurance. He had my camera.

Somebody else's face leaned over me, a black face full of concern, then another and another until I couldn't see the cameraman any more and I panicked that he might have gone. I felt the hand of the Latino cop and heard him talking to the emergency services. There was a microphone bobbing above us and a television camera pushing its lens between the shoulders of the crowd of faces. I could see myself lying on the sidewalk in the rainbow glass, my face swollen and elongated at one and the same time, as if I was looking into the base of a silver spoon.

'A camera got stolen,' I whispered to the policeman.

'Yeah, I know ma'am, don't worry about that now,' he said, holding my white hand in his cool brown one.

'I took photos with mine.' My lips were dry, my tongue thick as a cotton gag.

'Your camera was stolen, OK ma'am. You got ID?'

'They stole her camera,' someone shouted.

'Man, they shot her for her camera?'

'Says something for this country, don't it?'

I was dying. I could feel the sun but my body was growing colder than the Pacific. Last night, I'd watched children hunting sand crabs as the evening sun dissolved into that vast calm ocean while I ate fried oysters and drank salty Margueritas with crushed ice.

'Insurance,' I said.

'You got insurance. That's good. Take it easy now.'

'Insurance cover lets you split the profit of the sale,' I tried to say.

The siren cry of an ambulance grew louder and all the faces but that of the cameras cleared away.

'Hey, at least we got something today,' I heard someone say.

ALBERT'S LIST

MICHAEL Z. LEWIN

At the end of Called by a Panther *my Indianapolis private eye, Albert Samson, was in jail. Although he could envision a scenario which would get him out, he wasn't at all sure that he wanted to return to being a not-very-successful private eye.*

One scene in my next book, Underdog, *moved his story along. It took place in Posie Samson's luncheonette. Posie is Albert's mother, and the scene confirmed for faithful readers that their faithless author had sprung Samson from jail, although his PI license had been suspended. As to his future, well, Posie was worried.*

'Albert's List' is the first short story Albert Samson has appeared in. It may be taken to give a significant clue as to whether there will be another Samson novel, one day.

I want also to acknowledge the sources of the two jokes which are told in the story. I got them from Jim Maley, and from Marcel Berlins' 'Writ Large' column in the Guardian. *Jim is an Indianapolis politician, and as such would obviously never cause a body a moment's grief, but Marcel is a lawyer, so must be treated with with all due care and respect.*

MZL
Somerset
April 1995

'I'm worried about your father,' Posie Samson said. 'Don't forget the table behind the pinball machine, hon.'

'I have it, Grandma,' Sam said. She added two chili bowls to her tray of dirty dishes, complete with spoons and saltine cellophanes.

As Sam carried the tray behind the luncheonette's counter Posie said, 'I'm worried about him, Sam. I really am.'

Norman, Posie's tattooed griddle man, said, 'What's to worry, Mrs S.?'

'Well, for one thing, he's drinking,' Posie said.

'Daddy's always kept a bottle in his desk,' Sam said.

'That doesn't signify, hon,' Posie said. 'That's something he thinks a private detective should do, you know? But anymore he takes a drink most every day.'

'He's not a private detective now,' Norman said.

'Just get on with those soiled dishes, Norman,' Posie said.

It was Sam who replied to Norman's baiting. 'Daddy's licence is only suspended,' she said. 'He's bound to get it back.'

'Sure he is,' Norman said. He smiled and began to load the dishwasher.

'He *is*,' Sam said.

'What I'm worried about,' Posie said as she wiped the countertop, 'is that my Albert may not want his licence back.'

'Why wouldn't he, Grandma?' Sam said.

'I don't hardly ever know what's in that boy's mind nowadays,' Posie said, 'but I did find something that makes me wonder.'

'What did you find?' Sam said. 'Shall I sweep now?'

'Are the ashtrays done?'

'Yes.'

'And the sugar?'

'I refilled all the shakers while you had your afternoon rest,' Sam said.

'Then the floor's about all that's left now, hon. Thanks.'

Sam took the broom. 'No need to thank me, Grandma. It's what I'm here for.'

Norman caught Sam's eye. He winked, expecting her to smile back. But she didn't.

'Albert's been moping so much anymore,' Posie said. She shook her head. 'I so wish he'd get out more, and do things. If only Adele could find more time for him.' Adele was Albert's long-time woman friend.

'I do know that Adele's been very busy,' Sam said, though she was also aware that a moping Albert was not the best company for a busy social worker. 'And he is out now, isn't he?'

'Only because I gave him a list of shopping to do.'

'What was it that you found, Grandma?'

'When he went out,' Posie said, 'I stopped in his room to tidy things up.'

'Once a mother,' Norman said.

'And I found a list,' Posie said.

'What kind of list?' Sam said.

'Well, I'm not quite sure, hon,' Posie said.

'Do you have it? May I see?' Sam said.

'Oh, I didn't take it off the table,' Posie said. 'I couldn't do that.'

'So it's still in his room?' Sam said.

'It is,' Posie said. 'What time is our shooting lesson today, Norman?

'Same as usual, Mrs S.,' Norman said.

'Oh well, we can be a little late for once,' Posie said.

As Sam followed her grandmother to the stairs which led to the residential part of the building, she handed Norman the broom. 'Make yourself useful,' she said.

'It's on the table,' Posie said. She pointed to a notepad among papers on a card table that stood by the window that overlooked Virginia Avenue.

Sam studied the list without touching anything. It read, 'Gas jockey, hack driver, basketball coach, short-order cook, surgeon, priest, architect, lawyer.' The word 'lawyer' was underlined.

Posie said, 'I don't know what to make of it, hon. One or two are maybe things he thinks he could do. I mean, even Albert could pump gas, and he could probably drive a cab.'

Sam studied the list again. 'Surgeon? Priest? Architect? Lawyer?'

'Maybe he's thinking about going back to school. He never wanted to drop out of college, you know. He only quit because his dad died.'

'But Grandma,' Sam said, 'that was so long ago.'

'Or it could be they're things what he thinks is a joke,' Posie said.

'Basketball coach?'

'He used to shoot baskets in the park until that time he got stabbed,' Posie said. 'Oh, I do so wish I could convince that boy to carry a gun. I hate to say it, hon, but your father's always been a bullhead.'

'But Daddy couldn't coach basketball, could he?'

'He might think he could.'

Sam looked at the list again. 'Short-order cook?'

Posie said, 'Maybe he thinks I'd give him a job. Or maybe he thinks he could get work at the Tugboat by giving them my secret recipes. But either way, hon, what you don't see on that list is "private detective".'

While Posie was at the shooting range, Sam tried Adele's number.

'Hello?' Adele said cautiously.

'It's Sam.'

'Thank God for that. I was afraid it was my boss with another loose end to be tied. I would have let the machine take it, but then I thought it might be your father and these days he hangs up rather than talk to "a contraption".'

'It's Daddy I'm calling about,' Sam said. 'Grandma and I are worried about him.'

'He doesn't seem himself,' Adele said.

'Could we meet?'

The women met for a meal at Turk's. Sam recited Albert's list.

Adele said, 'At least he's abandoned the idea of fixing up old houses to sell.'

'Was he going to do that?'

'It's all he talked about when they first took his licence away. But it would have been a disaster. If he ever had started on a house, he'd have lost interest halfway through because he was planning what he'd do on the next one.'

'But you are worried about him,' Sam said.

'Of course,' Adele said. 'Heavens, the very idea of Albert not being a private detective . . .'

'It's absurd, isn't it?' Sam said.

'It's unthinkable. I mean, what else could he do? I'm not saying that he's too old to learn new things,' Adele said, 'except maybe for the piano or how to juggle. But Albert . . . A taxi driver? A cook? No, no. A list like that is a cry for help.'

*　　*　　*

The following morning Sam came down to help Posie during the breakfast rush.

'You're up and about early today, hon,' Posie said.

'I had dinner with Adele last night,' Sam said. 'She's worried about Daddy too, so we came up with a plan.'

A man at the counter said, 'How's about coming up with my flapjacks?'

'We'll talk later, hon,' Posie said.

The luncheonette cleared entirely by a quarter past nine, leaving just Sam and Posie and a lot of dirty dishes. Norman was not due until noon.

The two women loaded the dishwasher and then sat down to talk. But no sooner did they pour two cups of coffee and each choose a pastry, than a short man in his thirties slipped in the door carrying a sleeping bag under one arm and an accordion file under the other. He was clean but rumpled, and his jacket matched neither his trousers nor his sweater. He wore old Air Jordans.

Posie rose. 'Why hello, Mr Moro. Long time no see. How's things with you?'

'Oh fine, just fine, Mrs Samson. I find it pays to look on the side of optimism, because when you're in business, you never do know but when things might be about to pick up.'

'That sure is true,' Posie said.

'And I always know it's a good day when I can have one of your Breakfast Specials, if I'm not too late.'

'One Special coming up.' Sam began to rise, but Posie said 'Stay where you are, Sam.'

Mr Moro said, 'Is it OK if I use the washroom?'

'Feel free,' Posie said.

The small man left his sleeping bag by a table but he carried his file into the restroom.

'Who is *that?*' Sam asked.

'He comes in when when he's on this side of town and when he can afford a meal,' Posie said. 'And he's a nice young feller. Sometimes he even gathers up dishes for me. But you were saying about Adele.'

Sam described the meal with her father's friend. By the time she was getting to the conclusion of her story, a freshly scrubbed Mr

Moro was tucking into his Breakfast Special and she and Posie were again sipping coffee.

'The thing is,' Sam said, 'Adele had this idea for something we could do, but she doesn't know if we ought to try to interfere.'

'I'd do anything to cheer him up,' Posie said. 'Just look at the time.' They looked at the time, which was after ten. 'He's still in bed. Now that can't be right for a grown man.'

'Well if we want her to, Adele will call this friend of hers,' Sam said. 'But she didn't want to take the responsibility all by herself.'

'The responsibility for what?' a voice from the passage to the house said. The women – and Mr Moro – turned and watched as a sleepy Albert Samson scratched himself and walked into the luncheonette.

Posie said, 'We were just saying how the trouble in this world can mostly all be laid down to folks not taking responsibility nowadays. Don't you think, son?'

Albert yawned. 'I think . . .' he began, but he couldn't think of anything to think.

'Good morning Daddy,' Sam said.

'Morning.' Albert went to the pinball machine and put in some quarters.

'Do you want breakfast, son?'

'I'll get something later. Don't mind me.'

'How's about you, Mr Moro? Some more toast?' Posie said. 'It's not extra.'

'Yes please,' Mr Moro said. 'And some coffee, if you don't mind.'

When Posie brought him the toast and coffee Mr Moro said, 'You know, Mrs Samson, what you were saying earlier to the young woman put me in mind of something a guy told me in a bar one time.'

'It did?' Posie said.

'This guy was real hard up, so he got down on his knees to pray. "Lord," he said, "I have lost my job and can't pay for my wife to have the operation that will save her eyesight. And, Lord, my poor old father needs a new hip, and my sister's house went and burned down and she didn't have no insurance because her no-account husband ran off with the payment. Lord, I ain't never asked you for nothing before but, Lord, could you see your way clear, just this one time, to letting me win the Lotto? There's all kinds as win

210

that Lotto, Lord, and some of them is sinners and some is even unbelievers. It's not for me, Lord, but if you let me win this one time, I promise that I won't never ask you for nothing again. So please, Lord, the Lotto. Please."'

'What happened?' Posie asked.

'Well everything around the guy goes unnatural quiet, and then just as sudden the wind comes up and about tears all the leaves off the trees. And then this almighty voice from on high says, "For Christ's sake, at least buy a ticket!"'

Posie and Sam exchanged smiles. From the pinball machine Albert laughed loudly.

Mr Moro said, 'The reason I'm telling you the story is that I think it has a lesson in it for us all, including about what you and the young woman was talking about.'

'And what lesson might that be, Mr Moro?' Posie asked.

'You can't win if you don't play,' Mr Moro said. 'Do you see what I mean?'

'I believe I do,' Posie said. She nodded to Sam, who rose and went upstairs to call Adele, even though there was a perfectly good telephone behind the counter.

Albert played out his money and then poured himself a large glass of orange juice. 'Was there any mail for me?' he asked.

'Not today, son,' Posie said.

He cut a slice of pumpkin pie and was about to take his breakfast upstairs to his room when Sam reappeared. 'Did Grandma remember to tell you, Daddy? There was a call for you.'

'Who from?' Albert asked.

'A lawyer,' Sam said. 'He wants you to call him. He wants to hire you for something.'

'Hire me?'

'That's what he said.'

'Did you give him Bobbie Lee's number? Or some other PI with a licence?'

'He knows about your licence, Daddy,' Sam said, 'but it's still you he wants.'

'What for?' Albert asked.

'It's researching something. He said researching wasn't investigating so it wouldn't matter if you don't have a licence. And he is a lawyer. He ought to know.'

'Probably thinks it would make me cheaper,' Albert said. 'Huh. And he's not wrong.'

'I wrote the number down, Daddy,' Sam said. She brandished a slip of paper.

'Did you know,' Albert said, 'that lawyers don't cast shadows?' Nevertheless he allowed Sam to put the slip of paper in his shirt pocket as he carried his plate and his glass upstairs.

When she was sure her father was out of earshot, a beaming Sam came into the middle of the luncheonette, punched the air and said, 'Yes!'

As the lunch-time rush was beginning, Albert reappeared. He was on his way out. He was dressed in a suit. He even wore a tie, although the top button of his shirt was undone.

From the griddle Norman called, 'How you doing, Mr S.?'

'Dynamite,' Albert said.

Posie was at a table taking an order and Sam was making change at the cash register.

'Any news about your licence, Mr S.?' Norman called. 'You ever going to get it back, or what?'

'Or what,' Albert said.

'Where are you off to, Daddy?' Sam asked.

'To see a man about a job,' Albert said. He left the luncheonette without saying goodbye to Norman.

Posie did not go for a rest in the afternoon, even though by three the luncheonette had no customers. Norman invited Sam to come for a walk, but she declined. Norman didn't understand it, but he didn't try very hard.

Albert returned at about a quarter to four. He had a big smile on his face.

'Well, Daddy?' Sam said.

'Very well, thank you,' Albert said. He went straight to the pinball machine and fed it some quarters.

'How did it go, son?' Posie said.

'Splendidly,' Albert said. He put the first ball into play. 'I was given a very expensive lunch.'

Norman shook his head. 'What's been happening, Mr S.?'

'I was taken to lunch by a litigator – that's a kind of lawyer,

Norman. And this litigator offered me some work, not knowing that my true calling is as a pinball wizard who aspires to become a pinball warlock.' The pinball machine awarded Albert an extra game.

Norman looked from Sam to Posie. Both were smiling, but he obtained no clues. 'Well, that's great,' he said.

'Yes,' Albert said, 'and no.'

Sam heard something in her father's voice which made her uneasy. 'Daddy, tell us what happened.'

'It was much as you said,' Albert said as he played. 'This litigator litigates, and he has a long list of jurors he wants to know things about before it comes time for jury selection. He thinks I would be good at doing such research. He wants to employ me. He suggested that I try it for a month, and longer if it works out.'

'Why that's fine, son,' Posie said.

'Yes and no,' Albert said.

'Why "no", Daddy?' Sam asked, unable to wait the game out at her father's rhythm.

Albert paused as he played a particularly difficult ball. 'Hah!' he said, and won another game. 'No,' he said, 'because I turned him down.'

'You what?' Sam said.

'Well, first I told him a story about a lawyer. I've been having a lot to do with lawyers lately, what with my licence and all,' Albert said. 'I've got lawyers on the brain.'

'What story?' Sam said.

'You see, there was a surgeon, a priest, an architect and a lawyer and they were all at sea, sailing in a boat. And the boat capsized in shark-infested waters. Three of them were immediately attacked and eaten. But the lawyer was left alive and unharmed. Do you want to know why?'

'I want to know why you turned the job down,' Sam said.

'Mom,' Albert said, 'do you want to know why the sharks didn't eat the lawyer?'

'Why?' Posie asked.

'Out of professional courtesy,' Albert said.

Posie smiled. Sam frowned. Norman laughed.

'Why thank you, Norman,' Albert said.

Sam said, 'But you do a lot of work for lawyers, Daddy.'

'I used to,' Albert said, 'but never . . .' and then he paused to play a ball. 'But never to do something as slimy and diseased as to try to win a trial by getting a jury composed entirely of people who cross-dress, or people who pray to a plastic Jesus, or people who hate Mexicans. It's foul work, vile work, and I won't do it, and I told him so, and I told him why, and I told him loud enough that everyone in the restaurant could hear.'

Sam's shoulders slumped. Norman looked around, trying to understand what was happening.

Posie said, 'You said, "Yes and no", about the job offer being a good thing, son. We've heard the "no". What was the "yes"?'

Albert turned away from the pinball machine. He said, 'Having my licence suspended has been real hard for me, Mom. I've tried not to show it, but it shook me up. It's really made me think about what I've done with my life. What I've made of it, or not made of it. It's made me think about what I ought to do from here on.'

'I know it's been hard, son,' Posie said.

'But talking to this goddamn lawyer sorted a lot of things out. I loved talking to him, Mom. I loved telling him what he could do with his sushi and his crêpes. I realized that I could never handle any job where I'm not free to make my own mind up about what's right and what's wrong. I'm dying to get my licence back, Mom. I can't wait. There's nothing in the world I want so much as to become a private detective again.'

Albert kicked the pinball machine. It registered 'tilt'. 'Except,' he said, 'to get out of this goddamn suit and tie.' He left the room and went upstairs.

A RED CABRIOLET

ALEX KEEGAN

The hottest day of the year. I was out on the garage forecourt taking in the sun when I saw her. She was walking down from the town centre, tall, good-looking, a positive, long stride, slim, dressed like a professional.

We had the 318i cabriolet out front for show, a gleaming fire-engine red. I saw her step falter when she saw it, just the faintest check; she couldn't help. Instantly I thought 'Eh up, Ron, we could be in there.' As she came by I looked up and said 'Brilliant day!' half looking at her, half at the car. She gave me a tiny smile but kept walking.

'I should be out on the moors with Betsy.'

She stopped. 'I'm sorry?'

'The BMW,' I said. 'Weather like this, I should be out on the moors, cruising, the top down, music on the stereo . . .'

'But you're working.'

'I could be taking someone on a test drive.'

She looked at me, the car, me, the tiniest flicker of amusement somewhere in there. 'Not my sort of thing, I think,' she said. She went to move on.

'You really don't like it?'

'No,' she said. 'Definitely not.'

'Why's that then?' I said. She got talking.

'Too flash. It's a man's car. A boy racer.'

I grinned. 'Not many boy racers have got twenty-eight thou!'

'Ouch!' she said.

I told her, 'Quality costs.'

'You *do* surprise me!' she snapped back. There was an edge, but she was still there.

'You don't fancy a ride then?' I said.

'No.'

My suit jacket was on the back of a chair in my office but I was still reasonably presentable, white shirt, blue and pink striped tie. I was feeling the heat and I'd undone my collar button.

'My name is Ron Trier,' I said hopefully, standing, adjusting my tie. 'You don't fancy a cold drink, take a look at Betsy?'

She shrugged.

'Great!' I said.

I waved towards the car. As we walked across I said my name again.

'I heard you the first time,' she said coldly. I leaned my head a little to the side. She stared at me. I gestured with open hands.

She gave in. 'Virginia Cole,' she said firmly. Then she added, 'Mrs.'

I held out my hand. 'Mrs Cole . . .'

Virginia reached out and placed four fingers delicately into my meaty hand. I felt slightly awkward and held her hand a second too long.

'You can let go now,' she said.

We were by the car. I suggested she got in. I opened the door and she swished in demurely and sat like all punters do, hands on the steering wheel, moving between ten to two and twenty to four. She liked it, I was certain. 'Cash or credit?' I said, making sure there was a hint of a laugh in my voice.

'Don't be so presumptuous!' Virginia said. 'I've already told you, it's not my type of car.'

I smiled and said I was sorry. She could see the rest of our range when we'd finished with the cabriolet, if she had the time. It was her lunch-break, she said. She didn't mind looking if I didn't mind wasting my time. But she was definitely *not* in the market for a car, *any* car.

I told Virginia that the cabriolet had a top speed of a hundred and thirty miles an hour.

Virginia told me that its maximum speed was irrelevant with a statutory seventy-mile-an-hour limit.

What about travelling on the Continent, I asked.

She said she never would.

I said OK, and then I said the car could do 0–60 in 8.5 seconds. She said she didn't need that kind of acceleration. What was the point?

I said that fast acceleration was useful for overtaking and for getting out quickly at junctions. She said she was a very patient woman and that I sounded too pent up. *She* wouldn't need all that power.

Yes, she said, the car *did* look nice, but she'd seen better. Yes, it was comfortable, but only averagely so. She admitted that she liked the dashboard layout. For a second I thought I'd chalked up a little victory, but then she said that for twenty-eight thousand, the dashboard ought to talk! 'It does,' I said.

The sun was high and burning down on to my back. I suggested it was time for that cold drink. It was cooler inside.

'OK,' Virginia said, 'as long as you understand that I am not a buyer.'

I smiled. 'I'm not busy. But if I have to be here, I might as well keep my hand in.'

We went inside and through to my office. I gave Virginia a couple of brochures and nipped off to get the drinks. When I came back I thought she'd unwound slightly – nothing specific, just some body language thing, something about the way she was sitting. I still wasn't convinced I couldn't sell her *something*.

By way of conversation, I asked Virginia if she worked in town. She said she worked near the civic centre. I was gently ferreting, so I explained that my sales manager was a lady. Was she perhaps in . . . ?

'Sales?' she said quickly. 'I'm afraid not.' She was laughing at me. 'You're not even warm.'

'I didn't think so,' I said. 'The way you dress and the positive way you stand, I'd've thought a position of power. Maybe you run a company?'

'No,' she said flatly.

'Tell me you're not from the VAT!' I said.

'I'm not from the VAT.'

I wiped my brow. 'Oh, that's all right, then!'

We were drinking iced lemon-barley water. I told Virginia there were two coffees coming. I was desperate for caffeine, I said, would she like one? She nodded. While we were drinking the coffees, I tried again. Wasn't she even a *little* bit interested in a new car?

'I'm interested, Ron, if that means would I like a new car.' She spoke firmly now. 'But I am *not* ready to purchase anything now, nor will I be in the near future. I think you will agree that I have already made that abundantly clear.'

'I thought, perhaps with the budget coming up—'

'I am aware of what might happen, but this is not the right time.'

'And with the price-rise on BMWs next month—'

'I know about that too, but as I said—'

This time *I* interrupted, giving in. 'OK, OK, no more selling, I promise! I try too hard, I know. Even my name is Trier. You win. D'you fancy a spin in the fire engine as some sort of apology?'

She asked did I mean the red cabriolet? I said yes. She sipped her coffee and looked away, thinking. Then she said she wouldn't mind, and thank you. We went back out to the car. As we left, the sun hit us full in the face. It was glorious.

I told Virginia I'd drive the car out of town and that she could drive it once we were in open countryside. She simply nodded, and I opened her door. She slipped quickly into her seat and was buckled up before I'd walked round to the other side. As I slipped in beside her, she brushed lightly at her lap.

I drove down Kingsway and filtered on to the roundabout without a pause. I'm a fairly careful driver and was keeping my eye on the road, but I just caught a sideways glimpse of Virginia loosening her dark brown hair and letting it fall back. We were doing about thirty and it fluttered faintly in the breeze. Then she seemed to ease in her seat and her hips moved forward slightly. I think I probably smiled, but I doubt she saw me. Her head was back now and she was loving it, the sun on her face and neck.

Some urge stopped me thrashing the cabriolet. Instead I let its power ooze through it like a big cat. I'd switched the car stereo on and we cruised out towards the moors at about sixty with the slip-stream playing around our heads, Meatloaf throbbing in our ears. I knew my choice of music might not be Virginia's, but I was enjoying myself now. When we came up behind a slow-moving lorry, I dropped into third and roared past. The car was beginning to bring out the macho in me, so I pulled over before I started showing off too much. Virginia still had her head back, her face pink and glow-ing. She rolled her eyes towards me and asked, was it her turn now? She said it languidly, almost as if she were drunk.

I told her yes, put the handbrake on and stepped out of the car. As I walked round the front, Virginia quickly flipped her legs up and over into the driver's side with a movement so deft it both surprised and excited me.

'Hurry up,' she said, 'or I'll go without you!'

She was a much better driver than me. She drove fast, the wind rushing through her hair, but as soon as we reached a sign for a forty limit, she dropped back to regulation speed. We purred along with the air just a breeze waving at us again.

She turned the car up at the Old Cross, and as we headed back towards town, the sea to our right was glinting blue-green. Virginia asked me how did I justify a price tag of twenty-eight thousand pounds? I told her about the marque's superb engineering quality, the smoothness and raw power of its engine, its high resale value, the two-year warranty, the safety features, the excellent in-car hi-fi system.

'It's still too expensive,' she said.
'I know,' I said, 'but they sell at twenty-eight K. What can I do?'
'Give a girl *something*,' she said. 'No part-ex?'
'How much?' I said.
'A thousand?'
'And you'll sign now?'
'I'll sign now.'
'Pull over,' I said.

I always carry a contract with me. You never know when you might need one! Virginia signed. We shook hands and I knew she was delighted. As we dropped back down into town she was smiling, and I had the contract tucked safely in my jacket pocket. We were both satisfied. It was a nice day. I felt good, and was genuinely pleased for Virginia.

Before she left the garage I tried asking Virginia out. Despite the 'Mrs' she wasn't wearing a ring and there was something about her that really tweaked me. She was nice about it when she said no, but it was a real no and I knew straight away that it wasn't worth chasing. I put it down to a class thing.

On my way home I reported to the police station and signed up. It was part of my bail conditions. The court case was the coming Monday and I was looking forward to putting all this rubbish behind me. My brief was worried, but I wasn't. I was innocent. I was a decent bloke. I'd always been straight up and down, never bent my VAT, paid my tax. I didn't drink and drive, I'd never done drugs. I'd never even jumped a red light. The only thing I'd ever done that was illegal was going over seventy on the motorway!

The case was daft. When it came to getting the other, you know, well, I was a bit of a lad, pretty good with the patter. I wasn't that bad-looking and I worked out at the health club five days a week, so I'd never had a lot of trouble pulling when I wanted to. Even so, I'd never tried to pull another bloke's bird or gone after anything I thought was married. I'd always figured there was enough grief in the world, why add to it? As I said, I reckoned I was a pretty decent bloke.

But my brief wasn't so sure. He was giving me a really hard time. I'd told him exactly how it'd been with me and this girl Linda. We were both between partners. We'd got together one night, had a few drinks, a Chinese, gone on to a nightclub, bog-standard stuff. We'd had a few dances and Linda was up *really* close, stroking the back of my head and nuzzling into my neck. Everything was going really strong, and at about two I asked her did she want to come back to my place? I knew she'd just broken up with her fella so I didn't come on too heavy. If she wanted me to drop her off at her place instead, that was OK as well.

'No,' she said. 'I wanna be with you.'

You can probably guess the rest. We went back to my place for a coffee, stuck some music on, got pretty friendly. Linda was all over me. She knew I fancied her, a bloke can't hide it, can he? We were going to go to bed but she started getting weepy, something about the ex-boyfriend. So I stopped, said it was all right, we'd just talk. Maybe she still loved her ex. I wasn't into unfinished business.

Then she said no, we should go to bed. By this time my balls were aching. I said we could leave it but she said I was being so nice, she wanted to after all. So we did. Go to bed, that is.

If I was nice, she fancied me. We'd start necking and whatever. We'd be almost there. Then the tears would start. She couldn't. It was my house, I wasn't going anywhere, so I said let's go to sleep. She put her head on my chest; I could feel her still crying. I said something like 'It's OK, it's OK.' and she kept saying 'We musn't, we musn't. I can't.'

She's still crying when she swings up on to me. We're making love, she's still saying 'No, no. It's wrong.' She's on top but she's saying no. In the morning she's feeling guilty, thinking about Frank, her ex. Now she's saying I made her, forced her.

My brief says that if I admit Linda was saying 'no', or 'we shouldn't', and I didn't stop, then I'll go down for rape. He says they're rough on rapists in the nick. When I say 'But I'm not a rapist' he says that the court will decide that. He won't tell me to lie, but he's sort of suggesting that maybe I shouldn't be so clear about what Linda actually said. I've told him, look, I'm no rapist and I'm no good at telling lies either. He says in that case, at the very best I've got a fifty-fifty chance. I can't believe it. I really am a decent bloke.

My boss's name is Christine. About a year back, when we were both in sales, we were in a 'situation' and just about to go at it. She'd not long separated from her old man and at the last minute she said no. So I stopped, she said she was sorry. It was OK. A month or so later, we got it together and we knocked around for about three months. Then she got the sales manager's job. My solicitor tried to persuade her to be a character witness for me, but she said that if the firm found out about our relationship, she'd lose her job. She said sorry, but I was on my own.

I don't get women. Sometimes it's a clear-cut thing: 'Let's go to bed', or 'No thanks, mate, I don't fancy you', but most of the time they make you go through the hoops; it's part of the test. For every time it's been cut and dried there've been five times when it's been looks, feelings, code words. That's all right. That's just the way it is. And except for this thing with Linda, no one has ever accused me of anything.

So here I am in court. The prosecutor's a woman, tall, slim, wearing thick glasses. When she crosses the court she strides out. She's been going on at me for ages and I'm getting a bit confused. Then she says, 'Mr Trier, Ronald, do you think every woman has the right to say no?'

'Of course she does!' I say.

'And does no always mean no?' she asks me.

She takes off her glasses and looks at me with steely blue eyes. They're not even faintly languid now. Beneath her wig, her dark brown hair is pulled back tightly.

I know the only thing I can say is 'yes', and I know she knows.

Linda knows I'm not a rapist. Christine knows I'm not a rapist.

My brief doesn't think I'm a rapist, but in a moment the prosecuting barrister will *prove* I'm a rapist.

'*Does no always mean no*, Mr Trier?' she says again. Louder this time.

'Yes,' I say.

Now I know how she can afford her red cabriolet.

NO NIGHT BY MYSELF

MAT COWARD

'I've got to go into hospital straight after Christmas.'

'Shit,' says Diplomacy. 'Sorry to hear that, mate.'

'Yeah. Royal Free, second day after Boxing Day. For tests.'

'I'm really sorry to hear that, mate.'

'Mind you,' I say. 'Tests – they're test-mad these days, aren't they? I mean, you go to the doc with a mouth ulcer these days, they send you down the hospital for tests.'

'That's true,' says Diplomacy, sipping the top off his pint. 'There again, my brother-in-law had a mouth ulcer, wouldn't clear up, they sent him down the Free for tests, and we buried him six months later.'

What's so funny about that is, the actual reason they call him Diplomacy is because he used to be a chauffeur for some foreign bloke, some Arab who lived on Ambassadors' Row. That's what's so funny about that.

'And I'll tell you what,' says Diplomacy, 'he must've been a good ten years younger than you, my brother-in-law. Mid-thirties, he was.'

'Well, anyway,' I say. 'I haven't got a mouth ulcer.'

'So what you doing for Christmas, Madness?' he says. 'Usual is it, going over your gran's, as per?'

I shake my head. Not like *no*; more like *slightly annoyed*. 'Gran died, yeah? In the summer.'

'Oh Christ,' says Diplomacy. 'Sorry mate, of course. I hadn't really forgotten, you did tell me, I just wasn't thinking. Sorry, mate. June, wasn't it? Only I remember, because Wimbledon was on, Cherry watches it on the telly. So what you got lined up, then? Hotel room full of teenage nymphos, yeah?'

'I don't know,' I say. 'Nothing, really.'

Diplomacy wipes his hand across his mouth, picks up his lager and finishes it. Right down the hatch, fast as you like. He stands up to go. 'Well, whatever you do, I hope you have a good one, mate. Look, I got to be going. Wife, etc. Christmas Eve, you know – last-minute instructions and what have you.' He claps a hand on my shoulder, picks up his lighter and some small change off the counter. 'Be seeing you, Madness. Have fun, yeah? And don't get caught!'

And he's gone.

So has almost everybody by now, it's getting late. Few faces I half know over the other side of the bar, younger than me, they're getting ready to go, too. Buying bottles to take out.

I call over to them. 'Having a party, lads?'

They make out they haven't heard me. If they are having a party, it's not one I'm invited to.

There's never been a Christmas in my life I didn't spend with my gran. I've been inside a few times, yeah, but even then, as it happened, I was never inside at Christmas. Always at my gran's.

The boys go off to their party or whatever, and it's just me and the Paddy barman. He sees me still sitting there and brings over a parcel, a heavy cardboard box tied up with string.

'Jim said to give you this,' he says, putting it on the counter. I pick it up and put it down by my feet.

'Oh yeah, cheers son. I was expecting it.'

'Right,' says the barman, polishing the counter, collecting empty glasses.

'Jim say anything about it, did he?'

'No,' he says, 'only that you'd know what it was about.'

'Yeah, that's all right,' I say. 'I know about it.'

'Which I don't,' says the barman. 'OK? I don't know anything about it.'

I finish my drink, and I'm about to see what the chances are of getting another when the barman takes the glass from me and says, 'Right, cheers then, Madness. Mind how you go.'

He's in a rush. Not working tomorrow, wants to get over his girlfriend's for Christmas.

'Yeah, fair enough mate,' I say. 'Let me get a couple of bottles to take out, right?'

'No problem,' says the barman. 'What's your pleasure?'

A couple of bottles – Jesus. I have *never* spent Christmas on my own, not ever. Never alone.

I'm walking through Golders Green, walking home to my room, thinking maybe there'll be a message on the board by the pay phone in the entrance hall – 'So-and-so rang while you were out, can you come for Xmas dinner?' – but really, I can't think of anyone who might leave a message like that. If there is anyone, I've already rung them.

And all the time I'm walking, my mind keeps going: 'Never alone, never alone, *never* alone.'

The parcel the barman gave me is awkward to carry, and the bag with the bottles in it is clanking against my leg, so I stop for a moment, put everything down, light a fag.

I'm stretching my arms and I look round, and I'm standing right outside this really nice house. I've walked down this road thousands of times, and it is a nice road, all the houses look like quality. Detached, big garage to the side, an in-and-out gravel drive with a rose bush or something in a brown earth island in the middle of a tiny front lawn. The windows have that lead stuff on them, like old-fashioned houses, but they're not, they're younger than me, these houses. I remember when they went up.

They always look nice, but tonight, Christmas Eve, this particular house looks *really* nice. They've got a holly wreath on the door with a bright red bow on it, and I can see all lights through the windows, and a paper-chain. So I pick up Jim's parcel and the bag of booze and scrunch my way up the drive and knock on the door. I have to use my knuckles, because the actual knocker is covered by the holly.

It's gone midnight now, and I'm thinking maybe it's too late, maybe I shouldn't be knocking so late at night, everyone might be in bed. But almost immediately the door opens, opens wide and welcome, and I walk in.

225

'Hello?' says the woman who's opened the door. Pleasant-looking woman, very white cheeks with red dots on them and light, thin hair. Just a few years younger than me, I reckon. Wearing a dress, quite smart, and some tiny pearls round her neck.

'*Excuse* me,' she says, still holding the front door open. Then she forgets the door and calls out: 'Tony!'

Meanwhile, I'm opening a door off the hall, on the left, peering into a room which at first I think, from the smell of it, is empty, unused. A spare room downstairs – well, when you've got this many rooms, why not? No point heating them all up just for the sake of using them. But when I turn the light on I see a big, green-topped desk with a computer screen on it, and there's a swivel chair and a filing cabinet and that. Like an office at home. In case you get snowed in or something, I suppose.

'Excuse me?'

I look round. There's a man standing there, late thirties, bald at the front, wearing suit trousers and a striped, ironed shirt, but without the jacket, and no tie. I switch the light off in the spare office, close the door behind me and slip past the man – not pushing, not roughly – because I've just caught sight of the living room across the hall.

The man, the husband obviously, pinches at my sleeve as I walk into the big room – light's already on in here – and says: 'I *said*, excuse me! Do I know you? Can I help you?' The wife's standing behind him, the red spots on her cheeks getting bigger.

Beautiful room. Very good quality furniture, wallpaper, all that. Very warm, from an artificial coal fire at the far end. Really nice room. These people have got taste, not just money. Little framed pictures on the walls, of country scenes. No telly – they probably keep that in another room, a special TV room – but a huge Christmas tree in the corner behind the door, absolutely covered with flickering lights and tinsel, and presents wrapped up in shiny paper that reflects the room. One of the biggest and best trees I've ever seen. Mind, they ought to put it in the window in my opinion, not hide it away behind the door. Make the place more inviting from outside. I might mention that to the woman, if it doesn't seem rude.

'Look,' says the man, trying to stand in front of me, trying to bar my way as I start moving along the hall towards the back of the house. 'Now look here, I don't know who you are, but unless you

have some reason for being here I must insist you leave immediately.'
And he points towards the front door, which is letting in quite a
draught.

It's the kitchen I want now, so I duck under the man's arm – he's
shorter than me, but I'm quicker than him – and as I head down
the long hall, I hear him behind me saying: 'It's all right, Sarah,
you just stay there.'

Before you get to the actual kitchen at Sarah and Tony's, you have
to pass through the dining room. This is also beautifully laid out,
with a pretty red tablecloth over a big round table – it'd seat six,
easily – and there's decorations round the room and on the table
itself, and Christmas crackers by each table-mat.

But I'm concentrating on the kitchen for the moment, so I walk
straight through. The man's been following me, sort of snapping
round my heels from room to room, and I haven't been paying much
attention. Suddenly, now, I find his arm is around my neck and he's
trying to steer me out of the back door, the door from the kitchen
into the garden.

Too bloody cold for that, thank you, so I push him down on to
a stool – it's a big kitchen, you hardly need a dining room with a
kitchen this size – and he falls off the stool and bumps his bum on
the floor. His wife, standing in the archway that leads back into the
dining room, gasps, and cries out: 'Oh my God, what do you want
from us? It's Christmas, for God's sake!'

Funny thing is, I thought they didn't have Christmas, this lot. I
don't know, maybe that's the Muslims, or whatever. So I look at
them now, the man getting up off the floor, slowly, trying to get the
stool between him and me, and the woman standing in the archway,
arms crossed tight, shaking a bit. I look at them. Or, let *them* have
a look at me, really. I've already seen them, corner-of-the-eyes stuff,
now they can see me.

Now I'll listen to them. It's not that I haven't been hearing them
before, all their questions, it's just that I've been busy. Had to have
a good look around, see if this is the sort of home I thought it was.
Like, have they done the place up nice? Got all the right grub in?
Put up decent decorations, etc., like my gran would. I mean, not
everybody bothers these days, I don't want to stay if they're not
going to do it properly.

So I look at the man, look back at the woman, and now she's got a little boy with her. Behind her; don't know if she's seen him yet, I never heard him come in. About ten years old, just standing there, wondering what's going on. Pyjamas, dressing-gown, Fred Flintstone slippers.

'Hello, son,' I say.

They both swing round, look at the boy. The man says, 'Oh God,' and the woman grabs the boy, holds him close.

We walk back into the dining room. Well, I walk in, they follow me. I'll tell you what, people say they're mean, don't they? Jews and that. But not this lot – I can tell that by the Christmas crackers. I've never seen crackers like them! Much bigger than the ones you normally see, much fatter, and the paper looks really classy, dead expensive. Still, people come out with a lot of prejudices, and they're not always accurate in my experience.

I put the parcel the barman gave me, and the bag of booze, on a small table by the window. I unwrap the parcel, using my penknife to cut through the string. I don't bother saving the paper, because it's not that sort of paper. Just ordinary brown paper: I screw it up and chuck it in a little waste-paper basket under the table. I take the gun out of the parcel, and put it on the table next to the carrier bag.

So then I turn round, look at them, give them a big smile.

'Hello,' I say. 'Happy Christmas.'

'What do you want?' says the man. 'Just tell us what you want.'

'I've come to stay,' I tell him. 'I've come to stay for Christmas. Look,' I say, 'I've brought this.' And I pull the bottles out of the bag. A big bottle of Scotch – malt whisky, for Christmas – and one of ginger wine. Seasonal fare. I hold them out to the woman, and after a moment she comes over and takes them.

'Thank you,' she says, very soft, staring at me as she backs away.

'That's right, love,' I says. 'Just put them with the rest, eh?'

The boy's sitting on one of the chairs at the dining table. He'd better not mess up the place settings, they've been done beautifully. The man watches his wife take the booze, my festive gifts, over to a handsome sideboard behind the table, where there's bottles of every kind of booze you can imagine lined up in rows, glinting in the jolly light.

'Oh my God,' says the man, so quiet I can hardly hear him. 'Oh my God, he's mad.'

Now the funny thing about that is, the only reason they call me Madness down the pub is because I used to really like that pop group – the one that was called Madness. That's what's so funny about that.

The man looks at the gun, the pistol, sitting on the table. 'Just tell us what you want,' he says again. 'We don't even know who you are, I swear we don't!'

So I pick up the gun and point it at the boy a bit. My finger's nowhere near the trigger, there's no danger. It's not mine, the gun, I haven't used one of these since I was a kid. It belongs to a big noise called Jim, only he's made a date with some pal on the robbery squad to raid his house on Boxing Day, so could I look after it for a couple of days (which obviously I can, no one's going to raid my bedsit, are they?), and he'll owe me a good drink, mate. *After* Christmas, naturally, when things have quietened down.

I smile at the man, smile at the woman. The boy looks a bit scared. In fact, I'm a bit worried about the boy. I mean, I haven't got anything for him – the booze is OK for his mum and dad, but I never thought to bring anything for a kid. It was all a bit spur of the moment, if you know what I mean. Never mind – I've had a good idea. Yeah, he'll love that, that'll do nicely.

Meanwhile: manners, Madness, please! Introductions first.

'I'm your cousin,' I tell them. 'I'm your cousin Madness, and I've come to stay for Christmas, I've come to surprise you for a lovely family Christmas. Happy Christmas,' I say.

No response from the husband, but the wife – she's looking at the gun pointing at the boy – she walks over towards me, so she's standing between the gun and the kid, clever girl, and she says: 'Happy Christmas.' She swallows, there's a little tear there I think, then she says it again, louder: 'Happy Christmas. I'm Sarah, and my son's name is Daniel.'

'Happy Christmas, Daniel,' I says, giving him a grin.

He doesn't look at his mum or his dad, he looks straight at me and says, 'Happy Christmas, Cousin Madness.'

I say Happy Christmas again, and laugh. We'll all have a laugh about that, later on, the way he says it with that straight face, like he thinks maybe I really *am* his cousin, only nobody's ever thought to mention me before! Good manners, that's what that is. Good decent family upbringing. 'Good boy,' I say.

Sarah looks over at her husband, sort of nudges him with her eyes, and says, 'And this is my husband, Tony.'

'Happy Christmas, Tony,' I say.

He looks at his wife, looks at me, takes off his glasses and wipes his face with his shirt cuff. 'Happy Christmas,' he says.

He's got his hands underneath his armpits now, squeezing them, so I don't go to shake hands with him. Wouldn't be right, I don't want to embarrass him.

I put the gun in my belt. There: that's the formal part over with.

We're in the living room, the room with the beautiful tree in it, having a nice Christmas Eve drink. Wine, in fact; they've opened a bottle specially, which is only what you'd expect from this sort of person. People of this quality, they're never thrown by unexpected guests. Nice drop of wine, as it goes, not my usual tipple, but it's going down very pleasantly.

I feel good. Sitting here, enjoying the lights from the tree, curtains drawn, fire up, all cosy. Christmassy. Wondering about the presents under the tree although, obviously, I know none of them can be for me. They weren't expecting me, that'd be asking too much, but even so, it's fun to wonder. That parcel there – is that a book? A record? That great big one, what's that: a bike for the lad? A DIY bench for Dad?

Which reminds me: presents. 'I hope you like the Scotch, Tony? I see you're a wine drinker, if I'd known, obviously . . .'

'No, no, that's . . . that's fine,' says Tony. 'Isn't it, dear? That's, yes, that's lovely.'

'Lovely,' says Sarah. 'Very thoughtful.'

'It's a good one,' I say, not boasting, but, you know, it *is* a good one.

'Yes,' says Tony. 'No that's, really, that's fine. My favourite.'

'I am glad,' I say. 'We'll have a drop later, eh?'

Daniel's in bed. As he should be, of course, nearly one o'clock Christmas morning. Dreaming about his presents.

'Thing is,' I say, a bit embarrassed, even though it's hardly my fault, 'the boy – I just didn't think.'

'Doesn't matter!' they both say at once. I've still got the gun in my belt, but to be honest, what I always think is, after the first few minutes – whatever situation you're in – a weapon doesn't really make much difference. Things are either calm or they're not, and if they're not, a weapon's just going to make things worse, right? Tonight, I rather wish I'd left it in the bag. Didn't really need it, not really, and there's always a risk it'll cause an atmosphere.

'No, well,' I say, 'maybe, but I've had an idea anyway.' I reach into my pocket, bring out the knife, and chuck it over to Tony. He flinches: butter-fingers.

'It's not new, obviously,' I say. 'But it's in good nick, I've kept it nice. And it's a good knife, cost me a few bob. I was thinking, you know, perhaps Sarah could just wrap it up, bung it under the tree with the rest. I mean, I know it's second-hand, but I think he'll like it. Every boy likes a knife, right?' And then I look at Tony seriously, because it's his house, after all, his son. 'Unless, you know, if you don't think it's suitable. I mean, if you think he's too young or whatever.'

But no problem there, they're fine about it, thank me for the knife, Sarah says she'll wrap it, she's sure Daniel'll be delighted. So that's good. Anyway, it's getting late now, I'm feeling a bit knackered. Been mixing my drinks today, that's the truth, which is always a bad move!

'Well, all good things must come to an end,' I say, and I stand up, stretch my arms over my head.

Sarah and Tony leap up like they've been bit by a dog. 'Wait!' says Tony.

'Bedtime,' I tell him.

They look at each other. 'Oh my God . . .' says Tony, sinking back into the chair.

'Right,' says the wife. 'Fine. Well – Madness. Why don't you help yourself? Any room, they're all aired. And there's towels in the bathroom cupboard.' She looks down at her husband, then back at me. 'I think – Tony and I, we'll probably stay up for a bit, see if there's a film on or something.'

I give her a smile. 'I think we should all turn in, don't you? Late nights make cross mornings, that's what my old gran always said.'

So we all turn in. Just as well: don't want to be grouchy, Christmas morning.

About an hour and a half later, Sarah falls right over me, bang! Straight on the deck.

Not her fault – I'm lying on the carpet right outside their room, jacket for a pillow, gun in my hand.

She's got her dressing-gown on, and shoes. Outdoor shoes. And a torch. I help her to her feet, nothing broken, and we look at each other for a while. Slightly awkward moment all round.

She looks at the gun, can't help herself, then looks at me. 'Are you angry with me?'

As if! I mean, come on, it's her family, isn't it? She's got to have a go, right, got to keep trying, else how would she live with herself if anything happened? Fair enough, hell, I understand all that. But then that's her, see: thinking of me, has she upset me, not thinking of herself. Smashing lady, Sarah.

'I hope your Tony knows what a lucky bloke he is,' I say, but she pulls her dressing-gown round her more tightly and I think maybe she's got the wrong idea. So I take a step away from her, lean against the banister, light a ciggie, very casual.

'I usually go to my gran's,' I tell her.

She nods. I offer her a cigarette – better late than never, Mr Manners! – and she takes it, lets me light it, though it's obvious she's not a smoker. 'Did your gran die?' she asks.

See what I mean? Thinks of others, notices things, works it out. Sympathetic.

But this is Christmas, and I've imposed enough already. I wouldn't actually mind crying on her shoulder, I'm not ashamed to say it, but it's not actually mine to cry on, is it? So I sniff, pretend a yawn, and say: 'Well, better get some sleep, yeah? Big day tomorrow!'

I wake in the morning, rested and relaxed. Kipping on floors doesn't bother me, slept on more floors than beds, me. Anyway: it's Christmas morning! And there's that special feeling, I don't care how old you are, it never goes away, does it? The time ever comes when you don't feel that special excitement of Christmas morning – I don't care if you're nine or ninety-nine – then, son, you are ready for the grave!

Well let me tell you, no danger of Christmas morning not being special here, in this beautiful house, with these fine, kind people. It's like a dream! I wish my gran could've been here, she'd have loved it.

Great big breakfast, all the family together. Lovely grub. Nothing heavy, got to leave room for later, but very satisfactory. They both get the meal, Sarah and Tony, which is nice. Lady like that, she deserves a considerate husband, and I'm pleased to see she's got one. Because it can be a chore for the women, Christmas Day, if the men don't help out. So I volunteer for the washing-up, least I can do.

While I'm doing that, I take the gun out of my belt, slip it in my inside jacket pocket and hang the jacket behind the kitchen door. I feel better for that: guns and Christmas, you know, doesn't seem right, does it? Daniel sees me doing it – impatient to open his presents, he's come into the kitchen to find out what's keeping me – so I tell him he's not to touch my jacket, OK? And of course he says OK, good lad.

Opening the presents makes me a bit sad just for a while. Nothing for me, naturally, and that makes me think of Christmas at my gran's. She always got me a nice jumper, a record, whatever. Still, I cheer up when Daniel's so pleased with my knife. I don't think he's just being polite, I think he's really pleased. Well, it is a good knife, even if it is second-hand.

Before you know it, it's almost lunch time. We pull lots of crackers, especially me and Daniel – two daft kids! – and bloody good crackers they are, just as I thought. Really good gifts, things you can actually use, not plastic crap, and a big bang, and classy hats. But the jokes are still crap. 'What do you call an octopus with seven legs? A seven-legged octopus.' I don't think that's funny. I mean I *get* it, I just don't think it's funny. You pay this sort of money you should get a decent joke. Still, never mind. Minor point.

Daniel's allowed to put the telly on now, sits there in front of it playing with all his new stuff, as us grown-ups enjoy a little sherry while the meal finishes cooking in the oven.

Sarah coughs, clears her throat and says, 'Well, a Merry Christmas to you, Madness, and a Happy New Year.' She's looking more relaxed now, glad to have all the preparations over, I suppose.

'Actually, it's been a jolly bad year for me,' I say. Well, why not? I'm amongst friends, don't have to be shy. Say what I'm feeling. 'A jolly bad year all round. I'll be glad to see the back of it. Or at least, I would be if I didn't know that the next one will be just as bad, or worse.'

'I'm sorry to hear that,' she says. 'Why has it been such a bad year, if you don't mind me asking?'

'Not at all,' I say. 'Kind of you to ask.' But I don't really know what to say now. Don't want to tell them about the hospital, all that, don't want to put the mockers on. Ruin their Christmas with someone else's bad luck. So I say: 'Oh, just this and that, you know.' I put a finger in my mouth, waggle a tooth about. 'Bad teeth, for one thing. Feels like they're all about to fall out. Keeps me awake, sometimes.' Funny thing is, that's not a lie, I have had a lot of trouble with my teeth just lately.

'Have you,' says Tony, 'I mean, have you seen a dentist? I suppose you must have.'

'No, I don't like dentists.'

'My wife's brother's a dentist,' he says.

Whoops. 'No, no offence, I'm not prejudiced or anything,' I tell her. 'I'm sure your brother's a very good dentist, they can't all be crooks, can they? Anyway, I'm sure it wasn't your brother I saw last time.'

'No,' she says.

'Unless – he's not an Australian bloke, is he? Finchley Road?'

'No,' she says.

'Red hair, big ears?'

'No, that's not him.'

'Well,' says Tony, 'no, not Finchley Road. He's bald. He has got big ears, though.' His wife gives him a look, and he shuts up.

It's nice in here. Warm, cheerful, few friends having a drink, rattling their jaws, chatting about their little troubles. A thought strikes me.

'What you two doing for New Year's, then?'

She gurgles, just for a second, very quietly. He opens his mouth preparatory for a quick stutter, but she puts her hand on his arm, says: 'Well, you know, Madness, we, sort of, we don't in fact celebrate the same New Year. We're Jewish, remember.'

Embarrassing! 'Oh right,' I say. 'Sorry, no offence.'

'None taken,' she says, very gracious. 'I hope you'll have a very happy one, anyway.'

'Oh, sure,' I say. 'Well, never mind, New Year's different, eh? Pubs are open, last train on the tube's free. Go anywhere, New Year. Many options, several choices. Yeah, don't worry, won't be on my own New Year.'

'You don't like to be on your own, Madness?' she says.

Very perceptive, that seems to me. A very unselfish lady, very open to thoughts about others. 'Well,' I say, playing it down, like it's no big thing. 'It's just that, you know, I mean, you don't come into this world alone, do you? Your mum's there, and the nurse and that, and you don't go out of it alone, do you?'

'You don't?' says Tony.

'Actually, no,' I say. 'This bloke comes in the pub, he used to work in a crematorium, and he says they shove you through twelve at a time, saves on the fuel.'

Bloody nice thing to talk about on Christmas Day! *Idiot.* I try to think of some way to make a joke of it, without making it worse, when there's a knock on the door and my hosts freeze, staring at each other.

Christ, now that *is* embarrassing. They were expecting company! And I never thought to ask, and they were too polite to mention it. But now I think, yeah, six places set in the dining room. Hell's bells.

The really embarrassing thing, of course, is that there's nothing I can do about it, not given the circumstances. We're just going to have to hope the visitors go away, and then we'll really have to get our heads together trying to come up with some excuse for later, for why Sarah and Tony didn't answer the door. And that's not going to be easy.

They do go away, but not quickly and not for very long. The phone rings all through lunch (great lunch, even if we are all a little distracted), and then just as we're settling down in front of the box again, the visitors return. Well they would, wouldn't they, when you think about it? I mean, they certainly know they haven't got the wrong day! And if we don't answer this time, chances are they'll get worried, call the cops.

'Right,' I say, positioning myself in the living-room doorway. 'Look, I'm sorry about this, but this is what we're going to have to do. Daniel?' He looks up from the telly. 'Lend me your new knife a moment, will you? And come and stand over here with me.' Because I don't fancy nipping to the kitchen to fetch the gun; the people outside might see me through the hall window. 'Sarah, you stay there behind me. Tony, you go to the door, tell them they can't come in, you've got a contagious disease.'

'Contagious disease?' says Tony, almost laughing at the idea. He wants to take things more seriously that bloke, no criticism intended, but he does. I know it's not a great plan, but it might send them away for a few minutes at least, long enough for me to fetch my jacket, dash off out the back. No time for good manners now, unfortunately.

'Go on, love,' says Sarah. 'Tell them measles, we've all got measles, and could they come back later when we might be feeling better.' Good girl!

'And Tony?' I say. 'Don't mumble, please.' Daniel's standing right in front of me, I've got one hand on his shoulder, and the knife in my other hand. Obviously, I don't want to scare the boy, but Tony gets the message.

I keep out of sight, but I can hear him. 'Measles . . . blah blah . . . not to worry . . . blah blah . . . give us a ring later, Jeremy . . . blah blah . . .'

It's worked. Won't work for long, I'll have to get out sharpish, and carefully too, but at least there's been no need for any of the sort of unpleasantness which could have ruined Christmas for everyone.

The door shuts, I look round at the family – like, *phew*! Like, relax folks, panic over, back to the festivities. Only, I look at Sarah, and she's got that damn gun of Jim's – wish I'd never seen the damn thing, I really do – pointing right at me. Steady as you like, two-handed grip like the cops on telly, pointing right at the bridge of my nose. Well, fair enough, I didn't tell Daniel 'Don't mention it to anyone,' I just told him 'Don't touch it.' It's not like he's disobeyed me.

I look at Sarah's eyes. Red flush from chest to cheeks, very angry. The funny thing is, I don't think she's going to shoot me. I'm not an expert on people or anything, but I've looked at a lot of faces in my time, and I don't think she'll shoot me. What I think she'll do is, I think she'll lock the gun up in a cupboard upstairs, not showing me where it is, then I think she'll go outside and throw the key down a drain, and then she'll say, like, 'Right, let's all go back in and finish our cheese and nuts, and then I think you owe everybody an apology, Madness, don't you?' Maybe she'll even laugh and say, 'Get my brother round to look at your teeth, shall we?'

I don't know for sure, obviously, I'm not a mind-reader, but I *think* that's what she'll do. That's what my gran would have done, anyway.

LOVE IN VAIN

LIZA CODY

He was just another randy bar-room stud. That's what I told the cop. 'Just another stupid stud,' I said. 'I don't want to see him again. I don't know his name. I never saw him before.'

'Description?' the cop said. He looked as if he was checking my stockings for holes and it was a chore.

I said, 'I didn't look at his face.' Because that's what he was expecting me to say.

He smiled then. 'Don't you look at any of their faces?'

'Never,' I said. 'Then I won't blush if I run into them in the chemist.'

'You?' he said. 'Blush? Pull the other one.'

I am not what I am pretending to be. I am pretending to be what he thinks I am. It's the only way we can get along.

'What do you look at then?' he asks, not curious, just wanting to hear me say it.

'The colour of their money.' I am obliging. He obliges me by leering.

'Pull the other one,' he says again. He's daring me to make a dirty crack, and this time I won't oblige – there is only so much I'll do to please.

He says, 'So let's get this straight: he was with you from when you left the bar to half past one in the morning when the security alarm went off downstairs in Mr Petro's deli, and you never saw his face.'

'It was dark,' I say, obliging again. 'He wore a hat.'

'What am I thinking of? 'Course it was dark.'

It still is dark outside. I could have said, 'I'm hurting, I'm tired, I want to go home.' But that would have been the truth and I won't tell the truth.

'You never saw him before?' the cop says. 'And you never want to see him again, with or without a hat? Is that a correct interpretation of your statement – such as it is?'

I nod.

'For the tape!' he barks suddenly.

'Correct,' I say for the tape.

He says, 'Interview suspended at 02.47.' He switches off the recorder. He yawns. His teeth are brown, his tongue is sickly. He snatches his cigarettes from the table between us. The uniformed WPC sitting behind him stirs hopefully.

'Christ!' he says. 'I could do with a drink.' He gets to his feet. 'In lieu of that, let's have a cup of tea. I'm fuckin' sick of this.'

The WPC gets up too.

The cop says, 'Aren't you fuckin' sick of this old boiler thinking she can give us the finger?'

The WPC says nothing – bless her. They leave.

Contempt is always hard to take, even if you've worked for it. It is bitter medicine best drunk without witnesses.

I had a couple of drinks in Johnny's Bar. There was no one to talk to so I took my rum over to the piano. I played 'Love In Vain' and some on-the-road songs like 'Moonlight Mile' and 'Hobo Blues'. I played quietly. I wasn't drumming up any action: I'd made the rent for a month and I didn't need any. I can buy my own liquor if I have to.

No one spoke to me. No one gave me any hassle. I was minding my own business.

I was thinking, 'Just a couple more drinks and I'll sleep tonight,' when Cassie walked in.

It was funny because at the time I was playing 'Tell Me Mama', and that's something Cassie never says. She never says 'Tell me' anything – not to me. She says, 'Let me tell you,' or 'Listen to me,' but never, 'Tell me something, Mama.' It's been like that for a long, long time.

She didn't wait for me to finish: she practically slammed the piano lid on my fingers.

She said, 'You got to help me, Mama.'

I looked at her properly then. She had a black eye and her jaw was angry swollen.

I said, 'I'll kill him. I'll swing for him this time, so help me.'

'No,' Cassie said, 'that won't help. You've got to stop drinking that muck and listen to me.'

'I'm listening,' I said. What can you do but listen?

The doctor says, 'Some broken ribs – nothing we can do about those – bruising around the face and neck. No sign of concussion.'

'Is she fit for questioning?' the cop asks.

'And the hands,' the doctor says. 'She should have treatment for those.'

'Is she fit?'

'Get her to the hospital,' the doctor says. 'I wish you'd called me out sooner.'

'Shit,' says the cop.

Cassie had a canvas bag in the back of her little blue Datsun. I thought, 'She's leaving him, oh thank you, God.' I really thought that this time she was going to leave him.

'Don't be stupid, Mama,' Cassie said. 'I wish you wouldn't drink – you get so stupid.'

'What, then?'

'You've got to hide it, Mama.'

'What is it?'

'Don't ask,' she said, staring up into the black rain.

So I looked inside the canvas bag. Then I looked into her eyes. One was black from when he hit her, the other was red from crying. My baby girl.

'Cassie,' I said, 'you swore. You swore you'd never touch that stuff again.'

'I'm not touching it,' she said. 'Don't be stupid. We're selling it.'

'Throw it in the river,' I said. 'Leave him. Throw it away. Burn it. Come and live with me.'

'What?' she said. 'Live with you again? You've got to be joking.' She carried the canvas bag in her arms like a precious, precious child and we went up to my flat.

Cassie said, 'This little lot's worth thousands. We haven't paid for all of it yet.'

'Sweet Jesus!' I said. I opened my door and turned on the light. The cat scuttled out between my feet.

'Don't you ever clean up?' Cassie asked. She went over to the window. She hipped my keyboard out of her way and studied the street below. Satisfied, she closed the curtains.

'We'll be rich, Mama,' Cassie said. 'It's our one big chance.'

'You'll never be rich,' I told her. 'Because you'll never finish paying for it.'

'Why do you do that?' she said. 'Don't bring me down.'

'It isn't me who's brought you down,' I said. 'I told you he was trouble. I told you he was mean. I *told* you. Now look at you, girl.'

'Oh yeah,' Cassie said. 'You brought me up. He brought me down. What chance did I ever have?'

The cop licks his finger and turns a page of his notebook. He is sitting on my bed. The nurse said she'd bring a chair, but she never came back.

'You don't mind?' the cop says. 'Oh, I forgot – you're used to strange men on your bed, aren't you?'

I look him in the eye and I smile. He doesn't like that.

He says, 'What're you grinning at? Look at you – you're a mess. All beat-up and dirty.'

'I fell down the stairs,' I say, 'when the alarm went off.'

'Just shut the fuck up with that old song and dance,' he says. 'I'll tell *you*.'

He turns another page. He says, 'You left Johnny's Bar with a man. Witnesses say he was quite young and good-looking – too bloody young for you. Christ – he should see you now!'

'I'm not at my best,' I say.

'Do me a favour,' the cop says. 'You were never at your best from the day you were born.'

*   *   *

'I love him, Mama,' Cassie said. 'I know he's got a filthy temper. But he's under a lot of stress right now. If you'd only think of me for once in your life – just once in your life do something for me. Hide his stuff for me.'

'I'll do something for you,' I said. 'I'll kill the bastard.'

'Don't talk stupid, Mama,' Cassie said. 'It's just the pressure. He'd never really hurt me.'

'He will,' I said because I knew. But she wouldn't listen. She said, 'The supplier had to move this stuff out real fast. That's why we got so much for so little. But we owe him and the heat's still on. We can't start dealing till the heat's off. And until we start dealing, we can't pay what we owe. So you've got to hide it.'

'Do you know what you're asking?' I said. 'I mean truly, child, do you know?'

'Only for a few days, Mama. A week at most. I can't go home with it. Not now.' She sat on my sofa and rubbed at her swollen face. She was such a pretty child.

'He could be busted,' she said. 'He could be killed. And Mama, what would I do without him?'

Even the bruised eye wept for him.

We hid the canvas bag up in the loft under the water tank.

Cassie didn't want to leave it alone with me, but she had no choice. Who can you trust if you can't trust your mama?

I couldn't sleep with that stuff above my head. I got up and played the blues on the keyboard, watching the street till it came alive after dawn. And all the time, the stuff in the loft seemed to tick.

Then I took some: only a little – just enough for one hit, just enough to remind me.

But it had been too long. It made me sick. It made little puffs of smoke, little spurts of white fire, hiss out from between the keys when I played. After that I was sick for thirty-six hours.

Maybe it was bad gear. Maybe it was too good.

Maybe I'd been clean for too long. I don't know. All I know is I couldn't take it no more. I stopped when Cassie was a little girl and that was too long ago.

She says I never do anything for her.

The cop says, 'Why am I wasting my fuckin' time on the likes of you? Why?'

I'm hurting bad. I need something to take the pain away. But the nurse never came back and I'm damned if I'll ask a cop for anything.

He says, 'Why don't you want to help me? Look at your hands. You play the piano, don't you? They said in the bar you played piano. Well you've had your last tickle for a long time – if not for ever. Don't you want us to get the bastard who did that to you?'

The cop gets up and goes to the door. He looks up and down the corridor. Then he comes back. I think he's going to hit me too, and I don't care. But he just takes his cigarettes out of his pocket and lights up.

He says, 'Want a drag?'

For a moment he doesn't look like a cop. He looks like any old sad joe. If I met him in Johnny's Bar he'd be just another sad, tired joe and maybe I'd take him home with me. Or maybe I wouldn't.

I shake my head, but he puts the cigarette between my lips anyway. The smoke hits the back of my throat like a fist.

I say, 'You're tired. Go home. I haven't got anything to tell you.'

He takes his cigarette back, but he doesn't want to smoke it after it's been in my mouth. He throws it on the floor and stamps on it.

'Why're you protecting him?' he says. He looks like a cop again. 'He trashed your home. He trashed you. I wouldn't mind that so much but he trashed Mr Petro's deli too. And Mr Petro's on the council. He's a solid citizen and he's giving us hell. We can do without a councillor giving us hell.'

Mr Petro is a bonus.

The cop says, 'He's your landlord, isn't he? What's he going to do when we tell him what goes on when he closes his shop every night? What's he going to say when I tell him you won't help find the bugger who trashed his deli?'

I could tell him a thing or two about Mr Petro. I could tell Mr Petro's wife a thing or two as well.

'You'll lose your home,' the cop says. 'He'll kick you out on your sorry arse. If you don't want to help me, at least help yourself.'

'Listen,' I say. 'Listen one more time. I had a couple of rums. The guy was just another stud. He wore a hat.'

'I know about the hat,' the cop says. 'But he didn't wear it in bed. No one keeps his hat on in bed.'

'You'd be surprised,' I say, to please him.

'I'd be surprised if you told me the simplest fact. Not otherwise.'

'He left in a hurry when the alarm went off.'

The cop says, 'And you? Why did you follow him out?'

I tell him what he'll believe. I say, 'He forgot my money.'

'I don't believe you,' the cop says. 'And I'll tell you why – one of your neighbours was awake at one-thirty.'

I am feeling sick. This is the first time he's talked about a neighbour.

'Your neighbour was at the window when the alarm went off. You say your stud left when the alarm went off.'

I say nothing.

He says, 'If you are to be believed, there were two men on the premises: your stud *and* whoever vandalized Mr Petro's deli. The neighbour says only one man left. Therefore, QED, you are not to be believed.'

'The neighbour's wrong.'

'The neighbour's not wrong,' the cop says. 'The neighbour never left the window for a second. One man ran out. Only one.'

That's all it takes – one man.

I was in Johnny's Bar for the first time since I'd been sick. I played a little boogie, I played a little blues. There was a man at the bar who smiled at me. I smiled at him. I didn't want to go home alone.

Cassie's man came in when I was playing 'Love In Vain'. He was loose and strutting, lean and dangerous. I used to love men like him too. That's how I know he's no good.

He said, 'What's that you're playing, Mama?' They scare me when they talk softly.

I said, 'Where's Cassie?'

'At your place,' he said.

'She doesn't have a key,' I said.

'I don't need keys,' he said softly. 'Always the sad songs, Mama. Why? Anyone'd think you cared.'

'What've you done to Cassie?' I asked.

'She's waiting for you,' he said. 'At your place. I haven't done anything to her yet. But I might get angry if I don't find my stuff. It isn't where she put it.'

He tipped his hat at a jaunty angle and bowed to me. I left the piano and went with him. The man who smiled didn't look at me again.

My door was swinging open. The cat was cowering on the landing. The sofa was upside down. My keyboard was in pieces on the floor. All wrecked.

Cassie sat on a hard chair. She had no fresh bruises where I could see them.

She said, 'What have you done, Mama?'

'Leave him,' I said. 'Leave him now.'

'Don't be stupid,' she said, looking at him.

'She can leave whenever she wants,' her man said, softly. 'I'm not stopping her. Am I, Cass?'

'I don't want to leave,' said Cassie.

'Please, baby,' I said.

'What've you done with it?' said Cassie.

'I burned it,' I said.

'She hasn't,' Cassie said. 'She wouldn't.'

'She's stolen it,' her man said. 'She's keeping it for herself.'

'She wouldn't,' Cassie said. 'She knows what it means to me.'

'I *do* know what it means to you,' I said. 'That's why I burned it. You've got to leave him, baby.'

'You burned it?' Cassie said. 'You really burned it? Oh Mama, what've you done?'

'She's lying,' her man said. 'Tell me she's lying, Cass.'

Cassie was trembling. She said, 'It's not my fault.'

'She's *not* lying,' he said, as if he didn't believe that either.

Cassie said, 'What you going to do?'

There's a lot the cop wants to know from me, but there's only one thing I want to know from the cop.

I say, 'Why can't the neighbour give you your description?'

'The hat,' says the cop. 'The bloody hat.'

'What about the car?' I say, holding my breath.

'Wrong angle,' says the cop. '*You* tell me – it was your stud's car.'

'I told you,' I say. 'I'd had a couple of jars.'

'Fuckin' give me strength!' says the cop.

'It was small,' I say. 'It was blue.' And that was as much of the truth as I'd ever tell him.

'It was blue,' says the cop. 'Very bloody useful. It was blue.'

Well, it *was* blue. And so was I.

'There's some psycho out there,' the cop says, 'beating up on tarts

– wrecking innocent citizens' property – and you won't lift a finger to help. Even if some other poor slag gets it, you won't help. You slags are so hard – you don't give a flying fuck, do you?'

'No,' I say. 'I don't give a damn.'

'And that's the truth,' he says.

'You *see*,' I said to Cassie. I wanted her to see.

'You asked for it,' Cassie said.

I got up. I thought it was over, but I couldn't stand straight.

'Do you think I've finished?' Cassie's man said, softly. 'She thinks I'm done, Cass. Tell her.' Oh, they really do scare me when they talk sweet and husky.

He said, 'Wait in the car, Cass.'

But I wanted her to see. I said, 'Don't leave me, baby.'

'There's no use crying, Mama,' she said, as a matter of information. 'I can't save you. I don't even want to. You wrecked my life. You got to take what's coming.'

She went downstairs, so she didn't see what he did to my hands. She waited in the car like an obedient child, and she didn't see what happened when he got turned on. Maybe she already knew. She waited when he went berserk and trashed Mr Petro's deli. And when the alarm went off, she let him drive her home. She loves him. She believes he'll never truly hurt her.

I wanted her to see. I came down the stairs but I was too slow. I wanted to stop her but it was too late. She left me but she didn't leave him.

THE CASE OF THE LOCKED-ROOM NUDE

MAXIM JAKUBOWSKI

It all began with a mistake.

Or a bad joke.

Someone had given Chris my name, and recommended me as a person who could help him find his wife. We actually never did meet; it was all transacted over the telephone and I happily went along with the deception. He was a journalist at the BBC, specializing in business and financial matters. I knew what he looked like. Since my affair with Katherine had broken up, I'd somehow become a bit of an insomniac, waking up in the early hours of the morning when all you could watch on the box was a succession of pimply young reporters broadcasting live from the car parks of factories or some dealing room in the City, or pontificating in the studio about the coming of the information superhighway and its benefits to the business community. Business journalists? They knew as much about business as a Cambridge History graduate, and wouldn't last a fortnight in the real world of money. I suppose he was one of the worst. He'd done his pretty best to erase his northern accent but still stumbled on words like Vauxhall, Heathrow or Brighton, a wrong intonation here, a portentous tone of voice there. Anyway, he said that my name had been given to him by a contact in the arts department, a woman he'd come across on a trip to Oslo. He'd probably made a sad pass at her, and she thought it would be funny to put us together.

'They say you're the one person in London who knows most about crime,' he said.

'I suppose so,' I answered.

'Can you keep matters confidential and discreet?'

This was becoming most interesting. This guy thought I was some kind of private detective. And he wasn't just any old poor deluded guy, but actually Katherine's husband. Believe me when I tell you that when I answered his phone call, my heart began skipping the light fantastic for a moment. Had he finally stumbled on my identity?

So I nodded sympathetically, muttered a few uh-uh's over the phone, and he told me his story.

A few months back he had discovered his wife was having an affair. By then it was already over, but the thought of the four months of secret assignations, groping in hotel rooms, outright lies and her defiant and insufficiently apologetic stance afterwards had hurt him badly. Yes, he knew that one day when they were still young he had written to her that he would always stand by her and would even forgive her if she had an affair, but in practice it was different. In some colour supplement there had been an article on adultery, with a survey indicating that fifteen per cent of cuckolded husbands only would not forgive the errant partner for a one-night stand, but that nearly sixty-five per cent would not wish to continue the relationship if the affair had lasted over three months. He wanted to forgive her, to be in the minority, but it was so fucking difficult to accept; New Man, my ass!

She seemed sincere in wishing to patch things up. He had been taking her for granted, absorbed by his job and office politics at the Corporation: with the other guy it had just been lust, and lust alone. And she'd broken up with him a few days before anyway, as he was becoming too possessive. But she wouldn't reveal his identity.

Someone in publishing, he guessed, as that was where she worked.

'Is that why you're contacting me?' I asked, tickled by the prospect of having to investigate myself. Just like a Philip K. Dick novel . . .

'No, I don't think I want to know who the vile bastard is,' he answered.

Really, truly, he assured me, he had wanted to forgive her, to forget the whole sad episode, but every time he opened a newspaper, browsed through a magazine, randomly started a book, he was reminded of the fact that another man had touched her white skin, ruffled her curly hair, nibbled sensuously on her torn ear, licked her breasts, her sensitive nipples, spread orgasmic flush over the pale flesh of her neck and shoulders, fingered her cunt, entered her repeatedly in the missionary position and from behind, chewed on her labial folds, spent his seed inside the mad pinkness of her innards, as surely he had. Yes, I had loved her thus.

All this, Chris had guessed, I knew, from the look of loss in Katherine's dark brown eyes when she admitted to the affair and expressed her contrite regrets and a litany of 'Never again, never again, Jesus I swear.' But it was too late, he confessed quietly over the phone to me, the new priest in his confessional, the poison had been planted. And poison inevitably spreads. An awkward Christmas holiday divided into visits to sets of parents in Scarborough and Woking, an unreliable car which let the rain in to her irritation, the strain of seasonal jollity; later, a holiday in Tenerife where he felt awful pangs of jealousy every time a German tourist or a Spanish waiter watched over Katherine lounging in her swimsuit by the pool. This body had been shared by another. Defiled. Once, he was even physically sick.

Their rows became more frequent. It always began with a small thing. She'd forgotten to get salad or tomatoes at the Goodge Street Tesco's during her lunch-break and scorned his vegetarianism in the ensuing argument. Or she'd call to say she'd be home late and he would have to prepare his own meal, she had to see an author who was coming up from Wales after office hours – an excuse she had used often when the affair was in progress. Lack of trust, jealousy. It was eating away at him.

Last week, there had been another argument and she'd walked off.

'So,' I interrupted him, 'you need me to find her, is that it?'

'Yes,' he admitted sheepishly. 'I've tried her parents, and a few girlfriends. But nobody knows where she is. I fear she's gone back to this other guy.'

I knew she hadn't. My bed was as empty as my life, and I couldn't even sleep properly for thinking of her all the bloody time, and longing like a scream for the luminous whiteness of her nudity. Often, to find the solace of dreams, I would close my eyes and jerk off silently, remembering how her long legs moved and the shape of her backside and the taste of her cunt and her heartbreaker of a smile. None of which I could tell him. Or the fact that with several women since Katherine, I couldn't even achieve suitable erections . . .

'Maybe she has,' I told him, thinking all the time that I hated his guts: why does a Christopher shorten his name to Chris, what a silly affectation for God's sake. I hate it when people call me Max. 'Maybe she hasn't.' And fuck you, Chris, why did she have to choose you, and who has she gone with now? I thought. 'At any rate, it's not the sort of case I can take on. Too trivial, too ordinary; come on, adultery in media circles, what could be more full of clichés? Remember, I'm the one who knows all about crime, and this sure ain't crime by a long stretch. Sorry, find another cheap dick, try the Yellow Pages, there's a firm on Charing Cross Road.' I knew that because I'd paid these investigators to find Chris and Katherine's ex-directory number after she split, thinking maybe she'd listen to my pleading, my silly assurances of love eternal, but they couldn't even bribe a telephone company employee for the information and refunded my retainer. 'I'm sorry too,' said Chris. I put the phone down and left him with his cheap pain. Imagining briefly that soon he'd take to the bottle, sink to the gutter in the streets of the lost, just like in a novel by David Goodis.

Maybe it had started as a joke but, having betrayed both of us, where was Katherine now? Of course I had to find out; if she'd moved on to another man, I was already as much of a fool and as insanely jealous as Chris.

I sat back in the reclining black leather chair and pondered. What would Philip Marlowe do?

The evening sky outside was streaked with pink. Already spring again. My second spring without Katherine's wondrous face. I recalled our night in the Birmingham hotel. She had gone up to do a presentation to library suppliers and I'd joined her. It must have been two or three in the morning already, we'd somehow made love three times already and were drenched in sweat, my cock was aching and I knew it would be on the blink until morning, and full powers again. I cuddled up to her, warmed her cold feet, and we stayed there for ages, silent, flesh pressed against flesh, and we were so close I felt like crying, wanting her more than ever. Finally I asked her, as one does, 'What are you thinking of?'

In the darkness, she answered: 'We'll be back in London tomorrow. I'll be taking that train to Charing Cross station and the office, and looking at the faces of all the people, all so sad, feeling mediocre like them. Surely there must be more to life than this.'

I didn't quite know what to say in response.

I held her even tighter against me.

'Wouldn't you just like to run away, take a train, take a plane, and just go?'

'Yeah.'

'One day, we'll go off together.'

'No, we won't.'

'Yes, we will,' I said insistently. 'Where would you go?'

'When I was younger, I often thought of pissing off to India. But it would be too hot and dirty. You can't drink the water. You mentioned how much you liked New Orleans when you went to that convention there. Yes, New Orleans. That's where I'll disappear to.'

And she fell asleep in my arms.

How the hell was I to know it was to be the last time?

My friend O'Neil had worked on the New Orleans police force. He picked me up from Moisan airport and gave me a quick tour of the Crescent City before dropping me off at my hotel in the French Quarter. He suggested we talk over a meal. I insisted we visit the Pearl just off Canal Street where the oysters are just so juicy and pungent and cheap, and by the window they have framed pages of James Lee Burke novels, in which the restaurant is mentioned. I'd always promised myself that I'd get the Pearl into a story someday, too. And the bowl of gumbo was no disappointment either.

O'Neil gave me some useful names, as I had no damn idea even where to begin my search for a tall dark-eyed blonde in this city of dreams and sudden rains.

On my first night I had a series of nightmares, a sleeping prisoner

Maxim Jakubowski

in a Cornell Woolrich story where coincidences and the implacable finger of fate kept on evoking the faces of all the women I had known and loved. I waited for Nicole by a train station clock and a policeman came to announce her death and the fact that I was a suspect. I awoke, or thought I did, and there was Lois watching me, dressed in Liisa's clothes, and when she opened her mouth, her voice was that of Marie-Jo. The clock ticked away, and I guessed that somehow my time was running out and that I had to find a woman by daybreak or my whole world would come tumbling down, or worse. But I didn't know which woman I was supposed to find. I thought of the dimple in Lois's chin, the mole on Pamela's neck, the scar on Katherine's cheek, the gap between Nicole's front teeth, the smile of Julie Christie in *Billy Liar*, Jasmine's round glasses and Julianne Moore's orange pubic thatch in *Short Cuts*. Still the minutes kept on ticking by and I was tied to the bed, Sharon Stone's opulent shape straddling me with a knife in her hand, but her face was now that of Katherine. And I missed them all, and loved them all, I wanted to shout, but no sound would come from my lips. Tick. Tock. Tick. Tock.

Struggling with my past. With images of women long gone or unattainable.

Faces. Bodies. Breasts. Legs. Lips.

Save me, please, from the memories that hurt so much.

Forgive me for the lies, the betrayals, I didn't know what I was doing.

And somewhere inside me on that endless Dauphine Street night, the voice of reason kept on saying that the damned don't die, they just have nightmares that never end.

At last, New Orleans morning and deliverance from the devils. I ventured out. Municipal workers were cleaning up Jackson Square, shovelling the deadbeats' detritus from the previous night into black plastic bags. I had a coffee at Tujague's and collected my thoughts. If Katherine had never been here before, what would she do? Well, I didn't have a clue. What a lousy private eye I was!

If she'd left their south London home in a hurry, I assumed she wouldn't have taken much in the way of reading-matter. Maybe a few paperbacks at the airport. She would soon run out of things to read. I remembered the way she would cram two or three books into her bag even when we'd gone away for the weekend, although she

252

knew there would be little time to read – we'd spend all our time fucking, talking and fucking. I knew, I was the same and never went anywhere without a few days' reading just in case, you know. We had so much in common. I phoned Reage, the cop O'Neil had recommended, and obtained a list of the town's main bookshops, both new and second-hand. As I expected, there weren't that many. New Orleans wasn't that sort of city.

I spent a couple of days describing Katherine, the way her curls flowed down over her shoulders, the sort of clothes she would usually wear, her distinctive way of walking, hunched slightly forward, how her lips curled, the irregular teeth. Surely there could not be more than one British woman answering her description in New Orleans right now, and she was bound to visit a bookshop along the way.

I was almost ready to give up when, in the last shop on my list, a dusty emporium on Chartres with a cache of book-club editions of Rex Stout and Dell Shannon mystery novels, a customer who'd heard my forlorn inquiries came over to me and said he had seen a woman answering to my description coming out of a bar on Bourbon Street the previous evening.

'I thought she did look English, you know,' the old guy said. 'But you can't be sure, can you . . . And that place she'd been in, not very respectable, you know. No, sir, not a place for a decent woman, you understand?'

Full moon over Bourbon Street. The drunks roll up and down the noisy arcade holding their plastic glasses of beer in precarious hands, while up there on the forged-iron balconies revellers laugh aloud at the sinners beneath and black kids tap-dance on the pavement to the rhythm of beat boxes.

Topless. Bottomless. All Nude. Male. Female. The Orgy Room. Old-time burlesque. One-dollar beer.

At the door a tall Hispanic guy urged me forward.

'Best pussy in town, sir. Come on in, entrance is free, drinks are only five bucks a go.'

I inquired after Katherine.

'Tall, blonde, small tits, biggish ass. Yeah, man, we can supply it. We've got 'em in all colours, shapes and sizes.'

Inside.

There was a stripper dancing to a dirge of a Leonard Cohen song.

Her movements were slow and languorous. She moved with deliberation across the small stage like a swimmer through water or an astronaut in space. She was a small brunette, Italian-looking, couldn't have been much over five feet tall, her dark hair was bunched in a chignon, a few strands escaping from its clutch and reaching her shoulders. She removed her spangled bra and revealed an absolutely perfect pair of breasts, delicately rounded spheres, dark areolae pointing gently upwards, firm, creamy-skinned like the rest of her body. By the bar, there was a piece of cardboard on which someone had scrawled 'Monia' in thick red felt pen. This must be her name.

A brassy barmaid served me my Coke, no ice. Five bucks, the same as beer.

The song ended.

A strong beat rushed through the club and a louder song roared its way through the industrial speakers. The Walkabouts singing Townes Van Zandt's 'Snake Mountain Blues'.

Monia began to squirm to the accelerated beat, her legs dancing up and down the length of the miniature stage. She thrust her backside at some of the punters. Squatted on her haunches, projected her crotch forward, stretching the thin fabric of her G-string. Customers slipped dollar bills into the elastic holding up the small square inch of material. When she moved towards me, her body still twitching in spasms to the music, she smiled at me as she opened her legs indecently wide just a few inches away, but all I could see was the dead zone that surrounded her eyes. When I did not proffer a green bill she moved away, stood up and twirled her slight body around the central pole that anchored the stage, the smooth contours of the wood pressing between her perfect breasts, moulding sex. The song came to an abrupt end, and Monia walked away off-stage into an area of darkness.

'That's the one thing about Noo Orleenz I don't like,' a fat Texan still wearing a ridiculous cowboy hat and sitting on my right said. 'The law don't allow them to take off their panties and show us some real pussy, like in Vegas or LA.'

A new stripper took the stage. She had a tattoo of a rose on her right shoulder and another, of a snake, circling her left wrist. I sipped my Coke, thinking who I could ask about Katherine without giving the wrong impression. Monia reappeared, wearing a silk dressing-gown over her stripping apparel. She tapped my shoulder and flashed that all-purpose smile again.

'One-to-one?' she inquired. 'There's a room at the back. I'm sure we can agree on a price.' She had a strong European accent. I nodded back. Maybe in private, she might be willing to answer my questions.

The back-room walls were plastered with movie posters. Some new, some old. *Reservoir Dogs, Choose Me, Vertigo, La Jetée*. Monia slipped the dressing-gown off. She was only wearing the thin G-string. On her own, like this, she really appeared tiny.

'Wanna fuck? Blow-job? You can come all over my tits.'

I handed her a fifty-buck note and described Katherine.

'Why didn't you say so before that you wanted the English-woman?' Monia said.

'Is she here?' I asked her, a tightening in my gut, a twinge of fear and expectation in my heart.

'Well, she wasn't very good at dancing, was she?' the small stripper said. 'Hernandez gave her a try-out, but she had no sense of rhythm, you know, couldn't move her butt to the beat to save her life, and she sure spooked the punters, reading at the bar all the time between sets.'

'Where is she?' I asked.

'Hernandez has got this private joint off Toulouse, very private, where they go all the way. You know, live shows. Your blonde Englishwoman, he says she's pretty good at cocksucking, but doesn't shake enough when the men fuck her, says all she can whisper is "Jesus, Jesus" as they pound her meat, y'know, they want noise, a few screams, to make it sound real, but she can't even manage that.'

'Enough: tell me where to go.'

'Not so easy, man.'

I slipped a couple of green bills into her outstretched hand. 'Please.'

'You wait here. I'll bring her round. Hernandez doesn't like new faces at the other place.'

She moved towards the door.

'Wait,' I said. 'What if—'

'Trust me,' said Monia of the perfect breasts.

I imagine dark clouds occluding the full moon outside. The sounds of Bourbon Street reach me, quieter now, filtered through the buffer of my fear.

Katherine is in the room. Her make-up is clumsy, the gash of red over her lips isn't straight, there is a lattice of needle holes across her forearm, there are holes in her stockings.

'You?'

'Yes.'

'How did you know, how did you find me here?'

'I did. Why?'

'I had to get away. I had so badly betrayed the two of you. I hated myself. Felt guilty. Ashamed I had given in to lust and spoilt everything. Absolutely everything.'

'But this, Katherine, how could you? It's too much like a bad pulp novel. X-rated Willeford. Surely there were other alternatives?'

'Maybe. But what's the point? My heart has grown cold, so I've given myself over to lust. Perhaps I should have recognized the fact earlier, understood the nature of it. I try to forget, you, Chris, London! I take the cocks of strange men into my mouth and caress their purple crowns with the tip of my tongue and feel them grow larger and larger inside me to the point that sometimes I almost choke. None taste the way you did, though. For the right amount of cash they can fuck me, and if the money's good enough I'll take two at the same time. It doesn't make much difference, does it? And others can watch, can touch, can stretch me, tear at my orifices. It's nothing, it doesn't matter.'

'But Katherine . . .'

'You know, it's true what they say of black men, a lot of them here do have these huge cocks. But I can take it. The pain helps keep me awake. Look . . .'

She slips out of the cheap calico dress she's been wearing, unclips the garter belt and rolls down the black stockings. She's not wearing anything else.

'My skin is so very white. They like this here.'

There's a network of bruises over her thighs. Her pubic curls have been trimmed to a thin band above the lips of her bare sex.

'Is this what you remember?' she asks me.

I see the nakedness of her desire and absurdly realize that we never went dancing, and know that we shall not grow old together.

'Come,' I beckon to her. 'Let me hold you.'

I have locked the door from the inside. Her nude body moves across the purple carpet where so many others have fucked before.

256

I open my arms: she is cold, her hair needs a wash, her curls are impossibly tangled, I recognize the particular smell of her breath as she presses her face against my shoulder. We stay like that for what feels like an eternity. Finally my fingers move to her throat, hold her firmly, then press hard against her carotid. Katherine does not resist. A nervous impulse races through her and a pale nipple quickly brushes against my elbow. I keep on pressing. She closes her eyes, keeps on leaning against me. She dies. A small trickle of urine splashes my feet as her whole body at last relaxes.

It began as a joke and ends as a locked-room mystery. Just the way I always liked my John Dickson Carr stories. Soon, Monia or someone else will knock at the door to tell me my time is up.

I unthread the belt from my trousers and attach it to a steel hook protruding from the room's ceiling. Why was it there? SM games? I find a chair which I climb on to. One end of the belt around my neck, I tighten it by a few notches.

On the floor Katherine's body lies in repose, her splendid nudity for my eyes only.

When they batter the door down later, it'll be a perfect mystery.

I jump off the chair.

DOUBLE-TALK
BARBARA TAYLOR McCAFFERTY AND BEVERLY TAYLOR HERALD

My sister Glenda and I are supposed to be a policeman's worst nightmare.

That's what they said, anyway. I heard two of them talking out in the living room. They were already saying stuff like that, and they'd only been here just long enough to take a quick look at what was out in the kitchen and then hurry into the living room to make some phone calls.

I'm not sure who they called, but I guess it had to be the coroner and people like that. I didn't really start eavesdropping until the policeman with the beer belly hung up the phone. He turned to the guy next to him and said, 'Can you believe this? Identical twins, for crying out loud.'

It was probably the first time in my life I'd ever heard anybody say *identical twins* as if it were a curse. Except for Earl, of course. Earl didn't exactly count, though. Everything our stepfather ever said had sounded like a curse to me and Glenda.

Glenda was talking to the woman cop standing out in the hall, and I was sort of ignored for a moment. I don't think the policemen in the living room even noticed I was listening.

When Beer Belly said that about twins, the other policeman – the

259

one with the long sideburns that only geeks wear anymore – he made this real icky noise, clearing his throat. 'Yep, a cop's worst nightmare,' he said. 'Friggin' *twins.*'

If Glenda and I were a police nightmare, they sure didn't act like it. Oh sure, the police had done the usual staring at Glenda and me, their eyes bouncing back and forth like tennis balls the instant we opened the front door. But that was pretty much standard procedure for anybody seeing the two of us for the first time.

After seventeen years of walking around looking exactly like each other, Glenda and I have gotten used to the staring. First-timers, of course, are the worst. They always seem to immediately start running a mental checklist, their eyes darting from one of us to the other. Short curly brown hair. *Check.* Large brown eyes. *Check.* Freckles. *Check.* Tall and thin. *Check.*

Today, of course, the policemen probably also added: pale and nervous. *Check.* That was all right, though. Under the circumstances, Glenda and I ought to look pretty upset. After all, it wasn't every day Earl got himself murdered.

Lord. Just thinking such a thing makes me shudder inside.

I'd told Linda they would separate us, and that's exactly what they did. Right after the cops saw Earl lying on the kitchen floor in all that mess, Linda and I were hustled right out of there. The cops actually had the nerve to act as if they were doing it for our own good. Like maybe whoever had done that to Earl was still hanging around, waiting for the chance to do it to us.

Uh huh. Right. We were in danger, all right. In fact, we must've been in so much danger that they had to take us to the police station in downtown Louisville in separate police cars.

Once we got to the station, the danger must not have let up any, because they put Linda and me in separate rooms. Hey, I know Linda thinks I always leap to the worst conclusions, but I don't think there's any leaping going on here. The cops were isolating the suspects. Pure and simple. They were going to check our stories and make damn sure we didn't slip up.

Now that was the real danger.

If Linda had watched all the true-crime movies I've watched, she'd have known it too. But Linda has always been the squeamish one. Didn't it end up being me who had to wipe off that stupid knife? It had clattered to the floor and slid under the refrigerator, so that only a part of the wooden handle was still sticking out.

The part of the handle that you could see had all these dark splotches on it. It was gross.

And yet, what choice was there? Somebody had to clean that thing off. I knew damn well if I left it up to Linda, the fingerprints would still be there when they hauled us off to the police station.

What do you know, Glenda was right. The police separated us almost immediately. Of course, Glenda's the one who never once closed her eyes during the gory parts of all those awful Jason films – in fact, Glenda actually laughed a few times – so I guess I shouldn't be surprised. She's good at facing the worst that gets thrown at you.

I only hoped she was right about the rest of it. She said it didn't matter that we were only seventeen. What mattered was this: we looked exactly alike. Right away, according to Glenda, the cops had to be thinking, 'If one of these girls killed this guy, how will we ever tell which one?'

That's why Glenda had said they'd separate us. They'd think that separating us would get one of us to rat on the other.

A lot they knew about twins.

It looked as if they knew even less about decorating. I looked around the room they'd put me in – gray metal table, orange plastic chairs, puke-green walls and gray linoleum floor, yellowed and cracked – and I found myself blinking back tears.

What kept me from breaking down completely was knowing that, if Earl were here, how irritated he would be. Even when Glenda and I were small, Earl had said he didn't like 'bawling babies'. That's what he called you if you ever even looked as if you were going to cry in front of him. And then, of course, he followed that up with a slap to the side of your head.

Oddly enough, thinking about how mad my crying would make Earl sort of cheered me up. I straightened up some in that plastic chair, and I only jumped a little when the door in back of me suddenly jerked open.

'Sorry to keep you waiting,' boomed a deep voice. It was Sideburns – the policeman who'd called us a nightmare back at the house. Sideburns was followed by a uniformed lady cop and an older lady wearing a blue linen suit and carrying a tape-recorder. 'Now,' Sideburns said, 'which one are you?'

'Linda,' I said, and my voice shook in spite of myself.

Sideburns nodded and smiled at me, as if I'd just answered a difficult question.

I guess maybe it would've been a difficult one for him. I wasn't sure what he was smiling about. How could he even know I really was Linda?

I watched Sideburns turn one of the orange plastic chairs around, straddling it like it was a horse, while the older woman in the suit fiddled with the recorder. All the time she worked on the thing, she didn't look at me once.

In back of me, the lady policeman positioned herself by the door. I glanced over at her. She met my eyes with a flat, unemotional gaze.

Either she was supposed to keep people out.

Or she was supposed to keep me in.

Sideburns was now mumbling into the tape-recorder, saying what day it was and who everybody else in the room was. All I caught was his name. Detective Brady – like in *The Brady Bunch*.

Come to think of it, he even looked a little like the Brady dad on TV, with those long sideburns that had to be at least twenty years out of date. Leaning forward, Detective Brady gave me another smile. 'All right, Linda, honey, why don't you tell me exactly what happened?'

I swallowed past the lump in my throat. This was it. Lights, camera, action. I just hoped I remembered exactly what Glenda and I had decided to say.

The cop with his undershirt showing between the buttons of his shirt sat across from me at the table. Staring. I knew he was trying to look intimidating and all, but I could've told him, when you've got a beer belly poking through your shirt at every button, looking intimidating is going to be a stretch. No pun intended.

I think Beer Belly might've had some idea what I was thinking, too, because he sucked in his gut a little when he started talking. 'OK, Glenda, just tell us what happened. In your own words.'

I just looked at him. For a crazy moment, I actually thought I might giggle. I mean, whose words did he expect me to use?

Come to think of it, I guess I intended to use both Linda's and my own. Both of us had sat down on the living-room couch and come up with exactly what we were going to say.

For some reason, having this occur to me made me want to giggle even more.

I quickly cleared my throat. It didn't take a rocket scientist to know that snickering at a time like this would probably not be all that terrific an idea.

Shifting position in the metal chair I was sitting in, I could feel the gaze of the other people in the room. The young lady with the tape-recorder who didn't look much older than me, and the woman cop with her gray hair in a bun who was standing over by the door – both were looking straight at me.

Being a twin, I was used to being stared at, but this was different. Everybody in the room, including Beer Belly, seemed to be looking at me as if I were a bug. And as if maybe they were Raid.

I took a deep breath and looked away, picturing in my mind's eye Linda's face the last time I'd seen it. From the window of the police car as the car pulled away. Her eyes had caught mine, and I'd known instantly what she was thinking. There wasn't anything magical about it. When you know somebody's face as well as your own – mainly because it is your own – you don't have any trouble reading it.

Linda had been thinking: you can do this. We can do this.

Now I cleared my throat again, and looked back over at Beer Belly sitting opposite me. His collar was so tight his fleshy neck bulged around it. The man did not look comfortable.

Hey, join the club.

'I really don't know what happened,' I said, opening my eyes real wide. Some of the time this wide-eyed innocent look had actually worked on old Earl. Mom, of course, could see through me, but Earl couldn't always. Of course, those times he didn't end up hitting me for doing something, he'd end up hitting Linda for it. Watching Linda get hit was worse than getting hit myself. You never could win with old Earl. 'Our stepfather was dead when we got home,' I said. 'Linda and I – we found him like that.'

The instant I said the words I got a quick flash of Earl on the kitchen floor. With the butcher knife in his chest. And that almost black circle of blood soaking the front of his T-shirt and pooling beneath him.

For a moment, I felt a little dizzy.

I guess I must've been dizzy with relief. Because, take my word for it, nobody needed dying worse than Earl. Nobody.

I was glad he was dead. I was glad, and I only wished I could tell everybody just how glad I was. It had been the right thing to do. Hell, it should've been done a long, long time ago.

All this was going through my mind, and I think that's why I didn't realize how quiet it had suddenly gotten. I looked over to see old Beer Belly leaning back in his chair, looking holes right through me. Letting the silence build.

I swallowed, and tried to meet his eyes. But you know how it is when there's a long silence, and you start feeling as if you've got to rush in and fill it? Before I knew it I'd blurted, 'That knife was from one of our kitchen drawers, you know – I guess the burglar must've grabbed it when Earl surprised him.'

'So it was a burglar, you think?' Beer Belly just asked the question, but there was something in his tone. Something that should've been a red flag.

'Well, yeah,' I said. 'It looked to me like whoever killed Earl had already stolen some things when Earl came in. I mean, there was that pillowcase on the floor right beside Earl. You saw that, didn't you? It had some of our stuff in it.'

There was another silence after that. Just a beat this time, that's all, and yet I knew I'd said something wrong.

'How did you know?' Beer Belly asked.

I blinked. 'Know what?'

Beer Belly scratched his stomach, like all of a sudden he was just as relaxed as he could be. He could've been sitting at home in his damn Barcolounger. 'How did you know what was in the pillowcase?'

I felt the blush start at my neck and rush toward my forehead, just like it always does when I give the wrong answer in trigonometry class. I glanced at the other people in the room. The girl running the tape-recorder was staring at me, her large blue eyes looking kind of alarmed. Over at the door, the female cop with the bun might've looked motherly, except that now she was leaning in my direction, frowning.

I shrugged, trying a little smile. 'We peeked.'

God, I wished Linda were here.

'All right, Linda, you arrived home about five-fifteen,' said Detective Brady, glancing at his legal pad. 'After shopping at the mall—'

'For school clothes,' I added.

He glanced up at me. 'Right. School clothes. I've got that. Now where was your mother all this time?'

I just stared at him. 'I thought I already told you.'

'Sorry. Bear with me, OK? Just tell me one more time, honey.'

I was getting real tired of being called honey. I may be wrong, but I don't believe *honey* is what you call people you're trying to get to confess to murder.

'Linda?' Detective Brady said. He was looking less and less like the Brady dad all the time. 'I asked, where was your mom?'

I stared at him without blinking. How many times had I heard that little question from Earl? Let me see, he'd married my mom when Glenda and I were six, so I guess it probably numbered in the millions. Earl, of course, always yelled it. He'd come storming into the living room, smelling like he'd just gone swimming in Jack Daniels, and he'd start yelling. 'Twins, where's your mom? Louise, dammit, where the hell are you? Get your ass down here! NOW! Your man wants you!'

Mom always came running, her eyes darting all around like a caught animal, her thin lips quivering. A couple times lately Earl had started with her, pulling at her clothes and stuff, with me and Glenda still in the room. Mom had cried and tried to make him stop, but Earl had just laughed. 'Hell, they're old enough, they'll probably learn something!' he'd said.

Both times Glenda and I had run upstairs, and when we got to our bedroom, we'd locked the door, turned on the TV, and then sat there and watched it as if nothing was happening.

The Brady cop was starting to frown. I took a deep breath and plunged in. 'Well, like I said before, Mom left this morning for Cincinnati at the same time Glenda and I left for school. Mom was going to visit her sister Celia overnight, and then come back tomorrow.'

Detective Brady erased the frown and went for a smile. 'You know, Linda honey, we haven't been able to reach your mother at her sister's.' He glanced away, and then said, almost casually, 'Cincinnati's only a two-hour drive from Louisville.'

I didn't move a muscle. 'Oh, didn't I tell you? Mom won't get to Celia's until around nine or so tonight. She always goes shopping in

the city before she finally goes out to Aunt Celia's. Just ask her sister
– Celia will tell you.'

Brady's eyes didn't waver. 'We already have. That's what your
aunt says, too.'

I closed my eyes for a second. Thank you, Celia.

Brady was now making a big show of thumbing through his notes
in this little spiral notebook. 'Now, where exactly did you say you
were today, from 4.12 to 5.31?'

He'd asked me this back at the house, and again in the police car
on the way here. How many times would I need to tell him? I took
another deep breath. 'Glenda and I were at Town Square Mall. We
drove there right after school was out. We were looking for—'

'School clothes,' Brady finished for me.

I met his gaze head-on. 'Right,' I said.

Brady started to close his notebook, but then he flipped it open
again. 'Which stores did you go in?'

I swallowed, staring at him. Oh God. I certainly hadn't memorized
any stores. I knew Glenda hadn't either.

'I'm not sure if I remember,' I said slowly. 'Is it important?'

Brady leaned forward, all fatherly and earnest. 'Actually, honey,
it would really help us out. If you could let us know exactly where
you were, we can go right ahead and eliminate you and your sister
as suspects. This way we can concentrate all our efforts on catching
the real killer.'

Uh huh. Sure.

'But why do you want to know about that particular time period?'
I asked. I opened my eyes as big as I could and just looked at him.
Glenda can do wide-eyed innocence better than anybody I ever saw,
but I'm almost as good.

'Well, hon,' Brady said, 'it turns out that your stepfather had a
receipt in his pocket. From an automatic teller machine. It was
stamped at 4.12 this afternoon.'

I nodded, keeping my face very still. 'No kidding,' I said.

It was difficult not to smile. So the police had found the bank
receipt. Just like Glenda had said they would. So far, she was batting
a thousand.

Brady went on, 'Your call to 911 was clocked in at 5.31. So if you
could account for your whereabouts between those times . . .' He
let his voice trail off.

I nodded. Right. OK, so all I needed to do was rattle off a few store names. Then the police could go find out if the store clerks remembered twin girls being in there earlier today, buying clothes.

Even if the clerks didn't remember, the names of the stores were important. If Glenda and I didn't come up with the same names, it'd make us look that much more guilty.

I took a deep breath. We really should've gone over this. 'OK, let me think,' I said. Twin brains are supposed to think alike, aren't they? So, if genetics meant anything at all, Glenda should be thinking along the exact same lines as me. 'We went to The Gap. And, um, Bacon's. And then, The Limited. I think that's it.'

I sat up a little straighter. Now, let's see if Glenda picked different ones.

Beer Belly was doing his staring routine again, and his face was getting redder and redder. I thought about suggesting that he unbutton his collar, maybe let a little blood drain off before he had a stroke. I decided against it, though. Earl had taught me that smarting off was never a good thing to do. Not if you didn't want to get smacked.

Besides, if Beer Belly wanted to have a stroke, far be it from me to stop him.

Beer Belly cleared his throat. 'So, Glenda, let's hear it again. You'd gone shopping with your sister, and arrived home about 5.05. You buy anything?'

I thought of the new Pappagallo boots from Bacon's, bought with the money from Earl's bank machine. There didn't seem to be any reason not to tell the truth. 'Just some boots,' I said. 'In fact, we both got a pair. They're up in our closet.'

I realized I'd said too much when Beer Belly's head did this odd little jerk. 'You're telling me,' he said, 'you two came in, found your stepfather murdered, and then you went upstairs and put your boots away?'

I blinked at that one. I was getting tired, or I'd have been more careful. Hell, if I hadn't been so weary, I probably would've been scared, but it seemed like too much effort.

I mean, how many times was this guy going to try to trip me up? I suppressed a sigh, and said, 'Earl always insisted that the house be kept spotless.' This was the gospel truth. If old Earl found so much as a magazine out of place, he'd go on for hours. If you were anywhere near him while he was ranting, you not only heard him, you felt him.

267

I shrugged. 'I guess, even under stress, you still do like you've always been told.'

As tired as I was, I could almost hear Earl's voice once again. 'DO AS YOU'RE TOLD! Do you hear me? DO YOU HEAR ME?'

God, that man could be frightening when he yelled. Of course, that was why Mom never left him. She was too afraid.

The reason Glenda and I never left was exactly the same. We were also too afraid – for Mom. We sure couldn't leave her alone with that monster.

All this was going through my mind, so when the question I'd been waiting for all day came, it startled me. 'You and your sister didn't like your stepfather much, did you?' Beer Belly spoke softly, but his eyes were riveted on my face.

I lifted my chin and stared back at him. 'Earl was OK,' I said.

Beer Belly raised his eyebrows. 'You don't seem upset about what happened to him.'

I continued to stare right back at Beer Belly. God, I was tired. 'I'm upset,' I said. 'I just don't show my feelings much. Linda calls me the Great Stone Face.'

This was, once again, the truth. Linda used to worry out loud that there might be something wrong with me, the way I never got emotional. She was afraid maybe Earl had damaged me from childhood or something.

I've tried to tell her that it's not that complicated. I just think crying is for babies. That's all.

Beer Belly was now scratching his belly again. 'Your stepdad was a real jerk, wasn't he?'

I just looked at him. Did he think I was stupid? I mean, I may have been only seventeen, but I'd scored in the ninety-eighth percentile on the PSATs. I wasn't dumb. And even if I was, I'm pretty sure even an idiot would know that this guy was fishing for a motive. 'Earl was a prince,' I said. 'An honest-to-God prince.'

Beer Belly must've been holding his breath, because he let it out all at once. He sounded like a tire going flat.

He glanced over at the lady cop standing by the door. I don't know if it was a cue or what, but the lady cop spoke up for the first time. 'Did any of you ever report the abuse?'

I didn't even look in her direction. 'You know,' I said, looking at the table in front of me, 'you read in the paper every day about some woman who goes to the police to get an order of protection, and all that does is get her killed. Because it makes her abuser that much madder.'

Beer Belly leaned forward. 'So that's why none of you ever called the police when your stepfather got violent?'

I didn't hesitate. 'Nope,' I said. 'Nobody ever reported anything because nothing ever happened.'

You could've cut the silence with a knife after I told Detective Brady and the others what a nice guy Earl had been. And how awful it was that he'd been killed by a burglar.

You could tell not a person in the room believed me.

Oh, yes, Glenda continued to bat a thousand. She'd said they wouldn't believe me, but it didn't matter. As long as we didn't tell them anything bad about Earl, they wouldn't be able to come up with a motive.

Brady was starting to look impatient. 'Look, Linda, you know everything you're saying is just a lot of double-talk,' he said. 'You say your stepdad is a great guy, and yet you don't look all that grief-stricken.'

I did what Glenda had told me to do. I looked at him and shrugged.

Brady opened his mouth to say something, but he didn't get the chance. The door opened suddenly, and another policeman walked in. This one was in uniform and carried a manila envelope.

The uniform whispered something in Brady's ear, glanced over at me, and then they both got up and went out into the hall. I could hear the hum of their voices through the closed door, but I couldn't make out what they were saying. It must not have been good, though, because when Brady came back in, his expression had changed. His face looked a lot like Daddy Brady might've looked if the entire Brady Bunch had bombed City Hall.

Brady sat back down, placing a small, white piece of paper face down on the table. 'Let me ask you something, Linda,' he said. Judging from his tone, he was pretty much through with calling me 'honey'.

'Did either you or Glenda go to the bank machine earlier today?'

All at once, I knew what the piece of paper was. My heart started pounding so loud I was sure everybody in the room could hear it. Trying to calm myself, I took a moment before I answered. 'No, I don't recall going to the bank machine.' I started doing Glenda's wide-eyed look of innocence. 'Why do you ask?'

Brady actually sounded angry. 'I'll bet you didn't know that banks routinely photograph the users of their automatic teller machines. Ever notice that camera mounted at the machine?'

I stared at him, still doing Glenda. 'They do?'

Brady turned the paper over, so that I could now see the image I'd already figured out had to be there.

He put his finger on the girl in the photograph. A tall, thin girl with short, curly brown hair and big brown eyes stared back at me. 'Which one of you is this?' Brady asked.

I raised my Glenda eyes to his. 'You tell me,' I said.

When Beer Belly suddenly pushed back his chair and walked out of the room, I relaxed a little. Until I noticed the expression on the face of the lady cop still standing at the door. Her expression said, Not so fast. It ain't over yet.

I looked away, shifting position. Hell, it seemed as if I'd been sitting in that dumb plastic chair for weeks. My legs and back hurt, and no amount of changing positions seemed to help.

I wanted to get out of there.

I was looking at my watch when Beer Belly came back in the room. It was my guess he'd been out comparing stories with the cop who was questioning Linda.

Can you believe Beer Belly actually looked offended to see me checking the time? 'You got an appointment, Glenda, or what?'

'No sir,' I said. What I wanted to do was remind him what I'd read in the newspaper once. In this state, the news story had said, the cops couldn't hold anyone for more than twenty-four hours and not charge them.

Like I said, that's what I wanted to say. But, once again, that might come under the heading of smart-mouthing, and Earl had taught me well. 'It's just that you've kept us here for an awful long time—'

'Us?' He lowered himself once again into the chair opposite me. 'Why do you say us? It could be we've already let your sister go. Because Linda fingered you as the one who stabbed your stepdad.'

I know he was disappointed at my reaction, but I couldn't help it. I actually grinned at him. Because I knew, without a shadow of a doubt, that he was lying.

This guy didn't know twins. Linda would no more finger me than she would confess. 'Well, if Linda has fingered me, then I guess I better finger her real quick, huh?'

For a second there, Beer Belly looked excited. 'Are you telling me that your sister did it?'

I shook my head. 'My stepfather was killed by a burglar. My sister has told you the same thing.'

Beer Belly turned even redder in the face. 'Your sister has also said that she couldn't recall going by the teller machine earlier today, either. Did you two also forget about putting the bank slip into your stepdad's pocket?'

Living with Earl had taught me well. I didn't even flinch. 'I don't know what you're talking about.'

I wouldn't have believed it possible, but Beer Belly's face went even redder. 'You know, we're dusting for fingerprints right now.'

I just looked at him. Unlike what a lot of people believe, it isn't true that identical twins have identical fingerprints. I guess you'd expect the police to know that kind of thing. But, then again, if you wear gloves when you're wiping things off, it doesn't really matter.

Beer Belly was really working himself up into a snit. 'You know what I think?' he went on, his tone almost a growl. 'I think either you or your twin is a murderer. And the other one is her accomplice.'

I stared at him. 'Then why don't you arrest us?'

Now he looked like he might explode. 'I think you know why – it's what you two are counting on. We can't prove to a jury which one of you actually did it.'

I figured my best bet now was to say nothing.

Beer Belly stood up. 'So we're letting you go.'

'Go?' My heart leaped to my throat.

'We've gotten in touch with your mother, and she's waiting outside to take you two home.'

I knew I shouldn't do it, but I couldn't help myself. I started smiling.

Beer Belly glared at me. 'Your mom's pretty upset about all this. She could hardly give us a statement.' He cleared his throat one more time. 'You two ought to have thought about your poor mother before you did this.'

I met Glenda in the hallway as they escorted us both out to the lobby. When Glenda saw me, she grabbed one of my hands, clutching it like it was a life-preserver.

'Mom's out there, you know,' I said.

Glenda just shrugged. Leaning close to me, she whispered, 'If

271

Mom says anything different now, they'll just think she's trying to protect us.'

I glanced over at Glenda then, and once again I could see what she was thinking. We were both seeing Mom again, just like she'd been earlier today, standing in the kitchen when we came home from school. With Earl sprawled at her feet, his eyes wide and staring.

Mom had dropped the knife the second we walked in. Glenda and I had both jumped at the noise, but Mom didn't seem to hear it.

'He was saying that you two belonged to him, too,' she'd said, almost as if she were explaining it to herself. 'He was saying that you two were full-grown, and that he was just the man to teach you—' Her voice had trailed off, but she'd still stood there, her mouth slightly open. As if she didn't realize she'd stopped speaking.

She was calm enough, though. Calm enough for us to convince her not to say anything to anyone. Just drive straight to her sister's while we took care of things here.

Now, as we saw Mom, sitting all hunched up over in the corner, Glenda squeezed my arm. 'Mom's going to be OK now,' she said. 'We did the right thing. She could never have claimed self-defense – Earl hadn't laid a hand on her.'

I nodded. Once again, Glenda was right. The only way out was for the police to think we'd done it.

So maybe Brady was right. Glenda and I *are* a cop's worst nightmare.

These days Glenda keeps saying that we've won. That, at last, it's over. I want to believe her. I particularly want to late at night when I've been awakened once again by Mom crying in her room down the hall.

I've never told Mom that we can hear her.

Like I've never told Glenda that I, too, wake with a start almost every night, drenched in sweat, heart pounding, seeing all over again the way Earl had looked that last day.

I won't ever tell Glenda that. Or that, sometimes, I also hear her. Muffling her sobs with her pillow.

Oh, yes, as it turns out, I guess we twins could give the police lessons on worst nightmares.

BY HENDON CENTRAL STATION I SAT DOWN AND WEPT

MARK TIMLIN

Author's Note:Nick Sharman's brother is briefly mentioned in Romeo's Tune. *An extended version of this story was, in fact, going to be the third Sharman novel entitled* A Young Mod's Forgotten Story. *But the lack of mayhem precluded that. It's been kicking around in my mind ever since. So, six years later, and set in late '89, here it is under another title.*

It had been twenty-five years since I'd last seen Allie Parker, when I met his train that Monday at Waterloo station.

Then it had been a warm July afternoon in 1965. Now it was a bitterly cold December morning just before a new decade began.

Then I'd been eleven and Allie eighteen, the same age as my brother Bob. Allie and I both grew older, Bob didn't.

Allie and Bob had both been mods. Nineteen-sixties style-freaks, into amphetamines and sweet soul music, part of a loose gang of maybe fifty geezers, known locally as the Streatham Boys.

One night in that long-forgotten summer there'd been a ruck at the Lyceum in the Strand, where the faces gathered to admire the cut of each other's trousers, listen to the latest sounds, pop pills and pull birds. The fight was over a girl from Hendon who Allie fancied, but whose boyfriend didn't appreciate the competition. Some blood was spilled, and the following Sunday a dozen of the Streatham Boys got tooled up and made a sortie up to north London to sort out the aggro.

Bob never came back. In a running battle outside Hendon Central tube station he ended up with a knife in his chest. Allie's prints were the only ones found on the murder weapon. He was nicked and tried, pleaded not guilty, but was convicted and sentenced to life. He always maintained his innocence, but refused to identify who did kill Bob. He was doing his time in Strangeways a couple of years later when a fight broke out one lunch-time in the mess hall. Somewhere Allie had got hold of another knife and he stuck a fellow prisoner, killing him immediately. That time he did plead guilty and got another life sentence. Twenty-five years he did in all, and that Monday he had been released from Parkhurst and was coming home.

Although I hadn't seen him he'd sent me letters from day one, and I'd spoken to him on the phone. He called me regularly once prisoners got the privilege and always maintained his innocence, but wouldn't say more. At first I'd ignored his correspondence and been pretty short with him on the dog. But he persevered, and over the years as I took my GCEs, went to university until I was slung out, joined the police, got into bad company and did bad things and was slung out of the force too; got married, had Judith, then lost her and my wife to a dentist, and became a private investigator down in south London, we got as friendly as it was possible for us to be.

But I hadn't seen him. No. That was out of the question. However much he pleaded he was innocent, I could never be sure.

You see, a murder is like a stone tossed into a still pool. The ripples spread, and keep on spreading, for years.

My mum and dad were never the same after Bob died. Mum went a bit strange, and eventually Dad left and vanished out of our lives for ever. And we weren't the only ones to suffer. Bob had had a girlfriend, Veronica, Ronnie. They'd been together for a couple of years, and there was talk of an engagement. That's how they did things then. Ronnie took it hard when Bob died, and she killed herself a few years later with an overdose of smack. That was two families ruined. Then there was Allie's folks. They nursed a lot of grief too. They ran a little grocer's shop in the Old Kent Road. I went to visit them irregularly, but when the old man died I didn't go to the funeral. Allie was out on day release with an escort, and I still couldn't face seeing him. His mum told me he'd lost a lot of hair, but was cheerful.

I was made up.

Mrs Parker's still in the the shop every day, although she's close to seventy-five, and she's had a lot of offers for the place. Mostly from the Asian community, but she keeps saying no. She hired some staff and they do most of the work whilst she keeps an eye on them. She told me she'd keep the business for Allie to come home to.

And eventually he did. All things must pass.

I miss my brother. He was a good bloke. Kind. Let me tag along. I miss my dad as well. And my mum, in a lot of ways. And Ronnie too. Maybe if she and Bob had got married I'd have some nephews and nieces to spoil, and Mum would have more grandchildren.

Maybe if the family had stayed together things would've turned out differently, and I wouldn't be missing my own wife and child, Laura and Judith, so much.

Do all the things you love slip through your fingers?

I even miss Allie in a way. He was a laugh. Underneath it all.

When he got news of his release date he called me up and told me. After twenty-five years a lot of the scars had healed, and when his mum asked me to meet him at the station and bring him home I decided to find out how deep the scar tissue was.

So that's why I was standing at the barrier to platform twelve when the nine-fifteen arrival from Portsmouth came chugging in.

I never would have recognized Allie. By then he was almost completely bald, he'd put on a lot of soft weight, and his face was pale and lined from prison life. But he recognized me and came over. He was wearing a bomber jacket and jeans with trainers, and carrying a nylon holdall.

'Nick,' he said.

I looked into his pale blue eyes. 'Allie,' I said back.

We didn't shake hands.

'I would've known you anywhere,' he said. 'You look just like your old man.' He didn't add 'And Bob,' but I could see it in his eyes.

'Is that right? I can hardly remember. He fucked off.'

'I know,' he said. 'Mum told me.'

'It was a long time ago, Allie.'

'Yeah. Everything's changed. Even since I came up for the funeral. Everything's bright.'

'Is that right?' I said again. It wasn't bright at all that day.

'Yeah. There's not much colour inside. It's all grey.'

I almost found out for myself, I thought. 'I've got the motor outside. Your mum's expecting you,' I said.

'Can we get a drink first?'

'At this time?'

He glanced at the cheap Timex on his wrist. 'Sorry. I forgot. Licensing hours don't mean much inside.'

'They wouldn't.'

'Cup of tea then. I need some time.'

'There's a café on the station.'

'No – outside. There's too many bodies here. I'm getting a bit freaked.'

'All right, Allie. We'll stop on the way.'

I rescued the car from the short-term parking and threw Allie's bag into the boot, then turned the car south. We found a greasy spoon by the Elephant, and I stuck the wheels on a meter and we went in.

It was steamy and warm inside the restaurant, with a bunch of *Sun*-reading individuals tucking into their breakfasts. Allie ordered beans on toast and a mug of tea. I settled for the tea only, and lit a cigarette as we sipped at the boiling brew and waited for his food to come from the kitchen.

'Long time, Nick,' he said.

'Yeah.'

'I'm forty-three now. Don't seem possible.'

'Same age as Bob would've been.'

'Yeah.' He started to roll a needle-thin, jailhouse cigarette. 'I never done it, you know.'

'No Allie, I don't know. Not for sure.'

'But I never. He was my mate.'

'Then who did?'

He regarded me through the smoke, and the steam from his mug. 'I've never told a soul.'

I said nothing.

'But I want to show you. You deserve that at least. That's why I got Mum to get you to meet me.'

'Yeah?'

He nodded, and a middle-aged woman in a white overall called out his order, and he sloped off to get it. 'Fuck me,' he said when he got back. 'Nearly fifteen bob for a few beans and a slice. I don't think I'll ever get used to this new money.'

'It's been going for nearly twenty years, Allie,' I said. 'You'd better. So tell me about Bob.'

'In a bit,' he replied, finishing his snack fast, like the food might be swiped from under his nose if he ate slowly. 'Let's go and see Mum.'

The shop was open, with the two assistants busily serving, Mrs Parker sitting in the back with her eyes on the TV screens that monitored the shop.

'Allie,' she said, with tears in her eyes as she got up to greet us. 'Hello son. It's good to see you out. Cuppa tea?'

'Hello Mum,' said Allie awkwardly, as he dropped his bag and clumsily embraced her. 'In a minute, yeah. I've got something I want to show Nick here first.'

'Whatever you like, son,' she said. 'Your room's just as you left it, but I gave it a rub round.'

And it was. I'd been there a couple of times with Bob and Allie, when they let me come along during the school holidays, and it was like stepping back thirty years to a more innocent time.

The room was medium-sized, at the top of the house looking down at the dreary backyard full of crates of old bottles and other rubbish from the shop. The windows were streaked and dirty, but the curtains were clean, as if Mrs P. had made sure that her boy didn't come back to complete squalor. The bed was freshly made too, with clean sheets, and the place had been dusted, but otherwise it was just as I remembered it from all that long time ago.

One wall was taken up with shelves of LPs and singles, all pristine in their sleeves, as if they'd just come out of the shop. Against another wall was a chest of drawers, on top of which stood a Dansette record-player with an autochange. There was a big wardrobe against the third wall, and Allie opened the door to show off maybe twenty moddy-boy suits and close to a hundred shirts with tab or button-down collars on hangers, plus two overcoats and a mackintosh. Neatly lined up beneath them were a couple of dozen pairs of shoes and boots.

'All me old clobber,' he said proudly. 'But I betcha I couldn't get into them now.' He rubbed his protruding stomach. 'Prison grub. All carbohydrates.'

He went over to the record shelves and riffled through a few albums, then picked up a handful of singles.

'All mint,' he said, tossing them on to the bed. 'Tamla, Sue, Atlantic. Worth a packet now. I kept up inside. I still love this music. It's all crap what they do now.'

'Bob,' I reminded him.

'Sure. Sorry. Give me a hand with this.' He moved over to the chest.

'Do what?'

'Give us a hand. Pull it out from the wall.'

I did as he said, and it slid over the carpet. Behind it, the wallpaper had been stripped to the bricks, four of which had been loosened from their cement.

'Coppers never found this,' he said with satisfaction. 'I betcha Mum and the old bloke give 'em a right hard time when they came round.'

He pulled the bricks out of the wall, exposing a gap. 'Bathroom next door,' he said. 'This is where the pipes go.' Then he pulled out a sawn-off shotgun, a box of shells and two big jars. One was full of old banknotes, and the other, little blue and purple pills.

'This was what it was all about, Nick,' he said, hunkering back on to his heels. 'Our little earner.'

'What?' I said.

'Me, Bob and another geezer, Jimmy Gurney, used to do chemist shops and wholesalers. We nicked uppers and sold them round the clubs. Simple.'

'I never knew,' I said.

'You weren't supposed to, little brother. You worshipped Bob,

278

everyone knew that. He wasn't going to let on that he was a tea leaf on the side.'

He saw my look.

'Christ Nick, don't look so surprised. We never did any harm. We never hurt no one. A bit of thieving, that was all. We were innocent, mate. Innocent times.'

'But it ended in murder. My brother's murder. And that murder fucked up a lot of people.'

'Tell me about it. What do you think it did to me, and Mum, and the old man?'

'So why didn't you tell the truth at the time?'

'Because we didn't grass. The rules of the road. Nowadays the little scumbags will turn their best mates over for twenty quid. But we didn't. Innocent, see. And then when I killed the other fella . . . Well, I was up for life on that too, and it didn't seem to make much difference.'

'So who did it?'

'That bastard Gurney. He wanted to make a career of being at it. I didn't care one way or another. Bob wanted to knock it on the head. He had that bird. What was her name?'

'Veronica.'

'That's right, Veronica. They were serious. He didn't want to get caught. Knew it would do your mum and dad up. Whatever happened to the bird?'

'She's dead. She turned into a junkie.'

'For fuck's sake. Ironical, ain't it, Nick?'

He hefted the bottle of pills, then picked up the jar of money. It was all old notes, well out of date. 'You'll have to take those to the Bank of England,' I said for something to cover my confusion. 'They'll change them for new.'

'Hardly seems worth it,' said Allie. 'I bet there's not more than a couple of ton in here. And at more than a nicker for beans on toast and a cuppa, how far will that get me? A souvenir, Nick, that's what they are.'

'So what now?' I asked.

'Now I go and do for Gurney. That bastard killed my best mate and let me rot inside.' Allie hefted the shotgun.

I picked up the box of shells, opened it and took one out. The cardboard tube of the .12-gauge cartridge was crazed and cracked under my fingers, dropping shot on to the carpet. 'Not with these you won't,' I said. 'They've perished.'

'Shit.'

He knelt again, put his hand back into the hole and brought out a flick-knife and popped the blade. It gleamed in the dull morning light, still sharp after all that time. 'Looks like this'll have to do then. Poetical justice.'

'You can't just kill him.'

'Why not? Mum'll know where he is. She knows everything. Besides, I've been inside so long, outside is like a prison to me. In there I get three meals a day, don't have to worry about me laundry, and I've made a lot of mates. I don't mind going back.'

He made it sound almost desirable.

'I'm coming with you,' I said.

'Nah.'

'Yeah. Otherwise I'll set the Bill on you.'

'You wouldn't.'

'I was one, don't forget.'

'I always wondered about that.' He looked at me hard, then shrugged. 'All right,' he said. 'It's your funeral.'

He emptied his holdall and put the gun, the cartridges, the knife and the two jars inside.

We went back downstairs. 'Cuppa tea, son?' asked Mrs P., hopefully.

'In a bit, Ma. Me and Nick's got a coupla people to see.'

'Who?'

'Jimmy Gurney. Remember him?'

''Course I do. I ain't lost my marbles yet.'

I had to smile.

''Course you ain't, Ma,' said Allie. 'He's still about, ain't he?'

'Sure he is. Dirty little sluice. Lives down on the Walk Estate with that slut of a wife of his, and all them poor kids.'

Bandit country.

'Know where?'

'Hamlet House. Top floor. Number seventy as I recall.'

'OK, Ma,' said Allie, kissing her on the cheek. 'We'll see you later.'

'Mrs Parker,' I said.

'Nick.'

We went back to my car and I turned in the direction of the Walk Estate. We were silent on the journey, although there were a million questions I wanted answered.

When we got on to the estate I parked on the corner opposite Hamlet House and we got out. A cold wind struck hard and there was snow in the air.

Allie grabbed hold of my arm and said, 'When I was a little kid I used to go round my nan's. She had this kitchen at the back of the house. It had one of those big, old-fashioned stoves. And she did all the cooking on it, and all the boiling and washing and stuff like that. And she had a coal fire too, and she kept it on all the time. It was always hot in there, winter and summer. And in the winter, when there was nobody in the room but me, I used to open the kitchen door and there were three steps that went down into the garden. And it'd be cold outside, and I'd be warm inside. And I felt safe. I haven't felt safe since then. How long is it since you've felt safe, Nick?'

'A long time,' I said. 'Twenty-five years at least.'

He let go of my arm then, and we shuffled through the rubbish that was skinned with grey snow, to the front door of the flats. Miraculously the lift was working and we punched twelve.

When we got to the top floor we found number seventy at the end of the balcony. From next door the thud of over-amplified rap music shook the walls. The bell at the side of the door was broken and the knocker was missing, so Allie hammered on the hardboard that covered where glass had once been.

'Salubrious,' I remarked.

'Jimmy always had style.'

The door was answered by a slatternly-looking woman dressed head to toe in cheap catalogue clothes. She was about thirty-five, skinny, with big tits, and could've used a decent bra. She had long, lank greasy hair and pimples on her forehead. She was holding a young kid whose nappy needed changing, and a couple of dirty-faced toddlers clutched at her skirts.

'Mrs Gurney,' said Allie.

''S'right.'

'Jimmy in?'

'You the old Bill?' she said.

'Hardly,' said Allie. 'I just came out today. Is he in?'

She nodded. 'You'd better come in,' she said. Visits from old lags were obviously no novelty.

'In the kitchen,' she said.

We went through into a stench of old sweat, puke, pizza and piss. Nice ambience, I thought.

I'd probably met Jimmy Gurney twenty-five years before, but even if we'd been old mates I doubt if I'd've recognized the vision we found sitting at the kitchen table.

He had long, stringy, dirty grey hair with a big bald spot at the crown, an earring in the shape of a skull, a hippie moustache, and he was wearing a dirty vest and jeans. He was smoking a spliff and nursing another baby.

Jesus. Home sweet home.

He looked up when we entered. 'I've told you a hundred times I haven't got any money,' he said.

Debt collectors must've been a big feature in the Gurneys' lives too.

'No money today, Jimmy,' said Allie. 'We've come round to clear up another debt.'

'Who the fuck are you?' demanded Gurney. The music from next door was so loud that we had to shout.

'Don't you remember, Jim? Think about it,' said Allie.

Gurney looked from one of us to the other, but seemed to have a better handle on me.

'It can't be,' he said, his already pasty skin turning pale.

'Like him, ain't he?' said Allie.

'Bob,' said Gurney.

'Bob's dead, you cunt. You fucking know that,' said Allie. 'That's his little brother all grown up. But the resemblance's there.'

'Allie,' said Gurney, now growing even paler.

'Home from the war,' said Allie. 'Now yours starts. You never visited me, Jim. Shame on you.'

'I . . . I . . . I . . .' the seated man stammered.

'Shut up,' said Allie.

'Listen,' said the woman. 'What's going on?'

'You. Take those kids and go into the next room,' ordered Allie. 'And don't even dream of using the phone.'

'The phone's off,' said Jimmy Gurney dispiritedly.

'Fuck me,' said Allie as the woman took the baby from Gurney. 'I was living better inside.'

When the woman had gone, Allie put the bag on the table and opened it. He took out the jar of pills. 'Remember these, Jim?' he said.

Gurney obviously did. Allie put the pills on the table then took out the shotgun and said to Gurney, 'I brought this for you, son.'

Gurney cringed in his seat.

'Tell him,' he ordered, nodding at me. 'Tell him what you done.'

'I never done nothing.'

'Liar,' said Allie. 'Black liar.' And he pulled both hammers of the shotgun back for effect, even though it wasn't loaded.

'Don't,' said Gurney, covering his head with his thin arms. 'Please don't. My kids.'

'Then tell him, you little bastard.'

Gurney was nearly in tears. 'I never meant to kill him,' he said. 'Just frighten him into keeping on doing the jobs we were doing. It was good money. But he wouldn't listen. We was away from the fight at the back of the station. I was out of me head on them.' He pointed at the jar. 'I never knew what I was doing.'

'See, Nick,' said Allie. 'Told you.'

'But your prints were on the knife,' I said to Allie.

'It *was* mine. But I lent it to this git when we went up to Hendon that day. And Jimmy here always wore gloves, winter and summer. Thought it was cool. Right, Jim?'

Gurney nodded.

Allie looked round. 'Times have changed. This fucking place stinks like shit. And Jimmy, you look like shit too.'

'It ain't my fault,' whined Gurney. 'I can't work. Got agoraphobia and asthma. And the fucking social don't help much . . .'

'You killed my brother,' I interrupted, and I felt a red rage wash over me.

'I swear it was an accident.'

'But you let Allie go to jail for it.'

Gurney said nothing.

'Shall I top him now, Nick?' said Allie.

'No,' pleaded Gurney. Another minute and the stink of his shit would join the rest in the disgusting kitchen. 'The missus would be all on her own.'

'You'd rather be alive in this hole, with that slag,' said Allie disbelievingly. 'I reckon I'd be doing you a favour, topping you.'

'So do I,' I said. 'So leave him, Allie. That's the worst punishment you could dole out.'

Allie looked around again and grinned. 'I think you're right, Nick.'

So we left Jimmy Gurney there with his wife and children in that slum, in the stink, of old sweat, puke, pizza and piss with the music thudding through the walls.

We went for a drink at a pub down by the river. We didn't talk much about what had happened that afternoon in Gurney's horrible kitchen. When it started to get dark and the tide was out, we walked on to the flats. I ruined a good pair of shoes. We threw all the stuff in the bag way out into the water: the gun and the knife and the shells and the pills and the money. I think we'd all got too many souvenirs to want any more by then. When we got back to the shore, Allie said, 'You go on Nick. I can get back home on my own. I want to take a wander.'

That time we shook hands, and I drove home. We didn't make any arrangements to meet again.

The next day I went to Hendon. I'd avoided going there ever since Bob died. I mean, Hendon wasn't part of my regular manor, and even though the police college is there, where you do your induction into the Met, I'd always managed not to go to Hendon Central itself.

But that day I did.

I got up early, had some breakfast, got into the car and pointed it north. Headed over the river, and after a couple of false starts I found Hendon Central tube.

It had started snowing again.

By the station was a bit of a green and a bench that looked like it had been taken over by dossers, but that was empty now, so I used it.

And by Hendon Central station I sat down and wept.

THE BONE JAR
CANDACE ROBB

The tide was in. The Ouse River swirled round the small island of rock on which stood a solitary hut fashioned from bits of flotsam and jetsam, crowned by a much patched, no longer seaworthy Viking longboat from York's past. Owen Archer folded his long legs into the coracle left for him on the muddy bank. The back of his neck tingled, as if someone was watching him, but he turned too late to see clearly the dark figure that disappeared into the smoke of the cooking fires. He told himself it meant nothing, the man had no doubt been staring at the water, not him. But why had he then dropped out of sight when Owen turned? He was uneasy as he fought his way across the rushing current.

On the other side, Owen pulled the coracle on to the rock, tied it up, passed under the dragon that leered upside down from the prow of the longboat, and knocked on Magda Digby's door. When he received no answer, he opened the door gingerly, peered round it. As he had thought, Magda Digby, midwife and healer, was bent over a patient.

'Draining old Daniel's wound, Bird-eye. Thou canst wait quietly.'

The hut was smoky and dusty from the herbs that hung drying from the planks of the longboat. 'I'll wait without.'

Magda nodded, intent on her work.

As Owen sat down on a bench facing back towards York, he felt the watcher's eyes upon him, but could pick out no one on the bank. Though he breathed in the damp river air and tried to relax, a shower of needle pricks across his blind left eye revealed his tension. He rubbed his scarred eye beneath the patch that hid the worst of the disfigurement.

It was not the watcher on the bank that worried Owen. Magda's messenger had not known why the Riverwoman wanted Owen, just that 'thou must come today'. Owen feared Magda had bad news about his wife's health or that of the babe she carried. His stomach churned. He could not bear the thought of losing Lucie. And something of her spirit would die if she lost this child.

Not a man who could sit still for long in the best of circumstances, Owen rose from the bench to pace.

At last Magda appeared, rubbing her eyes, stretching with a satisfied sigh. She wore a colourful dress made from the squares of wool on which she tested dyeing plants. Sewn together they formed a shapeless gown that confused the eye of the beholder when Magda moved quickly, which she invariably did despite her great age. Her grizzled hair was tucked up into a clean kerchief.

'Old Daniel's shoulder will heal?' Owen asked.

Magda squinted up at him. 'Aye, Bird-eye.' Gnarled fists on hips, she leaned back and studied Owen's face. 'Such a frown thou wearest! Art thou so concerned for old Daniel?' Her deep-set eyes teased, though her mouth was stern.

Owen sank down on to the bench. 'In truth, 'tis your purpose in calling me here that worries me.'

'Magda might ask thee to imperil thy soul, is that what thou fearest?' She threw back her head and gave a loud, barking laugh.

'No. I fear you've summoned me because something is amiss with Lucie.'

'Thy child's coming is the centre of thy world at present.' Magda shook her grizzled head and sat down beside Owen. 'Thy wife is a master apothecary, Bird-eye, she knows to take care of herself. And with Magda assisting – who has delivered more babes than thou canst imagine – all will be well.' She patted his knee.

Owen closed his eye and said a silent prayer of thanksgiving.

Magda grunted, folded her arms, leaned back against the wall.

'Magda must go up into the Dales. She asks thee to guard her house for two nights.' She snorted as Owen glanced back at the ramshackle building with a puzzled expression. 'What is to guard against but wind and flood, eh? Magda reads thy mind, Bird-eye.' She rose, motioned for him to follow her round the house. Under the stern of the old ship that capped the hut stood a jar almost as tall as Magda herself. 'Magda's bone jar, that is what's to guard. The bone man comes in two days.'

Owen laughed. Who would steal such a thing? He had once shifted the jar for her and knew its heft. 'You fear the bones will walk before the relic dealer arrives, do you?'

Magda frowned. 'Laugh not. A man has been watching Magda's house, waiting for her to leave. He knows of the bone jar. He knows a leg and part of an arm wait in the jar for the bone man, who gives them a Christian burial.'

'You have the bones buried? Is that common practice?'

Magda shrugged. ''Tis Magda's way.'

'Why not make some profit on them?'

The sharp eyes bored through him. 'Thinkst thou art clever? Pah. Magda pities the poor wretches who pray to dried skin and bones, expecting miracle cures. She won't be part of such traffic.'

'This thief won't come for them while you're here?'

Magda shook her head.

'Why not?'

'Thou knowest why, Bird-eye. Some folk think that because they do not see Magda in church she is a spell-casting heathen. They fear Magda.'

Owen could not deny that. 'I could dispose of the bones for you.'

The Riverwoman shook her head. 'Magda's bone man prays over them as he buries them. Magda does not have the prayers. Nor dost thou, not the proper prayers.'

The Riverwoman's beliefs puzzled Owen, though Lucie seemed to understand them. She said that faith came hard to Magda. She must see to believe. But Magda understood that most folk needed the Church to comfort them and keep them on the path of righteousness. 'Your bone man is a priest?'

'A friar.'

Magda placed her trust in the oddest creatures. 'Friars are not opposed to relics. Why trust him?'

'He understands Magda removes cursèd limbs. They must be left in peace.'

Generous man; there was money to be made in relics. Owen hoped Magda was not being cheated. 'And you want me to sleep here and scare off anyone who lurks about?'

'Aye.'

'Why me?'

'Thou art a good man, Bird-eye. Thou'lt let thy God guide thee.'

God guide him in catching a thief. A strange way of putting it, but in the end it was God's hand that guided all men in their work. Owen shrugged. 'You have done much for me and asked naught in return. 'Tis time I returned the favour.' It was a change from the political webs in which the archbishop was wont to snare him.

The wrinkles deepened about her mouth and eyes as the River-woman smiled. 'Magda knew thou wouldst aid her. Though thou lookst a rogue thou art a gentle man, Bird-eye. See thou takest care. Thou hast a family would miss thee and curse Magda if aught happened to thee.'

'Lucie is close to her time. What if the babe—'

'Peace, Bird-eye. Magda knows the signs. Lucie is not ready. Magda will return in time. See that thou comest tomorrow evening.'

'This thief will stay away during the day?'

'Young Jack will watch during the day. Easy for the lad to draw attention in daylight if he needs help. Not so easy at night.'

Owen should have known Magda would think of everything.

Long before sunset the next day Owen passed out through the gates of the city. He picked his way down to the riverbank through mud and the ramshackle huts of the poor, looking for the man who had watched him the previous day. A cat sniffed and followed, hoping to trick him out of the sweet he carried in his bag. Children watched him uneasily, his height, his dark beard and the patch over his scarred face all fearful-seeming. Would his own child fear him so?

He searched the vermin city and found no one as well fed as a relic dealer. At last he gave up and rowed the coracle over to Magda's rock.

Young Jack had been waiting. He jumped up, eager to get off the island before dark.

'Did anyone bother you today, lad?'

'Nay, Captain Archer. 'Twas a quiet day.'

Owen drew a cup covered in oiled cloth from his bag and from it pulled a slice of angelica stem dipped in honey. 'Mistress Wilton thought you might enjoy this.'

The boy's eyes lit up. 'Thank you, Captain!'

Owen returned it to the cup and handed it to Jack. 'There's a cat waiting on the bank for it. Take care to hold it high.'

The boy carefully placed it on the floor of the coracle and picked up the oar.

'See that you return early,' Owen said as he untied the boat and eased it into the water.

'I won't fail you, Captain,' the boy cried as he paddled off.

Owen watched that Jack reached the riverbank without mishap, then walked round the outside of the house before heading in. Within, fresh straw had been spread on the mud floor. Owen wondered where Magda got so much energy at her age. Though no one in York knew how old she was, no one could remember her not being here. Even Bess Merchet, proprietress of the York Tavern and reservoir of city history, could not say how old Magda was or whence she'd come to the odd house on the rock. Magda was a good friend to him and Lucie, but they knew little about her. Owen might learn something of Magda's past with a careful search of the house. Tempting, but he would not so betray a friendship.

He went outside, settled on the bench facing back towards the city, poured himself some ale from the jug he'd brought with him, and settled in to watch and wait. He leaned back and looked up at the dragon's head silhouetted against the evening sky. What sort of folk went to sea with such a monster on their prow? Why did Magda choose such a thing to crown her house? She made a joke of it, but why had she really chosen it? To guard the jar?

For that matter, how did he know what was actually in the jar? A leg and part of an arm, would those call for a constant watch? What did Magda care whether the bones went to a relic dealer or were given a Christian burial? And what was the point of a Christian burial if the limbs were not with the rest of the body? When the bones rose up on Judgement Day, how were they to find the rest of the body and rejoin it?

Owen stood and shook his arms and legs to loosen them after his long sit in the damp air. Silly thoughts he was having. He looked about him. The stars were brightening in the darkening sky and the water lapped quietly away from the north side of the rock. He walked slowly round the house, listening for sounds nearby. Nothing but the water and his own footsteps.

He approached the jar, standing tall and silent, its lid secure. Perhaps he should have looked within while it was light. What if the thief had already struck? Owen considered getting a lantern and checking now. He put his hands on either side and gently rocked the jar. Felt much the same as the day Magda had asked him to move it for her. It had been empty then. Perhaps it was empty now and he was playing the fool. He rocked it again. Something shifted within.

No doubt he would be uneasy until he looked inside.

Owen continued his circuit of the hut, then went in to get a lantern. He cursed himself when he found the fire almost out. Had he come in much later he would have spent a cold night in the dark. Now he must take the time to stoke the fire.

By the time Owen had the fire burning once more, he was thirsty and hungry. He spread his cold meal of bread, cheese and meat out on a table and poured himself an ale. Sitting down, he stretched his booted feet out towards the fire and took a long, satisfying drink, then bent to the food. He was noisily chewing the hard-crusted bread when he heard a noise at the door. He stopped chewing, held his breath – heard nothing but the gentle lapping of the water and the far-off cries of the night watchmen. He had not realized how much time had passed. Perhaps he should make a circuit of the rock before he finished his meal. And take a look inside the jar. He lit a lantern and stepped outside.

Something came whistling through the air towards Owen's head. He stepped back and the missile flew past him, falling with a plop into the river. Closing the shutter on the lantern, Owen dropped down to a squat. It was now quite dark and a mist rose up from the river, not too thick, but just enough to shield him as long as he stayed low. He peered out into the dark but saw no one moving. Nor did he hear anyone. Staying low, he crept to the corner of the building and listened. The tide was out and the mud would noisily suck at a walker's feet. Nothing. His attacker must be on the rock.

Still in a crouch, Owen edged along the north side of the house towards the back. A scraping sound. He paused. Heard it again.

The sound echoed. He hurried round the corner, saw at first only the jar. But the scraping sound came again. Now he noticed motion at the top of the jar. The thief was working on the lid.

Owen sat back on his heels and considered his options. He could open the shutter and surprise the thief with the light. After all, where could the thief run? And how likely was it he could outrun Owen? But tackling him to the ground would be far more satisfying. Owen had worked up a lot of tension and a nice, physical attack would help work it off. But he must not be too violent; he wanted to find out who the thief was and why he attacked Owen but not Magda.

Inching closer, keeping against the house, Owen gradually saw the man's outline, smelled his fear. He waited – the thief was the same height as the jar and it would be difficult to keep his arms stretched up to work at the lid for long. When he lowered his arms, shaking them, Owen leapt. He knocked the thief to the rocky ground with a satisfying thud.

'Sweet Jesu, you've broken my limbs!' the thief cried.

'More for the jar,' Owen muttered. He rose and pulled the thief up by his clothes. The man wobbled and crumpled against Owen. For pity's sake, what was such a weak cur doing thieving? Owen grabbed him up and slung him over his shoulder. The man whimpered, but he did not struggle.

Inside, Owen dropped his limp burden on to one of Magda's cots and finally got a look at the thief in the firelight. He was astonished. 'John Fortescue! What does the clerk of the Mercers' Guild want with the Riverwoman's bones?'

The wizened face of the young man crinkled in shame. 'Captain Archer, forgive me.' He tried to sit up, winced, and fell back clutching his left arm.

Seeing John's pain, Owen regretted the fury of his attack. John was a frail young man, aged beyond his years by some curse that wrinkled his skin and bent his body like an old man. 'You fell on the arm and broke it, eh? I'm sorry. But I'll be damned if I can think of an innocent explanation for your activities tonight.' Owen searched Magda's work table for bandages and a splint.

John lay still. 'I was thieving, Captain Archer. 'Tis the unholy truth.'

Armed with the necessary supplies and a jug of brandywine, Owen knelt beside the cot. 'Let me examine your arm.' Owen handed John the jug. 'Drink some of this.' He felt round on the arm while John drank; a bone in the forearm had snapped like that of an old man. But it would not take much of a tug to set it. 'Brace yourself.' Owen tugged. John made a terrible face, but kept stoically silent. Owen splinted the arm and bound it close to John's body. 'What of the leg? You stumbled when you stood up.'

John wiggled his foot. 'It's my ankle. Sprained, I think.'

Owen examined it, nodded, sat back on his heels. 'You'll do best to keep off it for a few days.' He crossed his arms over his chest and studied the clerk's dark, mud-spattered clothing, his pale, wrinkled face, the frightened eyes. 'Why are you thieving, is what I wonder. You have neither the strength nor the temperament for it. Nor the need, I should think – the chief clerk of the richest guild in the city – surely you are well paid.'

'I am after health, not wealth,' John said softly, keeping his eyes downcast. 'But I did not start out to steal, Captain. I asked the Riverwoman if I might have the skin off the boy's arm. She refused. Said it must be given a proper burial.'

'Her arrangement for the bones is an odd one, I'll grant you that. But what did you want with the skin? And how did you know about the arm?'

John bit his lower lip, a naughty child explaining his behaviour. 'It is for a remedy – for afflictions of the skin. I must bind a piece of young, unblemished skin to my forehead for seven days and seven nights. At sunset on the seventh day I crawl the length of York Minster while chanting a Latin charm, and then I have a seventh son bury the skin that night – the seventh night.'

As his wife's apprentice in the apothecary, Owen had heard many such remedies. 'It sounds harmless enough; except that such charms usually call for the skin of a pig or some other flesh readily available.'

The clerk took a deep, shivery breath, crossed himself. 'So it has all been for naught. Blessed Mary, Mother of God, forgive me my sin.' He rubbed his arm; his eyes glittered with tears.

'What did Magda tell you?'

John wiped his nose on his sleeve. 'She said that I must accept the truth, that my affliction is not of the skin, but affects every part of me. My body is in haste to grow old and expire. There is no cure for it.' John picked up the jug of ale and drank, then passed it to Owen. 'But I thought, what harm was there in trying? The Lord might hear my prayer. Who was she to judge whether He would choose to bless me?' He sighed. 'Now I pay for my arrogance.'

Owen understood. Well he knew how desperate the afflicted one was to put his body right. The loss of Owen's eye had meant the loss of his world – no longer was he worthy to be Henry of Lancaster's captain of archers. Even after Lancaster's physician had declared him blind in his left eye, Owen had tortured himself with tests, thinking he'd seen a glimmer of light on the left. 'When I first came to York, I hoped Magda might cure my blindness. But she told me that there was nothing more to be done.' He took a drink. 'It was not easy to accept. She knew. She said I would ever after see her as partly to blame. And I do sometimes, God forgive me.'

'And why not blame her? She condemned me to sit and wait for an early death.'

'We all face death, John.'

The angry look surprised Owen. 'You don't understand. When an old man wrinkles and weakens into a shuffling gait, he thanks the Lord for a good life and looks forward to eternal rest. I am not ready for that. I have not yet lived.'

Owen pitied him. But surely it did him no good to brood. 'Seems to me you've done a bit of living tonight, haven't you now? Creeping out here, slinking round, attacking me.' He laughed, picked up the jug and drank again, waiting for an echo of laughter. But John had lain down and covered his head with his arm.

'What I've told you – about the pig's skin – it simplifies things, doesn't it?'

John shrugged. 'Maybe.'

'You didn't tell me how you learned about the arm, John.'

'A traveller. He delivered some items to the guildhall. He told me about the charm and said the Riverwoman would have what I needed.' The voice was muffled under the arm.

Suddenly Owen jumped up. 'He was your partner, wasn't he? He was out there tonight.'

John lay very still.

Good Lord, he'd been so stupid. 'I should have seen it was too easy. You were distracting me.'

'And all for naught,' the muffled voice whined.

'Not for your partner, you fool. He's got the bones and a good head start.' Owen took the lantern and rushed out into the night.

He shoved the flat stone lid off the jar and let it fall with a clatter while he trained the light on the inside. Empty. He shone the lantern out on the mud flat, but he knew it was useless. While he'd been playing the good Samaritan in the hut, the thief had taken the bones and escaped. He'd known Owen wouldn't be listening, thinking he'd caught his thief – and injured him. Furious with himself, Owen picked up the stone lid and threw it into the river. He wanted to put his fist through the wall of the house, grab John Fortescue by the neck and throttle him – but what would be the point? John was the victim as much as he. Owen sat down on the bank and tried to calm himself.

When his mind cleared, he went inside, seeking answers.

John sat up, waiting for him, his eyes wide with fear.

'Why did your thief put Magda on her guard?'

'He didn't know where she kept the bones, and he didn't want to linger here, searching all those boxes and jars piled up against the house. He said she would watch the bones if we worried her, and then we'd know. He was clever.'

'Easy to be clever when you're working with fools.' Owen sat down and glumly drained the jug of ale.

Owen went out to the rock as soon as he had word Magda was back. She sat on the bench beneath the serpent, mending a shoe. Without looking up, she said, 'Magda knows the worst.'

He sank down beside her. 'I failed you. I'll make no excuses.'

'Thou wert there to protect the innocent fool, Bird-eye.'

'But the bones are gone. Sold by now, no doubt.'

Magda chuckled. 'If only Magda might have seen the thief's face at dawn, when he took out the bones and saw his treasure. Or woke to its smell.' She was overtaken by a bout of mirth.

Owen had a sinking feeling. How many people had fooled him? 'What were they?'

'The bones of an old goat that strayed on to the mud flats and died.'

'And the bones for the bone man?'

'He came before Magda left.' She patted Owen's knee. 'Magda is not disappointed in thee. Thou hast done as Magda had hoped. John will heal, and he has seen the folly of his search for a miracle. The thief is gone, no more spying on Magda.'

'No doubt I've learned something, too, though I cannot see it. Why did you have me here?'

'If he had felt no danger, the thief would have examined the bones, Bird-eye, and spoiled Magda's fun.'

'But what of poor John?'

'Fortescue respects thee. He will not wish to appear a fool to thee again, so he will behave now. So.' She snipped the thread, squinted up at Owen. 'How dost thou like working for Magda? A nice change from politics?'

Owen rubbed his scar. 'In truth I'd rather a month on the road for the archbishop than another night in your hut.'

Magda turned the mended shoe inside out, tugged it on, stood up, hopped, nodded. 'Suit thyself, Bird-eye,' she said with a shrug and went inside.

Owen did not leave at once but sat there, staring down at the rising tide, trying to remember what it had been like to be able to see upstream as well as down. At last he gave up. A useless exercise. That had been another life. He headed for home.

QUIET PLEASE – WE'RE ROLLING

PETER LOVESEY

A naked man on a tropical beach was chasing a small white dog that had just run off with his swimming trunks. The scene was shot from the rear. Once in a while, a bare bum is acceptable for early evening viewing.

Albert Challis, in his bedsit in Reading, reached for another can of lager, his eyes never leaving the screen of the small portable TV.

'Jesus! I don't know how they get away with this. It's bloody obvious most of it is faked.'

His wife Karen continued mending the jumper on her lap, oblivious to Albert's ranting. She didn't enjoy the programme, and she had a long evening in prospect, repairing clothes. There was no escape from the TV when you lived in a bedsit.

Albert continued, after a belch, 'When this show first went out, I reckon most of the clips were genuine. Then they started offering a few hundred quid for new material. Stands to reason people are going to fake the incidents. They set up someone making a fool of himself, roll the camera and cash in.'

He watched in cynical expectation as a grey man in a grey room began painting a door-frame. A second later the door opened and the hapless decorator was doused in red.

'Well, knock me down with a feather,' said Albert with heavy sarcasm. 'I never saw that one coming. It's like I say, Karen. The whole thing's a set-up.'

Karen folded the jumper and placed it on her 'done' pile, then turned her attention to a black woollen sock. It was one of Albert's, the survivor of a pair he had worn so proudly on their wedding day eighteen years ago. Now it contained as much darning wool as original thread, but Albert insisted it wasn't ready for the rag-box yet.

On the screen a well-dressed woman in a stable yard started walking beside the half-doors where the horses were kept.

'Eh up!' said Albert. 'Watch what happens to her big straw hat. There it goes!'

Sure enough, a horse's head appeared suddenly from one of the stables and got the woman's hat between its teeth and whipped it off her head and out of reach.

'I bet they rehearsed it three times.'

Karen had looked up and watched the clip, prompted by Albert's 'Eh up!'. 'If they did,' she said, 'they must have got through more than one hat. It's very destructive. I've never had a hat as nice as that.'

Albert said, 'It seems to me all you have to do is buy one of these bloody camcorders and the money's yours. They'll take anything, slipping on some ice, falling into a pond, being hit on the head by a football, any bloody thing. You could make one a week, I reckon. Shoot it on Saturday, send it to the television people on the Monday, and bingo, the cheque arrives on Wednesday. We could live like kings on that sort of money, Karen.'

Karen looked down at her darning again. 'Well why not, if it's so simple? Why not get one of those cameras and try it?'

Albert had no immediate answer. He placed his can on the aged carpet and folded both arms across his ample beer belly. The best he could manage in response was a smile that was meant to be superior.

Karen said, 'You're all mouth and trousers, Albert Challis. You say it's all a con, but you don't have the bottle to prove it.'

Albert found his voice. 'I'm not sure I heard you correctly, my sweet,' he said. 'You did just suggest buying one of those camcorders, didn't you? When was the last time you looked in the bloody shop window? Have you any idea of the price of those things?'

Karen shook her head. They didn't have the sort of money most

298

other people seemed to have. Nothing in their household had been bought new. They got it all second-hand. Whatever broke, burst or wore out had to be repaired.

'They cost a bloody fortune, woman,' Albert ranted. 'Hundreds of pounds. Can you imagine that, a little piece of black plastic costing five hundred quid?'

Karen shook her head, returning to the rhythmical comfort of needle and thread.

Albert finished his lager, watching a fat woman being chased across a field by a goat while the studio audience guffawed. 'The point is,' he said in support of his apparent caution, 'I'm not prepared to splash out five hundred on a camcorder when we only stand to make two hundred and fifty back.'

'But you just said you could make one a week and we could live like royalty,' Karen reminded him. 'Soon as I call your bluff, you back off.'

Albert shot her a filthy look. 'Don't you provoke me.'

'It's not as if we haven't got the money,' Karen persisted. 'We must have more than five hundred in the bank.'

'Never you mind what we have or haven't got in the bank, Karen.'

'I do mind,' she said. 'It's mine as much as yours. I work to keep us going, same as you. The cooking, the cleaning, the mending. I think we ought to have a joint account and then I'd know how much we're worth.'

'You'd spend it in a week,' said Albert. 'Look, if anything happened to me, God forbid, that money goes to you, right? All my worldly goods. Satisfied?'

The programme was coming to an end. The grinning host was saying '. . . Be sure to keep your home-movie clips coming in, because you could be the winner of our Clip of the Series prize, and that's worth a cool ten thousand pounds.'

'Ten grand!' said Albert, deeply impressed. 'Now that might be worth splashing out for. The clip of the series. We'd have to think of something really brilliant. Get me a pen and paper, quick. I'm taking down the address.'

In bed, Karen was trying her best to sleep, drawing the thin blankets tightly around her, thinking of continental quilts, double glazing and central heating. She wondered how much they really had in that bank account.

Albert's voice broke into her fantasies. 'It would have to be a really great caper. Something completely fantastic. They wouldn't give the money for one more silly kid messing about with a hose-pipe.'

Karen said, 'Are you still on about that programme?'

'I'm on about ten grand.'

There was an interval of silence before Karen spoke again.

'It would have to be believable.'

'What do you mean?'

She raised herself on to her elbows, any hope of sleep impossible as long as Albert was preoccupied with the big prize. 'Well,' she said, 'when you see most of those clips, the situation is just unreal. You couldn't believe in it.'

The bed creaked and Albert rolled towards her. 'Go on. I'm listening.'

'Tonight, for instance,' Karen said. 'The chap who ended up covered in paint. You yourself said it was probably all set up for the programme. I mean, who would want to film a door being painted?'

Albert clutched her arm. 'You've hit the nail on the head. It's hardly a prime home-movie subject.'

Karen explained, 'That's why the ones they show at weddings work so well. You know, when they can't get the knife into the cake and they knock it off the stand. Or a breeze gets under the bride's gown and lifts it up to her waist. Stuff like that. People accept them as genuine accidents because a wedding is the place where you take your video camera.'

'But you can't mess up someone's wedding just to get a laugh on video,' Albert said, misreading the plot.

'That's just an example,' said Karen. 'All I'm telling you is that to win the big prize you'd have to find a situation when it would be perfectly normal to be filming. Then it looks genuine, and it's funnier, too.'

Albert pondered the matter further. 'Weddings, kiddies' parties, barbecues, village fêtes. Where else do people take these little cameras?'

'Holidays,' Karen dreamily replied. She yawned. 'Night-night.'

She turned over, trying to find a comfortable spot between the thinly covered mattress springs.

Albert's eyes were gleaming in the dark. He reached out and fondled Karen's rump. 'You're brilliant.'

'Shove off,' she said, pushing his hand away.

'What I have, I hold,' said Albert, replacing it. 'You and I are going to take a holiday, my sweet. A caravan holiday.'

'A *caravan*, did you say?'

'And I know where to get one. That bloke across the street who keeps it in his drive.'

'Mr Tinker? He wouldn't let us borrow his caravan.'

'I bet he will. He doesn't use it himself. Since the divorce, it's been stuck on that drive for two years. He'll be glad to be rid of it.'

'*Rid* of it?' said Karen, failing to understand.

'We'll be doing him a favour,' said Albert. 'What does he want with a caravan? He'll make a few quid on the insurance. I'll speak to him tomorrow.'

When Albert returned from his chat with Joe Tinker, he was practically turning cartwheels of joy. 'He couldn't be more helpful,' he told Karen. 'Like I said, he's got no more use for the caravan. We're welcome to do just whatever we like with it.'

'Take it on holiday?'

'We're doing him a favour,' said Albert. 'He won't have to park his car on the street any more. But that isn't all. I told him what this is about.'

'You told him?' said Karen, horrified.

'Everything. To get his cooperation,' said Albert. 'He's seen the programme and he thinks the same as us. He says this is one hell of a stunt and he reckons we can't fail to win the big money. I've told him I'll give him a couple of hundred if we do. Fair enough, eh?'

'I suppose so,' said Karen, 'but can we trust him to stay quiet about it?'

'That's why he gets a cut. He's part of the conspiracy, then,' said Albert. 'But I haven't told you the best part. Joe Tinker also owns a camcorder. Yes, I'm not kidding. He's going to lend it to us for nothing. For nothing, Karen! What's more, he'll show you how to use it.'

'Me?' said Karen.

'Unless you want to be making an idiot of yourself on television, you've got to be holding the camera, pointing it at me. And it's got to be done properly. Good focusing. No shaking. You only get one take, remember. It's got to be right first time, and it's got to be up to professional standard to win the ten grand.'

She said nervously, 'I don't think I can do it, Albert.'

''Course you can! They're simple, these camcorders, dead simple. I told Joe you'll be over for some instruction this afternoon. He's a good bloke, and he fancies you, anyway. He'll give you all the confidence in the world.'

'What is this stunt, anyway?' said Karen.

'We take a holiday, like I said, towing Joe's caravan.'

'Where to?'

'Some remote part of Wales. I'm going to study the map this afternoon while you're learning to be an ace camerawoman. If you get your certificate of competence we can drive down there next Saturday for the shoot.'

'The shoot?'

'Of the film,' Albert explained. 'Get with it, love. We're shooting a film, remember? Like I say, we hook the caravan to the old Cortina. Joe's lending me his tow-bar as well. He's great.'

'Is it strong enough?'

'The tow-bar?'

'The car. Those caravans are big things to tow.'

'No problem,' said Albert. 'We can take it gently, just tootling along. We'll be stopping every few miles filming bits and pieces of our journey.'

'What for?'

Albert sighed. Everything always had to be explained to Karen. 'Because it has to look like we're on a proper holiday. We need about twenty minutes of boring holiday stuff to divert suspicion from our real intentions. Can't you see how phony it will look if the only thing on the tape is the caravan going over the cliff?'

Karen gasped in horror. 'Over the cliff? Mr Tinker's caravan?'

Albert smiled. 'With only the seagulls as witnesses – apart from the camera and fifteen million viewers.'

'It's insane!'

'That's why it's going to win ten grand. What a spectacle! I'm going to look at the Ordnance Survey and find a bit of the coast with a gentle slope leading to the cliff edge, and a good long drop to the rocks below. We park the caravan thirty yards up the slope. That way I have time to get out.'

'Get out?'

'Before it rolls over. It's going to be sensational. You'll be outside filming the scenery from the clifftop. You pan around to me at the window of the caravan. I'll hold up a bit of metal and say, "What's this, love?" The caravan will start to move. I'll shout something the TV people will have to bleep out – the audience always loves that – then I leap from the door holding the broken handbrake of the caravan, to watch the thing roll over the edge.' He laughed out loud and raised his arms like a boxer who has just heard his opponent counted out.

'It's so dangerous,' said Karen. 'I mean, it's a tremendous idea, but . . .'

Albert brushed the objection aside. 'No risk at all,' he said. 'If you're nervous, we'll give the van fifty yards to roll, instead of thirty.'

In the week that followed, Albert planned the 'shoot', as he called it, with military precision. Having selected several possible clifftop sites, he drove down to Wales to make a decision on the most suitable. He found one on the Pembrokeshire Coast that was wonderfully remote, with a grassy slope leading straight to a two-hundred-foot drop. In his spare moments he worked diligently on the script that he and Karen would have to follow, complete with stage directions.

'We only get one shot at this,' he told her when he returned from scouting the locations. 'It has to go like clockwork, while appearing totally unplanned. How are the lessons going?'

'All right,' Karen said.

'You've been clocking in with Joe, have you, while I was away?'

She nodded.

'Mastered it yet?'

'I hope so.'

'Hope isn't good enough,' said Albert. 'You've got to be certain. Are you going over to see him again?'

'This afternoon.'

'Excellent. He's a good bloke, isn't he?'

'He's very good,' said Karen, and she meant it.

'While you're in there, I'm going to do a bit of work on the old caravan. It could do with a clean. The smarter it looks, the better the effect.'

So whilst Albert sponged and polished, preparing the caravan for its TV début, Karen had more tuition from Joe. Really, as Joe explained, the camcorder was a simple machine that almost anyone could use, but if the attractive Mrs Challis wanted more practice with the thing, he was only too pleased to show her how to hold it. No woman had been inside his house since his wife had divorced him two years ago.

For her part, Karen was not displeased to feel Joe's arm around her shoulders steadying the camera from time to time. He was a most considerate man, and not bad looking, either. And he had double glazing and central heating. 'It seems a real shame that you're going to lose your caravan through this,' she said.

'Not at all,' said Joe cheerfully. 'It's had its day. I've no more use for it. Besides, it's not in very good condition any more. The door has warped in the damp. You have to give it quite a tug to open it. Better mention that to Albert. A little grease around the sides will ease it.'

Extremely early Saturday morning, when it was still dark and nobody was about, Albert went over to Joe's to attach the tow-bar. He'd arranged to collect Karen at the last minute. She sat in their bedsit with the lights off, mentally revising the instructions for the video camera. She had collected the camera from Joe after one last session of instruction the previous afternoon. Joe had been a tower of strength.

After what seemed like a couple of hours, Albert drew the caravan from its mooring and swung the car across the street. Karen climbed in, camcorder in hand.

'You'll do no filming in this light,' Albert said tensely. 'I don't know what you're holding it for. Chuck it on the back seat.'

'It doesn't belong to us,' said Karen.

Instead of 'tootling along' as he'd promised, Albert drove fast for the first two hours. Two or three times Karen said she was nervous about the car, but he didn't slow down. Near the Welsh border, as dawn came up, she suggested a stop for filming. Albert said there would be opportunities later.

She reminded him of the reason for having some footage of other places as well as the clifftop, and he relented and let her film some sheep sheltering at the side of the road.

Albert looked at his watch. 'I want to get on,' he told her. 'The light isn't so good in the middle of the day. It gets too bright.'

'Joe said it doesn't matter what time of day you film with one of these.'

'Will you shut up about Joe?'

As they neared their destination, Albert made a couple of short stops to consult the map. The area was very remote.

'Mm.'

'Let's get on with it, then.'

She watched him walk to the caravan. He had some difficulty opening the door, but he managed it at the second attempt, climbed inside, slammed the door and took his place by the window, opening it wide.

'Can you hear me all right?'

'Perfectly, Albert.'

'Are we ready to roll, then?'

'Yes.'

'Remember what I said. Establish the shot with a view of that cliff to your left, showing just how big the drop is, then pan around slowly along the cliff edge and across the grass to me. Right?'

'Right.'

'Start the camcorder now. Action.'

Heart thumping, Karen pressed the red Record button, swinging slowly around to encompass the impressive-looking cliff. She didn't care any more that her hands were shaking. She watched the grass in the lens, then the white gleam of the caravan, then Albert at the window.

True to his script, he held up a piece of metal. The caravan lurched on its mooring feet and for a second, Karen feared that it wasn't going to move.

Albert spoke his words: 'Do you know what this is, love?'

The caravan began to roll.

'It's the brake, Albert! What is it doing in your hand? Get out – the van's moving!'

'Bloody hell!'

Peter Lovesey

She saw Albert move fast towards the door and waited for the panic to set in for real.

Thirty yards to the edge.

She screamed his name as loudly as possible, mainly to obscure his shouting. She had stopped filming, of course.

The caravan moved sedately on its way.

He was desperately trying to open the jammed caravan door. How many times had Joe stressed to her that she should tell Albert to grease the edges? Not once had she considered passing on the information. She wanted Albert to die.

Twenty yards to go, and it was picking up a little speed.

The worst thing would be finding a phone in this God-forsaken place. The closest must be miles away. Everything else would be simple. A few tears for the police. Then hand over the tape. 'It must be all on here, officer. It's been the most awful accident.'

Karen continued to scream, thinking of her future with Joe Tinker with his double glazing and his central heating and his modern fully sprung bed with the continental quilt.

Ten yards.

Five.

A moment before the caravan disappeared from view, the door burst open, Albert flung himself out and hit the turf a yard from the edge. He had survived.

Karen was devastated. She flung down the camcorder and stamped her foot.

Fortunately, Albert was too shaken to notice. He still lay face down, panting.

Eventually she drew herself together and went to him. She could probably have pushed him over, he was so near, but she couldn't bring herself to do it. That would be too direct, a hands-on murder.

Albert said, 'That was a bloody near thing.'

'What went wrong?' said Karen as innocently as she was able.

'Couldn't get the bloody door open. I knew it was difficult. Found that out when I was cleaning the thing. Put some grease on it yesterday, but it wasn't enough, obviously. Ended up kicking my way out.' He got to his feet. 'Look at me. I'm shaking like a leaf.'

Karen said, 'Let's get you to the car.'

'Where's the camera?'

306

'Oh, I dropped it over there,' she said. 'I'm not sure how much I got. God, I was frightened!'

'Doesn't matter, love,' said Albert with unusual tenderness. 'We can't use the video anyway.'

'Why not?'

'Evidence. If they ever find anything at the bottom of that cliff and come knocking on our door, the last thing we want is a bloody video of the event.'

She frowned. 'They could only find the caravan.'

Albert was shaking his head. 'There's something else. With luck, the sea will take care of it.'

'What on earth are you talking about?'

'Bloody Joe Tinker. When I went in to see him this morning, he said he wanted a half-share of the profits. *Five grand!* You know me, love. Mean as hell. I lashed out. Hit the bleeder against the kitchen stove and cracked his skull. Killed him outright. What could I do but shove him into his own bloody caravan and bring him down here for disposal?'

'Oh God, no!' wailed Karen.

'Don't shed tears over him,' said Albert. 'Didn't you ever notice he fancied you something rotten, the jerk? Like I told you the other night, what I have, I hold.'

LILY AND THE SOCKEYES

SARA PARETSKY

When Clementine DuVal took the job of managing public relations for the Vancouver Sockeye baseball team, the sports side of town buzzed. Nepotism, some said. After all, if her father hadn't been Hall of Fame shortstop Leon DuVal, the Sockeyes would never have talked to her. True, she was an athlete in her own right – women's NCAA strike-out leader when she played softball for the University of Kansas. True, she'd studied journalism and covered sports for several local papers for five years. But still – a woman handling the press for a men's pro team? If Leon hadn't bought a piece of the Sockeyes, the sportswriters said, it would never have happened.

Other tongues clacked about WXJ sportscaster Jimmy-Bob Reedy. Sixty if he was a day, fat, slack-lipped, with hands he couldn't keep to himself, he'd been chased out of Los Angeles by an angry Dodger franchise. Five years later, he had somehow ingratiated himself with the Sockeye front office and was the lead announcer on both television and radio. While loyal fans – and hapless color man Carlos Edwards – flinched, Jimmy-Bob lost track of the ball-strike count, forgot who was at bat, mispronounced names and droned on about his latest fishing trip.

Three WXJ women staffers had quit after doing technical back-up for him. The station and the front office gave handsome severance pay to stop possible attempted-rape charges, but the tales were known widely among sportswriters. How, they wondered, would Clementine react if Jimmy-Bob copped a feel? Known for her slow curve and her fast temper, she might well break his nose. However much that might please the fans, it wouldn't endear her to the front office.

The team gave Clementine mixed reviews. The fact that her college pitching stats were better than their two-million-dollar Cy Young starter was gleefully repeated in the papers. When Jason Colby gave up a walk and three consecutive doubles in a crucial game with Philadelphia, Jimmy-Bob talked on the air about little else for days.

'Why Carlos,' he'd say to his long-suffering back-up, 'our cute little Clementine could of got us out of that inning without a scratch. You see her working with the boys at batting practice? You should a caught her from behind on her follow-through.' Followed by a wet-lipped laugh.

Clementine had pitched for batting practice a couple of times as a publicity gimmick. She had a decent fastball and a good curve, but no one – least of all herself – thought she was any competition for Jason Colby. But the Cy Young winner was having a bad year, and he couldn't laugh off Jimmy-Bob's sniping. Even though he knew it wasn't Clementine's fault, he reacted by refusing her efforts to set up interviews and keep relations running smoothly with the press until his rhythm returned.

She had more success with young players still trying to prove themselves. She'd bring them over to her father's apartment for dinner, and they would sit stiffly on their chairs listening to Leon discourse on fielding and hitting: it couldn't hurt their chances in the majors for Leon DuVal to know who they were.

The other person who wasn't crazy about Clementine's sports career was her grandmother. Lily DuVal, a notable actress in her day, still carried considerable punch in film and theater circles. She had no use for sports, and had never understood why her son wanted to go into baseball when she'd lined up a couple of movie parts for him. Her daughter-in-law had even less love of baseball and had walked out on Leon and two-year-old Clementine. Lily took in her granddaughter and tried to instill in her a hatred of baseball and a love of theater. Alas, neither took.

When Clementine graduated from college, she returned to the

city to live with her grandmother in Lily's twenty-room mansion in suburban Fisherman's Cove. Lily, who adored her, swept magnificently through the house in emerald-studded caftans, entertained the theater and the press with panache, and loftily ignored her granddaughter's calling. 'Clementine is in entertainment,' she would tell people, smiling maliciously.

Lily was a vegetarian and a single-malt whiskey drinker. Loch Ness Distillers flew in crates of twenty-three-year-old Glen Moray whiskey for her from Scotland. Some people said that she and Sir Malcolm Darrough, Loch Ness's chairman, had been more than close friends in the thirties. All Lily would say was she judged a man by his taste in single malts, not how far he could hit a silly white ball.

Other dear friends said that despite her famed hatred of baseball, Leon got his start with the Sockeyes because of Lily's 'friendship' with Sockeye owner Teddy Wolitzer. After Clementine had been around the Sockeye dugout and front office for three months, she naturally heard these stories, which lost none of their zest to the tellers for being forty years old. With the same straightforward action that characterized her fastball, she asked Lily about it one night at dinner.

'I hope it's not true,' she said, her mouth full of lentil salad (with endive, tomatoes and onions – a summer treat, Lily called it). 'I mean, he may have been the world's biggest charmer when he was thirty, Granny, but he's almost as disgusting as Jimmy-Bob Reedy. And almost as fat, too. Around the newsroom, they call him Teddy Bear, not because he's cute, you know, but because of his paws. I believe the stories they tell about him and Jason Colby's daughter. He's just the type, you know.'

Lily raised her plucked eyebrows as high as the line of her brilliantly dyed turquoise hair. 'Really, Clementine. Isn't it bad enough that you bring home earned-run averages and at-bats, without dredging up all this ancient – and very dull – gossip? Could we change the topic, please? How's your Jock-Talk program going?'

This was Lily's name for Clementine's boldest PR venture to date. Clementine had done the traditional – bat days, glove days, autograph days ad nauseam. But she believed baseball's great untapped market was the woman spectator. In a survey of the ten most popular sports among women, baseball wasn't even ranked, while football was fourth behind tennis, ice-skating and gymnastics. How to get women interested in baseball? She had talked it over with Lily.

'Impossible!' her grandmother had snorted. 'The only thing even remotely appealing about baseball is the bodies of the players. And even those are only good on a hit-or-miss basis.'

Clementine's eyes lit up. 'Granny! That's it! We'll get cameras in the locker room after games. We'll have the jock-of-the-week, and we'll reveal everything about him. Everything!'

In execution, the idea had to be toned down a little. Ballplayers, while as graphic as the next man in their discussions of female anatomy, proved strangely shy about revealing all on national television. In fact, when Clementine came into the locker room for the first time after a brilliant 2–1 victory over Montreal, the speed with which everyone leapt to the nearest towel was twice as fast as they ever ran the baselines.

After overcoming the ballplayers' initial reluctance, the in-depth profiles, done by Carlos Edwards, proved very popular. They couldn't do one every week – there are only so many good-looking jocks, and they produce a limited number of heart-stopping plays. But every two or three weeks Clementine and Carlos Edwards would pick a player and produce an interview accompanied by candid photographs. Clementine's forthright, friendly manner got the men to reveal details about their lives that their wives and coaches didn't always know.

When Jimmy-Bob used his pressure at WXJ to keep the interviews off the air, the *Herald-Star* agreed to run the stories. The sports section included a poster-size picture of the player in uniform. The first thousand women to come to the ballpark on the next game day received a free copy of a candid glossy color shot, and the player would meet twenty women for drinks on the first following non-game day. The women's names were selected by a random drawing of their ticket stubs, so they had to come to the ballpark to participate.

The campaign proved so popular that other major-league teams soon started their own copycat programs. Lily was proud of her granddaughter's ingenuity. She secretly read the *Herald-Star* sports section on interview days. Teddy Wolitzer bragged openly, as did Leon DuVal.

The only person who wasn't happy was Jimmy-Bob Reedy. He

already worried that fans preferred Carlos Edwards's reporting style. Carlos had been a Cy Young winning pitcher himself in a brilliant career with the Kansas City Royals. He not only understood the game well, but could talk about it.

Until the Jock-Talk program started, Jimmy-Bob got his pals in the Sockeye front office to keep Carlos's air time to a minimum. Now, however, the younger man was getting a lot of publicity. The *Herald-Star* articles proved so popular that the paper got their TV station, WSNP, to run tapes of Carlos's interviews. Jimmy-Bob tried blocking this in court, claiming it violated his exclusivity rights for Sockeye baseball coverage. He lost the suit and the newspapers made him look ridiculous.

Angry and humiliated, Jimmy-Bob started ridiculing Clementine on the air. His beady, lecherous eyes had taken in the fact that Carlos and Clementine were spending more and more time in restaurants and bars discussing 'Jock-Talk'. He even happened to drive 'casually' by Carlos's apartment one morning in time to see Clementine come out, laughing, arm-in-arm with Carlos.

The sight added to his rage, because his early amorous efforts with Clementine had been soundly rebuffed. No one ever knew exactly what happened between them in private, but the day after Jimmy-Bob had invited Clementine to stay late to work on publicity, he had taken time off to treat an abscessed tooth. When he finally returned to the studio, his jaw was badly swollen. 'It might have been from dental work,' one columnist said dubiously. The other sportswriters had a field day ('NCAA Pitching Ace Connects', the *Province* gleefully reported).

Jimmy-Bob hoped that Carlos might react wildly to his attacks on Clementine. Then he could get the Sockeyes to cancel his contract. Or his attacks might provoke a response from Clementine herself that would turn the Sockeye front office against her. So he carolled happily about her possible sex life, insinuating that all women athletes were lesbians, discussed her probable drug habits, and how she wouldn't have a job at all without Leon and Lily's influence. He was even foolhardy enough to allude to Wolitzer and Lily's forty-year-old romance.

Carlos controlled himself with an effort. He had played second fiddle to Jimmy-Bob for two years, maintaining a cheerful camaraderie on the air. He reminded himself of the three years he'd played for a manager who hated him and still won twenty games each season. Off the air, he contemplated lying in wait for Jimmy-Bob and mugging him, or fiddling with the brakes on his car so that he would plunge into Howe Sound when he next went fishing.

Leon DuVal put in his two cents with Teddy Wolitzer.

'Come'n, Teddy. That lump of lard is screwing my daughter on the air. Not to mention what he's saying about Lily, who doesn't take too kindly to insults.'

Wolitzer lit a fresh cigar. 'Just be glad he ain't screwing her in the press room, Leon. Come'n. This feud is sweet music to my ears. TV ratings have never been better. The fans are pouring into the ballpark. I ain't gonna put a plug in the guy's mouth. He may be crazy, but he's selling ad time for the network.'

Word of Jimmy-Bob's attacks reached Lily quickly enough. Not from Clementine, who didn't pay much attention to him – she figured if he got too wild she'd just break the other side of his jaw – nor from Leon, who knew his mother's temper of old. But one or another of Lily's pals in the press corps came out for cocktails or dinner most days. And one of them, a drama critic, brought the word out to Fisherman's Cove.

Lily took the unprecedented step of turning on WXJ. In all the years Leon had played, when he batted .295 and won a Golden Glove three seasons running, Lily had never watched a Sockeye game. Now she spent all of one hot August week watching them in a road series with Chicago. Her eyes began to sparkle dangerously.

Clementine, dividing her evenings between Lily and Carlos – between tofu and hamburgers – came in one afternoon to find Lily pacing the length of the patio, green silk billowing around her as it sought to keep pace with the swift movement of her legs.

'That man is a menace,' she pronounced majestically.

'What man, Granny? You don't mean Carlos, do you? I thought you liked him. And don't tell me I'm not old enough—'

Lily cut her short. 'Don't be ridiculous. I'm delighted to see you having fun with a nice boy with good legs. I'm talking about that fat, slobbering ape on television.'

Clementine's eyes opened wide. 'Granny! Don't tell me you've been watching the games! You shouldn't, really. Jimmy-Bob is a jerk. Why, yesterday when Sergio Diaz was batting he called him Manford Yates, and when he took a curve that just clipped the inside of the plate, Jimmy-Bob started yelling that it was high and outside and should have been ball four!'

Lily snorted. 'Don't talk like that in front of me, Clementine. You know I don't care for it. I have no interest in anything Jimmy-Bob might say about any ballgame. It is his personal comments that disturb me.'

'You mean because he talks about me being a lesbian Communist? I don't care. If he bothers me too much, I'll just blacken both his eyes so he won't broadcast for a week.'

Lily came to a halt in front of her granddaughter. 'No doubt. I expect such a lack of subtlety from someone who eschewed the theater for a baseball scholarship. And what are you going to do to stop his innuendos against me?' Her nostrils widened. 'No, I'll think of a different way to cook his goose. Something he won't forget as fast as a black eye or two.'

Clementine put an arm around her grandmother. 'Whatever you say, Granny. Just don't be too rough with him – I think he's supporting a couple of ex-wives and three or four children.'

Lily decided her subtle silencing of Jimmy-Bob Reedy would take place in front of as many people as possible. She would invite the whole Sockeye front office, Jimmy-Bob, Carlos and the rest of the broadcast team, and of course the players, to a magnificent party out at Fisherman's Cove. A blanket invitation was given to reporters and TV personalities in the city.

Clementine told her the Sockeyes had a day off in a long home stand right after Labor Day, so Lily announced that as the party date. Only Carlos knew what she was planning, because she needed his help. He took to spending evenings at the mansion, huddled with Lily. Clementine found herself feeling jealous – after all, Lily had pretty nice legs herself. She might be seventy-five, but yoga and high spirits concealed the fact admirably.

Clementine tried to swallow her hurt feelings and took on her usual role at Lily's parties: managing all the practical details. All Lily would tell her granddaughter about the entertainment was that she wanted four five-foot televisions installed in the ballroom. Clementine sighed resignedly and called electronics shops: Granny only got worse if you acted as though you cared what she was doing.

Lily relaxed her strict vegetarian rules for the occasion, allowing Clementine to order fish and pâté to feed a guest list which grew with each passing day. Somehow a film producer just happened to be in town, the publisher of Lily's racy memoirs, the travel editor for the *New York Times*, and so it went. Sir Malcolm Darrough apparently had got wind of the affair and was jetting in on his company plane with a case or two of private label Glen Moray whiskey. And another old flame, head of a steel company, was flying in from Chicago.

For the bulk of the party Lily proposed champagne, so Clementine ordered thirteen cases of brut. Lily didn't waste her single-malt on the world at large. 'It's not for silly ballplayers who want to get drunk as fast as possible. Only those who have the palate to appreciate it will be given a chance to drink it.'

By the day of the party, the guest list had grown to three hundred. Since Lily always had everything her own way, even the weather cooperated: it was a sparkling September day, the leaves beginning to show hints of red and yellow, but the air kissed with the warmth of summer.

Guests began arriving in the early afternoon, laden with swimming suits for use at Lily's private beach. She managed to greet most people as they arrived. 'Champagne and food on the patio and in the ballroom. Now you must be in the ballroom at six for the entertainment. It's really special.'

Clementine herself served Glen Moray according to Lily's orders. Not even Teddy Wolitzer was allowed any – maybe, Clementine thought, all the tales about Lily and Teddy were so much smoke. Her grandmother's ex-lovers were always treated graciously, and the movie producer, Sir Malcolm, and the head of the Chicago steel company could be seen genially drinking and smoking in a corner together, with frequent visits from Lily herself.

By five p.m. it was clear that the party was one of Lily's major successes. Nine cases of champagne had already been disposed of, along with fifty pounds of shrimp, twenty of salmon, innumerable little cakes and giant bowls of fruit. While Lily, exotic in transparent silk and the emeralds which were world-famous, floated from one happy group to the other, it was Clementine who made the party tick. She kept a scrupulous eye on guests with a potential for battle, separating them dexterously into other groups, seeing that everyone was kept supplied with food and drink.

Jimmy-Bob, who had arrived early and was inclined to be aggressive, presented the biggest problem. Whenever Clementine tried to steer him from some prominent person whom he was offending, he would slip an arm tightly around her, squeeze her, and say, 'I'm working to convert our little lesbian here. Me and Carlos are working on it together. Who's winning, babe?'

Because it was a public occasion, Clementine restrained herself from slugging him. She did once dig her pointed heels into his instep with a happy smile on her face. He winced in pain and loosened his grip so that she could break away from him and redirect the people he was talking to.

At six, Lily and Clementine herded the guests into the ballroom. Lily attached herself to Jimmy-Bob. 'Now for my most special guest, a special place of honor.' While three hundred people disposed themselves around four wide-screen TVs, Lily made sure that Jimmy-Bob had a front-row seat.

The lights went out and the screens came to life. To the strains of 'Take Me Out to the Ballgame,' the words, 'Highlights of the Sockeyes' Man of the Hour' flashed on the screens. Then a close-up of Jimmy-Bob's face, red, veinous, slack-lipped. The crowd laughed. For the next fifteen minutes, they roared at a montage of Jimmy-Bob's greatest blunders, on and off the air.

Clementine watched silently. Lily had surely gone too far this time. Not to mention Carlos, who apparently had raided the WXJ tape library to pull the show together. Clementine wondered what she could do to stop it, and decided there wasn't a thing. She could only hope that Jimmy-Bob would feel too embarrassed to raise a legal stink, but knowing his temper, she didn't have much confidence in that. Carlos would lose his job; she'd probably lose hers, too. So maybe Lily could be persuaded to support the two of them. She was gloomily considering the possibility when a scream rose loud above the laughter, effectively shutting off the noise.

Clementine struggled to the wall where the lights were and turned them on. The ballroom was in total confusion. Some people were trying to leave, others to find what had caused the scream. As they pushed against each other, they created an immovable mass.

Clementine went behind the scenes where the A-V equipment was set up. She found Carlos doubled over with laughter.

'Enjoy yourself today, because tomorrow you're going to be out of work,' she advised him shortly, hunting around in the equipment for a microphone.

She switched it on and spoke into it. Using her summer-camp counselor voice, which effectively calmed screaming ten-year-olds, she asked for silence. When the room had quieted down, she explained where she was standing and requested anyone who knew of any problems to join her.

The ballroom promptly began buzzing again, but more quietly. She saw Leon work his way through the crowd to her.

'It's Jimmy-Bob,' he explained when he reached her. 'Someone stuck one of the carving knives for the salmon into him. I guess his blood seeped out to where one of the ladies from Los Angeles was sitting and she started to scream. I've already sent a waiter to call the police.'

By eleven o'clock the police had sorted through the bulk of the guests and had sent most of them home. The head of the investigating team, Lieutenant Oberlin, had asked Leon, Carlos, Lily and Clementine to wait for him in Lily's front drawing room. Teddy Wolitzer insisted on waiting, too, on the grounds that he needed to know any new developments which might affect the Sockeyes. A uniformed policeman stood guard, trying to control his awe at being with his childhood baseball heroes.

Every now and then, Lieutenant Oberlin sent in an additional suspect to wait. Jason Colby, the Sockeye starting pitcher, was among them. Sir Malcolm Darrough, although given permission to leave, hovered solicitously at Lily's emerald-laden shoulder. Lily herself, while losing none of her vivacity, had stopped trying to entertain her troubled guests.

When Lieutenant Oberlin finally joined them, his voice was hoarse from four hours of interrogations. He sent the uniformed man for a glass of water and settled back to talk to his chief suspects and their hostess.

'From what I have seen of the video, I'm surprised it was Mr Reedy who was killed instead of you, Mr Edwards, or – with respect – yourself, ma'am. I'd like to know what prompted you to show a libelous film like that to three hundred people with the subject watching.'

Lily's painted eyebrows went up. 'My good man – have you ever watched Jimmy-Bob Reedy's broadcasts of the Sockeyes? If you have, you know how he slandered everyone and anyone. I thought it was time to give him a dose of his own medicine.'

She turned to Sir Malcolm, who was trying to silence her, and patted his hand. 'Don't worry, Malcolm – I'm not telling the man anything he doesn't already know, I'm sure.'

Lieutenant Oberlin swallowed some water and leaned back tiredly in his chair. 'Now, I know Jimmy-Bob – Mr Reed – had been insulting you and Miss Clementine DuVal on the air: I heard him myself a few times. So the two of you were understandably angry with him. And Mr Leon DuVal wanted Mr Wolitzer here to take Reedy off the air. And Mr Carlos Edwards, who's pretty friendly with Miss DuVal, was angry with the deceased for insulting her. So any of the four of you might have been angry enough to kill him.

'Mr Reedy had also been insulting Jason Colby all year – saying that Clementine DuVal could out-pitch him and that he ought to be sent back to the minors. It's true Mr Colby has had a bad season. I suppose any athlete should be used to being insulted by the press. But maybe you weren't, huh, Mr Colby? I have statements from a couple of your team-mates who heard you threatening to kill the man a couple of times.'

Colby turned a painful red under his sunburned skin. 'I might've said something,' he muttered. 'You know, you get hot when you're not performing the way you think you should. But I didn't kill the guy.'

'What about you, Mr Edwards?'

Carlos looked embarrassed. 'I agree the video wasn't in the best taste, Lieutenant. But it was such a sweet revenge on that jag-off – better than murder. I sure didn't want to kill him this afternoon – I couldn't wait to see what he was going to do when the lights came up.'

Oberlin nodded. 'And I think the same could be said for Miss Lily DuVal. But you, Mr DuVal – you were really angry about the attacks on your daughter's character. You were seen near Mr Reedy before the lights went down. And as a trained athlete you certainly know enough about the human body to be able to stab a man to death. We're going to take you downtown for further questioning.'

Clementine turned pale under her tan. 'Wait a minute, Lieutenant. You're forgetting me: I'm a trained athlete, too, and it was me he

319

was insulting. Besides, I live here – Leon doesn't – and I know all the silverware and stuff. I knew which knife to use.'

Lily snorted. 'Do stop the heroics, darling. Even if you haven't been in the theater, a love of drama must be in your blood.'

She turned to the policeman. 'Lieutenant – could we use a little common sense? Let's talk about Mr Reedy for a moment – however ugly a topic that is. Is there anyone in Vancouver who could stand listening to the man? He was disgusting. He apparently tried to rape every young lady who had to work with him – I've heard about pay-offs from Teddy Wolitzer to several women to keep their mouths shut. In addition, according to the boring stories my granddaughter brought home, he knew nothing about the game he was supposed to report on. The fans apparently preferred Mr Edwards here, and it's not hard to understand why.

'Has it ever occurred to you to wonder why, in face of this concerted dislike, the Sockeyes let him announce their games?'

Lieutenant Oberlin looked at her intently. 'Go on, ma'am.'

Lily looked at Jason Colby. 'I'm sorry to have to bring this up, Mr Colby. But you have a daughter, don't you?'

Colby looked faint. 'Alison,' he said hoarsely. 'She's eleven.'

Lily nodded. 'Teddy Wolitzer assaulted the child, didn't he? Last year?'

Jason only nodded without speaking.

'I've known Teddy for forty years now. Not a man who likes things going against him, are you, Teddy? I can guess what happened – he told you if you wanted to continue to pitch in the majors you wouldn't press charges.'

Jason nodded again. 'We sent her to live with her grandmother in California. But I can't get it out of my mind. My pitching's gone to hell. Then Jimmy-Bob made things worse, harping on and on about my playing. It was driving me off my head, but I didn't kill the guy. If I'd killed anyone, it would have been Wolitzer.'

'Yes, dear,' Lily said briskly. 'Very upsetting. I don't blame you. But your daughter's story wasn't the well-kept secret Teddy might have hoped – Clementine brought home some garbled gossip about it earlier this summer. And presumably if Teddy did it once, there were other incidents with other little girls – right, Teddy? Did Jimmy-Bob find out about it? And use that information to force you to hire him and keep him in the lead announcing position?'

Leon nodded agreement. 'Makes sense, Lily. You wouldn't know it, since you don't like baseball, but the commissioner would force him to sell the franchise if the word got out. Moral turpitude. They don't like the all-American game smirched by slime like child-abusers.'

Lieutenant Oberlin got up and went over to Teddy. 'We have people downtown looking through everyone's private papers for signs of blackmail or fraud involving Jimmy-Bob. So maybe we'll find something in your office, Mr Wolitzer. Meanwhile, you have the right to remain silent, but if you give up that right, anything you say can be used as evidence against you . . .'

After the police had left with Wolitzer, Lily leaned back in her chair. 'Bring the Glen Moray, darling,' she said to Clementine. 'I think we all need a little drink.'

Carlos followed Clementine from the room. 'Listen, Clementine, don't be mad at me – I'm not in love with your grandmother – at least, I am, but not the way I am with you – I just wanted a chance to get revenge on that fat bastard. And you've got to admit – he died embarrassed.'

They were gone for a long time. When they finally returned with the bottle, Lily raised her painted brows, but said only, 'I thought you knew this house too well to get lost in it, darling.'

She waited until everyone's glass had been filled before speaking again. 'I spent several months with Teddy Wolitzer in 1946. I realized then what a vile man he was – which is why I never let him near my single-malt: that's for friends and whiskey lovers only.' She raised her glass in a salute to them.

They lifted theirs to her.

'Lily,' Sir Malcolm said, 'you're incomparable.'

THE WOMEN AT THE FUNERAL

ROBERT BARNARD

Alice Furnley closed her brother's eyes and turned to her sisters.

'He'll be in heaven now,' she said.

The two younger sisters nodded. There was no doubt about that. They went into the next bedroom to tell their mother, who had been expecting it.

'If only I could have gone first,' she said, tears running down her wrinkled cheeks. 'But there – it's God's will. He'll be one more saint in the holy choir.'

They all murmured their assent without hesitation or reservation. They knew their brother Roderick had been a man of singular gentleness and boundless charity. His consideration for his old mother and his sisters was much commended in the parish: the old lady was eighty-two, and very frail; two of his sisters were spinsters and the other had been widowed early. They all lived together in the large house and grounds in Acacia Avenue, in great harmony. 'We never had an unkind word from him,' Alice told the vicar, who had prayed for him the previous Sunday at St Michael's. He had described Roderick as a man of boundless goodness and of good works, an example to them all. His sisters, in the family pew, had nodded. They were women of faith, of certainties, and their minds were not inquiring ones.

Alice's first uneasiness came at the funeral service, or rather just after it. There had been many tears shed during the address and the prayers, for many at St Michael's, not just his sisters, felt they had lost a brother: he had been counsellor and confessor to many of them, had given solid aid to more than a few. The vicar had meditated, to no very good effect, on the ways of God, particularly in taking to himself so admirable a man at the early age of fifty-two. As the coffin was borne down the aisle and out to the churchyard for burial, the congregation held back to allow the mourning women of the family to follow it. Sarah and Emily, the two younger sisters, helped their old mother along, and were preoccupied, but Alice could look around her, could see that the church was three-quarters full, and, as she came to the pews at the back, could get a good view of the unknown women.

They were sitting together, nine or ten of them, and they were clearly uncertain what to do at a funeral, or even in church. They had gone to some effort to make their dresses appropriate to the occasion: black or brown skirts, little dark hats or headscarves. But they were not at all the class of women that Alice would have expected at her brother's funeral, and they were not – Alice found it difficult to find a way of putting it to herself – they were not, they didn't *look*, respectable. She went out into the bitter December wind.

There was no question of celebrating Christmas that year. Most of the customary seasonal indulgences were cancelled, and those that could not be were consumed soberly, often with sad comment about how much Roderick had always enjoyed this or that. Alice said nothing to her sisters about the women in the church, but she felt weighed down by her secret. On Boxing Day the tradespeople and roundsmen were tipped by Alice, through Cook, with particular generosity, which she felt her brother would have expected. It was on that day, in the late afternoon, that she had a visitor.

Mary, the little maid, quite new from one of Dr Barnardo's establishments, looked more than a little confused.

'Wouldn't give no name, Miss, said it wouldn't mean anything to you. But she asked special to speak to you alone, Miss. She's not—'

'Not what, Mary?'

'Not – not like one of us. Not a lady, Miss.'

And that, in the year 1891, presented a problem. *Where* was this talk to take place? Not in the drawing room, surely, especially as one of her sisters might come in at any time.

'Show her into Mr Roderick's study,' Alice said. 'And tell my sisters I am busy.'

Alice was not new to taking household decisions, but this one was unexpected, outside her usual scope. She felt almost nervous as she waited in the study. When the young woman was shown in she knew at once it must be one of the ones she had seen at the back of the church: she had on the same sort of dull, dun clothes and the same look of cleanliness achieved with effort. Now, as then, the visitor was not at ease.

'I thought as how I should come, Miss Furnley,' she said, from just inside the door, 'in case you were worried or upset about the will.'

'The will? My brother's will?' Alice heard uneasiness in her voice and repressed it firmly. 'We have had no time to see the family solicitor as yet. Christmas, you understand . . .'

'Oh, I see. Well, I'm glad, Miss, because you might have wondered . . .'

'Wondered?'

'Oh, no need to be uneasy, Miss.'

Alice drew herself up.

'I am not uneasy. Merely bewildered as to what my brother's will can have to do with you.'

'O' course, Miss. Well, you see, he told me as how he was going to leave me something. Oh, not a great sum. Something you could easily afford.'

'I see.' But it was said faintly, and Alice Furnley clearly could not see.

'And o' course it's not for me, not for myself.'

'He left you money, but not for yourself?'

'That's right, Miss. It's because he knew he could trust me, and because I know a bit about banks and accounts and that. It's for me to keep, to help any of us girls.'

'Any . . . of . . . you . . . girls,' said Alice, more faintly still.

'If we're in trouble,' said the woman, growing almost confiding. 'In the nature o' things, a lot of us get into trouble from time to time.'

'You do?'

'Us being independent girls, working on our own, on the streets a lot . . . There's a lot of rough men around in Leeds, you know, Miss.'

'I know *that*. I see them.'

'That's all you want to do, Miss. Anyway, there's lots of us girls have been helped over a bad patch by your brother – when we've been swindled, or beaten up, or put in 'ospital – that's when they'll take us in there. And he knew, when he was beginning to feel poorly, that if he left the money to me I'd keep it and give it or lend it as the need arose.'

'I see.' Alice began walking up and down the little room to get a better look at the woman. She did indeed look honest. Rough, but honest. 'Let me get this right: my brother has left you a sum of money—'

'A thousand pounds.'

'A thousand pounds! My brother has left this sum to you so that you may relieve the distress of your . . . sisters.'

'My friends, like. He didn't trust the churches and organizations. He said there was always strings attached.'

'That sounds like Roderick.' Alice was getting her confidence back. That did sound like Roderick. He was always direct and warm in his charities. This must be one he preferred – perhaps naturally – not to tell his womenfolk about. 'He was so generous,' she said. 'So open.'

'Oh he was! Is this his room?' The woman looked around the book-lined little office, with old copies of *Punch*, pipes and boots, and a chessboard by the fire. 'I can imagine him in it. We all worshipped him!'

'All?'

'All the girls he was kind to. He never gave a lecture with it, that was the great thing, and you knew he was there in need.'

'That's true.'

'And he was always very considerate and gentle in, you know, in personal things.'

Alice could not begin to think what she meant, so she stayed silent.

'Oh, you mustn't think badly of him,' said the woman, hurriedly. 'All he wanted was a bit of comfort, a bit of relaxation, like.' Seeing the bewilderment, then the horror, on Alice's face, she turned to go. 'I won't take up any more of your time. Oh – just one more thing. That business with Mr Johnston. He told me he was going to tell you about that, and I'm the only other one who knows. I swear to God it'll go no further. The man's quite safe as far as I'm concerned, and always will be.'

And she marched out, showing herself out through the front door. Alice watched her to the end of Acacia Avenue, then sank exhausted into a chair. What had she meant – *comfort*? *Relaxation*? Just when she had reconciled herself in her mind to the idea that Roderick had quietly been dispensing charity to women who – to *fallen* women (that must, surely, be what this woman had implied), then came this new revelation: that he had gone to this woman – these women – for comfort and relaxation. What could that mean except—? Impossible to believe!

Yet even as she told herself that, Alice remembered those late evenings of Roderick's at the Liberal Club twice a week. And remembered too that her brother had never felt the need to be particularly active in the party cause at election time, nor had he ever showed great familiarity with the Liberal candidate, or even with party officials when he met them.

Alice took the decision to go to the family solicitor next day, and take only her sister Sarah – her once-married sister – with her. When the main provisions of the will were read, the division of the estate into three equal portions for his sisters, the two women nodded: they had known that was what Roderick had intended. When the will said that the deceased trusted his dear sisters' generosity to give adequate remembrances of himself to the family's servants and dependants Alice whispered: 'We must give them something they'll be *very* pleased with.' And when one thousand pounds was left to Mrs Sally Hardwick, of Crow Lane, Armley, Alice whispered: 'One of the poor people Roderick was always so kind to – large family, father dead.' If Sarah thought that one thousand pounds was an awful lot of money to leave a poor family, even a fatherless one, she said nothing: it would have been unseemly, almost blasphemous, to question Roderick's judgement.

The next day Alice went to the bank and on her return gave seventy-five pounds to Cook, fifty pounds to the ladies' maid, the same to Frank the gardener, and ten pounds to little Mary, with strict instructions to save most of it against the time a respectable young man asked her to marry him.

Which left Alice with the problem of Mr Johnston. What on earth could the woman – could Sally Hardwick – have meant? The Furnleys had no close friends called Johnston. Racking her brains, Alice could recall that there was a Mr Johnston among the congregation at St Michael's. He was a bachelor and an elderly man, almost as old as their mother. Surely there could be no secret concerning him that Roderick had kept? She looked in trade directories, asked Walter Wakeham who now ran the family clothing manufactory if he knew of a Mr Johnston that her brother Roderick was close to. All to no avail. It was a blank wall. When she decided that the woman could have got it wrong, or she have misheard, and it was a Mr *Johnson* who was meant, her perplexity increased. There were just too many Johnsons around – and even so, no family or man of that name with whom the Furnleys had been close.

It seemed like an unsolvable puzzle. Alice could think of nothing more she could do, short of employing a private detective. But she had the impression that these were most unsavoury individuals who would not scruple to use any discreditable information they found out against their employer, so she put that possibility from her mind. Though she acknowledged to herself her own helplessness, she found that the name Johnston jumped out at her from the pages of the *Leeds Advertiser* or the *Yorkshire Post* in the way that names one is interested in have a habit of doing (other names which thus leapt off the page for Alice Furnley were the Prince of Wales and Marie Corelli, whose novels she found painfully exciting).

But it was not from the pages of a newspaper that the name of the Johnston she had been looking for sprang at her. She was sitting in the family pew at St Michael's in early autumn, praying for her mother whose life was drawing to a sad close, and the vicar was reading the banns of marriage:

'Francis Johnston, bachelor of this parish, to Ellen Currey, spinster of this parish . . .'

Alice had started involuntarily at the name and looked round. Her sister Emily smiled and patted her arm. 'Frank,' she said. 'Isn't it nice?' Alice nodded and subsided into her pew.

Frank the gardener. She knew he had got engaged to a girl – no, to a woman – who worked for old Mrs Macklin round the corner in

Galton Road. She'd heard the name 'Ellen' – that was why several bells had rung when the banns were read. Because she had never to her knowledge heard Frank's surname: he had always been 'Frank' to her, and nothing more. She might, if she racked her brain, remember little Mary's surname (probably a gift of the good Dr Barnardo): but Frank was outdoor staff, and as such she had had little to do with him beyond an occasional commending of his diligence or the excellence of his Brussels sprouts.

It was three days before Alice had matured a plan of action in her mind. Sarah was shopping in Leeds and Emily was nursing their mother when she ventured into the long, leafy garden that stretched from the back of the house. Frank was busy separating daffodil bulbs and she approached him circuitously, collecting a little bunch of autumn flowers in a basket. As she drew near him he straightened himself respectfully. He was about middle height, strong and capable-looking, but with strongly etched lines on his face that gave him an unhappy air.

'I was so glad to hear the banns read for you, Frank,' Alice said.

'Thank you very much, Miss.'

'You must be looking forward to a happier time ahead.'

There was a tiny pause before Frank said: 'I am that.'

'Because you've had a lot of trouble in the past, haven't you?'

This time there was a quite measurable pause before Frank said: 'Did Mr Roderick tell you about that? He said he was going to when he . . . took me on, then he changed his mind. Said he thought it would worry you, and you wouldn't understand.'

'Before he died he told me,' lied Alice, mentally excusing herself by her need to know. 'He thought it was his duty, you see, as we would be left alone.'

'I see, Miss. I'm sure Mr Roderick would always do what was right.'

'But it was a very brief account – him being so weak. I didn't really understand the *circumstances* of your . . . problem.'

'It must have sounded bad enough, Miss, without the circumstances.' Frank drew his sleeve across his forehead, which was beaded with sweat. 'And it *was* bad, I acknowledge that freely. We were farm workers, you see, from down Lincolnshire way, me and my wife.' Alice tried not to let it show that she was surprised he had

had a wife, having been proclaimed a bachelor in her own church. 'We were never well off, but when this depression hit the farmers we got poorer and poorer, hungrier and hungrier. I was just about to leave, to try and find work in the town, when it happened.'

He looked at her as if hoping that she would supply the words he didn't want to say. Alice could only nod.

'First the boy, then the little girl – the light of my life. I won't say they died of hunger, but they were powerful weak when the influenza struck. We'd been going to lose our cottage the week after, but the farmer gave us another month, out of compassion. My poor wife was mad wi' grief, tearing her hair, Miss, and crying from noon to night. As the time came for us to lose our home she kept saying "I don't want to live," and "There's nothing left to live for." And – to cut a long story short – we came to a sort of agreement.'

'A suicide pact,' whispered Alice, stunned by the wickedness of the idea.

'That's what they called it in court. We didn't have the words for it, not being educated people. I was willing, Miss – didn't take no persuading. I had nothing to live for either. We went down to a little coppice, I wi' my gun, we kissed for the last time, and I shot her. It were like putting an animal out of its misery. I were just seeing that she was really dead, not going to come round, when the farmer ran up, wrestled the gun from me, and forced me back to the farm. I pleaded with him to let things take their course, but he locked me up and fetched the authorities.'

'But you were not—?' Alice began faintly.

'Hanged? No, Miss. That were the sentence, but it was commuted. Maybe it'd have been better for all if it had been carried out. I got fifteen years' hard labour, and if my life had been hell before – pardon my language, Miss – it was double hell in jail. I served three years, and if I could have ended my life I would have done it. They made sure I couldn't. But I got away while I was in prison in York – escaped from a working party. It's easier if you don't care if they shoot you or not.'

'But how did my brother come to know about you?'

He twisted the cap which he was holding in his hand.

'That was through a . . . lady I knew and he knew. She told him my story, and he offered me this job. He was a saint, your brother, Miss.'

Alice made noises that she hoped sounded like assent. Once it would have been spontaneous, full-hearted agreement.

'I had my own contacts by then. I gave myself a new name, and got a birth certificate to prove it. I can never forget my poor wife, and my lovely children, but now I've got the chance of a new life. I'm very fond of Ellen, and I mean to take it.'

'Yes. Yes, of course. Thank you for telling me all this. I wish you luck in the future.'

And Alice made her way back to the house more directly than she had come from it. She went straight to her bedroom, sat by the little fire there, and tried to compose her thoughts. Her overwhelming feeling was anger: her brother had introduced into the house a murderer – a dreadful man who had killed his own wife, served only part of his prison sentence, and was in effect a convict on the run. And now a household of women – and Roderick had always been the sickly one, had often said he would be the first to go – had been left through his lack of thought or consideration with a brutal killer whom they daily came into contact with. She had not been able to say so to Johnston, for she would not have brought out into the open a disagreement with her late brother, but she thought it was *wicked*. It was contempt of the law, it was endangering his own family, it was condoning the sin of suicide. She could never, ever, think well of her brother again.

Meanwhile there was daily life to be got through, and a decision to be made about that. That decision bothered Alice sorely. She could hardly give Johnston up to the law, which was her first instinct: that would be to go against her brother's judgement totally and publicly, and she had always deferred to him as the eldest and as the head of the house. It would also reveal the shaming fact that he had connived in defeating the proper workings of justice.

And yet, to have the man *there*, working around the house, to see him every day, a man who had killed his own wife. Alice could hardly bear to go out into her own garden.

In the end it was Johnston who ended the awkward situation. He contrived to be in the front garden when she was coming home from a sewing bee at the vicarage a week after their conversation.

'Oh, Miss Furnley, could I have a word?'

'Well, er . . . I'm very busy . . . a *quick* one, Johnston.'

'I can see, Miss, that you're not happy about . . . what we spoke about. No reason why you should be. I should have told you when we were talking that before he died, when he knew the tuberculosis had come back, your brother talked to me, said he wanted me to be set up in a small way, so as to be independent. He gave me seven hundred and fifty pounds. Walked away when I tried to thank him. Well, there's a small market garden I've had my eye on, and I've managed to buy it with part of the money. My wife and I will be able to live off that, and I'll be out of your way, not in front of your eyes every time you look out of the window.'

Alice was surprised at the perceptiveness of this rough man, but of course she could not say so. She said: 'I wish you well in the future, then, Johnston, and I'll advertise on Saturday for a replacement.'

And that, though it did not exactly solve the problem, made it much less pressing. She had other things to occupy her mind. Her old mother died before the next Christmas, and the daughters were left alone in the house. Sarah married again, not wisely or well, and within five years was back again. The younger sisters died first, but Alice lived on and on, ramrod straight, sharp of eye.

She saw Johnston from time to time, sometimes with his wife, eventually with children. She nodded to him graciously, in a way that did not encourage the exchange of words. Johnston himself never attempted that. The only time they talked was when she was a very old lady, in her late eighties, still walking the streets of Leeds dispensing charity to the deserving poor and attending church as one of the dwindling congregation of St Michael's. The slaughter of young men which was the Great War had gone, and so had the influenza epidemic which had slaughtered less unfairly as to sex. It was in the middle of the gay twenties, which were not particularly gay in Leeds, that she came upon Johnston, now a bent man in his seventies, with a bright, forceful young man, walking down Boar Lane. On an impulse she stopped.

'It's Johnston, isn't it?'

'That's right, Miss Furnley.'

'And is this your son?'

'It is – Sam, our youngest.'

'A prop for your old age. You are so fortunate. So many of my friends lost sons and grandsons in the War.'

'I were just too young to serve, Miss,' said Sam. 'Thank God.'

'That is not a very patriotic sentiment,' said Alice Furnley severely. 'I sometimes think the dead were the lucky ones. *They carried back bright to the coiner the mintage of man*, as the poet says. They never grew old and tarnished, as so often happens.'

She looked meaningfully at Johnston. He stared doggedly back.

'If you mean your brother, Miss, he went to his Maker as bright as any man ever did.'

'Oh come, Johnston, you know that's not true,' she said, in a low voice, preparing to pass on. 'You of all people know that.'

And she marched on, serenely continuing about her business.

'Silly old biddy,' said young Sam. And for once his father did not reprove him.

ADVENTURES IN BABYSITTING

An everyday tale of Hollywood folk

IAN RANKIN

I thought it was the hotel's fire alarm at first, and shot out of bed to hide my clothes.

Then I remembered: I wasn't in the same hotel as the talent. Panic over, I slumped back on the bed.

To explain: I was once staying in the same hotel as the talent, and someone in the talent's entourage decided to set off the hotel's smoke detectors. This was one in the morning. Sprinklers came on all over the sixth floor. People were stumbling from their bedrooms soaking wet and screaming and swearing. The film company was inundated with compensation claims, not least from the hotel itself. I think it was the Fairmount in Glasgow. Nice hotel. I'd only just unpacked my suitcase; my clothes were ruined. Though the film company tried to put up the shutters, the story made several tabloids. Obviously someone had phoned the papers, probably anonymously. The talent lost a couple of big parts with Paramount after that . . .

My phone was ringing, that's what it was. Not a fire alarm; my phone. I picked up the receiver, knowing who'd be on the other end.

'Hello?'

I could hear sounds of a party in progress, then a voice. 'Jenny? Jenny, I need a big favour?'

Another big favour.

'What is it, Mr Claymore?'

'Todd, I told you, call me Todd.'

Todd. That's what the world called him. Todd Terrific. Todd-ally Tremendous. The new Stallone, Arnie with feelings. Todd Claymore, hunky but sensitive, loved by men and women. But to me, Mr Claymore.

'What is it?' I repeated.

He launched straight in, while a female squealed behind him, then burst out laughing. I knew who *that* laugh belonged to: Claymore's new wife, Sherilynne Tamasco. The one and only. 'A bow,' Todd Claymore was saying. 'I need a bow.'

'You mean like for your hair?'

'Hell no, I mean a *crossbow*.'

'Three in the morning and you want a crossbow?'

I'd turned on the bedside lamp and reached for my cigarette packet. Some people would think this scene surreal, but I'd experienced worse. I was a professional babysitter after all. That's what film publicists call it; we say we're babysitting the talent. And Todd Claymore was A-list, definitely not someone I wanted crying back to the producers and the company.

'See,' he was saying, 'here we are in *Notting*ham . . . ?'

'Yes?'

'Home of Robin Hood . . .'

'Ye-ess?'

'So I need a goddamned crossbow, Jenny!'

'Why exactly?'

'So I can shoot the damned apple off Sherry's beautiful head!'

More laughter behind him, pitched towards the hysterical. They were a noisy couple, Todd and Sherilynne, always to be placed in the middle suite – other members of the entourage either side to muffle them from other hotel rooms, other guests.

'Mr Claymore,' I said calmly, 'Robin Hood didn't shoot apples off anybody's head. That was William Tell. And Robin Hood wouldn't have used a crossbow, he'd have used a longbow.'

'Well get me a longbow then,' he snapped. Todd Claymore didn't like to be corrected, and he *definitely* didn't like not having his requests complied with immediately and to his full satisfaction. He was Californian, his parents had spoiled him, and now he was A-list, a financial hot property – he simply wasn't used to being denied.

He was recent A-list, and those are the worst. He was just learning to throw his weight around. He'd become A-list after the belated success – sleeper hit of the year – of his thriller *Untold Passion*. He was in the UK to promote the follow-up, *Crime Yellow*. We were in Nottingham because he was guest of honour at a festival which was about to have its UK-premiere, *Crime Yellow*. I'd tried briefing him in the limo on the way up from London, but his mind was on more important questions. Sample dialogue:

'Ever met Bruce Willis, Jenny?'

'Yes.' And the name's Jennifer.

'Tell me,' leaning forward, showing bulgy stomach and pecs which looked bigger on the screen, 'when he's in England, is his limo the same size as this . . . or is it *bigger*?'

'Same size.'

'Yeah, but how does he get here? Private jet, right?'

'I'm not sure.' Second lie.

Todd Claymore explodes. 'Well *I* know, baby. He flies private, and *I* have to fly public! Me, Todd Claymore!'

By 'public' he means Concorde, of course.

'And how big's his per diem, huh?'

And so it goes.

Cut to Nottingham, and Todd and his wife, plus his brother, a bodyguard, Sherilynne's dresser and make-up artist, their joint manager and a representative from Todd's Hollywood agent: they're all booked into the city's best hotel, while I settle for a three-star hovel a short distance away, guessing – wrongly – that if I kept my distance I might catch a full night's sleep.

'A longbow then,' Todd Claymore was saying. 'Yeah, like Kevin used in the movie. Jesus, they should've tested me for that.'

'You'd have been beyond belief,' I said, thinking if I did a bit of strategic toadying, maybe he'd—

'Hey,' he roared suddenly, 'I *want* a crossbow!'

I rubbed my face with my free hand. 'Crossbow or longbow?'

'Whatever Kevin used. Yeah, we'll take a car out to Sherwood Forest, do some arching.'

In an hour, I knew he wouldn't want to do that at all. In an hour, he'd have forgotten all about his request. He'd be asleep in his wife's arms, two babes together between the satin sheets Todd's agent had requested. Flashback: a sheaf of faxes from Hollywood – 'My client Todd Claymore requests . . .' – a fantasy list, everything from his favoured brand of mineral water (Calistoga, cherry flavour) to a daily diet of black satin sheets.

'Don't piss me off,' Todd was saying now. My hackles rose and I slammed down the phone.

So who else could I phone but Bunny? Bunny who knows everybody, who can put his hands on *anything*. Harrods incarnate. And – final blessing – an insomniac. So he sounded alert when he picked up the receiver in his Clapham three-storey.

'Bunny, it's Jennifer.'

'Jennifer Juniper,' he sang quietly. 'That was before your time, right?'

'Right.'

'Don't tell me another of your charges has woken you up with a teeny-tiny request?'

'He wants a longbow.'

Bunny didn't flinch. 'Who does?'

'Todd Claymore.'

'Hot Toddy himself, I'm impressed. I hear Disney are about to sign him for that new fantasy film.'

Bunny loved the business. 'It's called *Armour World*,' I confided. 'If Claymore signs on the line, he makes three and a half.'

As in, 3.5 million dollars. Hollywood figures made me queasy.

'I think I know a guy,' Bunny was saying. 'Lives in Nottingham. Runs an archery club.'

'Perfect.' I was no longer amazed at the stuff Bunny knew. I pulled a pad of paper on to my lap. 'Give me his phone number.'

And Bunny, dear Bunny, reeled it off.

An hour and a half later I was at Todd's hotel, knocking on his suite door. The chauffeur was outside with the limo. Hey, if you're having a shitty night, spread it around, right? The chauffeur had taken me all round the city till we found the right address, Mr Archery guiding us in, me on the cellphone passing his directions to the driver. Then back to the hotel with the longbow, at six feet high a full foot taller than me. Plus a dozen arrows in a mock-leather quiver. The whole package costing a cool grand. Mr Archery's out-of-hours fee.

I knocked on the suite door. I waited. I knocked again. I looked up and down the hallway. I swore. As I was walking away, I heard a roar from one of the other rooms. I followed the sound, longbow in hand, and knocked loudly. The door was hauled open by Todd Claymore, his teeth bared in a snarl. His face was puce with anger, beads of sweat on his high, tanned forehead. He wasn't acting.

'This whole damned thing is off!' he yelled. Then he pushed past me and stalked to his room.

I walked through the open door as Todd's door slammed shut. This was Chris Klamowski's room, Chris being Todd's brother – Klamowski being Todd's real surname. I liked Chris. He was young, goofy and enjoying the ride without thinking he could take too many liberties. Still, he was a Hollywood hanger-on, and therefore not to be trusted. Maybe his *niceness* was part of an act. They all had an act: the agents, producers, managers, accountants. They all had a face.

Chris was standing by his window. On the bed sat Sherilynne. She was in tears, her legs tucked beneath her. She wore a white towelling robe and looked to die for. Matthieu Preene, the agent, handed her a box of tissues he'd brought from the bathroom. At this time of night, Preene still wore his suit, a three-piece at that. But he'd taken off his tie and undone the top button of his shirt. In his books this probably counted as 'casual'. I'd take bets Matthieu wasn't spelt that way on his birth certificate.

Standing near the bed was Chuck, the Claymore–Tamasco bodyguard. Usually Todd and his bride were inseparable, which made Chuck's job a cinch. But now he didn't know where he should be. He cracked his knuckles and belched. Like most men who spend time in gymnasia, Chuck possessed the social grace of a lipid.

Seated at a table was the last member of the group, the Claymore–Tamasco joint manager, 'Howie' Malamud. Like Chuck, Howie didn't know where to be: here, comforting Sherilynne (who might soon sign opposite Sly in next year's high-tech, low-IQ blockbuster), or by Todd's anguished side, protecting the Disney deal?

At our first meeting, Howie had pulled me to one side and told me he hoped together, as a team, acting in the best interests of everyone, we could keep Todd out of trouble. Press stories had to be OK'd before publication. Ditto photos. And any unseemly scenes were to be kept under wraps. Howie was small and fat and hairy with a perspiration problem.

I knew why he was sweating. Disney's contract would allow them to pull out should the talent cause embarrassment to the company in any way. This meant: no drugs, no boozing, no extramarital rumpy . . . not in the public domain.

'Well,' I said, beaming a smile to the assembly, 'the gang's all here. Suppose you tell me what's going on?'

'What the hell is that?' Chuck asked. 'That' was the longbow. I rested it against the wall. A cool grand of the film company's cash. I laid the quiver of arrows on the floor.

'Could we do with some coffee?' I suggested. The group perked up at that, and Chris called room service. Requests flew at him. Cream . . . low-fat sweetener . . . ice (Howie was nursing a whisky from the suite's fridge) . . . some sandwiches, ham and French mustard . . . Finally, he was able to put the receiver down.

'So?' I hinted.

'So,' Matthieu Preene said, 'there has been a robbery.'

'Jesus, Matthieu,' Howie Malamud interjected, 'we haven't even searched his room yet.'

'Todd says he's turned that room upside down.'

Oh great. 'What's missing?'

Everyone looked to Sherilynne, who sniffed and knew what was expected of her. She took a deep breath.

'His lucky mascot. He never goes anywhere without it.'

'Well, can we replace it?'

She shook her perfect locks. The room watched her hair move like they'd paid for the privilege. In front of men – especially *Holly-wood* men – Sherilynne did her act. But it *was* an act. We'd had a ten-minute conversation in London, just the two of us, and she'd been very different, cool and sussed. Flashback:

'You and me,' she'd told me, 'we're alike in a lot of ways.' Like, we were both in our twenties and blonde . . . 'Me,' she said, 'I'm playing the system the only way they'll let me. Let's face it,' running her fingers through her insured tresses, 'I'm never going to be cast as the rocket scientist. As long as I look like this and want to be in movies, I'll be the villain's babe or the easy lay next door . . .'

Cut to a hotel suite in Nottingham:

'Do you mind me asking what exactly this memento is?' I was thinking of Bunny, of replacing the item without Todd ever knowing the truth.

Sherilynne took another exquisite deep breath. 'It's a polyp,' she said.

I kissed the notion of Bunny goodbye.

We finally got Todd to open his door and initiated a search of the room, which looked like a tornado had been through it. Todd refused to help. He glared at everyone in turn and wouldn't take a ham sandwich.

'It was in the drawer of the bedside cabinet,' he told me, like he was explaining something to a child. 'I put it there myself. Then Sherry and me went to dinner, came back, invited everyone in for a drink.'

'I heard on the telephone.'

'Yeah, and just after I phoned you, that's when I pulled open the drawer, wanted to show Chuck . . . and it wasn't there. So some asshole's taken it, and it must be one of you!' He pointed his finger at all of us. 'And you,' he spat at me, 'you're supposed to look after me!'

To which I should have replied: 'But not your polyp.'

This was no polyp *ordinaire*. It had been removed from Todd's father's rump during extended surgery in Our Lady of Aloysius General Hospital in Eureka. I got the details from Chris as we stood in the hallway.

'And he kept it?' I asked.

'Had it preserved in formaldehyde in a little glass phial,' Chris confirmed. 'When the old guy died, it was all Todd wanted by way of a keepsake. He said it would remind him of the motivation that had taken him out of Eureka and into the movies.'

'And what motivation was that?'

Chris sniffed. 'Our father,' he said, 'was a royal pain in the ass.'

Back in Todd and Sherilynne's bedroom, I noticed two things. One, that it was growing light outside. The other was that there was someone missing.

Ludmilla, Sherilynne's dresser and make-up woman.

*　　*　　*

Ian Rankin

We knocked on her door, but got no response, then tried rousing her by telephone. We summoned the night manager, who was polite but looked as sorely pressed as if we'd put his legs into a Corby. Finally, he agreed to unlock Ludmilla's door.

She lay on her bed, fully dressed and pretty well dead.

An ambulance rushed her to hospital. The prognosis was not great: if I didn't keep this out of the papers, I might not keep my job.

We were eating breakfast in the hotel restaurant when Howie came with the news.

'They think there may be brain damage. Lack of oxygen or something.' He took off his glasses and wiped them. His eyes were red-rimmed. Our large table was the only one occupied at this hour. Normally, breakfast started at seven, but hotel kitchens made allowances for talent.

'What had she taken?'

Howie smoothed his hairy arms. 'Cocaine maybe, and some tablets – amphetamines.'

'Was Ludmilla at the party?' I asked Todd. He nodded. Sheri-lynne was clinging to his arm and crying softly. She'd dehydrate soon, the liquid she was losing.

'Drinking heavily,' Chris added.

'She left early though,' Matthieu Preene said. He was the only one at the table managing a cooked breakfast. He'd put his tie back on.

'This is a nightmare,' Todd groaned.

'Don't worry,' Howie said, patting his shoulder, 'we'll keep the lid on it.' He looked at me. 'Right, Jennifer?'

I excused myself and went back up to the suites floor. I had to get that damned bow back by nine a.m. or there'd be another day to pay on it. Plus I wanted to telephone my boss in private.

Chuck was coming out of Ludmilla's room.

'Hi,' I said, 'lose something?'

His face reddened, an actor with no cue-board. 'Can you keep a secret?'

'Usually.'

He looked down at the floor. 'Ludmilla and me, we . . . you know, had something going.'

'Nice,' I said. It hadn't stopped him propositioning me that first night in London.

'But I swear I didn't know she did drugs. Thing is, if the police start asking questions, I don't want them to know about Ludmilla and me.'

My mind clicked. 'You take drugs?' I examined his physique: made by chemists.

'Only,' Chuck said, 'I ain't sure what's legal in this country and what ain't.'

I nodded. 'You were checking there was nothing of yours in Ludmilla's room?'

'Hey,' he growled, 'I'm sorry she's dead and all, but I've my career to think of.'

'Don't we all,' I said, making for Chris's room and the longbow.

'If this gets out,' Todd Claymore said, 'I can kiss Disney goodbye.'

We were in conference in his suite, just the two of us, despite Matthieu Preene's protests.

'I'll do my best.'

His face darkened. 'But I mean it about that polyp. As long as it's missing, that's it, tour over. This is non-negotiable, understand?'

'Any idea *why* someone would want to steal it?'

He shook his head. 'Not a damned clue. But you can forget England, you can forget France.'

France: after the English tour, Todd and his retinue were flying to Bordeaux, another film festival, another premiere. Only this time he was joint guest of honour with his musclebound *arriviste* rival, Jeremiah Tang. Tang was an American with a Hong Kong mother, and boasted martial arts training to make up for lack of acting ability. Todd Claymore, it was accepted, could act Tang off any film set. But Tang, one-time video star, had yet to make a film which didn't recoup its cost ten times over. Age twenty-five, Todd Claymore could hear the youngster's footsteps taking the stairs two at a time towards the A-list.

I wasn't accompanying Todd and Co. to France, my boss was. Sore point.

I'd spoken to my boss in London. He'd been in the bathtub and furious. So now I was trying to keep the media away from Ludmilla, and track down the missing polyp. I even considered visiting the hospital, not to see Ludmilla but to talk to staff about the possibility of purchasing a small lump of extraneous gristle, preferably in for-maldehyde, money no object.

But I had to keep close to Todd. We had a press conference in the ballroom at eleven, then a TV interview at three, and selected individual media interviews from five till seven. The premiere was at nine. Always supposing Todd deigned to go. I had Matthieu and Howie pressuring him to carry out his prescribed duties. He'd signed up to everything, and if he backed out, there'd be a financial penalty. It was in neither man's interest to have *that* happen.

'Hey,' Hairy Howie said, pointing a small fat finger, 'much as I like you, Jennifer, if anything screws up around here, I'll see to it that the closest you ever get to the industry again is renting a video.'

Matthieu Preene nodded, checking his cufflinks.

'I admire your candour, gentlemen,' I said, standing up, head high as I walked away. It felt like a move from an old film.

Chris was in the lounge, reading a comic book. It could be boring, touring with talent. I sat down and asked him what he thought of Ludmilla.

'I guessed she was on dope,' he confessed, 'I just couldn't figure *what*. I mean, she never spoke much, kept herself to herself except when she was in Sherry's room. She'd be in there for *hours*.'

'What about Ludmilla and Chuck? Weren't they . . . ?'

He snorted. 'Are you kidding? She couldn't stand him. I think he was putting the make on her again last night, that's why she left the party early. Maybe she went out to get away from him.'

'Went out?'

Chris had rolled the comic into a cylinder, and peered down it at me before panning the lounge. 'I had to go to my room to get something. I saw her disappear into the elevator.'

I left Chris and went to speak to the day manager. He was dubious about giving me the names of the night staff, never mind home telephone numbers. I dug into the dwindling film company pot and salved his professional conscience.

Five calls later, I knew that Ludmilla had come down to the lobby. She'd been drunk, or acting drunk, weaving from wall to wall, looking for the bar. When told it was closed, she demanded it reopen. The night manager explained that room service would be pleased to furnish her with any refreshments. She'd remonstrated, stumbled, knocked a wastebin over, and eventually retreated to the elevator.

And presumably to an accidental overdose.

I checked the ballroom and saw that the press conference was going ahead. Preene and Malamud flanked their property, both men with mobile phones on the desk in front of them. There was no sign of Sherilynne, but Chuck – liar and phony – was seated off to one side, arms prodigiously folded. There was a good crowd, including a few foreign journalists. I recognized one from Denmark who always asked the talent the same question: 'What in particular greatness are you thinking merits of that actor is Robert deNiro?'

While answers varied, the most frequent was 'Excuse me?'

I went to talk to the cleaning staff, but first I phoned Bunny and managed to set something up. He made me promise it wasn't for my own personal use. After talking to the cleaners, I went up to my room and changed into my scruffiest clothes, then went back down to help sift last night's cleaning-bags.

I needed a shower after that. Everyone was lunching in the dining room, tab to be picked up by the film company. They invited me to join them, but I shook my head, giving my professional smile. I said I had somewhere to be.

'Just don't go talking to any damned journalists,' Preene warned. Most of the ones from the press conference were still in the hotel bar.

Todd was chewing bread and staring at the walls from behind tortoiseshell Ray-Bans.

'You know,' he said, 'I really want to work with Quentin. Quentin *knows* actors.'

'Well, he knows a few,' I said into the silence. 'By the way, I'll have that polyp for you this evening. I'll hand it over at the premiere.'

Then I turned and walked away, knowing I look good from the back.

I visited a flat on one of the city's less salubrious schemes, then got my driver to stop outside a video rental shop, and had the pale-faced teenage manager do some cross-referencing for me. Cut to: the hotel, where Sherilynne was casting prospective replacements for Ludmilla. It was short notice, and the contenders milling in the hallway looked unconvincing. I knocked and entered her suite. A girl with

Ian Rankin

pink dreadlocked hair and several nose studs was just leaving.

'I'm exhausted,' Sherilynne said.

'You must be.'

She looked up at me, studied my face, then narrowed her eyes. For a second, we knew one another, and then she twitched and showed me the fingers of her left hand.

'I had that last one give me a manicure and varnish. Painful *and* amateurish.'

I stuck the phial in front of her nose and she flinched.

'Look what Ludmilla dropped in the foyer,' I said. 'And guess who had to sift a dozen hoover bags to find it?'

Sherilynne's face had gone so pale I could make out the individual specks of make-up.

'Do you want me to give this to Todd?' I asked.

'Of course,' she said, not at all convincingly.

'That line doesn't fit the script, Sherry.' I sat on a chair. 'You took the polyp from the drawer and told Ludmilla to get rid of it, or maybe just to hold on to it. She didn't have any reason to steal it for herself. Then she OD'd, and you didn't know what she'd done with it, so you talked Chuck into searching her room – not hard to sweet-talk Chuck, is it?'

'I don't know what you're . . .' She corpsed, and took a moment to compose herself. Maybe she was switching to another act, but I didn't think so.

'I don't want us to go to Bordeaux,' she said.

'I know.' Her eyes widened. 'When we spoke in London, you mentioned the kinds of role you were given, including a villain's babe. But you've only once played that role. *The Knife That Bled.* It went direct to video and from there to the dumpster.'

'You've seen it?' She sounded amazed.

'I love films, Sherry. There was a time I rented maybe fifteen a week. I had a vague memory of *The Knife That Bled.* Your boyfriend the bad guy was a then unknown called Jerry Tang. So I put two and two together . . .'

Her voice was dry and quiet. 'It only lasted the length of shooting, maybe three weeks. Nobody knew except for the cast and crew, and they've been surprisingly reticent. But I just know that when Todd and Jerry . . . I know that if they get into some macho I-can-beat-you bullshit, then Jerry will use his ultimate weapon.' She looked up with wet eyes. 'Me. And Todd will hate me for that, I know it.'

I got up to leave. I didn't like seeing this woman in front of me, the one with tears streaming down her face. I didn't like the bruised, frightened voice. I like her better bold and bitchy, with a snarling comeback line in almost every scene she played.

'What will you do?' she said.

'Todd's bound to find out. You two are so big now . . . eventually someone will talk, either for money or just from jealousy.' But she knew that already. She just wanted more time, real time. 'You know, I could have lost my job over this,' I told her.

'I'm sorry.' But she wasn't.

'I'll see you at the premiere,' I said. 'And Sherry, you won't be going to Bordeaux.' I winked at her. 'Trust me.'

There was a big crowd on the pavement outside the theatre, with crash barriers and police to keep them in check. They didn't pay me much attention as I walked up the red carpet and through the doors. They were waiting for a Hollywood couple. I wondered why. I wondered what the attraction really was. But then some people like to visit zoos, too.

There was a standing ovation as Todd and his glittering wife entered the auditorium. They were late, and had arrived by limo despite their hotel being next door to the theatre. They walked hand in hand, waving to the fans. Todd pecked Sherry on the cheek to cheers and renewed applause.

When Todd saw me, he squeezed Sherilynne's hand and came over. She stood frozen as I handed over the phial. He checked it before slipping it into his pocket. Then he gave me his big, warm, film-star smile and hugged me, whispering, 'You did all right, Jenny. You did all right.'

Caught in his cologne embrace, I slipped something into his other pocket, then watched him take his seat.

The film was no more enjoyable for me fourth time round. The holes in the plot gaped wider, a change of takes in the middle of one scene screamed from the screen, and the dialogue was all paste and scissors.

There was another standing ovation at the end, and a rush of autograph hunters. But Todd and Sherilynne couldn't hang around.

347

They had a private plane to catch. It was taking them to Paris, where my boss would join them for the trip down to Bordeaux.

Their bags had already been packed, and the retinue proceeded straight to the airport from the theatre. Nobody said goodbye to me, or thanks or anything. Not even Chris. I returned to my hotel, undressed and lay on the bed. I was returning to London in the morning. By train. Second class. I picked up the telephone and dialled the number I'd been given, the one for Customs & Excise. Using a voice from my repertoire I told them that the actor Todd Claymore would be attempting to carry cocaine into France. I knew the message would be passed along, and that the drugs squad would be waiting. I'd slipped just enough coke into Todd's pocket for there to be embarrassment, disquiet, a certain *interest* in the event.

My second call was to a stringer on the *Sun*. Now he owed me *two* favours. The exposure would be bad for Todd. Disney would not be amused. Malamud and Preene would be *extremely* unamused. And my boss's Bordeaux trip would be cancelled. I didn't know if Hollywood would rate that a happy ending.

Closing credits.